RED SKY OVER HAWAII

Center Point
Large Print

Also by Sara Ackerman and available from Center Point Large Print:

The Lieutenant's Nurse

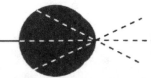

This Large Print Book carries the Seal of Approval of N.A.V.H.

RED SKY OVER HAWAII

SARA ACKERMAN

CENTER POINT LARGE PRINT
THORNDIKE, MAINE

This Center Point Large Print edition
is published in the year 2020 by arrangement with
Harlequin Books S. A.

The text of this Large Print edition is unabridged.
In other aspects, this book may vary
from the original edition.
Printed in the United States of America
on permanent paper.
Set in 16-point Times New Roman type.

ISBN: 978-1-64358-704-2

The Library of Congress has cataloged this record
under Library of Congress Control Number: 2020942111

For my beautiful mother,
Diane McFaull, who planted all the seeds.

LOVE & MAGIC

When I close my eyes, I still see the fiery glow of lava in Halemaʻumaʻu crater. Sometimes if I'm not careful, I find myself walking through the clouds while the honeycreepers build nests in my hair. I can't see where I'm going, but I don't care. To be there with my boots crunching on lava is sweeter than any honey from the hives. Bees swirl around me. I still feel my hand in his and the sound of his voice whispering in my tired ear.

In the end, we remember those slices of time where we *feel* the most—love, anguish, joy, sorrow, fright. I don't care what the reason. Maybe it was the day you first realized you were mortal or that first moment you saw love walk in the door. Or that no matter how many years passed, you would still be that girl, the barefoot one with long brown hair and a penny in her pocket. Maybe it was when you suddenly realized you had everything to lose and you were too blind to notice. What matters most is what lives in your heart, and if there is one thing I know, it is this: love is the only way.

And magic.

I guess that's two.

THE ROAD

December 8, 1941

With every mile closer to Volcano, the fog thickened, until they were driving through a forest of white gauze with the occasional branch showing through. Lana considered turning the truck around no less than forty-six times. Going back to Hilo would have been the prudent thing to do, but this was not a time for prudence. Of that she was sure. She slowed the Chevy to a crawl and checked the rearview mirror. The cage with the geese was now invisible, and she could barely make out the dog's big black spots.

Maybe the fog would be to their advantage.

"I don't like it here at all," said Coco, who was smashed up next to Lana, scrawny arms folded in protest. The child had to almost yell to be heard above the chug of the motor.

Lana grabbed a blanket from the floor. "Put this over you. It should help."

Coco shook her head. "I'm not cold. I want to go home. Can you please take us back?"

Goose bumps had formed up and down her limbs, but she was so stubborn that she had refused to put on a jacket. True, Hilo was insufferably hot, but where they were headed—

four thousand feet up the mountain—the air was cold and damp and flimsy.

It had been over ten years since Lana had set foot at Kīlauea. Never would she have guessed to be returning under these circumstances.

Marie chimed in. "We can't go back now, sis. And anyway, there's no one to go back to at the moment."

Poor Coco trembled. Lana wished she could hug the girl and tell her everything was going to be okay. But that would be a lie. Things were liable to get a whole lot worse before they got any better.

"Sorry, honey. I wish things were different, but right now you two are my priority. Once we get to the house, we can make a plan," Lana said.

"But you don't even know where it is," Coco whined.

"I have a good idea."

More like a vague notion.

"What if we don't find it by dark? Are they going to shoot us?" Coco said.

Marie put her arm around Coco and pulled her in. "Turn off that little overactive imagination of yours. No one is going to shoot us," she said, but threw a questioning glance Lana's way.

"We'll be fine," Lana said, wishing she believed that.

The girls were not the real problem here. Of greater concern was what they had hidden in the

10

back of the truck. Curfew was six o'clock, but people had been ordered to stay off the roads unless their travel was essential to the war. Lana hadn't told the girls that. Driving up here was a huge risk, but she had invented a story she hoped and prayed would let them get through if anyone stopped them. The thought of a checkpoint caused her palms to break out in sweat, despite the icy air blowing in through the cracks in the floorboard.

On a good day, the road from Hilo to Volcano would take about an hour and a half. Today was not a good day. Every so often they hit a rut the size of a whiskey barrel that bounced her head straight into the roof. The continuous drizzle of the rain forest had undermined all attempts at smooth roads here. At times the ride was reminiscent of the plane ride from Honolulu. Exactly two days ago, but felt more like a lifetime.

Lana's main worry was what they would encounter once in the vicinity of the national park entrance. With the Kīlauea military camp nearby, there were bound to be soldiers and roadblocks in the area. She had so many questions for her father and felt a mixed ache of sadness and resentment that he was not here to answer them. *How were you so sure the Japanese were coming? Why the volcano, of all places? How are we going to survive up here? Why didn't you call me sooner?*

Coco seemed to settle down, leaning her nut-brown ringlets against her sister's shoulder and closing her eyes. There was something comforting in the roar of the engine and the jostle of the truck. With the whiteout it was hard to tell where they were, but by all estimates they should be arriving soon.

Lana was dreaming of a cup of hot coffee when Coco sat upright and said, "I have to go tinkle."

"Tinkle?" Lana asked.

Marie said, "She means she has to go to the bathroom."

They drove until they found a grassy shoulder, and Lana pulled the truck aside, though they could have stopped in the middle of the road. They had met only one other vehicle the whole way, a police car that fortunately had passed by.

The rain had let up, and they all climbed out. It was like walking through a cloud, and the air smelled metallic and faintly lemony from the eucalyptus that lined the road. Lana went to check on Sailor. The dog stood up and whined, yanking on the rope around her neck, straining to be pet. Poor thing was drenched and shaking. Lana had wanted to leave her behind with a neighbor, but Coco had put up such a fuss, throwing herself onto her bed and wailing and punching the pillow, that Lana relented. Caring for the girls would be hard enough, but a hundred-and-twenty-pound dog?

"Just a bathroom stop. Is everyone okay back here?" she asked in a hushed voice. Two low grunts came from under the tarp. "We should be there soon. Remember, be still and don't make a sound if we stop again."

As if on cue, one of the hidden passengers started a coughing fit, shaking the whole tarp. She wondered how wise it was to subject him to this long and chilly ride, and if it might be the death of him. But the alternative was worse.

"Deep breaths . . . you can do it," Lana said.

Coco showed up and hopped onto the back tire. "I think we should put Sailor inside with us. She looks miserable."

"Whose lap do you propose she sits on?" Lana said.

Sailor was as tall as a small horse, but half as wide.

"I can sit in the back of the truck and she can come up here, then," Coco said in all seriousness.

"Not in those clothes you won't. We don't need you catching pneumonia on us."

They started off again, and ten seconds down the road, Sailor started howling at the top of her lungs. Lana felt herself on the verge of unraveling. The last thing they needed was one extra ounce of attention. The whole idea of coming up here was preposterous when she thought about it. At the time it had seemed like a good idea, but now she wondered at her sanity.

"What is *wrong* with that dog?" Lana said, annoyed.

Coco turned around, and Lana felt her hot breath against her arm. In the smallest of voices, she said, "Sailor is scared."

Lana felt her heart crack. "Oh, honey, we're all a bit scared. It's perfectly normal under the circumstances. But I promise you this—I will do everything in my power to keep you out of harm's way."

"But you hardly know us," Coco said.

"My father knew you, and you knew him, right?" Lana said. "And remember, if anyone asks, we tell them our story."

They had rehearsed it many times already, but with kids one could never be sure. Not that Lana had much experience with kids. With none of her own and no nieces or nephews in the islands, she felt the lack palpably, smack in the center of her chest. There had been a time when she saw children in her future, but that dream had come and gone and left her sitting on the curb with a jarful of tears.

Her mind immediately went to Buck. Strange how your future with a person could veer so far off course from how you'd originally pictured it. How the one person you swore you would have and hold could end up wreaking havoc on your heart instead. She blinked the thought away.

As they neared Volcano, the fog remained like a curtain, but the air around them brightened. Lana knew from all her time up here as a young girl

14

that the trees got smaller as the elevation rose, and the terrain changed from towering eucalyptus and fields of yellow-and-white ginger to a more cindery terrain covered with red-blossomed 'ohi'a trees, and prehistoric-looking hāpu'u ferns and the crawling uluhe. At one time in her life, this had been one of her happiest places. Coco reached for the letter on the dashboard and began reading it for the fourth time. *"Coco Hitchcock. It sounds funny."* The paper was already getting worn.

Marie swiped it out of her hands. "You're going to ruin that. Give it to me."

Where Coco was whip thin and dark and spirited—a nice way of putting it—Marie was blonde and full-bodied and sweet as coconut taffy. But Lana could tell even Marie's patience was wearing thin.

"Mrs. Hitchcock said we need to memorize our new names or we'll be shot."

Lana said as calmly as she could, "I never said anything of the sort. And, Coco, you have to get used to calling me Aunt Lana for now. Both of you do."

"And stop talking about getting shot," Marie added, rolling her eyes.

If they could all just hold it together a little bit longer.

There was sweat pooling between her breasts and behind her kneecaps. Lying was not her strong suit, and she was hoping that, by some strange miracle, they could sail on through without anyone stopping them. She rolled her window down a couple of inches for a burst of fresh air. "We're just about here. So if we get stopped, let me do the talking. Speak only if someone asks you a direct question, okay?"

Neither girl said anything; they both just nodded. Lana could almost see the fear condensing on the windshield. And pretty soon little Coco started sniffling. Lana would have said something to comfort her, but her mind was void of words. Next the sniffles turned into heaving sobs big enough to break the poor girl in half. Marie rubbed her hand up and down Coco's back in a warm, smooth circle.

"You can cry when we get there, but no tears now," she said.

Tears and snot were smeared across Coco's face in one big shiny layer. "But they might kill Mama and Papa." Her face was pinched and twisted into such anguish that Lana had to fight back a sob of her own.

"We're Americans. They would never kill them—or us, for that matter," Marie said with pure confidence.

A split second later Lana blinked several times to make sure she was seeing straight. Her foot pressed hard on the brakes. Up ahead were two guards standing in the middle of the road with rifles aimed at the truck. Shrouded in fog, they looked like ghost soldiers. All along the side of the road were sandbags piled high with what appeared to be machine guns set up behind them. The sight quieted Coco right down.

"Oh hell," Lana muttered.

She rolled down the window and waved, wondering if she should get out or wait for them to come to her. "Hello, there," she called. "Just a woman and two girls here."

Outside, the world seemed very small, pressing in from all directions. The way her heart was skipping along at two hundred beats per minute, Lana wondered if she would even be able to talk in complete sentences. She let out a big breath and opened the door.

One of the men moved toward them. "Civilians are not supposed to be out driving around, ma'am. What's your business here?" he said.

She stood up and forced a smile. "We just need to get home. We were trapped in Hilo for the past few days after a trip to Oʻahu, and I got clearance from the head of the Territorial Guard to come back up here and stay put."

With limbs he still needed to grow into, the guard looked to be no older than eighteen. He came and stood just to the left of the truck. "You have proof of that?"

She handed him the letter, signed by one Deputy Chester Hoʻokano, a neighbor and friend of her father. Chester was *in* the Territorial Guard but certainly not in charge of it. He'd scribbled his name so it was nearly unreadable.

A low growl started up in the back of the truck. Then a cacophony of honking and strange hissing followed.

The man craned his neck. "What the dickens you got back there, ma'am?"

"Just a dog and two nene geese. I couldn't leave them behind. My friend was watching them while we were away," she said.

He hooked his fingers in his belt loops and seemed to contemplate her story. She noted his name tag said *Pvt. Smith*. After a moment the animals settled.

Cigarette smoke wafted over from the other guard, who said, "Everything okay, Jimbo?"

"Appears to be," Jimbo said as he leaned down to glance into the cab.

The two men had probably been standing out here for hours with nothing to do. Now they had a diversion to keep them occupied and seemed in no hurry whatsoever.

"Hey, ladies," he said to Coco and Marie.

Marie and Coco both said hello in unison, their hands folded neatly in their laps.

Lana gave him her license. "There was no room for us at my friend's house. We were all sleeping on the patio with the cockroaches and mosquitos, and we were told we would be much safer up here."

The soldier raised a brow, his eyes lingering on Marie. "These your girls?"

As it turned out, Coco was eight but looked five, and Marie was thirteen but could have passed for seventeen, and was a real stunner.

Lana felt like she was swallowing a huge wad of gum. "Yes."

"You look young enough to be their sister, and funny, they didn't get that dark skin of yours . . . at all," he said.

His boots crunched on the cinder as he stepped back to assess them. He seemed half nervous teenager, half authority figure, and Lana couldn't figure which one to appeal to.

Lana faked a laugh. "My husband and I adopted them when they were wee little things. Long story. Look, Private Smith, the girls are cold and scared, our dog is shivering in the back and we would like to get to the house before dark. If you wouldn't mind letting us be on our way?"

He paused for what felt like an hour. "Where is your husband?" he finally asked.

"He stayed on O'ahu for business and now he's stuck there."

"Shame. Where's the house?"

"Just up ahead at the edge of the village."

By now the other guard had sauntered over to participate in the questioning. He was as compact as the other one was gangly. "Just the three of you ladies, all alone?" he said.

This one felt more dangerous.

"Just the three of us, and a dog and two geese. I am perfectly capable of taking care of us, if that's what you mean?"

"You know there's a lot of Japanese farmers in the village. You own a gun?" Private Smith said.

That was when she heard a muffled but distinct cough coming from the back of the truck. Not a whole string of coughs, thank heavens, but one was bad enough.

The second guard, Private Lowry, cocked his head and motioned toward the rear. "What was that?"

Lana's cheeks heated up, and if the guilty looks on the girls were any indication, they had heard it, too. She waved it off. "Oh, those nene geese, they make all kinds of peculiar noises."

She said a silent prayer to the goose god. *Now would be a good time to start honking and hissing again. Please!* Lowry walked around to the back, keeping a wide distance. Sailor had sat down earlier when she realized she wasn't getting out and continued a low-pitched whine, but now she stood up and glared at the man.

"What's under the tarp?" Lowry said.

"Supplies. Food, clothing, blankets and some gardening supplies. We're going to work on planting more edibles."

"Mind showing me?" he said.

He struck her as the kind of man who once he got on the scent of something, would follow it to the ends of the earth. It seemed at that very moment the sky around them condensed, turning four shades darker and making it hard to see one's own feet. She was trying to figure out which side of the tarp to pull up when Coco climbed out and started wailing. As if on cue, the geese started up again and Sailor turned her snout to the sky and let out a gut-splitting howl.

"Auntie, if we don't go now, I'm gonna wet my pants," she sobbed. While she had hardly allowed herself to be touched by Lana earlier, she now wrapped her arms around Lana's waist and pressed her face into the side of her chest.

Lana pulled her in and smoothed her hair. To Lowry, she said, "Forgive us, since the attack, she's been having night terrors and a bad case of nerves."

Amid all the commotion Lana thought she heard another cough. If they didn't get out of there soon, the men would surely uncover the extra cargo, and who knew what would happen then. Lana felt the weight of the impossible promise she'd made to Mrs. Wagner, the girls' mother. Of course she had said yes—what else could she have said? But with so many unknowns, the yes was as good as a lie.

She let annoyance creep into her voice. "Fellas, please just let us pass," Lana said. "It should be obvious we are no danger, and once we get home, we'll stay put. I can promise you that."

Smith shrugged and glanced at Lowry. "What do you think, Skip?"

Coco was now tugging at Lana's arm, trying to pull her toward the open door.

Lana gave it her last shot. "Our tarp is tied down to keep our belongings dry, and if I open it, everything will get wet."

Lowry threw his cigarette stub down and stepped on it. She thought he was going to demand to inspect what they had in the truck bed, but instead he said, "You ladies need an escort?"

She slipped onto the wet seat behind Coco before he could change his mind. "I would never impose on you like that. We'll be just fine."

The engine roaring to life was about the sweetest sound she had ever heard. They rode in silence for a full minute before Lana said to Coco, "You were brilliant back there—you even had me fooled."

Coco gave her an inch of a smile, which was more than she had seen in all the time she'd known her. "It was Marie's idea."

"I like how you girls think. Watching each other's backs is exactly how we're going to get through this."

Maybe there was hope for them after all.

THE KNOWING

December 5, 1941
Honolulu

For the past several days there had been the kind of faint buzzing in the air that preceded a tragedy. Lana could explain it no more than she could say why the sky was a deeper blue in December than it was in May. But the feeling was there, like static on a radio coming from someplace down the street. Though it had happened only a few times in her life, she recognized the signs. Hair standing on end, metallic taste, a humming along her skin and the feeling that life was about to spin off into a whole new direction.

In an effort to ignore it, she busied herself in the yard, pruning the gardenia and cutting back the liliko'i vine that was threatening to overtake her roses. Plants in Nu'uanu could be counted on to run amok at this time of year. At night Lana lay awake listening to the bufo toads croaking and the wash of water over stones in the stream. She often wondered how many stars were out there and if perhaps she had just not found the right one to wish upon.

Most people thought she had an idyllic life. So had she, at one time. And then she and Buck had tried to have a baby. Tried, tried and tried some more. Once, long ago, someone had told her she would have difficulty conceiving again, but she had promptly filed those words away. Nope, not Lana Spalding. Lana was going to have a house full of children and be the mother that she never had. Now it looked as if the doctor had been right. She might have been able to live with it, had Buck not done the unthinkable.

And there she was, sitting on the patio contemplating how to escape her life, when the phone rang. Two short bursts, which meant the call was for her house. A feeling of *knowing* settled over her. Here it came.

"Lana, is that you?" said a voice through the line.

"Daddy?"

Even after all these years, through broken hearts and across oceans and even despite their so-called estrangement, she couldn't call him anything else. In the long pause between words, she heard ragged breathing coming through the line.

"Wouldn't you know it, I might be dying."

Picturing her father anything other than fit and strong was impossible. He had always had triple the energy of most people she knew and always looked ten years younger than his age. Granted, she hadn't seen him in six months, but she was having a hard time reconciling the Jack Spalding she knew with the voice on the phone.

"What's happened?" she asked, unsure what to say or how to feel.

"Some kind of infection—meningitis, Dr. Woodell thinks. I'm trying to fight it." He coughed and struggled to continue with a throat full of phlegm. "Could you come to Hilo, dear?"

The quiver in his voice made him sound like an old, broken man. And maybe he was. Thanks to the full moon, Lana could see her hands resting on the table next to her glass of red wine. Her fingers trembled. She took a sip. Oak and cinnamon mixed with notes of blackberry. *So much hurt.*

"Are you at home or in the hospital?" she asked, needing time to gather her wits.

"Hospital."

That meant it was bad. Her father hated hospitals.

"How long have you been there?"

"We can talk when you get here. Please. I want to make this right . . ." His voice trailed off and the line grew staticky.

The strange thing was that in recent weeks she had been dreaming of her father almost every other night. He had been surrounded by honeybees in flight, as if he had a buzzing full-body halo, and he was showing her various new inventions—a car that doubled as a boat, a new kind of beehive, glass-and-rubber goggles to see with underwater. She didn't like the dreams of him, because they made her think about him, and she didn't want to think about him.

Despite it all, Lana had begun to wonder if the time had come to return to Hilo. But was forgiveness even possible? The way she saw it, everything was his fault. That iron will of his, the calamity that could have been avoided and the fact that she had a stubborn streak just as formidable as his. A big seed of anger was still planted deep inside her. Ignoring him kept the seed from sprouting.

With a flurry of thoughts racing through her mind, Lana surprised herself by saying, "I'll make arrangements first thing tomorrow morning." She had been asking God for some kind of reason to get out of town. Here it was, fallen neatly and tragically into her lap.

A sniffle came through from her father. "I love you, Lana. Always have and always will."

"I'll see you soon, Daddy" was all she could muster in reply.

These days the fastest way to Hilo was by plane. Lana would have preferred to go by steamer, but she'd been hearing about the fancy new DC-3 airplanes that Hawaiian Airlines had recently brought in from the mainland. Now was her chance to take a flight on one, even though airplanes gave her the jitters. She climbed out of the car holding a small suitcase in one hand and box of sugary malasadas in the other.

After a night of fitful sleep in the guest room—where she had taken up residence the past month—and a cool argument with Buck before the roosters were even up, she felt like hell. He hadn't wanted her to go, and though neither of them said it, her leaving felt final and lonely and as necessary as the air in her lungs.

The final unspooling between them had begun three months prior, on a storm-drenched August afternoon. One of those moments that would be forever branded into her mind. In fact it was the third-worst day of her life.

Lana had been rained out on a drawing trip to Waimānalo where she had planned to sketch the Makapuʻu Lighthouse, and she had arrived home half a day early. Buck's blue Ford coupe was parked in the turnaround, and it seemed strange that he was not at work as he always was on a Thursday at noon. She figured he must have forgotten something, so she tiptoed into the kitchen to surprise him, when she heard muffled sounds coming from the bedroom. Fearing he was ill, she hurried in and came upon a blonde woman sitting on the couch with her husband, drink in hand. One look at the bed, as rumpled as the woman's hair, and Lana knew.

For a full week afterward she had refused to speak to Buck or even look at him, but slowly he'd begun working his way back in. Writing her sappy love notes, bringing home roses and new pens for her to draw with, and pleading for forgiveness. Like a fool, she felt her resolve cracking. Most men made mistakes; it was in their nature. And then he did something that turned her insides to ice.

He blamed her.

"You lied to me. You knew you were sterile and you never told me. What did you expect me to do?" he had said.

That was when she understood that Buck was her past, not her future. He might see it otherwise, but he was a man used to getting whatever he wanted.

Not today, Lana had thought as she slid into her car.

Poha, their live-in maid, had insisted on stopping for malasadas on the way to the airport. "They won't turn you away with these in your hand," she said, since who knew if the flights had any open seats.

Lana's suitcase contained enough clothing and supplies for a few days away, and that was all. Anyway, she could buy more if she needed to.

The John Rodgers Airport was dry and dusty, with a few twisted kiawe trees scattered here and there, and a lazy black cat stretched out across the entry door to the building. Lana had to step over it to pass. The place smelled of fuel and salt water with a hint of kiawe pods. A group of men in suits, plantation managers by the looks of it, stood off to the side of the counter smoking cigarettes and looking serious.

A big sign announced the brand-new planes and that Inter-Island Airways had just changed its name to Hawaiian Airlines. Lana set her suitcase on the ground and said to the man at the counter, "I need to get on the first flight to Hilo, please."

He eyed her suitcase. "Do you have a reservation?"

"I don't."

"Flights are full today. Sorry, ma'am," he said with a shrug of his shoulders.

"I'll pay extra, but I need to get to Hilo before the end of the day. My father is very ill."

A feeling of urgency swirled in her chest. All these years of hardly seeing her father, by her own choice, and now there was the sense that she absolutely *had* to be there.

"There's no room for you, even if you had all the money in the world," he said, voice rising in annoyance.

One of the suited men came over. "Excuse me for butting in, but I couldn't help but overhear you need a flight."

"Badly," Lana said, on the verge of tears.

"In the next hangar over, there's a chap named Baron that runs a small charter. I've used him a few times in a pinch. Wave a few greenbacks in his face and I reckon he'll fly you to the north pole if you asked," he said with a friendly smile.

Whatever it took.

"Baron?"

The man laughed. "Honest to God, that's his name."

"And he's trustworthy?" she asked.

"He can fly blindfolded, if that's what you mean."

She wasn't exactly sure why she'd asked but suspected it had to do with her distrust of hurtling through the skies in a heavy metal object.

Over in the other hangar there were three planes. Two larger and one small enough to be an automobile with wings. A radio on the back was blaring the Andrews Sisters.

She stopped in the open doorway. "Hello?"

A young man with a clipboard appeared from behind one of the planes. He wasn't wearing a shirt and couldn't have been a year over seventeen. For such a young fellow he was broad shouldered and chiseled and probably too handsome for his own good.

"Can I help you?" he said.

"I was told I might be able to get a flight to Hilo here."

"You were told right. The plane leaves in ten minutes," he said matter-of-factly.

"How much is the fare?" she asked, looking around for any signs of other passengers or a pilot.

"How much you got?"

What kind of business was this? "If it's not too much trouble, may I speak to your boss, or even the pilot?"

Without answering, he walked over to a chair, grabbed a shirt and slowly slipped it on. Lana wasn't quite sure where to look, so she riffled through her purse, pretending to search for her wallet. When his shirt was buttoned up, she saw the name *Baron* embroidered in red across the front.

He laughed. "Today's your lucky day, then, since I'm the boss *and* the pilot."

This plan was sounding worse by the minute. She debated marching back to Hawaiian and begging one of the plantation men to switch places with her. Getting to Hilo alive with Baron seemed like a remote possibility, at best.

She nodded to the small plane. "Is this the plane we'd go in?"

"Nah, we're taking the Sikorsky. Got a drop at Kalaupapa along the way."

While she stood there trying to tame her overactive imagination, he must have sensed her fear. "I've been around planes since I could walk, so you're in good hands, Mrs. . . .."

"Hitchcock. Lana Hitchcock. Oh, and here, these are for you," she said, handing him the malasadas.

Anywhere in Hawaii when you said your last name was Hitchcock, people paid attention.

31

But Baron seemed unfazed. Buck's father was actually the face behind the name of J. Hitchcock & Co., though Buck was likely to follow in his footsteps. Except that he was half as smart and twice as lazy. Lana had learned that the hard way. Sometimes money did that to a child.

"Well, Mrs. Hitchcock, I'll take your suitcase, and let's get going. I like to leave at 8:00 a.m. sharp." When he tried to lift her suitcase, his arm sagged. "Whoa, you dragging gold bullion to Hilo with you?"

Lana offered her first smile of the day. "Books, which to me are better than gold. Oh, and speaking of gold, don't I need to pay you?"

He winked. "You can pay me once we get there."

What on earth was that supposed to mean? When she stepped into the plane, she immediately thought, *How will this thing even get off the ground?* The entire back section of the eight-seater was full of boxes and crates. Everything from giant bags of rice, pickle jars, and Wesson oil to decks of playing cards and toilet paper. There were also rolls and rolls of army blankets. If Baron hadn't been right behind her, she might have turned around and called the whole thing off.

"They have a barge come in once a year at Kalaupapa, so we supplement when they need stuff. Those poor folks out there . . . breaks my heart every time I go," he said.

"Have you heard about the new medicine for leprosy? People are saying it's a miracle, even though it hurts like the dickens," she said.

He nodded toward a box. "It's the main reason I'm going. Last time I was there, I was watching these young kids running around playing soccer looking like regular kids, then you know some of them were probably ripped away from their families. Can you imagine?"

Lana had never been there, since the whole community on the peninsula was quarantined, but she had heard the unfathomable stories. Scouts sent to look for infected people. Families hiding out in remote valleys—Waipi'o and Kalalau—so they wouldn't be separated. The sad thing was she almost *could* imagine. And if Baron was kindhearted enough to be flying them supplies, the least she could do was trust him.

Soon after they took off, they banked to the right and headed toward Diamond Head. Typical morning rain clouds blotted out much of the Ko'olau range, but along the shores of Waikiki, skies were clear and seas turquoise and balmy. Lines of coconut trees snaked just inland from the beach. It was such a pretty sight that for a moment she forgot to be scared, and her worries about her father slipped away.

Baron held the box of malasadas in his lap. He had polished off two in under a minute. He wiped the sugar from his lips and yelled to be heard above the engines. "Beautiful, ain't it?"

From above it looked even dreamier. "Like a painting."

All these white-sand beaches had taken some time to get used to after coming from Hilo, where the sand was the color of black lava. The water there was different, too. A deeper, more solitary blue. Not that she spent much time in the ocean anymore. Her life had become one big affair of dinner parties and functions, polo matches, lunches and teas and an endless procession of houseguests. All part of the duty of being Mrs. Hitchcock.

"You see the headlines from the *Hilo Tribune-Herald* on Sunday?" Baron asked.

Everyone seemed to want to talk about the Japanese these days. "My husband brought one home. Scary business."

Japanese May Strike over the Weekend.

"Really gets your hair up to hear that, especially being right next to Pearl. I've been keeping an eye out lately when I fly for any signs of trouble."

"Sounds like they're more interested in the Philippines or the East Indies, though," she said, having listened enough to Buck and his army friends talking late into the night about what might happen with Japan and trying to anticipate their next move.

"Don't be too sure."

34

"What makes you say that?"

He shrugged. "Common sense, I guess. Look where we are. Smack in the middle of the Pacific, halfway to America from Tokyo. Hawaii would be strategically perfect for them. And since FDR moved the whole Pacific Fleet out here last year, I'd say we're a pretty nice target."

"They'd have to be pretty stupid," she said, picturing the formidable row of battleships lined up in the harbor.

"Or bold."

As if she didn't have enough on her mind already. A Japanese invasion was more than she could bear to think about at present, so she turned her attention at the scenery below. Once they flew past Koko Head crater and into the Kaiwi Channel, small whitecaps swirled in the sea below and the ride grew choppier. She tightened her seat belt against her hip bones. Forget about her white dress.

"Say, how long have you been flying?" she asked, afraid to hear his answer and yet needing to know.

"Nine years."

She pulled back to get a better look at him. "Wait a minute—how old are you?"

"Twenty-four. I know I look young, but I'd rather look young than old, wouldn't you?" he said with a lazy smile.

Her shoulders relaxed, and she let out a breath she hadn't even realized she'd been holding.

Baron offered the box of malasadas and she took one. With her stomach in a knot this morning, she had skipped breakfast and now realized she was famished.

The skies were clear, and they flew directly into the morning sun, which scattered a web of gold on the tips of the waves. She could almost see how one could get used to this. All was smooth until the approach into Kalaupapa, when the plane started dipping and diving erratically. She snuck a nervous glance at Baron.

He was facing straight ahead, calm as could be. "Relax, this is nothing," he said.

Closer to the spit of land that is Kalaupapa, Lana could make out the zigzag of the mule trail down the cliffs. A memory suddenly arose from over twenty years ago. The first time she had felt a strange prickly feeling in the air that preceded a tragedy.

One morning during third grade, a Hawaiian girl named Mele showed up to school with a rosy spot on her cheek. A few of the kids were teasing her about it, but Lana was scared for her. Everyone knew what a spot could mean. One of the teachers must have reported it, because just after lunch two men in suits came and hauled Mele off. For days and weeks afterward, Lana kept a lookout in the morning before school, hoping to catch sight of the girl's long, thick braids. But Mele never came back.

If you were Hawaiian, you had no immunity. And since Lana was part Hawaiian, she was convinced that she would end up with the sickness. She took to inspecting her entire little body several times a day, until her father informed her that, with his haole blood, she need not worry. Still, the look of pure terror on Mele's face was forever etched in her mind.

From above, with all the whitewashed plantation-style cottages, churches, rock walls and the lighthouse, it appeared a more bucolic settlement than anything. Then she noticed the runway. If you overshot it, there was a good chance you'd end up in the ocean. Lana closed her eyes and prayed.

They touched down without incident, and a cluster of men immediately came out to help unload. These were workers, not patients. Lana stood off to the side, wind tossing her hair in every direction. The air was ripe with salt. Onlookers crowded along the field: little kids, teens, men, women. Some stood; some were in wheelchairs. They all waved, and Lana and Baron waved back. People shouted *aloha* and *thank you*. She strained to see their faces. Would she even recognize Mele? But there were too many tears to see through.

A realization smacked her in the side of the head. All this time she'd been going about her life the wrong way. Here she was, distanced from her own father and refusing to come back home for how many years now? And the whole thing was self-imposed. These people would have given their lives to be together, in fact many had, following their diseased loved ones to Moloka'i and contracting leprosy themselves. A chill traveled up her spine.

Now, for her, it might be too late.

Midway between Maui and the Big Island, the weather took a frightening turn. Baron had warned her that the 'Alenuihāhā Channel was the windiest in the islands, and boy, was he right about that. The plane bucked and dipped like an angry wild bronco. Probably a good thing they had dropped off the cargo. Below, the ocean was a frenzy of white, and Lana wasn't sure if she'd rather be on a steamer or in this flying can of tin. The only thing for certain was that she would kiss the solid ground if they made it to Hilo alive.

"Hang on tight, there. Those clouds up ahead may cause some bumps," Baron said.

"Aren't we already in the bumps?" she asked, blood pressure rising by the second.

Just north of Upolu Point, everything was swallowed by an ominous wall of charcoal-and-navy storm clouds. Raindrops showed up on the windshield a few moments later, streaking up like tiny water snakes.

"Don't you need to be able to see where the cliffs are?" she yelled.

From there to Hilo the coastline was mostly deep valleys and sheer cliffs, thousands of feet high.

"It helps," he said, taking off his sunglasses and smoothing down his hair.

Five minutes into the wall of clouds, the plane went into a free fall. Lana let out a small scream. The box of malasadas hit the roof and rained down sugar. She looked over at Baron, whose face was unreadable. He made a wide turn. "I'm going to swing farther out to sea just to be safe," he said.

Safe was a poor word choice. In fact nothing about this whole experience felt safe. "Should we turn back?"

"You need to be in Hilo, don't you?"

"I do."

"Then why turn around?"

Baron must have been born with an extra helping of confidence, for which she was grateful. Her father always said that confidence was catching. Spend enough time with confident folks, and some would rub off on you. Lana began reciting the words *have faith* over and over in her head. But that ended with the first flash of lightning and a clap of thunder loud enough to drown out the engines.

Suddenly the plane went into a steep dive. If it

had been possible, she would have curled herself into a tiny ball and squeezed her eyes shut. She had no desire to watch the ocean come up on them. But her eyes refused to follow orders. Through breaks in the clouds, black and angry seas appeared here and there, waiting to swallow their little plane. One glance at Baron and his chalk-white face told her more than she needed to know.

"Just hang on, Mrs. Hitchcock," he said, somehow managing to level the plane out.

"But the ocean is right there," she said in a strangely high-pitched voice.

"Not for long."

Every hair on her body was standing on end. Another flash. They banked left and climbed a little. It was one of those strange moments when the entire world narrows to a pinhole. The slamming of her heart against its walls. The gasping for air, as though they had already gone underwater.

"Say, does this plane float?" she managed to ask.

Baron risked a glance her way. "I've never tested it out."

It seemed unlikely, as rainwater had made its way in through one of the window cracks, and the whole right side of her dress was soaked. Something funny happened then. A sense of calm started off in the middle of her chest and spread out in all directions. Like someone flipped a switch on the inside of her ribs. That rapid pounding subsided. Her hands stopped gripping the armrest.

Now she knew. This was the tragedy that had been buzzing through the air in recent days.

Dying might not be so bad after all. If there was a heaven, her mother might be there to welcome her in, and they could have all those mother-daughter conversations she'd missed out on throughout her life. Her father might even be there soon, too. Nor would she have to suffer any more heartache about Buck and that dumb Alexandra woman, and feeling like a failure in love. Granted, she didn't have the energy to care anymore, but the sad fact of the matter was that life was extremely overrated.

As luck would have it, the clouds began to thin. They were about a half mile offshore, safe from the cliffs but close enough to see waterfall after waterfall emptying into the ocean. The bumps lessened. Ten minutes later Hilo Bay came into view. Lana felt a surge of pure relief at being wrong. Apparently this wasn't her time.

Baron let out a huge exhale. "Now that is a damn happy sight."

Lana felt like cheering. "A miracle."

He patted the dashboard lovingly. "I'm a firm believer."

THE HOUSE

December 8, 1941
Volcano

The sky could not make up its mind. Rain turned off and on every thirty feet or so, and once they had put some distance between themselves and the guards, Lana pulled over to reexamine the directions.

Follow the road past Kano Store (29 miles). Turn up first side road, then at second cluster of Sugi pines turn right onto dirt drive and follow it about a mile or two. At fork, veer left. Watch out for cracks—and goats.

"Clear as mud," Lana mumbled to herself.

"Mud is not clear," Coco said.

Lana debated explaining but was too worn out. They rolled past Kano Store, which looked abandoned, though every place along the way had seemed the same: dark and closed up on the outside, while you knew there were people inside huddled around the radio, hanging on any and all news. In this case, though, she wondered if the Japanese owners had been hauled away.

Coco sat forward and looked out, her little button nose sniffing the air. "Where is everyone?"

"People are being cautious."

"It smells spooky here, don't you think?"

Marie jabbed Coco in the ribs. "She does this,

talking about smelling things, like she thinks she's a dog or something."

It *felt* spooky everywhere, though Lana couldn't attest to it smelling so. Air-raid sirens, convoys, armed men spilling through Hilo town. The fact that an invasion seemed imminent was enough to keep the whole island chain on the edge of their seats. But Coco was right—up here so far out in the sticks in a universe of fog, there was an extra feeling of unease.

Coco argued, "No, I don't. It just smells weird here, like something rotten."

A light went on in Lana's head. "Oh, that. It's the sulfur. Not far ahead, there's what they call the Sulphur Banks, where the whole ground is full of yellow crystals and seeping gases. Fun to visit as long as you have a bandana or something to put over your nose."

"Can we go?"

"Maybe once we settle in."

They came to a side road on the right that might have been a driveway, but fifty yards up and to the left, Marie spotted another road.

"What about that one?"

Of course the directions *had* to be missing that one crucial piece of information. But the road heading right, toward Mauna Loa, looked more like a real road, so Lana ventured that way.

"Keep an eye out for the Sugi pines," she told the girls.

Not far in they drifted past several tiny red houses surrounded by neat rows of vegetables and vine-covered fences. Not a leaf was out of place. Two fat and muddy pigs stood on the side of the road staring at them. But again, no people in sight. And no Sugi pines. Without the fog they would have been able to spot the towering trees from a good distance, but not today. They headed toward the last remnants of soggy light. Lord, she just wanted to get there already. All this fear was causing her stomach to twist in on itself.

Coco pointed to a tangerine tree. "Stop! Let's pick some."

"We have to keep going. Sorry," Lana said.

The temperature had gone from cool to icy in the past few minutes, and Lana felt for those in the back. It was likely to get worse quickly. The nene geese were probably the best off, but even they were accustomed to Hilo and its sea-level air.

When they'd gone farther than seemed right with no pine trees in sight, Lana turned the truck around and headed back toward the main road, silently cursing—or so she thought.

"My mother would not approve of that kind of talk," Coco announced.

Well, your mother isn't here, is she? almost came out, but Lana was aware her temper had whittled down to a nub. Instead she said, "Your mother would be right not to. Sorry. It's just that

I'm extraordinarily tired, and now add cold and hungry to that." She left out *scared* and *uncertain* and *alone*.

"My dad would call that an unhappy sandwich," Marie said.

Lana laughed. "Your parents sound like good people, and you know what?"

"What?" both girls said.

"As soon as they're back, we'll make them a big welcome-home dinner and—"

Coco drew the scratchy blanket up around her and cut Lana off. "They aren't coming back," she said, as though she knew something that Lana didn't.

Note: do not bring up the parents if you can help it.

"Your folks will be back once everything is sorted out. I promise you that. We just need to be patient."

More empty promises being made, and in all honesty she had no idea if the Wagners were helping the Germans in any way or not. She hardly knew them. But they were probably innocent, in which case they'd have to be released sooner than later.

"They haven't done anything, so quit your worrying. The people in charge will know that, won't they?" Marie said.

"Definitely."

"Who's in charge?" Coco asked.

"I believe it's the FBI and the US military working together. Right now their main concern is to keep everyone here in Hawaii safe. And in wartime that sometimes means acting first, asking questions later."

They were back on the main road, and Lana checked to make sure no cars were coming, then crossed and headed the other way, downhill from the volcano.

"Sailor wanted to go with them, to help protect them, but I asked her to stay with us instead," Coco said.

They hit a rut and all went flying.

"That was sweet of her," Lana said.

"She loves me the most is why."

"I'll bet."

On one hand Coco seemed like such a cute and delicate child, and on the other, precocious and strong willed and rather unpredictable. Either way, she was Lana's responsibility for the time being. It was all so surreal, how life could upend with the swish of a horsetail. One day enjoying the garden in Honolulu, the next on a harrowing plane ride to Hilo, and after that, war with Japan. Just the thought caused a line of perspiration to break out along her hairline.

A minute later Coco bounced up and down. "Look, over there, the big trees!"

Sure enough, there was a grove of Sugi pines. Their distinct cedar smell came in through the cracks. They went past it and kept an eye out for the next one, which they soon came upon. But there was no road in sight.

"It says right side, doesn't it?" Lana held the paper up for Coco, who passed it to Marie.

"Yep."

Lana backed up the truck, careful to stay on the road, which was already muddy enough. Getting stuck out here would be cause for a mental breakdown, for which there was no time. "Keep an eye out. It has to be there," she instructed.

This time she thought she saw a narrow opening in the bushes, barely wide enough for a car, with ginger crowding in on both sides and tall grass down the middle. A couple of lava rocks had been placed across the front, almost as a deterrent. As if anyone would be driving down this overgrown corridor on the side of an active volcano. Darkness was closing in fast.

Marie saw it, too. "That?"

"Has to be. Can you guys get out and move those?"

Much to her relief, the girls did as they were told. Coco also said to Sailor, "We'll be there soon, so don't worry."

Lana swung the truck wide and gassed it. They could put the rocks back later. Or not. Her father always leaned toward being overly cautious, but maybe in this case that had been in their favor. And as much as she was hoping that the house would be just what they needed, a small voice reminded her that this was Jack Spalding they were dealing with. Nothing involving her father ever went as expected.

After moving through dense 'ohi'a and tree ferns the size of giraffes for what seemed like an hour, they suddenly came upon a clearing. For as far as they could see—which wasn't saying much—there was only lava and tiny 'ōhelo berry bushes. Lana came to a stop.

"Is this it?" Marie asked.

There was no sign of a house. And almost no sign of a road across the lava. In this part of the volcano, there were newer flows over older flows, and you could have a barren rock desert next to a rain forest.

"Maybe this is where the road forks," Coco said.

Lana climbed out and noticed what could have once been a dirt road off to the right, and straight ahead there were signs of crushed lava and an ahu, a small piling of rocks the Hawaiians used to mark the trails across the lava. Earlier she had wondered about the cracks and goats comment. Now it made sense.

"I guess we go this way," she said, watching her words come out in small puffs of steam. "You guys okay back there?" she called.

A muffled *yes*.

The truck creaked and groaned along as they

crept across the lava flow. Coco sat at the edge of the seat. "Why would you put a house here?"

Lana had been wondering the same thing. Everyone with houses at Volcano built them mauka—toward the mountain—from the main road, where rich soil and rainfall made for an enchantingly rich landscape, with rhododendrons, blackberries, 'ōhelo berries, plums and wild strawberries dotting the forest. As a girl, Lana and her best friend, Rose Wallace, used to make up stories about the wild bands of fairies that traversed the area.

"I guess we'll see." It was too late to turn around now.

The ahu rock piles were helpful when one could see, but between the fog and the oncoming night, they came to a standstill. If it had been just her, Lana would have curled up with exhaustion and closed her eyes until the morning. In the past week her total hours of sleep had been less than twenty.

"We need to put the covers over the headlights so I can turn them on," Lana said.

"Even out here in the boondocks?" Marie asked.

"Better safe than sorry. That's our motto now, okay? You saw how jumpy everyone was back in Hilo. And we don't want to call attention to ourselves."

Lana hopped out and secured the heavy blue

cloth with slits down the center over each light. She kept the lights off until they were absolutely necessary. But with the fog, the lights only magnified the white. She imagined going off into a tantrum, just like Coco had earlier, but thought the better of it. *You're the adult here; you need to act like one.*

At several points they passed steaming cracks in the lava, and the girls hung their heads and arms out the window, and Sailor began another round of barking. At least they knew where they could find warmth if they needed to. Apparently the girls' parents had never brought them up here to see the volcano. Marie said it was because they spent every spare moment working.

They came to another abrupt switch in terrain, where they were back at an old-growth forest with strands of yellowish-green lichen hanging down from the branches. A group of small black animals scattered at their approach, revealing a narrow road.

"Pigs," Lana said.

"Ooh, I love pigs," Coco said, sounding delighted.

"Not these kind."

At long last the fog thinned and so did the foliage. At a small grassy clearing, another fork in the road showed up. The path they were on seemed to keep going downhill, while another one curved in. Visibility had gone from bad to worse, and Lana's eyes burned from all the squinting. For all she knew, they had driven ten miles, not one or two, so she took the turn and circled around a large cluster of cedar trees. If this wasn't it, well, they would pull over and camp.

Then Coco and Marie both screamed, "There it is!"

There, just beyond the trees, was a long one-story structure. Untreated wood siding, with an olive tin roof and rust-colored trim, a big deck out front and an empty trellis to one side. It looked large enough to house several families at once. A hand-painted sign said Hale Manu. At least they were in the right place.

"Is that a tree coming out of it?" Marie said.

From where they were, it did appear that a large tree was coming out of the roof. "I think it just looks that way."

"Do we get to choose our room?" Coco asked, as if they were on a Girl Scout adventure or at summer camp. She certainly had perked up in the last ten minutes, and Lana prayed it stayed that way. The mood swings were wearing on her.

"Of course."

The driveway ended in the grass, and she pulled up as close as she could get. With the motor turned off, the quiet was an eerie contrast. That was when they noticed the side of the house. Or rather, the lack thereof.

Coco's little face scrunched up. "Where's the wall?"

Lana mustered every ounce of strength she had to sound upbeat. "Well, that is a wonderful question. What do you say we go find out?"

THE HOMECOMING

December 6, 1941
Hilo

It was a strange and wondrous thing to approach Hilo from the air. The large crescent bay spanned out before them, as did the massive breakwater, Coconut Island, and the harbor full of colorful sampans and boats of all shapes and sizes. And over land, large swaths of cane as far as the eye could see, rows and rows of two-story buildings, and patches of rain coming down in big gray bursts.

Stepping off the plane was like walking into a wall of moisture. The kind that leaves a permanent sheen on your face and frizz in your hair. For a half second Lana thought about kneeling down and kissing the ground but decided to wait until later, when no one was watching. And, oh, that familiar scent of fish and burning sugarcane. She felt as though she was plopped right back to the moment she had left. Then, she'd traveled not by plane but by steamer. And not just to Honolulu but all the way across the cold Pacific to a strange and foreign land called California. She had known this trip would dredge up memories but was wholly unprepared for the jumbled mess of emotions she felt at that moment.

Images of her father suddenly came to light. Letting her stick her whole fist into a jar of honey they'd just harvested. His goofy grin when he'd come out of the water with a lobster in each hand and chased her around the beach while she screamed half in terror, half in delight. The way his voice lulled her to sleep reading *The Lilac Fairy Book* while he patiently answered endless questions. And then the look on his face when she'd told him the news. *Daddy, I have something to tell you.* They had been sitting on the porch listening to the roar of rain on the tin roof, but the cozy afternoon turned disastrous in five seconds flat.

So much love, spiked with anguish and one big wrong turn.

Baron was kind enough to arrange a ride for her to Hilo Memorial, and she slipped him a big tip as they parted ways.

"Keep yourself safe and happy," she said.

His eyes got wide when he saw the extra green. "Say, I usually come in around lunchtime Mondays, Wednesdays and Fridays, if you want to hitch a ride back."

"I'll look for you next week, then."

Hilo was nowhere the size of Honolulu, but it was the second-largest city in the territory and had grown since she'd left. There were more cars on the road now, and far fewer horses. Lawns were so lush and green they almost hurt your eyes to look at, a byproduct of the frequent rain.

The hospital was a one-story wooden building with elegant white stairs and a welcoming facade. Nevertheless, as she approached, Lana felt a squeezing in her chest. She had first agreed to see her father five years ago, when he had traveled to Honolulu for an engineering convention. He had asked if she would meet him for lunch. She'd reluctantly accepted his offer, but the lunch turned out stiff and awkward and painful. And when they parted, she promised she would try to visit. But whenever he called, she always had an excuse, sometimes real, sometimes manufactured. They still met up when he came to Honolulu, but it never felt right.

"Avoidance is the easy way out, Lana. Remember that," he had finally said, sounding ready to give up.

Over the years those words had bored into her psyche, keeping her up at night. Because, on some level, she knew he was right.

Inside the hospital there was no one at the front desk.

"Hello?" Lana said into the hallway.

Moments later a nurse came out of the nearest room. "Can I help you?"

"Yes, I'm here to see my father, Jack Spalding."

The woman stared at Lana a little too long, then said, "Hang on. Let me get Dr. Woodell."

A feeling of dread arose. Lana sat. Fiddled with

her hair. Watched a spotted gecko on the screen.

You're too late.

He's gone.

Stop.

He'll be fine.

Heavy footsteps announced Dr. Woodell, an impeccably dressed bald man with a mustache large enough to house several birds. His hands were clasped and his face unreadable.

"Would you come with me, Mrs. . . . ."

"Hitchcock. But call me Lana," she said.

He walked her into a small office lined with framed degrees and shut the door quietly behind her. "Is my father okay?" she said, antsy and suddenly out of breath.

"Have a seat."

Again, she sat. He sat across from her and took her hand. His palms were warm and clammy. Or maybe hers were the clammy ones.

His watery eyes said it all. "I'm sorry, dear, but your father did not make it. He succumbed several hours ago to the meningitis."

The words refused to register, hanging halfway between her and Dr. Woodell. Suspended midair. She fought them off. Her stomach felt an awful turning.

"Wait, no. But I just spoke with him last night," she protested.

"It's been touch and go for several days. Problem was he came in too late. We gave him the serum, but the swelling had already taken hold."

"No!"

"I'm sorry."

She wondered about his last moments. Had he known? "How did he die?"

"He went into a coma early this morning. And once that happened, it was a matter of hours," he said, squeezing her hand and covering it with his other one.

This had been the one thing she had not counted on to happen. Her father had been a young and active fifty-two. In fact she always knew he'd be a young eighty, when the time came. Or even a young one hundred. In some small corner of her mind, there had been the rock-solid belief that when she was ready to patch things up, he would be there.

How selfish and stupid and naive.

Small, choking sobs wanted to come out but lodged in her windpipe instead. Lana buried her face in her hands. This was not supposed to happen. She'd come to be with him. She was a lifetime too late. Tears turned on and flooded her cheeks. Someone must have made a mistake.

"Are you sure he's dead and not still in a coma?" she found herself asking.

Dr. Woodell, bless his heart, pulled her in and gave her a hug, and not the fake kind where someone just pats your back and says *there,*

there. Her head rested on his shoulder and she inhaled starch and something sharply medicinal. "You can see him, if that would help," he said.

That made her sit straight up. "He's still here?"

"Downstairs. They are readying him for the mortuary. From his file, you're his only next of kin," he said.

"He has a sister in California."

"Well, you were the only one he talked about. From what I gathered, you are quite a gifted artist. You were at the top of your class, and you had big dreams of being a volcanologist," he said.

Lana had to laugh at that. "I do enjoy drawing, and those dreams of being a volcanologist were quite far-fetched. As a girl I was enamored with Thomas Jaggar and his wife, Isabel. I met them only a couple of times, but they left a lasting impression, especially Isabel. That was a long time ago, though, and you know how it goes with dreams."

His eyes sparkled. "Dreams are what hold our world together."

"In my experience, dreams don't usually pan out." She realized she sounded harsh, but this was not the time to talk about old dreams and missed opportunities. Outside, a mynah bird screeched. "Please take me to see my father and then I'll be out of your hair."

He led her down the hallway, and she focused

on his scuffed cowboy boots. They didn't match the starched coat and polished man. *This is Hilo,* she reminded herself. The minute they reached the back door, a downpour started. Dr. Woodell stopped on the small porch, and Lana held out her hand to catch the drops, which felt warm and reassuring on her palm.

The doctor pulled an envelope out of his pocket. "I guess I'll give you this now. It's from your father. He actually had one of the nurses write it out, but these are his words."

She slipped the letter into her pocket, unsure of when she would have the courage to open it. Right now she wanted to get this horrible thing over with and get to his house. Their house. Her house, now. And then catch the next flight back to Honolulu. Hilo without her father was unthinkable. But who would make arrangements for his funeral? The thought made her dizzy. *Take a breath, one step at a time.*

The rain let up a few minutes later, as it usually did here, and they went into the basement. The room was cool and dimly lit. Her nose picked up a sour and waxy smell, mostly masked by a strong chemical odor. On one side there was a large steel table with a sheet draped over what could only be a body.

Dr. Woodell stood next to it and fingered his stethoscope. "Are you sure about this? The choice is all yours, but I do know that sometimes it helps with closure. And I can leave you alone, too."

The truth of the matter was Lana had never seen a dead person, and she was terrified. "I need to do this," she said.

When the sheet came off, she saw a pale and much too thin version of her father. He was wearing an orange aloha shirt and his hands were crossed over his midsection, as if he had just lain down for a nap. Would it be strange if she climbed on the table with him and rested her head on his chest and told him that, despite it all, she loved him? She was so caught up in persuading herself that he was dead that she forgot to breathe.

"I'll step out for a minute," Dr. Woodell said, leaving her alone with the body.

The body.

Lana moved closer and bent down, placing her hand over his heart. She half expected to feel a beat. "Daddy," she whispered.

No answer.

Outrage threatened to split her down the middle, coupled with a bone-weary sadness. Her whole body trembled. "Daddy." There were so many things to say, and instead, huge gasping sobs overcame her. Before she knew it, her ear was flattened against his chest and she listened to the silence of a still heart. This life was done. Her father, gone on to heaven or one of those strange other worlds he used to talk about. Strings of her snot dampened his shirt. She had no idea how long she stayed like that. Her neck ached but she didn't care.

Eventually Dr. Woodell came back in, placing his hand on her back. "Dear, your father will always be with you. It's time to go," he said.

Outside, the air was still buzzing, which Lana found curious, since the tragedy had already happened.

THE GERMANS

December 6, 1941
Hilo

Life in Hilo revolved around sugar and fishing, and Lana was surprised at how many people milled about the sidewalks—Hawaiian, Japanese, Filipino, Portuguese, Chinese, haole and everything in between. Maybe because it was Saturday afternoon, *pau hana* time, and everyone was eager for a cold beer and the weekend, or maybe there were just more people now. She half expected to see Mochi or any of her father's other friends in the mix. Tall blue shadows from a row of two-story buildings fell on the far side of the street. The sun went down early, behind Mauna Kea, on this side of the island.

At her father's place, down Kīlauea Avenue, the mango tree had nearly doubled in size, but otherwise the house looked exactly the same. Red roof and siding, white trim. Ti leaves galore. Grass had grown knee-high in some places, matching the Ramirezes' horse pasture on one side. On the other side, where Mr. Young used to live, Lana noticed two blonde haole girls riding their bikes around a newly paved circular drive in front of the house. Never mind the wet grass and salty rain.

Whoever the family was, they had done a massive cleanup. Mr. Young had not believed in throwing anything away. Old cars, cable drums, furniture, lumber, fencing, an antique icebox, you name it. Her father had found more than his share of treasures there, and come to think of it, so had she.

Lana waved at the girls, who had stopped their riding to gawk at her. The older one waved back and gave a shy smile, but the younger one looked down. In no mood to socialize, Lana hurried up the steps and onto the lanai. The door was unlocked, as usual, and the moment she stepped inside, she felt a trembling under her skin. She fought the urge to turn around and run back out the door.

While Mr. Young had kept absolutely everything, her father had kept everything he ever made. Light fixtures made from wood and Hawaiian print fabric, driftwood creatures with copper wire limbs and *puka*-shell eyes, a bench designed for opening coconuts, gadgets that served a purpose only he understood. *Organized chaos,* he used to say.

Now the house was nearly empty, but for the furniture and books. It felt as though its soul had been removed. She went into the bedrooms. Same thing. Had someone come and taken his stuff, or had he moved it somewhere? Strange, he hadn't mentioned it on the phone. Lana sunk into a chair, perplexed.

As she sat there, the letter in her pocket felt as heavy as a lead fishing weight. To read or not to read? On the one hand, she was curious and knew it was the rational thing to do; on the other, reading the letter would be like reading the last page of a beloved book. Once those words came out, there would be nothing more. She pulled it out and set it on the table.

Someone rang the cowbell at the door. "Hello?" A tall woman stood outside the screen peering in, a girl on each side of her.

Lana greeted them and invited them in. The woman introduced herself as Ingrid Wagner, and the girls as Marie and Coco. Ingrid wore a stylish blue-and-white sleeveless dress, and all three of them were barefoot. "We are so sorry about your father. Dr. Woodell called us this morning to break the news." She had a strong German accent. "Jack felt like family to us," she said with genuine sadness.

The older girl said, "We help him feed and take care of Gin and Tonic."

"Gin and Tonic?"

"The geese. Your father had a sense of humor, didn't he?"

"Oh, the geese, that's right," Lana said, laughing nervously.

Up until this moment, there had been no mention of geese. And how much did these people know about her anyway? Surely if they had lived here any amount of time, they would have known that Lana had not set foot on the property recently. The ungrateful daughter.

"Anything that walks on four legs, swims or flies, and my girls want to be involved," Ingrid said, glancing at the girls with adoration plastered all over her face.

"How long have you folks been here?" Lana said.

"In Hilo for six years and this house for four. My husband struck up a friendship with Mr. Young, who used to come into our store, and he agreed to pass on the house when he died."

How anyone could have seen through all that junk, Lana would never know. Mr. Wagner must have a good imagination.

"What kind of store do you own?"

"Oh, dry goods of all sorts. We specialize in watches and radios, too."

A strange racket started up outside.

Marie smiled. "The geese want their dinner. Come meet them!"

"Honey, she probably wants to be left alone," Ingrid said, then turned to Lana. "We'll leave you, but I just wanted to say hello. And if there is anything at all we can help you with—"

"You know, I'll come see the geese," Lana said.

As much as she wished they would leave her alone, it felt good to have people around. Despite being a knockout who looked like she belonged in a *Vogue* magazine, Ingrid seemed very motherly.

Something Lana could use about now. They went out back to a large fenced enclosure, complete with a small pond. Leave it to her father to begin collecting nene geese. Whatever struck his fancy, he would dive in up to his teeth. You never knew what strange notions would take up residence in that overactive brain of his.

Coco opened the gate and waltzed in, ignoring the honking and flapping and threatening-looking behavior. She held tight to her bucket.

"Careful," Lana said.

Ingrid waved her hand as though it were nothing. "He's just posturing."

Next to the pond, Coco emptied out the bucket, and the geese converged on the berries and grass as though they hadn't eaten in weeks. The little girl crouched down and began stroking the smaller goose on the back.

Ingrid leaned close and spoke quietly. "Coco may have her quirks, and she's not an easy child, but boy, does she love these geese. And they love her back."

Lana decided that the woman smelled like marshmallows. This was the perfect solution. "I suppose I should ask, then—would you like to keep them? I wouldn't have the faintest idea what to do with them, and I certainly can't take them back to O'ahu with me," Lana said.

"I can ask Fred. I know Coco would be devastated to see them go."

"And for now, they could stay here at the house."

Ingrid looked as though she had swallowed a plum. Her sky-blue eyes widened. "You don't know, then. . ."

"Know what?"

"*Meine liebe*, your father sold us his house, too."

An invisible hand slapped Lana across the face. *"What?"*

This house that she had purposefully stayed away from suddenly seemed essential as air, more valuable than every other possession. This would have to be undone.

"It was your father's idea. He said he needed the money for a project, and that you had no interest whatsoever. We want more kids and horses and dogs, so it made sense," Ingrid said, her singsong voice now strained under the weight of bad news.

"When did he do this?"

"Earlier this year, but we said he could stay for a while."

All worry about pretenses evaporated. "What was the project he needed money for?" Lana asked.

"He kept it to himself, but he did say he would tell us when the time was right. He would disappear for stretches of time. A week here, a few weeks there."

Jack had gone through an assortment of

obsessions, always the next big invention, and usually ended up more broke than when he started. Pulley systems for cane, earthquake warning systems, amphibious vehicles. What would have made him sell off the house?

"Would anyone else know?"

Ingrid shrugged. "Beats me. He had that old fisherman friend, Mr. Mochizuki, I think? And a few others I saw around here. But most of my time lately has been at the shop."

Hawaii had a knack for attracting adventurous and ambitious people, the kind who would move clear around the globe for a better life. Lana admired that. The slamming of the enclosure gate startled her back to the geese and tall grass. Coco skipped past them humming.

"Look, feel free to stay as long as you need to. To sort out your father's affairs and figure out what to do next. Will your husband be joining you?" Ingrid said.

Lana winced at the word *husband*. For so many years now she had been known as *Buck Hitchcock's wife*. All around town that was how she was introduced. Never just *Lana*.

"We're separated."

Spoken aloud for the first time, it was like hearing the words from someone else. Yet this was her life. She was now a family of one.

"What a hard time this must be for you. I'm sorry."

"Feast or famine, you know how that goes," Lana said, though it was quite possible that Mrs. Wagner did not know. She seemed like *that* kind of person.

"Would you come for breakfast in the morning? I hate for you to be handling this alone. And your father was like family to us."

Lana wasn't in the mood to socialize but couldn't come up with an excuse fast enough. "Thank you. I'd like that."

The whole thing felt like a sad dream. Just then a shiny black car turned up the Wagners' drive. A massive dog hung halfway out the window, pink tongue flapping in the wind. Both girls took off running.

"Here's Fred," said Ingrid, waving as though she hadn't seen him in weeks.

Lana said goodbye and made a hasty retreat into the now dark house. Before reading the letter, she needed food. Someone had emptied out the fridge, and the cupboards were nearly bare, but she found a can of tuna, a bag of stale Saloon Pilot crackers and a startled cane spider. One thing she had not missed about Hilo. There was also a big bottle of gin staring her in the face. She wasn't much of a drinker but poured herself a shot. *Why the hell not?*

Within ten minutes she was more than a little woozy and lay down on the *pune'e* with the letter in hand. She pulled down the string for the light.

My dear Lana,

In case I don't make it through, the first thing I want you to know is that I never once stopped loving you, not for one second of one minute of one day. I wish we could undo stupid decisions, but we can't. For that I am sorrier than I hope you will ever be, and here is my advice to you: always put people and love first. I don't care what the circumstance. No amount of pigheaded ideals are worth it. I should know. Damn, my head hurts and I wish I could say more right now. Just know that you will always be my little girl.

Be careful, Jack
PS Check the inside
of your favorite book.

Was that it? Lana flipped the paper over. There had to be more. The back was blank. *Be careful?* Her mouth went dry. What about the house? A burning need to know filled every pore in her body. She glanced over at the bookshelf. *The Education of Henry Adams, Pragmatism, The Sound and the Fury, The Theory of Continuous Structures and Arches.* She stood, then walked over to the shelf, inhaling the musty book smells. Mixed in with his books were a few she recognized as hers. *Riders of the Purple Sage,*

The Secret of the Old Clock, *The Secret Garden*.
She opened these and leafed through them, even
though none had been her favorite. Her hand
shook with each turn of the page. Nothing. And
then a small slip of paper fell out of *The Call of
the Wild*.

She picked it up. It was a drawing of a girl
standing on a dappled horse, with what looked
like honeybees, or maybe fireflies, swarming
around them. She had no memory of the drawing
but recognized it as her own. What was she even
looking for? Her father's vagueness bothered her,
and she was ready to give up, having scanned
every row. Then, on the bottom shelf, pushed
back and shadowed by two other books, she
spotted *The Wonderful Wizard of Oz*. A tingling
ran across her skin. As a girl, she loved this book
so much that the minute she finished, she would
go right back to the beginning and start again.

When she cracked it open, a manila envelope
stuffed with papers dropped into her hand. *Hale
Manu* was scrawled across the front—"house
of birds." The name made her smile. Jack was
bird obsessed, and he had passed his love onto
Lana, who at a young age had memorized every
Hawaiian bird in the forest. She went to the table
and dumped out the contents: a folded-up sketch
of a house, rough but elegant; a piece of paper
with directions written on it, starting at Kano
Store in Volcano; a key; and a piece of card that

read "When the time comes, all are welcome."

The room was full of orange light from the homemade lamp and the whirring of moth wings against the screen. She had no idea how long she stared at the words. *When the time comes.* She thought back to what Ingrid said, about telling them when the time was right. Had her father built a house and said nothing to anyone about it? At the volcano no less. There was only one Kano Store that she knew of. None of it made any sense. Especially the cryptic nature of it all.

Perhaps he was worried about a tsunami. Or maybe another eruption from Mauna Loa but this time actually reaching Hilo and wiping it out. The only other possibility that came to mind was the attack or invasion by the Japanese that everyone was talking about. What they had done to China was unthinkable, and rumors and headlines had been storming around town, increasing by the week. She felt a strange, heavy feeling inside. Her father had lots of Japanese friends. What if he knew something? The newspaper headline came back to her then: *Japanese May Strike over the Weekend.* All the more reason to get back to Honolulu, which had a good portion of the US Navy there for protection.

She had two hundred more questions, but her eyelids kept shutting. It was as if the whole world had tilted under her, and if she didn't lie down now, there was a good chance she would collapse. No teeth brushing, no changing, no using the bathroom. She fell to the dusty sheets of the *pune'e* in slow motion and curled into a ball. There was a hollow spot on the mattress in the shape of her father, and the house was so quiet she could almost hear the sound of his knife on a plate, or the shaking of ice around his glass when he'd finished his drink. All of his noises suddenly filled the room.

As bone tired as she was, Lana lay awake for hours, tossing and turning and crying. Apologizing, rewriting their history, and telling him how mixed-up she felt. She was mad at him for going and dying, mad at herself for not coming back to Hilo sooner. The sad truth was she was the world's worst daughter.

THE NEWS

December 7, 1941
Hilo

Lana woke to the sound of roosters. For a moment she had no idea where she was, not to mention a terrible case of cotton mouth. As it turned out, gin and tuna were a poor dinner combination. Now her stomach growled with hunger and her temples throbbed. There were so many odds and ends to tackle today that she ordered herself not to think about any of them until after breakfast.

Coming up the Wagners' steps with a bouquet of freshly picked ginger, she smelled bacon and something fresh-baked and cinnamony. "Hello," she called.

A sudden roar of barking stopped her in her tracks. The door opened and a black-and-white dog bounded out. All paws and limbs, it came nearly up to her waist. Lana wasn't sure whether to turn and flee or greet the dog in her most assured voice.

Marie was behind the dog. "Don't worry, she's friendly."

The dog sniffed and licked and leaned with her whole hundred pounds against Lana, making it impossible for her to move.

"Sailor, stop," Marie said, laughing.

Lana had never encountered such an enormous house pet. So much tongue and slobber, now transferred to her skirt in frothy strings. She enjoyed dogs as much as the next person, but why would anyone want such a huge one?

The Wagners' whole house was unrecognizable from the way Lana remembered it, especially the kitchen. Shiny white paint, eyelet curtains, black-and-white checkered linoleum on the kitchen floor, and a spanking-new red refrigerator. Ingrid stood beside the stove in a peach-colored apron, waving around a spatula and singing to the radio when Lana walked in. Mr. Wagner lowered his newspaper and stood to shake her hand.

"Well, I'll be damned, you look Hawaiian," he said, as though this were some huge revelation.

Ingrid shot him a look.

"My father never mentioned it?" Lana said.

"I could ask Jack why my engine was idling high, how to unstick the lawnmower blades or what ships were in port, but we drew the line there. Man talk," he said, grinning with a set of orderly teeth.

It sounded exactly right. "My mother was Hawaiian, from Kaua'i. She died in childbirth," Lana said.

That shut him up fast.

"Now losing Jack must be doubly hard on you. I'm so sorry," Ingrid said, though Lana guessed that she already knew the story, as a mother herself. Women had a knack for uncovering all kinds of details that wash right past the men. Mothers especially. It seemed as though being a mother elevated you into a special club where you suddenly developed superhuman skills. Lana was not a part of that club and felt like half a woman because of it. By all appearances the Wagners were the perfect family. If Lana hadn't liked them so much, she would have been wallowing in envy.

"Coco, come help set the table," Ingrid called.

A minute later Coco pranced in with a lizard on her shoulder. She made no eye contact with Lana and announced, "I hear airplanes."

Fred peered out from behind the newspaper with slate-colored eyes and bushy brows, tilting his head. "Do you, now?" He and Ingrid exchanged glances.

It was possible that Lana missed it, with the sizzling bacon and conversation. But everyone quieted. The only sounds were the rustling coconut fronds and cooing doves. She listened hard for engines.

"Our Coco has an active imagination. Don't you, dear," Ingrid said, ruffling up her daughter's hair.

Coco went to the window, stood on her tippy toes and looked out. "I'm not making it up, and there are lots of them."

A peculiar feeling of unease circled through the room.

"Honey, maybe you did, or maybe it was just car noise. Now please get the silverware out."

The little girl did as she was told, and Lana hoped that the speckled gecko would stay put on Coco's arm and leave the freshly cut papaya and banana for the people. Coco moved around Lana as though she wasn't there.

"Is that a pet?" Lana asked.

"No, it's a friend."

"Does your friend have a name?"

Coco looked straight at her and said, "Jack."

Lana commanded herself to hold it together.

Ingrid jumped in. "She really looked up to your father. He talked to her as a real person, not just a kid. And her favorite thing was when he cut open coconuts for her. It got to the point where she would wait on his deck for him to come home in the afternoons. She could never get enough. In fact that's how she got the nickname Coco. Her real name is Berta."

Marie came in with Sailor just then and filled a bucket with water. Sailor drank noisily and then went to a rug and lay down without even being asked. This kitchen was like a warm and cozy center of the universe—you could almost feel it pulsing. No wonder her father had befriended the Wagners.

"Do you have plans for a service? I would be more than happy to help," Ingrid said.

"I haven't had a chance to think about any

of that yet. When I flew over yesterday, I was expecting to be nursing him back to health, not planning a funeral."

"You must still be in shock. We all are," Fred said.

"It feels that way."

Numbness was better than the alternative.

"I had a dream about him last night," Coco said.

"Oh?" Lana said, not quite sure she wanted to hear.

Coco went on. "He and a Hawaiian lady were riding a big horse down the beach and they went into the water. He was waving at me and yelling something but I couldn't hear. I ran down to try to get in the water to follow, but the water turned to lava, and when I looked up again, they were gone."

No one said anything for a moment, and the scene that Coco described filled Lana's mind perfectly. She had the experience of watching a full-color film of her parents, so real she could smell the seaweed on the sand and hear her mother's laugher in the wind. She almost called out.

Ingrid's voice brought her back. "I imagine we all may have dreams of Jack in the days to come."

Fred steered the conversation to safer ground, wanting to know all about Oʻahu and how it was to live in the hub of the islands, with the world at your fingertips and opportunities around every corner. She was thankful for the change in subject, far less likely now to break down into a teary mess.

Soon the meal was served, and if Lana had ever eaten a more delicious breakfast, she couldn't remember it. Crisp bacon and fluffy eggs, golden scones and guava jelly with just the right tartness, and cream-topped milk. Lana was tempted to bring up the house and find out how much they had purchased it for but figured there would be time for that later. Instead they made small talk about the latest happenings in Hilo. Marie talked about her upcoming Christmas concert and Coco picked at her food and remained mostly silent. Once they finished eating, Lana offered to do the dishes and Ingrid turned the volume on the radio back up.

"In this household, music rules the roost," she said, swaying her hips from side to side and trying to pull Coco into a hug. But Coco stood ramrod straight and looked like she was about to cry. "What's a matter, *Mausi*?"

A burst of static came over the radio, and then Webley Edwards, in that unmistakable baritone, was saying, "All right, now, listen carefully. The island of O'ahu is being attacked by enemy planes. The center of this attack is Pearl Harbor, but the planes are attacking airfields, as well. We are under attack."

Lana glanced around at everyone frozen like statues in a pool of sunlight. Ingrid was tomato red, while Fred had turned white. *We are under attack* echoed around the room. Everyone stared at the radio, except for Coco, who was looking right at Lana. In that fraction of time, something strange passed between them. A flash of knowing, and then it was gone.

Webley's voice droned on. "There seems to be no doubt about it. Do not go out on the streets. Keep under cover and keep calm. Some of you may think that this is just another military maneuver. This is not a maneuver. This is the real McCoy! I repeat, we have been attacked by enemy planes. The mark of the rising sun has been seen on the wings of these planes and they are attacking Pearl Harbor at this moment. Now keep your radio on and tell your neighbor to do the same. Keep off the streets and highways unless you have a duty to perform. Please don't use your telephone unless you absolutely have to do so. All of these phone facilities are needed for emergency calls. Now standby, all military personnel and all police—police regulars and reserves. Report for duty at once. I repeat, we are under attack by enemy planes. The mark of the rising sun has been seen on these planes. Many of you have been asking if this is a maneuver. This is not a maneuver. This is the real McCoy."

After a moment of shocked silence, Fred,

Ingrid and Lana all started talking at once, words layered on top of one another in a semipanicked jumble.

"It was only a matter of time, those bastards," Fred said.

"Lord, have mercy on us all. We need to find shelter," Ingrid blurted out, grabbing hold of the girls and pressing their heads to her chest. She rattled off a long burst of words in German.

Lana was thinking of immediate safety, if Coco had indeed heard airplanes. "I know of a lava tube nearby. We can hide in there if we have to."

Time went thick as molasses, and in one second Lana managed to think of Buck in Nuʻuanu and pray that he was okay, as well as picture her best friends—Mary on Diamond Head and Alice in Mānoa valley—with a quick flash to Baron and his little airplane not too far from Pearl Harbor, along with all the other people she knew and cared about. The human mind was a mysterious and wondrous thing, how it took over in a catastrophe.

"Stay here," Fred said. "I'm going to get my rifle."

Ingrid grabbed his arm. "Hang on—what should we do?"

"See if there's any more news on the other station," he said as he ran out the door.

Lana felt as helpless as a baby, turning the knobs but coming up with only static and

Hawaiian slack-key guitar. "How did those Japanese pilots fly all the way over here? This has to be some kind of mistake," Ingrid said, voicing one of the many questions Lana had.

"Mama, they wouldn't broadcast that to the world unless they knew for sure," Marie said, sounding like the most levelheaded of the bunch.

Over Sunday morning breakfast, the world had up and gone to war. Surely FDR would not take this lying down. Lana looked at the phone. She would have given anything to pick it up and call someone—anyone—who could tell them what was happening. Sailor, clearly aware that something was going on, came over leaned against Coco and started panting. The clock read 9:05.

Nothing will ever be the same. This was not how Lana had planned to begin her Sunday. There were too many other things to attend to, and a flash of anger ran through her.

"How dare they!" she said.

Ingrid went to the window. "I don't see any planes, but Coco, you were right about hearing them."

Had the planes passed right over Hilo on the way to Pearl Harbor? Possibly, but it would have taken them hours to get there. It sounded as though the attack was still ongoing. If only her father were here, he would know exactly what to do.

Two seconds later the telephone rang.

Ingrid grabbed it. "Hello? He went out back for a moment. Who's calling, please?"

The line went dead.

"Who was it?" Lana asked.

"It cut him off. I'm not sure. Say, girls, would you mind going into the living room for a moment?"

"Why?" Coco said with a frown.

"We need a few minutes of adult talk. Go now."

Both girls did as asked, though Coco lingered at the door.

"Scoot," Ingrid said. As soon as they were gone, she began wringing her hands and pacing. "This won't look good for us, you know that, right?"

"You folks are members of the community. I'm sure you have nothing to worry about," Lana said.

"We're German, Lana. And Germany and Japan are allies."

"But you've been here a long time. And you aren't Nazis . . . are you?" the last words came out of their own accord.

Ingrid made a face as though she had just drunk a spoonful of vinegar. "Of course not. We abhor what Hitler is doing over there. It's why we left."

"Okay, so one thing at a time. Right now we need to focus on whether to stay put or seek shelter, and whether or not there are Japanese planes coming to Hilo," Lana said.

"Maybe we should move farther from the harbor. If they come in anywhere, it'll be here."

She had a good point. Lana had had friends from Wainaku and friends in Hakalau and Kaumana, but who knew if they were still around. Young people who went off to college and moved onto bigger and better things often never returned.

"It makes sense, but the radio said not to go into the streets," Lana said.

Ingrid looked as though she was about to hyperventilate. "Dear God, please keep my girls safe. We are sitting geese."

If there were Japanese planes nearby, that meant Japanese ships and Japanese submarines loose in Hawaiian waters. And Japanese ships and submarines meant a Japanese invasion. Where were the American forces? Lana tried to remember seeing any ships on the plane ride over, but her mind had been so busy trying to keep calm that she had no recollection.

Fred burst back in, slinging a rifle, with both girls at his heels. Not much that was going to do against a Japanese fighter plane, but Lana held her tongue. A rifle was better than nothing. They all sat back down, except for Fred, who paced the kitchen and ducked down to check the skies out the window for airplanes every thirty seconds. His nostrils flared and he looked ready to shoot the next pigeon that flew by.

"My dad has one, too. I can grab that," she said. He nodded.

Outside, nothing seemed any different. A butterfly hovered around the pikake bush and the doves went about their usual business of sitting on tree branches, wing to wing, and catching sun. Lana listened for the roar of engines but heard only the radio blaring from the Wagners' window. Maybe she ought to go check in with the Ramirezes, but Mrs. Ramirez would want to know every last detail of the past ten years, and Lana didn't have it in her. She also thought about Ryo Mochizuki—better known as Mochi—her dad's fishing buddy who lived on the next street over, a quick walk through a pasture and over an old rock wall.

After leaving her father's Winchester with Fred, Lana set out to look for Mochi. Out of all the people she'd left behind in Hilo, he had been one of her favorites. He had big teeth and a bigger smile, with a laugh that sounded like a lonely donkey. His folks had come over to work on the sugar plantations when he was just ten. One dip in the warm Hawaiian water and he never looked back. Her father and Mochi shared a love of fishing and became fast friends. After breakfast she had been planning on visiting him anyway, so why let an air raid stop her? What else was she going to do?

As usual the grass in Mochi's yard was clipped

an even two inches, and there wasn't a ti leaf out of place. The trim on his tiny white house was red and the hedge freshly cut. Lana had never once walked into the house and not smelled fish, and in the late afternoons, in the glow of sunset, there was often such an accumulation of fish scales that the whole place shimmered silver.

This morning the curtains were drawn and the house felt empty. She knocked anyway. "Mochi, it's Lana Spalding. Please open up if you're here!"

There were no signs of movement. Maybe he was out fishing, but she sure as heck hoped not. She pounded again. "Mochi?"

Six seconds later, the door sprung open and a teenage boy was staring her in the face. Lana was shocked. Had Mochi had a son in her absence? The boy said nothing but motioned her in.

Smells have a way of transporting you back in time, and here was no different. *Sashimi, poi and laughter.* Fish tails and lures and glass balls in nets lined the walls. Mochi was sitting at the card table in the middle of the room. A radio played music in the corner.

He didn't stand. "Lana-san," he said, his voice hoarse.

From the dark skin beneath his eyes, and the way his cheekbones and collarbones stood out under his leathery skin, it was clear he wasn't well. "Mochi, have you heard? My father."

One nod.

"And the attack?" she said.

Another nod.

All at once Lana burst out in tears. Life was blowing up around her, and it only seemed to be getting worse by the minute. She pulled out the chair next to him and sat. He reached out and held her hands, their warm calluses a familiar comfort on her skin. Mochi had been here as long as she could remember, a fixture in the neighborhood.

"Mochi, what's happened to you?"

"I could ask the same of you," he said gently.

"We can talk later. I just feel at such a loss, like I need someone to tell me what to do. Have you heard anything other than what's on the radio, maybe from your fisherman friends?" she asked.

"Judge Carlsmith called and said the lobster traps are full. It was our code if they started rounding us up."

Her stomach fell to the floor. "You had a code?"

Mochi's voice caught. "They already assigned him to keep an eye on me. The feds made lists months ago of anyone they suspected might be dangerous if a war broke out."

"Who are *they,* and why you?" she asked.

"The FBI, army, police. Because I have a boat and because I play cards with some of the Japanese leaders in town. Who knows exactly?" he said, moving a puzzle piece into place.

The weight of his words glued her to the chair.

On one hand, it was not entirely unexpected; she had caught wind of these kinds of ideas. On the other, it seemed impossible and unfair. "What are they planning on doing with the men on these lists?"

"Arresting, holding, I don't know."

"So you're on the list and that means you're going to be arrested?" she said, her voice cracking.

His withered shoulders shrugged.

Lana glanced over at the boy, who was in the kitchen making tea. "What about him. Is he your son?"

"I took Benji in after his parents were lost at sea on a trip back to Japan. He had no one here."

"How long has he been with you?"

"Seven years."

Mochi had had this boy for seven years, and Lana had not even known. She felt more ashamed than ever at her absence. As much as she wanted to find out more about Mochi and why he was as thin as a blade of grass, a voice inside was screaming that they needed to get away from Hilo Bay. Her father's neighborhood was only two blocks from the water, and if the Japanese army attacked, they were likely to be flattened. Mochi's house was even closer.

"Come to my house," she said.

His watery eyes met hers. "Why?"

"You'll be safer there, and if we need to

evacuate, you can come with us. I'm going to load up the truck when I get back."

"Where are you planning on going?"

"Away from the water, up mauka someplace," she said, with nowhere specific in mind.

"I can't run away."

"You're an American fisherman, and from the looks of it, you aren't well. You're no threat, Mochi, and I can help take care of you."

He looked up at Benji, who had just set down a mug of steaming tea. "You go on. We'll be fine."

Mochi was not the kind of man you argued with. His word was immovable stone. There were so many questions she wanted to ask about her father, and if she didn't ask now, she might not have another chance. But fear won out in the end. "If you change your mind, you know where to find me."

THE VISITORS

December 7, 1941
Hilo

The telephone sat on her father's desk, begging to be used. More out of duty than anything, Lana wanted to call Buck. Not to mention needing to hear a firsthand account of what was going on in Honolulu. But when she picked up the phone, there was a conversation between the operator and an irate neighbor demanding to get through to his son on Oʻahu. She set down the receiver. Had Buck even tried to reach her? Odd to think that at some point in the future their lives would not even touch.

It wasn't long before Lana found herself back in the Wagners' kitchen. Human contact was what she realized she craved the most, even if it was with people she had just met. Fred had gone to town to secure their store and collect all the money, and Lana sat with Ingrid and Marie, while Coco was on the porch reading to the geese from a picture book. She had insisted on bringing them up under cover, and Ingrid apparently had a hard time saying no. Sailor eyed the geese through the screen door.

Bursts of radio news came in between a church sermon. *"The attack was wholly unexpected, five*

93

civilians killed in Honolulu, Japanese paratroopers spotted on Oʻahu's north shore, and a direct hit on Hickam Airfield resulted in at least three hundred and fifty deaths." Bombs falling in Honolulu seemed so far-fetched that Lana was having a hard time believing. Her town, her people. Every update caused another round of tears, and she wondered how much more she could take.

The big question remained: When were they coming for Hilo? Fred came back in the middle of the afternoon with an armful of metal boxes and more bad news. "Marie, would you fill up the bathtub? They're saying the Japanese are poisoning our water supply. Ingrid and Marie, come with me."

They disappeared into the bedroom, leaving Lana alone with her vivid imagination. Her mind pulled up pictures of whole towns in flames, soldiers going door-to-door raping, killing and looting. Accusations of slaughter in China had been plastered across the newspapers, leaving her with the taste of blood in her mouth. Being stuck on an island with an invading army was about the worst fate she could think of.

To avoid dwelling on such horrors, Lana walked outside onto the porch. A light drizzle had started, causing steam to rise on the driveway. The horses in the pasture across the street grazed and swished their tails as though it were any old day in paradise.

"The geese seem quite comfortable with you," she said to Coco, who had one goose in her lap and the other at her side. The one on the ground ruffled up her feathers and hissed at Lana, so she stayed back.

"I knew them since they were eggs," Coco said.

"They're like your babies, then."

"No."

"Why not?"

"They were Jack's babies. I'm their aunt."

"Okay, that makes sense. Now that Jack is gone, though, how would you feel about adopting them," Lana said.

"They'd like that."

"The geese, you mean?"

"Yes."

Out front, a black car slowed to a stop and just sat there idling for a good minute before finally turning up the driveway. Lana turned to Coco, who had stopped petting the goose. Her little nose twitched. Behind them, Sailor started growling through the screen door. Two men wearing tailored suits climbed out. Neither waved.

"You know these fellas?" Lana said, trying to sound casual and hoping for a yes.

"No."

"They must be going door-to-door. Perhaps they have some information for us," Lana said.

The two men paused at the top of the steps. Something about their demeanor told Lana they were not here with happy news. The men gave her a puzzled look, then glanced down at Coco. The older one with a sheen on his bald head spoke first, while at the same time flipping out a badge. "FBI. Are you Mrs. Wagner?" he said.

"No, I'm a friend," she said as she tried to make out the faded words on his badge.

Federal Bureau of Investigation. US.

The younger one had enough hair to donate to his partner, and then some. It was slicked back with a whole jar full of oil. "Our business is with the Wagners. Are they in?"

Lana looked toward the door and there was Fred, standing behind the screen. The air was thick enough to slice up with a cane knife and serve on a platter.

"Can I help you?" he said, not coming out and not inviting them in.

The men stepped up onto the porch. Both geese by now had had enough, honking and fluffing. "Coco, take the geese back to their cage," Fred said.

"But, Papa—"

"Go," he said.

Coco rounded up the agitated geese and led them away.

"We need to have a few words with you, Wagner. Let us in, please. I'm Cash and this is McMurry," said the shiny one, again flashing his badge.

Both men wore revolvers on their hips, clear as

day. As soon as Ingrid had secured Sailor in the bedroom, Fred and the two men went inside, and Marie came out. Lana sat with the two girls.

"What kinds of words are they having?" Coco said.

"Probably just routine information gathering, you know, wondering if they have seen anything suspicious," Lana said.

Marie gave her a look that said *yeah right,* and Lana turned to look out on the lawn so the girls wouldn't be able to interpret the concern on her face. These men felt very Eliot Ness, and it did not bode well for the Wagners. "Then why didn't they ask you anything?" Marie said.

"Probably because I live in Honolulu."

Coco and Marie pressed themselves up against the screen door, listening to the rise and fall of muffled voices coming from the kitchen. *Fritz . . . Why did you change your name . . . Nazi meetings. . .*

Coco's yellow dress had smears of dirt all along the side, and her ringlets stuck out in forty different directions. You could see her breaths coming fast. Two minutes later Fred and Ingrid walked out with two agents trailing behind.

Fred said to the girls in a clipped voice, "These men want to ask us some questions at the station."

Ingrid said, "Mrs. Hitchcock, would you mind staying with Coco and Marie until we get back? I'm sure we won't be long."

"I'm sure she's busy. I'll call Dutch London. They know him," Fred said.

Lana insisted. "I don't mind at all."

"No offense, but I'd feel better with a man around," Fred said.

Lana felt slapped. "I'll stay until he comes to get them, at least."

Ingrid gave Marie the kind of hug that meant she feared she might never see them again, and when it was Coco's turn, she clung to her mother like a baby monkey.

"I want to come!" she said.

"*Mausi*, someone has to stay with the animals."

Cash jumped in. "No German," he said, making a cut-it sign at his throat with his hand.

Lana wanted to smack him but reminded herself that they were only doing their job. Hawaii was under attack after all. Ingrid gave her a hollowed-out and haunted look.

"We'll have supper ready for you," Lana said, forcing a smile.

As the Wagners walked down the steps, escorted by the two federal agents, Coco flung herself after them, grabbed her mother's arm and pulled hard. "Don't take them!" she screamed.

Cash peeled her little hand off. "Kid, we're at war."

Marie came after Coco and wrapped her from behind in a full-body hug. "Our parents are model citizens. You'll see," she said to the men.

Coco began to sob in earnest and stomped her feet. "No! You come back here this minute." The last part morphed into a high-pitched wail.

Fred turned and, with the saddest eyes, said, "This will all be over soon, I promise. Just do as Mrs. Hitchcock says."

A loud groan came out of the bedroom from Sailor, and Lana and the two girls watched as the car slowly drove off. She tried to remain stoic, but she was pretty sure they all had the same dark feeling: this was only the beginning.

It turned into the longest afternoon on record. Coco sat on the porch with Sailor counting the minutes and every car that passed. Every now and then on the radio, the program was interrupted for a quick announcement. *"Martial law has been declared, blackout ordered, stay in your house unless you are an essential worker, FDR will address the nation tomorrow."* Lana got busy in the kitchen making roasted potatoes smeared in butter and rosemary, and mixing meat loaf with fresh tomato sauce. Who knew if anyone would eat it or not.

When night approached and the Wagners still weren't back, she decided to hell with not using the telephone. Over at her father's house she dug up Deputy Ho'okano's number. If anyone, he would know what was going on.

He picked up before the phone even rang, with a booming "Ho'okano here."

"Chester, it's Lana, Jack Spalding's daughter. I need your help," she said, wasting no time on small talk.

"What do you need?"

"I flew in yesterday to see my father, but I missed him. I'm with his neighbors, the Wagners, and two FBI agents took the parents away earlier for questioning and left me with the girls. They aren't back yet and the girls are scared. Hell, we're all scared. Do you know anything?"

There was a long moment where all she heard was breathing. "Hard to talk on the phone, Lana, and I'm sorry about Jack—he was a good friend. People are being arrested. Anyone who might be a threat. Japanese, German, Italian."

"I doubt the Wagners are any kind of threat."

"They aren't taking chances."

His voice was grave.

"So if they arrest the parents, what happens to the kids?" she asked.

He cleared his throat. "Orphanage, most likely. Unless they have other family here."

This was not the kind of casualty one first thought of in war, but here they were. The thought of the girls in an orphanage made her sick to her stomach. "What are they doing with people they arrest?"

"Best you stay out of this, Lana. It's not your business. And it's serious. Rules have changed. You don't want to be associated with suspected Nazis."

From the window she could see Coco's profile, with her button nose and bony shoulders, keeping a pained lookout for her parents. Lana's heart lurched. This most certainly was her business.

"Is there anything else you can tell me? About the invasion?" she asked.

"Not on the phone. Just go somewhere safe, away from Hilo, somewhere your father might have gone," he said, drawing out the last words like they were taffy.

Did Chester know about the house at Volcano? "But we aren't supposed to drive."

"Type up a letter and sign my name."

Lana hung up the phone feeling worse than before the call. How was she going to break the news to Marie and Coco? Marie was levelheaded enough, but Coco seemed like a different breed altogether. Chester could be wrong, but she doubted it. When she walked back up the steps to the Wagners' house, Coco glared at her in the fading sunlight.

"I'm not eating until they get home," she said, folding her arms across her chest and sinking farther back into the chair.

Sailor, on the other hand, looked ready to swallow the meat loaf whole. With one ear up and one ear folded down, Sailor was awfully cute, Lana had to admit.

"Honey, food is your friend right now, and your parents would want you to eat."

By now only the faintest glow remained in the sky. A light went on in the kitchen and Lana yelled. "Turn it off!"

The last thing they needed was another round of police showing up.

It went right back off. "Sorry, I forgot," Marie said.

Lana was about to sit down with Coco to persuade her to eat when a black car zoomed into the driveway. A wave of relief flooded in. All this fretting and the Wagners were back already. Thank the heavens above.

"Would you look at this?" she said.

Coco perked up for all of five seconds, and then retreated into a ball once she saw a man waddling up the path. His suit was several sizes too small and he had one long stripe of hair pulled over his head. "That's Mr. London. I hate him," Coco said.

Mr. London stopped one step short of the porch and said, "I got a call from Mr. Wagner informing me of the situation here, and I came straight over. You must be Lana Hitchcock. I'm Dutch London."

Marie rushed out, then froze when she spotted him. He eyed her up and down, with a pause at her breasts, then did the same to Lana. Oddly, he was holding a yellow plumeria flower in his left hand.

She nodded. "Mr. London."

"Call me Dutch. Looks like we'll be spending some time together," he said.

"And why is that?"

"Fred said they're holding them indefinitely."

Lana glanced over at Coco, who was all ears. "Say, why don't we go inside to chat. Girls, wait out here, please."

Lana went to the kitchen and sat. She waited a few moments, but Mr. London did not appear. She went back to the screen door just in time to see him slipping the flower behind Marie's ear. He gave an approving nod and said, "Sure looks pretty on you."

"Mr. London. Shall we have a word?" Lana said.

He turned to follow Lana, but not before letting his hand drift across Marie's shoulder.

The kitchen was dark enough now that she could make out only his outline. He smelled like rotten cheese and she almost gagged when he opened his mouth.

"We need to get this place boarded up on the double," he said.

We?

"So tell me, what exactly is going on?" Lana said.

"Freddie called—wouldn't say from where— and said they're having him sign over power of attorney to me on account they're being hauled away to some kind of prison. He asked if I would watch over the girls and keep 'em safe. You know, these Japs'll be landing in Hilo anytime now and young girls will be in trouble."

Lana could hardly believe what she was hearing. Surely the agents must have a reason to believe the Wagners were dangerous, but they seemed like such good people. "How are you and the Wagners acquainted?" she asked.

"We do business together. I'm in real estate, and I live just down the way. He trusts me."

A red flag shot up in her head. In her experience, when someone has to inform you that you can trust them, you usually can't.

"Are they Nazi supporters?" she had to ask.

"Not that I knew of, but people do things behind closed doors that would shock even Adolf Hitler. Know what I mean?" he said, taking a step closer.

Lana moved back until her hip hit the counter. "Look, I don't mind watching over the girls. I promised Fred and Ingrid I would, so that lets you off the hook," she said.

"Oh, but he asked me just an hour ago. Help run the store and keep the household in order. That makes me responsible, and I don't shy away from duty, no sirree. And better to have a man

104

around—you never know when those Japs are coming ashore."

Having this man in her face all day, so-called caring for the girls, seemed unthinkable. Had Fred been so stupid to really ask this? "Don't you have your own household to worry about?"

"I'm between places. Mine just sold."

"So you'll be living here until further notice?"

"The girls are familiar with me, and we all get along just fine."

If only she could phone the Wagners to double-check his story. It sounded off. "Tell you what. Why don't you give us one night here alone, and I can break the news to the girls. Coco has had several bouts of hysteria since the agents were here, and it might be better if I handle it. You know, woman to woman. Then you'll have time to gather your things," she offered.

He made a weird grunting noise, then said, "Deal."

After he left, Coco interrogated Lana about his visit. *Why was he here? What does he know? He's not coming back, is he?* Then she said, "He looks at Marie like she's a bowl of chocolate pudding with whipping cream on top."

That did it. Lana spent the next couple of hours loading up the truck under the light of a waning gibbous moon. To the girls she gave the lame excuse of having the truck packed and ready to go in case the Japanese showed up.

"What about our parents?" Marie asked.

"We'll pack enough for them, too."

She could not bring herself to say, *Your parents might not be coming back and you could end up in an orphanage or with Dutch London.*

Coco spoke up, too. "We can't leave Sailor and the geese."

"We won't, don't worry."

Lana felt like the worst kind of liar as she went around in both houses and collected blankets, as much food as she could fit into boxes, lanterns, matches, though there would be no fires at night. Being at the volcano without fires was not a pleasant proposition. She had the girls pack their warmest clothes, and Coco was in charge of packing a bag for her parents and putting a box of dog food and Milk-Bones together.

All the while Lana was trying to make sense of the madness. All this time hearing about the war raging in Europe, the horror stories had belonged to other people. Now the war had come to her hometown.

Throughout the night she faded in and out of sleep, dreaming of bombers and submarines and soldiers sneaking into the house and climbing into her bed. One of them smelled like fish and seaweed. He was shaking her shoulder and trying to wake her up, but she couldn't open her eyes. Horsefeathers, they were blindfolding her! All at once she was wide-awake with fear snaking around her throat and squeezing. Her eyes shot open, but the room was early-morning blue. Someone was sitting on the bed next to her, slanting it down from his weight.

"Marie?" she said, knowing full well it was not Marie.

"Lana, it's Mochi," he said softly.

A thick wave of relief. "What are you doing here?" she whispered.

"We want to go with you."

THE WALL

December 8, 1941
Hale Manu, Volcano

A house without a wall. If that was the case, what else might be missing? Lana hadn't even given thought to beds and furniture, assuming the place had been at least minimally outfitted. Her first concern, though, was getting Mochi and Benji out of the back and warmed up.

Sailor jumped out first and immediately put her nose to the ground, sniffing and snorting and following an invisible scent that wound around the whole front of the house. Lana wondered if this far out anyone would notice a lantern, but she wasn't willing to risk it. She peeled off the tarp, and Mochi and Benji both sat up. Mochi rubbed the back of his head.

"We can unpack all this later, but grab your blankets and let's go inside," she said.

Coco rubbed her arms. "It's freezing. The geese should sleep inside with us."

Marie nudged her. "The geese have down feathers—they'll be fine."

The key was in Lana's pocket, but they hardly needed it. They walked around the deck to the side missing the wall and stepped inside. Dark and shadowy, the house felt like a cold wooden shell. The sharp smell of cedar and paint still hung in the air. Lana froze. Something moved in one of the far rooms. *Thud, rustle, scrape.*

"There's someone here," Benji said.

"Hello?" Lana said, her voice an echo in the emptiness.

Just then Sailor came bounding in and shot past them into the dark. A second later a squeal, and what sounded like a stampede, came toward them. Lana jumped out of the way in time to avoid getting run down by a massive pig and several smaller ones. Thunder filled the house.

"Sailor, no," Coco said, as calmly as she would ask for a glass of water.

Lana thought there was not a chance the dog would stop, but she did, just at the edge of the deck, as though she had come up against an invisible wall.

"Thank you," Coco said, wrapping an arm around the dog's neck.

The girl had her quirks, but she also clearly had a way with animals that went beyond the usual. Less work for Lana, since she had a whole crew of humans to worry about now.

"We need light," Mochi said.

"We can't."

"Just for a minute, so we can see what we got here."

He was right. They could be walking through a pig den with droppings over every square foot, though there was no foul smell. "Okay, but hurry."

A beam of yellow light cut through the darkness, showing a stone fireplace and a long great room with a wide door to what appeared to be a kitchen, if the glimmer of stainless steel was any indication. Trusses crisscrossed the high space above their heads, making the room feel twice the size that it was, and it was already large. The only piece of furniture was a table twenty feet long, with two benches instead of chairs. Lana saw right away Jack's stuff on the built-in shelves. Driftwood creatures, light fixtures, big koa and Norfolk calabashes and gadgets. It was so like him to bring the impractical stuff first.

They moved as a group, arms brushing up against one another as they bumped their way down a hallway. Mochi led the way. Four smaller bedrooms and one master, with a pop-out window and a double mattress on the floor. A bookshelf full of books lined one side. None of the rooms had any doors, except the bathroom. Thank goodness for at least that.

Lana turned on the shower, and a few pipes banged. She held her hand under the water. It never got warm. Cold air and cold showers were not a great combination.

"Where are we going to sleep?" Coco asked.

Five people, one mattress. The odds were not looking good.

"You girls take the mattress. Benji and I have our sleeping bags," Mochi said with his hand over the light so they were back in darkness again.

At least the mattress looked new, but three of them on a double? Mochi led them back out to the truck, where they began unloading by moonlight. They moved the geese onto the porch, and Coco fed and watered them and Sailor. They honked in protest at being stuck in the small cages. If anything, the Japanese would be led right to them from that god-awful noise. Lana would be happy to set them free in the morning and let them fend for themselves.

Unable to light a fire, they huddled together at the table around a basket of crackers and sardines, corned beef hash, and mandarin oranges. Lana had long given up trying to keep her skirt clean. They had placed a lantern on the table with a shirt over it, so the room glowed blue. Mochi unwrapped tinfoil with strips of dried *ahi*. Coco would have none of it, although Sailor circled around them waiting for something to drop.

"You have to eat *something*," Lana said.

Coco shook her head, then held up a handful of sardines to the dog, who swallowed them whole and then hovered, waiting for more.

"Don't feed her our food!" Lana said.

"But she's hungry."

"She just ate."

"Not enough, I guess."

"This may not seem serious to you, but we have no idea how long we need to ration our food for, no idea about anything, really. So we need to be careful with what we have now and not waste anything. Even if you don't like something, you may have to eat it," Lana said.

"She likes peanut butter. Maybe some of that on the crackers?" Marie said.

Mochi spoke up. "The girl will eat when she's ready. Won't you, *Mausi*?" He looked at Coco.

Her eyes grew wide. "How do you know my nickname?"

He smiled. "We share the same field and rock wall between our houses. Maybe you haven't noticed me out there. I have a way of blending in."

Coco stared at him as though her little mind was making a determination. *Good guy I can trust, or crackpot?* "My mother calls me that because I always bring home baby mice who have lost their mamas."

"You must have a good heart, then," he said.

"It beats pretty hard, I know that."

Lana had to laugh. "He means you seem like a caring person. I notice you always put the animals first. That's a wonderful quality that shows you think about others. And I didn't mean to get on your case for it—it's just that things are different right now and we have to be careful with what we have."

Mochi rested his hand on her knee. "This place has a good feeling about it. I think you can relax a little, Lana-san."

Funny, she had felt the exact opposite. At the moment it felt far away and cold and lonely. A different planet from where she had been three days ago. After they finished eating, they outfitted the mattress with sheets and blankets and Coco's stuffed owl, Hoot. Along the opposite wall Lana lay down two pillows end-to-end on a towel and spread out her father's plaid flannel blanket, which still smelled like him. That blanket had been around. It had seen them through camping trips all over the island and been a bed for stargazing countless times. Having it there brought a warmth that couldn't be manufactured.

They said good-night to Mochi and Benji, who posted up on the floor of one of the other rooms. Lana hated to think of his skin and bones on the floor, but he had insisted he would be fine.

Bone tired as she was, the minute Lana settled into her nest, she felt painfully awake. Every cell in her body was on edge, and the blunt force of the wood beneath her did not help. She got up to put on another sweater and fold another towel under her lower half. She guessed the temperature to be somewhere in the low fifties, and it was likely to get a whole lot colder.

"Good night, girls," she said.

A sniffle. Whispers. The sound of a dog panting and then licking. Giggles. Then wretched sobbing. What did someone do in a situation like this? Lana felt woefully unprepared.

"Things will work out. You'll see. Try to get some sleep," she said. Though the minute the words left her lips, she knew how unconvincing they sounded. The girls might be young, but they were not dumb.

More sobbing. The choking, full-bodied kind. Lana sat up. A pale moonlight poured through the window, outlining the lumps on the mattress. Marie looked to be spooning Coco. Something about their sisterly bond tore open a wound inside Lana. She had always wished for a sibling, secretly hoped her father would marry again, but he never had, young as he'd been. *For some, one great love is all you need,* he used to tell her.

Over the years with Buck, Jack's words would spontaneously pop into her head. Especially when things had begun to spiral downhill. Had Buck been her one great love? It certainly didn't feel that way now. In fact it felt like a one great love was completely out of her reach. Spinsterhood was more likely.

"Mrs. Hitchcock?" Marie said.

"Yes?"

"What are we going to do tomorrow?"

Coming here had been the wrong thing to do, Lana realized now with perfect clarity. She found herself unable to say, *I made a mistake. What do you say we head back to Hilo as soon as we wake up?* The hideaway house was a romantic notion at best, a nice idea but implausible when she really thought about it. In the middle of nowhere, unfinished, ill equipped and full of pigs. They would leave first thing in the morning.

Instead she said, "Let's talk about it tomorrow. I'll fix a nice breakfast and we can all decide together. How does that sound?"

"Okay, I guess."

She didn't sound convinced.

"We are safe. Your parents are safe. Trust me," she said, hoping it was true.

In the morning Lana's neck felt as though someone had tried to saw it off in the night, and her left hip was tender and throbbing. She opened one eye. Across the room the lump of the girls had doubled in size, and when she propped herself up to get a better look, she saw that Sailor was tangled in between them. All peacefully asleep.

She unfolded her stiff limbs and tiptoed out of the room, down the hallway and out to the porch. The fog was so dense she could taste it on her tongue. And it was cold, but at least the moisture trapped some of the heat, and it wasn't as icy as the volcano could sometimes be. The whole world seemed to still be sleeping, even Gin and

Tonic, who were snuggled together, with their necks turned back and their heads tucked onto their backs.

"Good morning."

Lana jumped and looked to the far end of the porch, where Mochi sat cross-legged on a pillow. "You scared me half to death," she whispered.

"How did you sleep?"

"Terribly. You?"

He looked awfully serene for someone who had slept on the floor all night. "I slept," he said, shrugging.

A typical Mochi response. He was, one might say, in tune with some higher power.

"Coming here was a mistake, but I don't know how to tell the girls we need to turn around and go back to Hilo. It was such an ordeal getting here," she said.

"Why go back?"

Tears threatened. "Because the house isn't finished and we have no furniture. I should have thought it through more carefully, but I was scared and feeling desperate."

"First reaction, best reaction."

"I suppose that means you think we should stay?"

Mist settled around him, blurring his lines. "A wall can be built, furniture found. We came up here for a reason. Let's not give up so easily," he said.

"I'm not giving up—I'm being rational. Who's going to build the wall, and where will we get the wood? We aren't exactly in Hilo anymore, and Volcano has no stores that sell furniture, last I checked."

"You know people here, don't you?" he said.

She immediately thought of Mr. Spain and his dahlias, or the Holzmans, who sold plums and mulberries at their roadside stand. "Maybe, but most of the people I came up here with only lived here in the summers."

"Go into town and see." He started up a coughing fit, then once it had passed, he continued. "We can put together a list."

"Mochi, how bad is it?" she asked. She remembered him with a cigarette hanging out of his mouth most of the time. He didn't have one now.

The purple smears and puffiness under his eyes looked worse this morning, and she feared having him up here, so far from any medical attention or hospital.

"It is neither bad nor good. It just is. I cough blood and my bones ache, if that's what you want to know," he said.

"Even more reason for us to go back. I'm going to start packing up," she said, spinning to go back into the house, surprised to find Coco standing there wrapped in a plaid wool blanket.

"Sweetie, I didn't hear you get up," Lana said.

She wanted to take the girl into her arms and give her a warm hug but sensed a wall of resistance around her, solid enough that she could have knocked on it. Coco's ringlets had been mashed and matted in the night, creating the appearance of a bird nest on her head, which Lana was sure Coco actually would have loved to have on board.

"We're going back to Hilo?" Coco asked.

Lana glanced back at Mochi, whose face was unreadable. "Right now we're going to get this fire going and then start fixing some breakfast. I could use your help."

"I've never lit a fire."

"That's no problem. You can just help pick out what you want to eat and set the table."

Coco pulled the blanket in around her neck. "Maybe you can go back to Hilo and pick up our parents and bring them here," she said, her voice so small and earnest.

Not what Lana expected to hear. "Why do you say that?"

"So we don't get hit by the submarines. And Mama and Papa will be safe."

How much could Coco know about submarines? Though of course talk had been everywhere in recent months. Those damn subs made everyone jumpy. In fact they should turn on the radio and find out the latest news, if they could pick up a signal this far out.

"I would drive back and get your parents in a heartbeat if I could. But right now we have to wait until they're done being questioned. I'm sure the FBI has them in a safe place, though."

Coco's whole face scrunched up. "I hate those men that took them."

"I can understand that. But those men were doing their job. Once they find out your parents are not dangerous, they'll let them go. You'll see."

"Today or tomorrow?"

"Maybe."

"How will you know?"

"We can call them."

"But we don't have a phone."

"I'm going into town later," Lana said, realizing that her answer implied they were staying. At least for the moment.

Once everyone was awake, Benji got the fire going, Marie and Lana fixed breakfast, and Coco tended to the animals. After much debate they decided to turn the geese loose. Coco sat down and had a long talk with Sailor about not harming them, emphasizing that they were part of the family and not to be eaten. The matter-of-fact way she spoke to the dog came so naturally that Lana half believed the dog understood every word.

Thank goodness the kitchen was well equipped, with stainless-steel countertops, an industrial-sized sink and a wood-burning stove with an oven drawer. There was a small basket of chopped wood, but they would need to gather more. With no electricity there was no point to having a fridge, but her father had built a large wooden icebox lined with tin. Fortunately the Wagners had had an extra icebox outside full with blocks of ice, and Lana had confiscated as many as would fit in her Coca-Cola cooler. Kerosene lights were placed strategically around the room, but a lot of good they'd do now.

When Lana and Marie came out to the picnic table, Mochi and Benji had pulled it closer to the fireplace and were warming themselves. Lana set down a plate of scrambled eggs, grilled spam and salted rice balls.

"Have a look at those wooden shutters," Mochi said, pointing to the walls.

In the black of night they hadn't noticed, but to the side of each window was a thin rail with a big piece of plywood attached.

"It slides over and clips on," Benji said, getting up to demonstrate.

"Well, I'll be," Lana said.

"Jack would have thought of everything," Mochi said.

"Everything but a wall. A lot of good these will do with a gaping hole on one side of the room."

Mochi rubbed his back. "He had planned on coming up here long before he got sick. Death snuck up on him. He knew about me and my situation, and we had even planned on where he and Benji would scatter my ashes if I didn't pull through. Out beyond the breakwater. I never thought he would go first."

"None of us did," Lana said.

Coco hurried in, her cheeks flushed pink. "I found something interesting out back," she said.

Lana and Marie followed her around to the rear. The sun was out there somewhere, behind the thinning fog, turning the landscape a fuzzy gold. Spindly vines climbed the trellis but had made it only halfway up. The grass felt like spongy carpet under their feet, and lava rocks littered the area. Lana heard it before she saw it. A hum that filled every square inch of air around them, a purring in the trees. At first she thought it might be airplanes and grew panicky, but the pitch was all wrong.

"What is that?" Marie asked.

Coco led them along, past a covered enclosure with a shower and what appeared to be a heating contraption. Lana was buoyed by the sight. Sailor was at her heels but then sat down with her tongue hanging out and a concerned look on her face.

"Come on, girl," Coco said.

But the dog was planted like a black-and-white rock. Up ahead several honeybees floated about, and then Coco pointed into a eucalyptus tree.

Hanging from one of the branches was a dripping, oozing honeycomb and a swarm of bees the size of a whiskey barrel. The vibration of thousands of tiny wings, all beating madly with their own specific job. Beneath the tree was a row of hive boxes, Jack's design.

"I'm not going any closer. Bees always seek me out and like to sting me for some reason," Marie said.

"Have you ever seen bees swarm before?" Lana asked.

Both girls said, "Nope."

"They're not interested in us, as long as we stay down here and mind our own business. The other part of the equation with bees is that if you approach them with love, they leave you alone."

Marie turned away and led Sailor back toward the house, and Coco stood staring. "I think they're happy we're here," she finally said.

"Oh?"

If believing that made her feel better, Lana was all for it.

"At least, they don't mind it," Coco said.

"Not in the least."

Lana envied Coco her ability to be distracted and her youthful innocence, but she knew all too well that the sadness would show up again with a vengeance.

They continued around the house. Her father had done a beautiful job in the construction. Lap siding with wide planks, and window trim painted a rusty red. A lava-and-concrete foundation that gave the house a very solid feel. If someone had the time and money to outfit the place, it would be lovely, if isolated. A refuge from the outside world. Lana realized how accustomed she had become to a busy social life and all the comforts of a modern home. Along the far side of the house, under the eaves, they found a big wood pile, presumably for the wall, and an area set up with tools.

"We should have Benji and Mochi get to it right away," Marie said.

"Mochi is in no shape to do any building. But we can help," Lana said.

Marie looked at Lana as though she were crazy. "I think I would be more hindrance than help. I've never built anything in my life."

"I'm sure there's plenty of other stuff we can find for you to do. Let's go see if Mochi has the radio working."

Back on the front porch, Benji was carrying firewood up and stacking it neatly, while Mochi fiddled with the dials on the radio. Jack was a radio buff, and they had brought his Zenith with them. There was a lot of crackling, some bursts of music and then a familiar voice booming through the space. Everyone stopped what they were doing, riveted.

"*. . . Japan has therefore undertaken a surprise*

offensive extending throughout the Pacific area. The facts of yesterday and today speak for themselves. The people of the United States have already formed their opinions and well understand the implications to the very life and safety of our nation. . . . No matter how long it may take us to overcome this premeditated invasion, the American people, in their righteous might, will win through to absolute victory. . . . The fact that our people, our territory and our interests are in grave danger. . . . I ask that the Congress declare that since the unprovoked and dastardly attack by Japan on Sunday, December 7, 1941, a state of war has existed between the United States and the Japanese Empire."

Lana looked at Coco and Marie, whose faces were five shades whiter than they had been a minute ago. *We are at war, all bets are off.* No one had seen Pearl Harbor coming, at least not as such a violent surprise. If the Japanese navy was capable of pulling that off, what did they have up their sleeves next? Being trapped on an island only made it worse. There was no place to run.

To Lana's relief, Mochi spoke up first. "This means we stay put. At least for another few days. If we get another air raid, Hilo won't be safe."

"Do you know any of these people, who attacked us?" Coco said to Mochi.

"I left Japan when I was ten, and I haven't been back since. Usually it's the young men sent to fight the wars, but could be I know some of their fathers, or grandfathers." He shrugged. "I might look Japanese, and have some Japanese thoughts and beliefs, but my heart is in Hawaii. Like your folks."

Coco went and stood in front of the fireplace. "Our folks aren't Japanese."

"No, but they came here from another country, and now they've made it their home."

"But why are they in trouble?"

"Because Japan and Germany are friends," Marie said.

"It's stupid. Why can't we all just be friends?" Coco said in all seriousness.

"Sometimes you get a bad person in power, and they start doing things to hurt people. What they believe in is corrupt. And then other countries try to intervene. But you have alliances already formed and it gets complicated," Mochi said.

Outside, the fog lifted, revealing a low layer of silvery clouds spreading up toward Mauna Loa and down to the sea. If they were going to stay, she had better get moving. "Tell you what—let's get started making this place more comfortable, and we can answer all your questions later."

THE ENCOUNTER

Lana parked the truck a little way in from the beginning of the road and pulled the bike out of the back. Tiny water droplets fell from the Sugi pines onto her shoulders, but thankfully there was no rain. On the radio more information had been given about staying off the roads. Complete blackouts were ordered, all schools were closed and suspicious aliens were being rounded up. *Not just aliens,* Lana thought. Food was to be rationed, as Hawaii had only enough provisions to last just over a month, and anyone found disobeying rules was subject to being shot. The worst part of it all was that more attacks were expected.

Every single clothing item she had brought on this trip was wrong. From the white dress, skirts and blouses for ninety-degree Hilo life to her scant supply of toiletries. For lack of options she had on her beige skirt, pink checkered button-up and white tennis shoes. All of that was hidden under her father's heavy army jacket. As she pedaled along, water from the wet road sprayed up on her. There was no point in trying to stay clean. All of this was fine, as long as she wasn't arrested for being out and about.

The gloom did not help her mood, and she fought back tears several times as she rode toward 29 Mile. Houses along the main road were mostly summer houses. Not a soul was in sight. She passed a little red-and-white schoolhouse. The sign read Volcano House Japanese School. Two men in military uniforms stood outside by an army jeep, reading a piece of paper. Lana put her head down and rode past on the far side of the road, fearing for whoever ran the school.

A little way beyond that, she came upon Kano Store, which to her surprise was open. There were cut anthuriums and red ginger out front on the wooden porch, and baskets of oranges, plums and tangerines. When she walked in, the cracked wood beneath her feet creaked and groaned, announcing her arrival. The place smelled of kerosene and boiled peanuts, of childhood and better times. A radio blared from behind the counter.

"Hello, is anyone here?"

Lana remembered old Mrs. Kano from when she was a girl but doubted the woman was still around. She had been ancient even back then. Tiny, generous, and full of spunk, she always handed out an extra few pieces of gum, or, Lana's favorite, the rice candy with paper that melted in your mouth.

A white head suddenly appeared behind the counter, and Lana found herself looking down into a set of watery black eyes.

"Mrs. Kano? My goodness, you're still here!"

"What did you expect?"

"I . . . um . . . well, it's just been so long since I've been up here."

"You look familiar. Where you from?"

"I'm Lana Spalding from Hilo. I used to come up here when I was young. Jack was my father. Maybe he's been in here lately?" Lana said.

"What you mean *was?*" Mrs. Kano said, in her own variation of pidgin English.

"He contracted meningitis and died several days ago. I'm sorry to have to tell you. It was a shock to everyone."

The old woman huffed. "Damn that man, he was my best customer. When he was up here. I could tell it was him by the way he always came skidding to a stop out front, like his car was on fire. He brought me things from Hilo, too." She shook her head. "Plenty bad news today."

Lana sighed. "To be honest, I can hardly remember a worse few days."

Though of course that wasn't entirely true.

"Stupid Japs," Mrs. Kano said, a drop of spit landing on her chin. "Bombing all their own countrymen, and pissing off America. Don't they know Hawaii is mostly Japanese? Big mistake, you watch."

The word *Jap* coming out of her mouth like that momentarily stunned Lana. People had been bandying the word around so much lately that it had become commonplace—and yet still disturbing—but hearing it spoken by a local made her realize how many of the people here identified more as Hawaiians than anything. There was a huge blending of the lines.

"Any updates?" Lana asked.

"Word is the water is poison. So they say to fill up your bathtubs. Lucky up here we catch our own damn water. You staying at Jack's house?"

"For now. Before we got here, I had no idea it wasn't finished. So I was hoping to find some much-needed supplies."

Mrs. Kano came around the front of the counter. She was a tiny woman but still moving well for someone well into her nineties, at least. "Who is *we?*"

"My two girls and our dog. We have a Great Dane who eats more than two men do."

"Just the three of you?" Mrs. Kano said, squinting at her as though she could see right through the lie.

"Yep. Just us."

"They say that rations are starting up, so get what you can now. I had a rush earlier this morning, and plenty goods got cleaned out."

Lana glanced around. The shelves were still stocked, though somewhat sparsely. "What I really need most are mattresses and maybe a few extra blankets. And any leads on where I might be able to pick up some furniture around here."

130

Just then the door to the back opened and a young woman stepped out. "Can I help you, Baba?"

"This lady wants a bed."

The young woman said, "I'm sorry, the Volcano House is just up the way. I would suggest you go there, but from what I hear, they're closed to civilians since Sunday."

"No, no, I have a house, I am looking for mattresses or beds—"

Mrs. Kano butted in. "She's Jack's daughter."

A look of confusion passed over the woman's face. "Jack?"

"Hilo Jack."

The woman's face brightened. "Oh, a pleasure to meet you. I'm Iris, her granddaughter."

Outside, a car door slammed. Iris peered out the window, as men's voices carried up through the open glass with no screen. "Oh hell, Baba, let me do the talking, okay?"

The three of them stood there staring at one another, fear and tension emanating from the two Japanese women, and Lana on edge herself, heart thumping and palms sweating. Two men entered, both in uniform. One young and blond, with overdeveloped biceps, the other tall and wiry and serious-faced. The younger one ran his finger along a shelf and held it up to reveal a layer of dust when he reached the end.

"Dirty," he said, looking directly at the women.

"Mrs. Kano, Iris," said the older one with a small nod, not acknowledging the comment from his peer. "We have to ask you to come with us to answer some questions."

Lana felt herself nearly gag. *Not again!*

Iris appeared to be working hard to breathe, a flush spreading across her cheeks. "Major Bailey, can you please ask us here? We have nothing to hide, you know that. And my grandmother, she puts up a good front, but she's old."

Mrs. Kano swatted at her hand. "Don't call me old."

"Please don't make this harder than it already is. I have my orders," Bailey said more gruffly than necessary.

These poor women.

"You taking all us Japanese in? Gonna arrest the whole island?" Mrs. Kano said.

"Depends on what happens next. Maybe your comrades will do another raid and then we won't need to," the blond one said.

Major Bailey shot his friend a look. "Snyder, enough."

Snyder saluted. "Sorry, sir, it's just hard when it's personal, you know?"

"I do know." His jaw clenched.

Lana felt invisible, until the younger one turned his gaze on her and looked her up and down. "And who might this be?"

"I just stopped in for a few supplies."

"Your name?"

"Mrs. Hitchcock. I live just down the way."

Major Bailey also seemed to notice her for the first time. The way his eyes finally locked onto hers caused a swishing of her insides. His brown eyes were set wide apart, beneath unruly brows, and the corners of his mouth turned down slightly.

"I haven't seen you up here before. I'm Major Bailey," he said.

"I just returned from O'ahu. I was there for a while," she answered. Her voice was shaky, even though she was innocent of any crime, at least in her mind. She kept waiting for him to look away and get back to business, but he just stood there, staring at her in the most awkward way possible. It was both intimidating and perplexing.

"Is there a problem, Mr. Bailey?" she finally said.

"Forgive me. There's no problem, ma'am. And it's *Major*."

He turned his attention back to Iris and Mrs. Kano. "We'll wait out on the porch. Take a minute or two to close up and we'll head out."

The two men walked out, leaving a chill in the air. Lana wanted to head outside and give them a scolding for being so rude and insensitive. How could they think that taking Mrs. Kano could do any good at all? She was about to march out there, then stopped. Calling attention to herself was a dumb idea and could lead to trouble down the road. There were others to think about.

Iris said in a hushed voice, "Mrs. Hata just called and said they took away the Shigetanis, at the Japanese school up the road. What do you think they are going to do with us?"

Mrs. Kano apparently did not feel the same need for privacy, and said in a voice even louder than usual, "Nothing, that's what. If they take us away, who you think gonna grow their food? The menehune? Pele?"

An excellent point, actually.

Lana whispered, "The FBI took away a German couple, my father's neighbors, yesterday, and I have no idea where they took them. I was going to ask to use your phone and see if they've returned home yet."

"Come back tomorrow. You can use it then," Mrs. Kano said.

If they were back tomorrow. She hated to leave them, but there was nothing else to do. "Thank you, and good luck," she said, giving them both a quick hug.

Snyder leaned against the railing sucking on a cigarette as though his life depended on it, and Major Bailey stood with his hands in his pockets watching the rain fall. Light enough that it could have been snow, it had already soaked Lana's bicycle. She was not looking forward to the ride back to the truck. Not to mention the fact that she had accomplished nothing she had come to do.

Lana hoped to make it past the soldiers without having to speak to them, but Major Bailey said, "What were you doing on Oʻahu, Mrs. Hitchcock?"

She turned in time to catch him looking at her hand, which was now ringless. She had left her wedding band in her jewelry box in the bedroom she used to share with her husband and now regretted the decision. There were likely to be enough lonely men around here in the upcoming months to be an annoyance.

"No offense, sir, but how is that pertinent to what's going on here?" she asked, stopping underneath the eave and holding her hand out to catch the droplets.

"Just covering all my bases," he said, tipping his hat.

"If you must know, I used to live on Oʻahu, and I just moved back here."

"When did you leave?"

"I flew over on Saturday."

He whistled. "That was cutting it close. Mighty lucky you weren't up in the air yesterday morning."

It felt more like small talk than questioning, and she was about to step down into the cold when the thrum of engines stopped her. Something big was coming their way. "Are you fellas bolstering troops at the military camp?" she said.

"The whole Volcano area is on high alert, and we're mobilizing troops and national park rangers and civilians, you name it. Every side of the island is vulnerable to attack or invasion, even up here."

That got her attention. Volcano felt so far removed and so unimportant in the large scheme of things that coming here seemed a safer bet than staying in Hilo. Perhaps that wasn't entirely the case. A moment later a line of police cars came into view, rattling and rumbling their way up the road.

Lana muttered to no one in particular, "What the dickens?"

The cars moved at a crawl, and when they passed, she saw with shock what they were hauling—Japanese men, all crammed into the back seats, eyes blank as they looked out the windows. The faces of men who had just lost their freedom and families and livelihoods, and had no idea if and when they would ever get them back. Freedom, it turned out, came in many shapes and sizes.

"Important Japanese. It's just a formality," Bailey said, as though he needed to explain.

"Where are they taking them?" she said.

"The camp."

If Mochi had stayed in Hilo, would he be in one of these cars now? As soon as the last car passed, she made a beeline for her bicycle. "Good day, gentlemen."

"You take care now," Bailey called after her.

She rode off, spokes whirling. Who would have ever imagined Volcano would be where they brought suspected . . . sympathizers? Spies? Saboteurs? The only thing for certain was that being of Japanese ancestry automatically made you a person of interest. It made you dangerous, and it made you untrustworthy in the eyes of the government.

She no longer cared about being splattered with rain or mud or fragments of leaf. Maybe she ought to investigate the new Volcano House lodge and see if they had any spare mattresses there, now that there would be no visitors coming to the park. Quite a shame, since the hotel had just had a big fancy opening in November, the old one having burned to the ground the previous year. And from all accounts, Theo Karavitis was still running the show in grand fashion.

Tiny red 'apapane flitted through the trees around her, the whir of their wings one of her favorite sounds. Lost in thought about what to do next, and only several hundred yards up the road, a tire burst and Lana suddenly careened off the road. Metal screeched against stone just before she flew headfirst into a bush. Her arm folded up under her at an awkward angle, and she tasted tree bark and moss and possibly blood. Before moving, she took stock of all her limbs. Other than a throbbing knee, everything seemed in order. She rolled over and sat up, wiping her mouth with her sleeve. It came away red.

Dazed, she remained in place for another minute or so, and as luck would have it, a car pulled up and stopped next to her bicycle. She waved them on. "Carry on, I'm fine."

"You're bleeding. Have you hit your head?" said Major Bailey. He'd already opened the door to get out.

"It's just my lip. I must have bitten it on the way down."

He came over, kneeling next to her. She squinted and rubbed her eyes. Were his edges a little blurry? She glanced over at the car and saw Iris and Mrs. Kano in the back seat.

"Major, or whatever it is, please let me be," she pleaded.

"My name is Grant. How about you stick with that?"

This kind of fall was nothing more than an embarrassment, the kind you hoped and prayed that no one was around to witness, so you could pretend it never happened. The timing could not have been worse.

"It would be remiss for us to leave you here. Look at your knee—it's badly skinned."

A big strawberry, smudged with dirt.

Grant pulled out a handkerchief and held it up to her lip, dabbing with surprising tenderness.

It smelled of cinnamon. "You're hurt," he said softly, as though this was news to her.

"Darn flat tire," she said, looking at her knee, which seemed the safest place to look right now.

"I have a repair kit," he said, still one foot away.

"Oh, that won't be necessary. I don't have far to go. I can walk the rest of the way."

A wave of dizziness hit her and she closed her eyes for a moment. Surely she hadn't hit her head hard enough for a concussion. Or had she? When she opened them, there was Grant, eyeing her with concern.

"How about we give you a lift, and I can come back for the bike later with the jeep?"

Lana held out her hand. "No, thank you. Help me up, if you wouldn't mind?"

He pulled her to standing as though she were a doll, his hand big and warm and full of some invisible current that ran from the top of her head to the tips of her toes. As much as she wanted to let go, she couldn't. Looking up at him, she saw for the first time a hint of a smile. Just the very corners of his mouth turned up, the sides of his eyes crinkling.

"Mrs. Hitchcock, I won't take no for an answer."

This time she pulled with more force, and her hand came away. Hot and tingly. She wobbled, slightly unsteady on her feet. "Maybe you're right."

She climbed in next to Mrs. Kano, who said, "Need one of those army helmets."

"You're right about that."

It felt strange to be a free person riding along with two women who, given a choice, would not be in this vehicle. The car smelled like cigarettes and damp socks, strong enough that she kept her head halfway out the window as they cruised down the road, Grant working hard to avoid any potholes.

No one said anything until Snyder asked, "So what does your husband do, Mrs. Hitchcock?"

Anyone who had been around Hawaii long enough had heard the name, but Snyder appeared fresh off the boat from Middle America.

"He's in business," she said.

"Not a lot of business in these parts. He connected with the Volcano House somehow?"

"No, but speaking of—what are they going to do now that we're at war?" she said, happy for a chance to switch subjects.

"We have more troops heading in soon. Likely we can house them there," Grant said.

In that case she had better hurry up and finagle mattresses. She was curious to see the new building, and also Uncle Theo, who may or may not remember her from her scrawny young teenage days. As they drove, Lana did her best to avoid looking at Grant.

"You can drop me off at this next corner," she

said as they approached the road to Hale Manu.

"We'll take you to your house."

"The truck is parked just down the way. I thought it would be safer to ride around town on the bicycle, though I guess I was wrong about that," she said.

She saw his eyes smile in the rearview mirror. He pulled into the road and cut the engine. "If you have any ice, I would ice that bump on your head, and take it easy for the next day or two. In case there's a concussion. Is your husband home to help you?"

"Not at the moment."

He paused, looking like he wanted to pursue that line of questioning, but instead said, "Hey, let me have a look at your eyes."

Before she could say anything, he jumped out of the car and came around to her side, opening her door. She stood right up, in order to avoid touching him again, wiping her palm on her muddy skirt to erase any residual static from his hand.

He bent down slightly and stepped closer. "A little that way, toward the light."

Lana turned her head and showed him her eyes. He stared into them, unflinching and very doctor-like. "Hmm. Your pupils look normal, but your eyes are two different shades of brown—did you know that?"

She laughed. "I do. They've always been that way."

He reddened. "Of course you would. Just making sure it wasn't some odd reaction to bumping your head."

Where earlier she had wanted to get away from him as fast as possible, now she wanted him to keep talking, to invite all of them down to the house for an afternoon picnic, where the men could ask their questions and see that Mrs. Kano and her granddaughter were nothing but hardworking community members trying to make a living. And then they would return them to the store and life would go on as usual.

"Well, then, you have a nice afternoon, Mrs. Hitchcock, and get some rest. Doctor's orders," he said.

"What about my bicycle?"

"How about I leave it at the store for you tomorrow," he said.

"Will it be okay for me to drive? They're asking people to stay off the roads."

"Anyone gives you a hard time, tell 'em you're meeting me on official business."

Before turning away, she stooped down and spoke into the car, to the women in the back seat. "I'll look forward to seeing the both of you tomorrow, back at the store." And to Grant she said, "Thank you for your help, sir."

THE COLD

The house was empty. Lana found Mochi and Benji cutting wood out back. Or rather Benji was cutting it and Mochi was supervising from a homemade bench. Benji was slight of build in the same way that Mochi was, but she'd seen Mochi hoist a fish bigger than she was right into the boat and knew that looks could be deceptive.

"Have you seen the girls?" she asked.

Mochi pointed toward a grassy path that led away from the driveway. "They walked that way about twenty minutes ago. What happened to you?"

"I had a flat, no big deal."

She was glad Marie and Coco had Sailor with them, but still, it was easy to get turned around out here, not to mention hidden cracks in the lava, and tree molds—gaping holes that were once trees. And once the sun came out in the Kaʻū Desert, temperatures soared. Though today they'd be more in danger from fog than overheating.

"Did you find what you were looking for?" Mochi said.

"Nope." She suddenly thought of Major Bailey.

Holding the handkerchief up to her mouth, his strong hands and that funny way her hand had stuck to his. "Not at all."

"Something happened," Mochi said.

Lana hesitated. "I should find the girls. I'll tell you when I get back."

She followed the overgrown path that wound around a grove of young cypress trees. Their tangy scent reminded her of California, and of another lifetime, when she herself had been a lost young girl with a big hole in her heart. Her aunt had taken her in after the incident, but she never felt at home there. Being *sent* somewhere did that to a person.

Upon learning that she was with child at the unripe age of seventeen, Jack went from an eccentric and loving father to a red-face maniac who then broke down in tears and that night ordered her to the mainland on the first available ship. Ironically the main issue wasn't the pregnancy: Jack was convinced Lana would die during childbirth, as her mother had. But abortions were more dangerous than childbirth; anyone knew that. Lana begged and pleaded and stomped her feet. She tried to reason with him, but he wouldn't hear it. He knew a doctor who could save her.

Before the trip, she'd dreamed of running off and having the baby in Kona or Honolulu. She brought it up to Alika, the father, but he went pale and told her a baby wasn't in his plans. Two days later he moved to Waimea. She was terrified to go to California but didn't know what else to do. When she left, she swore she would never go back to Hilo.

On the wintery crossing, the seas were rough and frothy. Lana, who was already nauseated, became even more ill. She spent all day in her bunk, unable to keep anything down, not even saltines. More troubling were the red spots that began peppering her body and others' aboard the ship.

The day before they made it to port, Lana woke in a pool of blood with sharp pangs in her abdomen. By the time they docked, she had a high fever and was in and out of consciousness. She remembered being carried out first on a stretcher, with rain snaking down around her. Several days later she woke up in a hospital room. Aunt Ginger sat by her side. Lana heard the words *measles, hopeless, lucky to be alive.* She closed her eyes and slept for another two days.

When she finally came out of it, the doctor told her they'd had to remove one ovary, and during the procedure to save her, damage had been done to other female parts that may render her sterile. But the good news was she was going to be okay. Well, that was easy for him to say.

True to her word, she stayed away. Worked

herself through two years of college and then met Buck. She was drawn to his confidence and the way he knew what he wanted in life. Not only that but he was a Hawaii boy, and when he persuaded her to come back to Honolulu with him, she couldn't refuse. The islands were in her blood, and she had missed them terribly. There were things about California she liked— the wide-open skies and the cool air, the endless supply of fresh oranges and strawberries, and how you could drive flat across the country if you wanted to—but nothing compared to home.

And now she was *really* home, though for all the wrong reasons. She called out to the girls, but only birds answered back in chirps and squeaks and wing flutters. How far could they have gone? Clumps of grass had grown as high as her knees, but at one point someone had mowed a trail through here. The surrounding 'ohi'a and koa trees were huge, an area missed entirely by recent flows. One would never know that less than a mile away the whole forest had been covered over with fields of crisp black lava. A little way on, she came upon a big open barn-like structure and a paddock.

Somewhere up ahead, there was a commotion in the trees. "Girls, is that you?" Lana shouted.

The ground beneath her feet rumbled, and two horses came galloping out through an opening, manes flapping and nostrils flared. One painted, one black. They were coming right at her, and instead of jumping one way or another, Lana was fastened in place. They went around her as though she were a stone in a river. Their sweaty, dusty and familiar scent swept past her. A strange place to see wild horses, but Keauhou Ranch was not too far away, as the crow flies. Perhaps they had gotten loose from there.

A moment later Coco and Marie came traipsing out of the trees with Sailor at their heels, looking a little sheepish. Both girls had rosy cheeks.

"Did you see the horses?" Coco said.

"They almost trampled me flat."

Marie pointed behind them. "There's a pasture back there. They were grazing and I think Sailor scared them. Even though her tail went between her legs the minute she saw them."

"Sailor is a scaredy-cat," Coco said.

"Horses are big animals. She has a right to be frightened. Say, it's not a good idea to go off on your own until we set some boundaries together. It's easy to get lost out here. Okay?" Lana said.

"We stayed on the trail."

"That's smart of you. How far down does this go?"

They turned around and walked through the trees, showing Lana where they'd found the horses. At the far end of the well-grazed pasture was a line of pine trees, and beyond that it was hard to tell.

"On this end, how about you don't venture past that tree line, until we know."

"What are we going to do all day?" Coco asked.

With the schools closed indefinitely, Lana had wondered the same thing. "We have your books, we have my dad's books, and there's much to be done around the house. I promise you won't get bored."

Coco's little mind was elsewhere, Lana could tell by the way she chewed her lip and got a faraway look in her eye. "Can we ride the horses?" she finally said.

"Did you bring a saddle?" Marie asked Coco.

"I don't own a saddle. You know that."

"Well, then, how are you going to ride them?" Marie said.

Coco looked to be on the verge of tears.

"They seemed kind of wild. But maybe we can make friends with them. Would you like that?" Lana said.

Coco nodded.

After polishing off a late lunch of peanut butter–and–marmalade sandwiches, which Coco willingly ate, Lana wanted nothing more than to take a hot shower, climb into her own bed, pull a pillow over her head and go to sleep. Instead they all went out back and got to work on the wall. Benji had cut studs to nail into place, and after that someone could hammer on the slats. The problem was they had only one hammer.

"Good work, Benji. We may not freeze to death here after all," she said.

"What about beds?" Mochi said.

"I got a flat tire before I could get to Volcano House. Iris Kano said to check there since there won't be any guests. Do you know her?"

"Never liked the cold, so I stayed Hilo side."

"You mean you've never been up here?"

Everyone had been to Volcano. It was Hawaii's most popular destination. Who wouldn't want to see an active volcano? Though eruptions came and went throughout the years, the otherworldly landscape remained.

"Nope."

She noted how some people were such creatures of habit, happy in their own small corners of the world, day in and day out. Others were not content unless they were sailing across the globe to faraway lands. Lana fancied herself somewhere in between, though to be honest, Buck was always too busy to travel, and she had been stuck on Oʻahu for longer than she cared to be.

"Well, I'm glad you're here now. With us. I know it's under the worst of circumstances. But at least we're together," she said.

Minus a few people.

Mochi was sitting on a stump. "So where's your bike?"

"Two soldiers helped me. They were at the

store and they passed when I fell. They said they'd take it back to the store for me."

"Why are there so many soldiers here?" he asked.

"It sounds like the Kīlauea Military Camp is going to be turned into headquarters of some kind. There are troops on the way."

Coco, who was intent on building a tower out of wood scraps, said, "Can we use their phone?"

"We can use the phone at the store tomorrow. I need to go back and grab my bike."

"Why not today?"

"Mrs. Kano closed up the store early today."

Coco bit her lip and went back to work.

"Japanese?" Mochi said.

"Most people who live up here year-round are Japanese."

Marie and Lana took turns holding the studs in place while Benji hammered. No one said much as they worked, and Lana got the impression that Marie and Benji were avoiding each other in that awkward teenage way. By the time they had all the studs up, her arms were burning. And they still had the siding to attach. Darkness would be here soon.

"We only have one more box of nails, and this won't go far," Benji said, searching the area for more, with no luck. The boy looked exhausted.

Another cold night on the hard floor. *Wonderful.* At least they weren't sleeping in a makeshift prison cell, she reminded herself. "Why don't you and Marie hold the boards, and I'll hammer, just until we get this one row on. Then we'll eat."

Benji sighed. "Thank you."

Lana was no stranger to a hammer. Having a father who built everything himself would do that to a girl. Over the years she'd helped him build a tree house, beehives, special racks on the back of the truck, bookshelves, light fixtures, you name it.

When the gray light faded to near darkness, they pounded in the last nail. Lana let the hammer fall from her shaky hand. Sawdust mixed with sweat covered her arms, neck, face—any exposed area. The lump on her head throbbed.

Stepping back to survey their work, she said, "Not bad, for a bunch of amateurs."

"The boards are crooked," Coco said, pointing to the higher ones that were clearly not level.

"Adds charm, don't you think?" Lana said to Mochi with a wink.

"Best wall in town," he said.

"Half a wall," Lana corrected him.

Tomorrow, scrounging up nails would be top priority.

The geese were on the porch, after spending the day roaming the yard and resting under a small Norfolk pine. True to her word, Coco had kept Sailor from going after them with a few reminders. *Sailor, they're our friends.* Now Sailor got too close to Tonic, and Gin came at the dog, flapping wings and hissing like a banshee. Sailor put her tail between her legs and backed away.

"Looks like Sailor is more bark than bite," Mochi said.

Coco looked offended. "She would never bite."

Marie explained, "It's a saying, Coco. It means she acts a lot tougher than she really is."

"Yeah, she's a big baby."

With one blue eye and one brown eye, each in a black spot of fur, Sailor had a unique look. She also seemed to know exactly when they were talking about her, like right now.

"Yes, we're talking about you," Lana said, rubbing the dog's bony head.

Sailor leaned in for more, almost knocking Lana over in the process. Lana wondered how they were going to manage to keep her fed if they stayed up here for any length of time, and the thought put a damper on her already bleak mood.

The fire had gone out earlier. Until that wall was on, they wouldn't be able to light it at night. The temperature plummeted again and it was too cold for a cold shower, but Lana suggested it anyway.

"Anyone want a rinse?"

"No way," Marie said.

Coco assured her, "I don't think I'll be showering while I'm here."

Understandable. "Tomorrow we can take a look at that outdoor shower. I have a feeling you may change your mind," Lana said.

They cooked up spaghetti and meatballs, which she had brought from the Wagners' refrigerator. If someone noticed the fire from the stove, well, tough luck. They were not going to eat cold food for dinner, and that was that.

Again, no one was much in the mood to talk, and they listened to the radio after dinner for any updates. Lana was of half a mind to put the kids to bed first, to spare them from any frightening information. But what was the point? They would find out anyway, one way or another.

The White House has announced casualties in Hawaii are now estimated at three thousand, with fifteen hundred deaths. At least one old battleship and a destroyer have been blown up. Residents are still being ordered to stay indoors and fill up bathtubs with water. No water is safe. As of the top of the hour, fifty unidentified planes are headed toward San Francisco. People living along all coastlines are advised to be on guard for imminent invasion.

The newsman droned on with more details of curfew and blackout and orders for rationing, and how Singapore and Hong Kong had been bombed, and the Japanese were attempting landing at Malaya. It sounded to Lana as though the Japanese army was at full throttle, ready to dominate the whole Pacific.

"I've heard enough for tonight," she finally said.

• • •

Another night of tossing and turning, and hearing strange noises outside—squeals, footsteps, grunts, screeches. And inside there were sniffles and sobs and whispers between the girls, and snores and ragged breaths from the other room. The only difference was that, at some point in the early-morning hours, the air grew so cold Lana could scarcely feel her toes. For what felt like hours, she lay there shivering and trying to curl up into the smallest ball possible. She was tempted to call Sailor over for warmth, but she didn't want to wake Coco and Marie.

In the morning, not even sure if she had slept, she climbed out of her bed, wrapped herself in the blanket and went out to the porch. A wide-open sky was there to greet her, baby blue and cloudless. She rubbed her eyes to make sure she was seeing clearly.

"Thank you," she whispered.

She brewed a pot of coffee, then sat on the one corner of the porch with sun. It was a new world, achingly beautiful in its sharp edges of greens pressed against the sky. The geese were up, waddling through the dewy grass, searching for bugs, and the honeycreepers were out in force. The forest sounded like one big concert of chirps. She waited for the rest of the house to get up, but no one stirred. Worried about Mochi, she poked her head into their room. Benji was sitting up, bleary-eyed, and Mochi was still lying down, scrunched into a ball.

"Are you all right?" she asked.

"Mochi couldn't get warm last night. I'm going to light a fire right now," Benji said, standing up and heading out.

"You should have come and gotten me," she said.

"I was asleep, and when I woke up, I found him shivering like this," he said as he passed.

"I half thought it was going to snow," she said.

Lana came in and bent down next to Mochi, feeling his forehead, which was hot and clammy.

"I'll be fine," Mochi said, turning to look up at her. His lips were the color of blueberries and his face pale.

She placed her blanket over him. "I'll fix you some tea, and once we get the fire going, you are to stay next to it all day. And that's an order."

"No fussing over me."

There was a commotion in the hallway, and Coco and Marie appeared in the doorway, wearing knitted hats and scarves and gloves. Sailor had a scarf wrapped around her neck, too, and did not look pleased. They might have been in the Swiss Alps for all anyone knew, with their pink noses and rosy cheeks.

"Good morning, ladies," Lana said.

Coco held Hoot in one arm and a small torn

blanket in the other. Her big blue eyes were rimmed in red. "I'm ready to go home now," she whimpered.

"No offense, Mrs. Hitchcock, but maybe we ought to reconsider. I've never been so cold in my life," Marie said.

"I take it you two have never been to Germany?"

Both shook their heads vigorously. In truth, Lana had never been so cold in Hawaii, even up here at the volcano. Without a thermometer it was hard to tell, but she wouldn't have been surprised if it was in the high thirties.

Coco blew out. "Look, there's smoke coming out of my mouth."

"It's just your warm breath mixing with the cold air," Lana said.

"I wanna go home." Tears streamed down her cheeks, and she turned and buried her face in Marie's side, her little fingers gripping Marie's sweater.

Just when Lana had come to terms with making this plan work, the world was throwing in another wrench.

"Listen, let's get some hot cocoa and light a fire and we can talk about it." *Again.* She rubbed Mochi's back, feeling his protruding spine. "Mochi, I'll bring you tea and honey—this honey here is healing—and grab you when the fire's going."

In the kitchen she sat the girls down. "I know this is hard on all of us, but right now we need to make sure that Mochi is okay and get the fire going for him. He's not well. Marie, can you and Benji drag the mattress out from the bedroom and set it in front of the fireplace? I can make some hot cocoa. Once that's handled, we can go make some phone calls," she said.

"Is Mochi going to die?" Coco asked.

"Why do you always think everyone's going to die?" Marie replied.

"I heard people talking last night about it. And he looks dead."

Marie held her finger up. "Shh, don't say that so loud."

Heard people?

"There was a man and a lady arguing about bringing him over. The woman wanted to and the man kept saying not yet," Coco said, as though this was perfectly normal.

"Sounds like a vivid dream," Lana said.

"It wasn't a dream."

Marie stood up. "I'll go grab the mattress," she said, leaving Lana alone with Coco.

Lana knew about the extra senses from her father. His favorite book on the subject was *The Call of the Soul*, full of the unexplained and psychic phenomena. She was intrigued by these so-called voices. "Have you always heard things that other people can't?"

Coco shrugged. She was chewing on her lip again, which had developed a small raw patch. She looked ready to burst into tears again and stared into her lap.

Lana got up and stirred the warm milk, giving the girl some space. "It's not that I don't believe you, honey. I'm just curious. There have been times over the years when I had that sense, too. Just not as strong."

That faint buzzing before tragedies, and how the air changed color. These were things she spoke about only to Jack, who believed the human mind was largely uncharted territory. As a girl, she loved to sneak her father's books when he was out and read about life's mysteries—the transference of thought, memories of past lives, and quantum mechanics, among others. The questions had always been there.

"It seems ordinary to me," Coco said, in a small voice.

"I'm sure it does, but since not everyone can see or hear what you can, it's truly extraordinary. Think of it as a gift, something special."

"My dad never believed me."

"Some people only believe in what they can see. Say, would you like some cinnamon in your hot cocoa?"

Here she was talking to Coco as if she were some kind of expert, when the truth was she was unsure herself. Maybe having kids around forced you to straighten out your beliefs. Above anything, Coco deserved to feel safe here. And Lana wanted to keep an open mind. Lord knew that Jack would have.

"Yes, please."

Lana placed a hand on her small shoulder. "I believe you. Whenever you hear something or see something, you can tell me, okay?"

Coco nodded.

Once they got Mochi out by the fire and onto the mattress full of blankets, his lips returned to a normal color and he finally stopped shivering. The sun was also high enough to cut through the window and send tendrils of warmth through the room. Eventually Mochi sat up for his tea and managed to take small sips. Benji looked more frightened than Mochi throughout the ordeal, and once Mochi was resting again, Lana pulled Benji outside.

"How long has he been like this?" she asked.

"A couple of months ago he got skinny, and then he'd wake up all sweaty. The cough has been at least six months."

"Has he seen a doctor?"

"I tried to make him go, but he refuses."

Men and their stubbornness. Or maybe it was just older people. Or maybe it was just people in general who held on to their notions and beliefs with the grip of an angry two-year-old, herself included. Why was it so hard to just let go?

"We have to finish up this wall today," she said.

"I'm on it, Mrs. Hitchcock."

"You're a lot like him, you know."

Unassuming, efficient and dependable.

He wiped a tear with the back of his hand. "Thanks."

THE VOLCANO HOUSE

Coco put up a huge fuss and was ready to stow away in the truck, but Lana swore on a stack of Bibles she would come back and get the girls if their parents answered the phone.

"At this point, the less attention on us, the better. And plus, you two can keep an eye on Mochi. He could use the company," Lana said.

Along the drive she caught herself holding her breath on several occasions, fretting over her phone call going unanswered or finding Kano Store deserted. Wondering how long they could stay out here without anyone noticing, or without Mochi dying. Once she reached the paved section, she checked herself in the mirror. What a wreck—ugly blue bruise on her forehead, shadows under her eyes and cracked lips. Not that any of that mattered.

With the sun dazzling, it was easy to forget there was a war going on around them. The birds went about their business fluttering through the forest canopy, the 'ohi'a blossoms kept right on blooming, and a mother and three baby spotted pigs were rooting up a patch of ginger.

She slowly rolled past the Japanese schoolhouse, where there was no sign of life, and a few minutes later pulled up to Kano Store. The door was open and someone had set out bunches of anthuriums. Lana let out a small sob of relief. She rushed up the steps to find Mrs. Kano sitting behind the counter in the exact same spot as yesterday, plucking stems from ʻōhelo berries.

"Mrs. Kano, thank heavens you're here," she said.

"I told you."

Iris walked in from out back carrying a bucket. "Beautiful morning. Would you like some plums?"

Lana couldn't care less about the plums. "If you don't mind my asking, how did it go yesterday?"

Iris set down the bucket on the counter, her pretty face looking tired.

"They already had my father there. They'd picked him up in the fields and took him to the military camp. We each went in separately, and two men in suits searched us and asked us every question in the book. Wanting to know every detail about where my grandparents came from. If my grandmother sends things back to Japan. If my father attends secret meetings and if we've been in communication with Japanese spies. They kept pushing for answers that we didn't have."

"What did they say when they let you go?" Lana asked.

"They assigned us to Mr. Dunn, who will be dropping in to check on us regularly. And Baba was right—I think they would have held on to my father if they didn't need him to grow their food. They kept Mr. Shigetani from the school."

"What a fiasco. Did you see where they had the prisoners?"

"No, but a crew of workers was busy putting up a fence around the barracks, so I'm guessing there."

"What do you think they're planning on doing with them?" Lana said.

"Gladys Tatsui has been sneaking around saying they're going to be executed and that we need to break them out. Her husband was head of the judo group and is now being held."

Lana gasped. "Surely they won't be executed."

Talk like that wasn't going to help anyone. But Lana felt for the woman and tried to imagine herself in her shoes. How many of these men were guilty of spying or aiding the homeland, and how many were just going about their lives trying to survive? Like Mochi.

"You never know."

The weight of it all settled like a lead ball in her stomach. "Did you see any Germans?"

"Germans?"

"German prisoners. My dad's neighbors."

"I was told to look straight ahead while we were walking," Iris said.

Lana glanced at Mrs. Kano. "Did you?"

"I could only see the big back of that army man. He dropped off your bike this morning, by the way," the old woman said.

Lana had been half expecting the bike not to be there, since it sounded like Major Bailey had his hands full. Iris led her out back, with Mrs. Kano shuffling after them. The bike was propped up against the wall, in top shape. It almost looked as if he'd polished it. She was ashamed to admit it, but a small part of her had been hoping to run into him here.

"He must not be all bad," Mrs. Kano said.

Lana felt herself blush slightly and hoped they didn't notice. "Thoughtful of him, certainly."

"He left a note taped to the seat."

She waved it off. "Probably just being polite."

"The man isn't blind."

Iris jumped. "She's married, Baba."

"Look, I'm just happy that my bike and I are okay, and, more important, that you two weren't kept. I also came to ask if I could buy some nails and use your telephone."

The phone was behind the counter, and Lana squeezed in next to Mrs. Kano, who busied herself with the 'ōhelo berries again. Lana hoped and prayed that Ingrid or Fred would answer. If Iris and Mrs. Kano had been released, there was a chance the Wagners had been, too. But she still had a sense that their case was different. She dialed. The phone rang and rang, and she was about to hang up when someone answered.

"Wagner residence," a man's voice said.

Caught off guard, Lana lowered her voice and said, "Is this Mr. Wagner?"

"Who's calling, please?"

Dutch London.

"This is Dottie Laird, a friend from Kona. Are they in?"

"I'm afraid they aren't. Mr. and Mrs. Wagner were taken in by the FBI and have not returned."

His voice boomed through the phone, hurting her ears, and she had to hold the receiver several inches away from her head.

"Oh, my! Is there any word when they'll be released? And what about the girls?"

"Your guess is as good as mine on that. The girls are another story. They were kidnapped by a neighbor," he said.

The back of her knees felt hot. "Kidnapped, you say? How dreadful."

"They're on my watch and they were taken without my permission. Where I'm from, that amounts to kidnapping. But I'll find 'em, rest assured, ma'am."

"Perhaps the neighbor has only good intentions, like keeping them safe," she couldn't help but say.

There was a pause on the other end, and she could hear him breathing. "Where did you say you are, Mrs. . . . ."

"Laird. I'm in Kona. Well, thank you for the update. I must go now."

She hung up the phone. Would he be able to determine where she'd been calling from? Had she given herself away? Even though it was called the Big Island, it really was a small island. With so few people compared to Oʻahu, a person in Hilo could easily find out information about someone in Kona. All it took was a phone call. Up here at Volcano was different, though; most of the new population was military, with a few old-timers hidden away in the rain forest.

Mrs. Kano didn't look up but said, "Mrs. Laird, in Kona? And who was kidnapped?"

Lies did not come naturally to Lana, and here were people she felt she could trust. "Oh, Mrs. Kano, it's a long story. The man I was talking to is not a good man. I promise I will explain soon, but I need to get over to the Volcano House as soon as I can."

"I have plenty of time."

Lana had a sudden thought. "I don't, not right now, but can you do me a favor?"

"Sure."

"Will you keep an eye on police cars coming by? See if there's any haole in the back, would you? Mr. Wagner has light brown hair, and Ingrid has shoulder-length wavy blond hair."

Iris said from across the room, "We're not always up front, but we can try."

They said their goodbyes, and Iris helped her load the bicycle into the back of the truck. She pulled the note off at the last minute and shoved it into her pocket. She wanted to know what it said, and yet she was more afraid of what it might not say. Her heart sped up. The paper burned against her thigh as she drove.

Volcano House was only a few miles up the road from Kano Store. As she neared, the smell of sulfur wafted through the windows. At the front gate two sentries stopped her.

"Ma'am?" said one, leaning down to get a better look.

She handed over her driver's license. "Hello, gentlemen. I'm here to see Theo Karavitis."

"Business or personal?"

She was about to say personal, but thought the better of it. "Business. Major Bailey has sent me on a mission."

The guard handed back her license, stepped aside and waved her in without another word. Since her last visit, roads had been improved and there was a new stone Volcano Observatory and Naturalist Building, almost completed. As she came around the corner to the Volcano House, a wave of nostalgia rose up. Memories of the big stone hearth and the fire that had by all accounts been burning there since 1877. Of moonlit walks along the crater floor and being scared silly but too afraid to walk back alone.

The new structure was a red two-story, no-nonsense affair with an even grander stone chimney than the last, and the most spectacular view in the world. Perched on the rim of the caldera, one could have a front-row seat to whatever was happening in Halemaʻumaʻu—the smaller crater within the caldera—at the time. Halemaʻumaʻu was where the lava lakes formed. Had she been here yesterday, the fog would have blocked everything, but today she could see the whole outline of Mauna Loa and alternating landscape of lava and forest.

Lana had expected the place to feel like a ghost town, but there were a handful of employees and a few uniformed men riding on horseback. She waved as she walked past. No one was at the front desk, so she walked out to the vast lobby. The old fire burned hot. Walls were lined with framed photographs of spewing fountains of molten lava. She walked over to a glass table, which held green olivine crystals, lava bombs, and Pele's hair and tears—strands and pieces of volcanic glass.

"Can I help you?" said a booming voice behind her.

She jumped. "I'm looking—"

Recognition dawned in the old man's eyes when he saw her. "Miss Spalding? Can it be you?"

"Uncle Theo! I was hoping you'd remember

me. It's Lana, Jack Spalding's daughter," she said.

He held out his arms and pulled her into a bear hug, his waxed mustache tickling her forehead. "Of course, you are a sight for these old eyes, my dear. But please don't tell me your father has run out of kerosene again, or wants help rounding up those darn horses."

The room suddenly felt colder.

"My father contracted meningitis. He passed away on Saturday. I'm sorry to have to tell you." She spoke as few words as possible to avoid breaking down and sobbing.

His whole face wrinkled up. "My condolences. I had no idea."

"It was a surprise."

"The best way to go—at least that way you live fully until the end. In fact when he was up here a few weeks back, he was raring to go and making plans to start a small horse ranch, taking tours and that kind of thing, at least until the invasion— which he swore was coming—after which his horses would be a means of evading the enemy," he said, pulling her over with gnarled hands to a table.

"My dad wanted to do horse tours?"

In her experience Jack had always been spooked by horses.

He nodded. "The horse tours are, or were, I should say, one of our main attractions. If you can believe it, we had nearly thirty thousand visitors last month alone."

She whistled. "That sounds like half the population of the island."

He stared off toward the crater. "You know, a lot of people laughed Jack off as being paranoid, but not anymore."

"He had a tendency to get a little obsessed," Lana said.

He threw his head back and guffawed. "Don't we all. I'm guessing you didn't come here for a social visit with this bloody war going on. What can I do for you, Miss Lana?"

She wanted to know more about the horses and where they'd come from, but that could wait. "I need beds, and Mrs. Kano suggested I check here."

"How many?"

"At least two, three if you can spare them."

He leaned close. "I'll tell you a secret. There's a whole new troop of soldiers on their way up here, and Major Bailey asked if we could put some up, so you take what you need, but take it now before they arrive. You at your father's hideaway?"

"I am."

"We may need your help around here in days to come. Rangers, wives, residents, you name it, all chipping in."

"I'm happy to," she said.

"Not just you alone, I take it?"

"I have my girls with me." She could explain more later, if pressed.

Voices echoed in the lobby behind them, and Uncle Theo held his hand to his head in salute. Lana turned to see Major Bailey walking toward them with a bouncy young blonde by his side. Lana waved lamely.

"Look who it is. We were just talking about you," Uncle Theo said, standing and bowing in his usual dramatic form.

"All good, I hope?" Grant said, as though he really wanted to know.

"Lana, may I introduce Major Grant Bailey and my lovely secretary, Cora."

To her surprise, Lana was envious of this red-lipped Cora woman, who was quite a dish. Lana stood. "Actually, Major Bailey and I have met," she said, afraid to touch his hand again after the last episode, so she reached out and shook Cora's instead. "A pleasure."

Grant gave her a look. "Lana? Your name is Lana?"

"Did I not mention that yesterday?"

"You introduced yourself as Mrs. Hitchcock. Wait, you're not Jack Spalding's daughter, are you?" he said, with a touch of wonder.

"I am . . . I mean I was . . . I mean my father died several days ago."

Grant's face went white as a tropic-bird feather.

She had expected the reaction from Uncle Theo, but Major Bailey?

"Jack and I became close over the past year. I can't believe this. How?"

Lana explained again. With each retelling, she was reminded of how Jack had a way of endearing himself to people from all walks of life. And how, in his last year alive, all these strangers got to be close with him while she was on O'ahu being stubborn.

"He spoke about you often."

She wondered what all these people knew about their estrangement. What a wicked and heartless daughter she was, leaving her old man to forge on in the world without her. And forge on he had.

"I hope good things?" It was more wishful thinking than anything.

"Always."

There he went, staring at her again. Or rather it felt more like he was staring into her and taking a leisurely look around, reading her thoughts and worries and, God forbid, half-formed desires.

"How were the two of you acquainted?" she asked.

"We met on the golf course, of all places. But it wasn't until he found out I knew my way around horses that we really hit it off. He begged me to teach him everything I knew, on account of him not being a real horse expert, as he put it," he said, and for the first time she noticed a slight twang. *Horse* came out like *hoss*.

Picturing Grant Bailey as a cowboy gave her a shiver. He was appealing enough in a very rugged way. Warning bells clanged in her head. And yet she had so many questions and wanted to know every detail of his time with her father.

"Have you been to the house?" she said, as casually as possible, though her heart was pounding. The last thing she needed was any unexpected visits from an army man, especially one who was in charge of interrogating suspected sympathizers. Now she just prayed that Uncle Theo would not mention her wanting three beds.

"Helped him design the barn and paddock. I was down there a lot."

"How generous of you."

Uncle Theo cleared his throat. "Excuse me, but I'm meeting with Wingate in ten minutes. Lana, take what you need from the rooms at the end of the hallway. Bailey, what can I do for you, sir?"

"I wanted to warn you we'll be doing some work on the roads and the airstrip. Precautionary measures," he said.

"Fine by me."

"Also, we need to talk about bunking arrangements."

"Come back at four o'clock," Uncle Theo said, standing up and kissing Lana's hand. "Come back tomorrow, lunchtime, Miss Lana."

Cora trailed behind him, leaving a cloud of perfume in her wake. Lana stood and straightened out her skirt, antsy to be far away from Grant. "Well, I guess I'd better be going."

Sunlight poured in the window, lighting him up from all angles. "Can I help you? It sounds like you came to get something?"

She flinched. "Oh, no. Thank you. You've already been a big help with the bike and all. You didn't have to clean it up like that."

His hands went into his pockets. "You got the bike. Did you see my note?"

The note was still there, a warm spot on her cool thigh. She pulled it out and held it up. "I did but I was in a hurry, so I haven't had a chance to read it yet."

He acted unaffected. "By the way, how's the head? Looks like you got a small shiner."

"I think I'll live."

Now that she was waving the note between them, she felt obligated to read it. Grant wrote in mechanical block print, like her father.

> Mrs. Hitchcock,
> I hope you don't mind my taking the liberty to give your bicycle an overhaul and a shine. Also, the darndest thing has happened. My hand has been itching incessantly since yesterday—the one I pulled you up with. I'm trying to make

sense of it. Could you have been wearing some kind of funny lotion? Anyway, please don't hesitate to call on me for any help you might need during these tough times. I can be reached at 885-6930.

Yours truly, Grant

Lana felt a plum pit in her throat and a blush spread across her cheekbones. She should have read the note sooner.

"It must have been your imagination," she said.

When she looked back up at him, he smiled sheepishly and flashed his palm. Red and welted. "Not my imagination."

The electricity that had passed through them came to mind. Perhaps there had been lightning that no one had noticed, or a volcanic charge from the rocks he had stood upon. Or an as-yet-undiscovered chemical reaction.

"It must be from cleaning the bicycle. Maybe a reaction to a substance you used?" she suggested.

He looked unconvinced. "Just some good old-fashioned grease and soap and water. Never had a reaction like that."

"My hands were clean," she said.

"A mystery, then."

Words came out that she didn't expect. "Some things are beyond explanation."

A flicker of a smile. "You got that right."

"Now, if you'll excuse me," she said, turning to leave and bumping into a chair instead, stubbing her toe and cussing under her breath.

"Hang on a minute. You planning on staying up here a while? At Volcano?" he asked.

"That depends."

"On?"

The way he looked at her made her feel as though the world hung on her answer. *Choose your words carefully, Lana.* "For one, the war."

He cocked his head. "What else?"

On how long you folks decide to keep the Wagners, or detain innocent men on account of their skin color. "It's personal."

"What about the horses? I'd love to keep working with 'em," he said.

"The horses are running wild right now, which is probably how they like it. So for now I think I'll let them be," she said.

"Fine. You change your mind, you let me know," he said, and she thought she was off the hook, but then he added, "I know it's none of my business, but are you alone up here?"

"I'm not alone."

After a moment of awkward silence, he said, "You said your husband was on Oʻahu. You have kids?"

Under normal circumstances, Lana would have welcomed the conversation. His strong presence, resonant voice and eyes a person could

176

drown in made her want to talk, and yet there were too many complications to even consider getting friendly with the man. Still, she found it impossible to walk away.

"I have two girls, a dog and two nene geese with me, so we've been keeping each other warm at night. Unbeknownst to me, my father hadn't finished the last wall, and it's been colder inside than out," she said.

As soon as she'd spoken the words, she regretted it.

"Dang, I could send some boys down to get that taken care of," he said.

"Thank you, but we've got it almost finished."

He raised an eyebrow. "A woman and two girls?"

She felt defensive, holding up her arm and showing her bicep, well formed from tennis and swimming. "You think we aren't capable? My father taught me well, and Uncle Theo is lending us more blankets. Which reminds me, I better grab them and get home."

"It's my nature to want to help, I guess. Especially now that I know you're Jack's daughter."

"You two were that close, huh?"

Age never mattered to her father. You could be fifteen or one hundred—if he liked you, you were a part of his circle. *When you get on with someone right off the bat, chances are you have a history with them in a past life,* he used to say.

Grant nodded enthusiastically. "He pulled you in. Even with all his absentmindedness and harebrained schemes, you wanted to be around him. I reckon he was that way with a lot of folks?" he said.

"Always."

"How long had it been since you last saw each other?"

She glanced out over the caldera, her eyes following a white-tailed tropic bird riding the thermals. "Too long" was all she could muster. "Take care, sir. I need to go."

She pulled the truck around as close to the exit at the end of the hall as she could get, went into the room and sat on the bed until she heard Grant's jeep start up. At the window she cracked the curtain and watched him drive off.

In the future she'd do her best to avoid all contact with him.

THE HORSE

The sharp blue of the sky seemed in direct contrast with life below. At least the sunshine would bring warmth to the house and help Mochi thaw out. Lana worried about him as she drove home across the last stretches of lava. Maybe Mrs. Kano would have suggestions on who could help him. Behind her, the mattresses and bed frames she had dragged into the back of the truck flopped around, the ones on top ready to bounce right out. Once in front of the house, she honked.

Sailor, who had been perched on the porch like a sphinx, stood up and bounded down the steps, barking as though Lana were a dangerous stranger come to steal all the dog food in the house. The three kids rushed down to get a better look at the cargo.

"A successful mission! I got nails and beds," Lana said, happily.

Coco was holding her stuffed owl. "What about our parents?"

Every time Coco asked about Fred and Ingrid, Lana could feel the pain oozing from that little heart of hers. Mentioning Mr. London would only cause them more apprehension, so she left that part out. "There was no answer, which for now just means they aren't home. I wish I had better news."

"Can we try tonight? With curfew, they would have to be home, wouldn't they?" Marie asked.

"True, but we're stuck out here at night, so it'll have to wait until tomorrow."

Coco put her head down, shoulders shuddering. Lana made a move toward her. Just before her hand touched her shoulder, Coco spun and took off in a sprint down the path toward the horse paddocks. She wasn't wearing shoes. A moment later Sailor followed.

"Coco, come back here!" Lana yelled.

"She does this," Marie said. "At our place, when she's upset, she goes into the field behind our house and either sits in the tall grass or climbs the old lychee tree. Sometimes she stays out there for hours."

Lana thought back to her own childhood. Without a mother, when her father wasn't quite enough, she had found solace with the crabs and the shorebirds. Or searching for shiny cowrie shells and blue eels in the tide pools along the bay front. All her cares and worries soaked up by the sea. On sunny days she would lie down under a coconut tree and watch the clouds change form. Whales, dragons, waves. This sometimes went on for hours, and when she was done, the world seemed back on its axis again.

"I just don't want her venturing off too far and getting lost," Lana said.

"She'll probably find a comfortable spot and hole up. Let her be for a bit," Marie said.

Good thing one of them knew what to do. Inside, Mochi was reading by the fireplace with a steaming mug in his hands. Somehow life had been breathed back into his thin body. Lana got busy fixing lunch, determined to put some weight back on his rack of bones. Thick slices of bacon sizzled in the skillet, while she fried rice with bell pepper, chopped green onion and eggs. Hopefully Mrs. Kano or Iris would know where to get a couple of hens, since she had only six eggs left.

When they were done eating, Marie offered to help Benji finish the wall. The boy seemed to go mute in her presence, though she hardly seemed to notice. Lana gave them the nails, then set out with a peanut butter sandwich and a tangerine in search of Coco.

The kikuyu grass had dried out and she marched down the pathway, enjoying the burn of sun on her shoulders. Little red blurs sped past every so often, wings whirring. If things had turned out differently, Lana would have wanted to be an ornithologist *and* a volcanologist. Wings and lava were two of her favorite things, and fortunately, both were plentiful here. The creaks and groans of trees and the scent of fresh foliage

181

helped her forget the outside world and all its troubles, if only for a moment.

At the barn, if you could call it that—it was really more of a giant shed—there was no sign of Coco. Under the roof, though, she noticed fresh manure and the recent smell of horse. Her mind immediately went to Major Bailey. In his buttoned-up uniform, he was intimidatingly appealing, but in jeans and on a horse, well, that would be another matter altogether. She walked on, lost in a daydream, past the paddock and into the pasture.

Once she rounded a small bend, she spotted Sailor sprawled out under a towering Sugi pine, while Coco sat on a fence post stroking a black horse. Lana stepped back against a tree trunk and watched for a while. Coco's lips were moving and her head bobbed along in conversation. The horse stood completely still, ears and tail twitching every so often. Lana wanted to bring Coco her lunch, but she hesitated to interrupt. Several times Coco leaned over and wrapped her arms around the horse's neck. The horse stood there and let her.

Rather than announce her arrival, Lana walked toward the center of the pasture where she would be easily seen, making a point to step on twigs and dried leaves. The horse heard her first and spun her head around. Coco's followed.

Lana waved. "Hello, there! I brought you a peanut butter sandwich."

Sailor sat up, looking dazed, and the horse

raised its head and trotted off into the forest with a pronounced limp. Even from a distance, the swelling in its knee was noticeable. The animal was small enough to be an adolescent, and so shiny it looked to be oiled.

"Sorry to scare away your friend," she said.

"Her name is 'Ohelo."

"That's a cute name. Did you pick it?"

Coco stayed on the fence with her back to Lana and didn't respond. From the back, she looked as though she could have been a feral child—curls smashed up and sticking out in twenty directions, no shoes, and overalls that were four inches too short.

Lana tried another tactic. "Do you think 'Ohelo would like some apples?"

A small nod.

"I know where we might be able to find some." Lana leaned against the fence several posts away. "Tomorrow we'll go look, how's that?"

"Her knee hurts," Coco said.

Lana hadn't been able to tell the sex, but she trusted that Coco knew the difference.

"I noticed that, poor sweet girl."

This time Coco looked right at Lana with pleading eyes. "We have to help her. I promised I would."

There was absolutely nothing they could do to help this horse, but Lana found herself nodding anyway. "A promise is a promise. I guess that means we have to try."

"Promises have to happen, don't they?"

"Promises can be tricky things. Sometimes the maker of the promise has every intention of following through, but the world gets in the way and complicates things."

"My dad promised this would be over soon," Coco said, in a very small voice.

Out of nowhere, an 'alalā—a Hawaiian crow—landed on a branch not ten feet in front of them, on the other side of the fence. The soot-black bird watched them intently, ducking and nodding its head. Lana had never seen one this close or at the volcano. They tended to be seen down south. Coco seemed unfazed and greeted the bird with a nod of her own head.

"He meant that with every bone in his body, but right now it's not up to him," Lana said.

"But my dad is always the one in charge."

"Right now the government is in charge."

Coco jumped off the fence and moved toward the crow. "Well, I hate the government."

Lana thought the bird would fly away, but it merely fluffed its feathers and settled onto the branch.

"I can see why you'd feel that way, but things will work out, you'll see," Lana said, silently praying her words to be true.

Coco walked right up to the crow on the branch and said, "What's your name?"

Lana half expected the crow to answer. "These

crows are quite rare. Did you know that?" she said.

"I've never seen one before."

"They don't live in Hilo. Seeing one is a good sign."

Coco went quiet for a few breaths. "Not this one," she finally said.

A chill ran down Lana's neck. "What makes you say that?"

"I just have a feeling."

By the time Lana, Coco and Sailor returned to the house, Benji and Marie had made great progress on the wall. Some pieces were nailed on crooked, but no one cared. When it got to the last nail, they still had a one-foot space to fill. They all scrounged around for nails or screws or anything to plug the hole with, and it was Marie who found a narrow piece of corrugated roofing that they managed to wedge in for the time being.

"My father would be proud, and so would yours," Lana told her.

It was hard to know whether to talk about the Wagners. Sometimes when she brought up their names, the girls perked up and wanted to talk about them, while other times, mentioning them seemed like rubbing grit in a wound.

After a dinner of meat loaf, steamed sweet potato and rice dripping in butter, they huddled by the fireplace and stared into the flames. No one said a word. The wood spit and crackled. Just to be sure the wooden shutters worked, Lana slipped out the front door and walked into the yard, looking back at the house. Only on one side, a thin sliver of light escaped. This far out in the boondocks, she'd risk it. Anything for a warm night's sleep.

Nearby, the bushes rustled. Something big was out there with her. She turned and bolted back into the house, skipping all the steps and slamming the door behind her. Everyone in the room turned to stare, eyes wide.

Lana waved it off. "Probably just some pigs. They startled me."

"It was 'Ohelo," Coco said.

" 'Ohelo?"

"The horse."

"I wasn't going to wait to find out. And what makes you so sure it was 'Ohelo?" Lana asked.

Coco just shrugged.

"In Japan, people believe there are places that have a very sacred spirit about them. Places where you are closer to the great Mystery. And there are animals, too, protectors and holders of the divine that have influence over us. There is a strong sense of that here. Any of you felt it?" Mochi said, looking directly at Coco.

"Like an aumakua?" Marie said.

Mochi nodded, and for a moment, Lana was surprised that a German girl would know about Hawaiian animal guardians, but then she

186

remembered that the girls had been born and raised in Hilo; they were kama'āina. Hawaii would have rubbed off on them by now.

"There's a crack in the sky down that way, that's why," Coco said, pointing south.

Lana tried not to act surprised, though half the things that came out of Coco's mouth surprised her. "I've always been drawn to the volcano, even when I was young. So that makes perfect sense. Though I haven't noticed a crack in the sky. How do you know about it?"

"I saw it today."

Mochi glanced at Lana, a thin smile forming.

"Maybe tomorrow you can show us," Lana said.

Marie put her arm around her sister. "There's that overactive imagination again. Remember what Daddy said about talking like this, *Mausi*."

Coco's shoulders wilted.

"What did he say?" Mochi asked.

"That the *crazy talk*—as he calls it—makes her sound crackers. The kids at school started calling her names, and my parents got called in every few days because of one squabble or another. She's supposed to keep the crazy talk to herself."

Lana could feel the shame radiating off Coco in thick layers. "That's plain wrong. I think what you have is a gift. When people don't understand something, they sometimes get frightened and react badly."

Marie looked taken aback.

Mochi spoke softly. "This war is a good example of that."

"Exactly. Your parents and all our neighbors being rounded up like cattle . . . The whole thing is about fear and people not stopping to try to understand," Lana said.

Coco's lower lip trembled, and she bolted from the room. Sailor, who had been lying on the warm planks next to the fire, followed Coco with her eyes, then got up and slowly trotted after her. *Thank goodness for this dog.*

At every turn, Lana felt inadequate to help this poor child, but she felt she had to try. When she moved to stand, Mochi held her arm. "Let me," he said, and went.

Lana stretched and said to Benji and Marie, "Lord only knows how long we're going to be up here together, so let's make the most of it. Whatever quirks we all may have, get used to them, I say." They both just stared at her, mute. This whole kid and teenager situation was going to take a lot of practice. "Come on, let's get ready for bed."

Earlier they had set up the girls in their own room with the queen mattress from Volcano House and given Mochi and Benji the twins, and Lana kept the master bedroom with the mattress on the floor. Heat from the fireplace had made it into the far reaches of the house, but there was no light. She ran her hands along the walls in the hallway, hearing whispers from Mochi and Coco as she passed. In her room she shuffled along until her foot hit the side of the mattress. Weariness pulled her down. And then a sound. Someone was snoring in her bed.

Sailor.

THE LUNCH

The following morning, as they drove toward Volcano House, the air was still clear and full of winter light and tiny white puffy clouds. No sign of Japanese invasion, but in just two days' time, a string of 'ōhelo berry bushes on the lava had turned red and purple, heavy with ripe berries.

Lana remembered how the old Hawaiian woman who lived on the lodge grounds used to tell her and Rose not to pluck the berries on the way to Kīlauea or rain and fog would engulf them. *You can pick once you get to the crater, but you must offer the first to Pele.* None of the kids had known her name; everyone just called her *Auntie.* One of her eyes was pale blue, which gave her a haunted look.

The first time Lana had seen her, she felt her skin itch. The woman had interrupted them as they played on the wall outside of Volcano House. Her words scratched at the back of Lana's mind. "We finally meet," she had said, even though there were no introductions made.

Once she had left, Rose whispered, "What if she's Pele?"

Coco and Marie were piled in the truck beside

her, with Sailor in the back, howling for no apparent reason each time they came across a patch of open sky.

"She misses home," Coco informed them.

"We all do, and that is perfectly understandable. But is there anything she likes about it here?" Lana asked.

From the side, Coco's little nose turned up slightly and a peppering of pale freckles dotted her cheeks. Lana could almost hear her unique little mind ticking. "She likes the warm fireplace and the pasture with wild horses. Sailor has always wished she was a horse, so now she can get to know a few and pretend."

Lana laughed. "Maybe we can make her some saddlebags."

"She would love that!"

Lana felt herself wanting to do anything to keep Coco happy and hear that sweet tone in her voice. Maybe joy was catching, and all it required was a well-meaning heart and plenty of friendship. Maybe it was something that couldn't be stamped out, even in the worst of times.

"When we go out to pick berries or gather honey, she can help transport," Lana said.

"We're going to do that?" Coco said, looking up at her with wide eyes.

"We have to keep ourselves busy somehow, don't we?"

Marie added, "What about helping out with the

war? On the radio last night, I heard they need volunteers to knit sweaters and socks and scarves or make bandages or to help spot Japanese submarines or ships."

"You ladies know how to knit?" Lana said.

Both girls shook their heads. "Our mama said all good German girls should know how to knit, but then she taught us how to bake instead," Marie said.

"Hilo is too hot for knitting," Coco said.

Boy, was that the truth. "Jack never taught me, either."

"What about your mama—how come she didn't teach you?" Marie asked.

"My mother died when I was born, so Jack was my mom and dad all wrapped into one." No matter how many times Lana had spoken those words, her heart iced over.

Coco turned. "What happened?"

I happened.

"There were complications with my birth, and they couldn't stop the bleeding. She died a few hours later."

"You mean you never knew her at all, like you were motherless?" Coco asked.

"I lived inside of her for nine months. I did know her, and I can still hear her when I close my eyes. I remember that after I came out, the nurses put me on her chest. My ear was over her heart and she was humming 'The Queen's Prayer' in the most beautiful voice you've ever heard. When I first learned the song in school and came home and told Jack it was the same song Mama was humming before she died, he went white as a ghost."

"How is that possible?" Marie said.

"For a long time, my father tried to convince himself that I had overheard him talking about the morning she died, even though he never shared it with anyone. But I had one other piece of proof."

By now, Coco was sitting facing Lana with her mouth agape. "What was it?"

"I knew her final words."

These were not the kinds of things Lana normally shared with people, but the girls deserved to know. They had lost their own mother, after all, if only for the moment.

Coco could not contain her curiosity. "Can you tell us what she said?"

"She whispered to my father, 'She is my *ha*,'" Lana told them.

"What is *ha*?" Marie asked.

"It's Hawaiian for life or breath." The rattle of the truck got louder as they all sat quiet for a bit, Lana thinking about how she had managed all those years. "I know it might feel different right now, but there really is no such thing as being motherless. Whether they're gone from this world or still alive, with you or not with you, it doesn't mean they stop being your mother. It's not something that is reversible. They are always right here." She placed her hand over her heart and patted it a few times. A few beats later, Coco did the same.

They pulled onto the main road. Heading south, Lana questioned her choice in bringing the girls and passing them off as her own, adopted or not. Hawaii was a small place, and although no one up here knew her business, word had a way of traveling from one town to the next faster than you could say *Halema'uma'u*. But if they were going to stay for any length of time, she couldn't leave them locked away in the house all day.

"Say, can you still see the crack in the sky?" she asked Coco.

Over the tops of the trees, an expanse of blue filled the windshield. Coco looked from left to right. "Not right now. I think you see it when you look up accidentally."

"What exactly does it look like?" Lana asked.

Coco shrugged. "Hard to explain."

Marie folded her arms and grunted. "That's because there is no such thing as a crack in the sky, silly."

"Let her finish. If she saw it, I believe her," Lana said.

Marie mumbled something that Lana couldn't hear.

"What was that?"

"Nothing."

After that, Coco refused to speak until they pulled up to Volcano House. A thin trail of smoke rose from the chimney. Sailor jumped down as soon as they climbed out and ran a big figure eight in the parking area. There were several army vehicles in the lot, and Lana felt herself tense.

"Let's go around," she said, ushering them around the side of the building and down a rocky trail to the side that overlooked the massive crater.

As soon as Coco caught sight of Kīlauea, she started running to the overlook, ringlets bouncing like coiled springs. "Will we see an eruption?" she called back.

"She's been quiet for a while, but you never know."

"Why do you call it a she?" Marie asked.

"Everyone does. Probably because Kīlauea is the home of Madame Pele, the Hawaiian goddess of fire."

"You don't really believe in Pele, do you?"

This was something Lana had grappled with as a young girl. "I respect the ancient Hawaiian myths as stories to make sense of the world around them. As I see it, Pele represents Mother Nature herself. Volcanoes are awfully powerful. Remember what Mochi was saying last night?"

Marie looked skeptical. "About the spirit in places and things?"

"Exactly."

"It seems to go against God."

A pair of tiny 'apapane swooped low, wings humming as they did a flyby. "God *is* nature, Marie. You can't separate the two."

Lana was no religious expert, but one thing she was sure of was that being in the salt water of the ocean or the warm green of the rain forest was as close to heaven as she'd ever felt.

When they caught up to Coco at the overlook, she asked, "Can we go down into the crater?"

"Not right now, but maybe one of these days." They were all in their fine dresses, Lana in newly washed white, Coco in pink seersucker and Marie in a sea-blue number that matched her eyes.

The sound of a door closing behind them had all three swinging around. Uncle Theo walked down the steps. "Not just one beauty, but three today. Who do we have here?"

Lana introduced the girls. Marie greeted him with a smile, and Coco hardly noticed him; she was too busy trying to locate a route to the crater floor. "Does this trail lead to the bottom?" she asked, pointing to a narrow break in the uluhe fern.

"That's for pigs and menehune," Uncle Theo said. "The one we use is over there toward the steam vents, and it takes you on the World's Weirdest Walk."

Coco looked intrigued. "Why is it called that? And are there really menehune here?"

He winked at Lana. "You'll have to see for yourself, my dear."

Coco bounced up and down on her tippy toes, and Lana had the thought that she might tear off on her own and follow the switchback to the crater floor in search of miniature Hawaiian men and molten lava. "Let's go inside, shall we?"

Sailor was allowed in, too, and promptly made herself comfortable in front of the fireplace. All stretched out, she was longer than the hearth itself. Given the chance, Uncle Theo would never stop talking, and he explained to the girls about the fire that had never gone out and which famous people had visited in recent years. Lana stared into the flames, happy that someone else was there to answer the endless questions.

"What about now that the war is here and we have blackout?" Marie asked.

"We can close off this great room."

Coco piped in. "Like our house. We almost froze to death two nights ago. Especially—"

Lana swore the next word out of her mouth would be *Mochi*, and so she cut her off. "Poor Coco, her lips were blue in the morning. Even with Sailor for warmth. She hasn't a lick of body fat to keep her warm."

"We can help with that. Do you like macaroni and cheese?" Uncle Theo said, bushy mustache covering up a smile.

"Yes!"

"And pie?"

"Yes!" both girls said in unison.

Men's voices drifted out of the dining area, and Lana caught herself listening for one in particular. Theo led them all in, and when they reached the entryway, Lana spotted a group of uniformed men circled around a table at the far end of the room. All conversation ceased when Lana and the girls walked in. Heat pricked the back of her neck, and she made a point not to look their way again.

At the nearest window table, Lana stopped. "Can we sit here?"

Every other table was empty.

"Make yourselves at home. I'll let the kitchen know you're here. Obviously we aren't doing a regular menu, but I bribed a few ranger wives to come in and cook for us. And I might be able to sneak a scrap or two for the big fella," said Uncle Theo.

"Sailor is a girl," Coco said.

Theo smacked his forehead. "Ah, forgive me."

The chairs were plush and the view magnificent, but the giant room felt oddly empty and quiet. She imagined it bustling with visitors from all corners of the earth. Coco sat quietly with her hands in her lap. Instead of looking out at the view, her eyes were on the door.

"Are you okay, sweetie?" Lana asked.

Coco appeared not to hear.

"*Mausi?*" Marie said.

Coco returned from wherever she'd gone off to in her mind. "I'm fine."

Lana faced the window, but her left cheek buzzed and her neck felt a strong urge to turn toward the table with the men. Not looking was taking so much effort that she finally relented. When she glanced over, her eyes found Major Bailey straightaway. The thick brown hair with its slight wave, strong chin, big hands. Even the sight of his profile made her slightly light-headed. There were four other men at the table, all sitting behind a curtain of cigarette smoke. They still had food on their plates and they looked deep in conversation. *Good.* Maybe the meeting would drag on so Lana and the girls could slip out before the men were done.

Coco excused herself to use the restroom, and Lana explained to Marie about Mauna Loa, which was spectacularly clear from where they were sitting, and how it was a different volcano from Kīlauea. People claimed that Mauna Loa—Hawaiian for "long mountain"—was the largest volcano on earth. Sitting there, feeling very small in its shadow, one could see why.

"Both are active, but Kīlauea is a lot easier to get to. You'd have to hike up thirteen thousand feet where the air is thin and there's nothing but jagged lava for miles."

"You've been?"

"Nope. My father has, though. He said it was the longest night of his life. Numb from cold and sick from altitude, he had to nearly crawl back down in the morning."

"It sounds horrendous. Why would anyone want to go up there?" Marie asked.

"Human nature, I suppose. Men love a challenge."

Lana looked over at Major Bailey again. Now he turned in time to catch her watching him. He smiled and tipped his glass. Several hundred moths took flight in her chest. She smiled back, and before she knew it, her hand was up and waving like an eager schoolgirl.

Marie followed her gaze. "Who is *that*?"

"No one."

"He doesn't look like no one," Marie said with her lips curled up.

"What do you mean?"

"Your face is bright red, for one. And the way he smiled at you? You must know him."

Lana took several gulps of water, spilling some down the front of her dress. "Hardly. I met him the other day when I fell off the bike. He gave me a ride. Say, where's Coco?"

"With her, there's no telling."

Lana stood. "I'm going to check."

Just outside the door and to the left was a bamboo hostess stand. Lana passed by and then did a double take. There was Coco, standing behind the stand with a phone to her ear. Her back was to Lana.

"I just want to talk to my parents," she was saying.

Lana ran over, grabbed the phone and slammed it down. "What are you doing?" she cried.

Coco turned beet red and fought back tears. "I was calling my mama and papa."

"I told you we would call them after lunch. Together. Who was that?" Lana said.

"Mr. London."

She should have seen this coming. "Did you tell him where we were?"

"He said he could take us to them."

She knelt down and grabbed Coco by the shoulders, looking into her watery eyes. "What did you tell him, sweetie? I need to know."

"Nothing. I just said I want to talk to them."

Marie came running around the corner. "What is it?"

"She called home and was talking to Mr. London."

Coco pleaded, wringing her little hands. "But he said he can take us to them. He knows important people."

Mr. London was the kind of man who could seamlessly lie to a child. "You let me do the calling, and if I feel like he's telling the truth, we will go right away to see your parents."

"Why would he lie?"

So he can have two beautiful young girls under his thumb?

"Who knows, but he could get us all in trouble, and even worse, separated. I don't trust him."

Marie stood beside Lana with her arms folded. "Neither do I."

Just then a figure in khakis walked out the door. Lana hardly noticed, until he spoke. "Do you ladies need some help here?"

Lana pulled Coco in to her side. "Oh, hello, Major. We were just borrowing the telephone, since we don't have one at the house."

"These your girls?"

"They are. We took them in when their parents died." She squeezed Coco's shoulder when she spoke the word *died.*

"Sorry to hear that, but I imagine they're lucky to have you," he said.

He stuck out his hand to Coco. She stared at it for a moment and then reached out and shook, her tiny hand pale against his olive skin. "A pleasure to meet you. I'm Major Bailey, but you can call me Grant."

"Are you in the war?" she asked him.

"You could say that. I'm part of the United States Army, which makes me active duty," he said.

"Do you know important things?"

Once again, Lana worried where this was headed and was about to interrupt, when Marie stepped in. "Hello, I'm Marie. My little sis here would ask you questions all day if she could. I'm sure you have more important business to attend to."

Grant grinned. "Trust me, seeing the three of you gals is a burst of sunshine. And to answer your question, Coco, I do know a thing or two. What did you want to know?"

Lana held her breath. No matter how many times she had coached the girls about what to say and what not to say, she got the feeling that Coco would give voice to whatever came to her at the moment. But Coco was no longer looking at Grant's face. Instead her eyes were focused on his smooth inner forearm, which Lana noticed for the first time was covered in a finely drawn tattoo.

"I want to know about the horses on your arm," Coco said.

He held his arm out. Lana was not a fan of tattoos, but the sketch of three horses galloping in a line was more like artwork on skin. So simple, and yet the horses seemed to be moving across his arm. Coco reached out and touched the first horse.

"In my other life, I was a cowboy in Wyoming. Horses were my thing, so when I joined the army, I had these beauties inked onto my arm," he said, sounding like a proud father.

Coco took her hand away, and without thinking,

Lana touched the first horse and traced her fingers across the others. Grant shivered. Lana yanked her hand away in embarrassment. "I'm sorry. It's just so beautiful," she said.

Grant held her gaze for a second too long. "Sorry for what?"

She looked away and didn't answer, heart galloping wildly.

Coco seemed wound up, too, speaking so fast her words overlapped. "I found a horse yesterday down by our house, actually a few horses, but one that I really like. Her name is 'Ohelo and she told me she wants to be friends."

He chuckled. "I'll bet she does. Horses make great friends. And you know what?" he said.

"What?"

"Once you earn their trust, they never forget you."

"Like people," Coco said.

"Tell me, what does this 'Ohelo look like?"

Coco pointed. "Just like that last horse on your arm. She's small and black and delicate, with an extra-long tail. And she has a sore knee."

Grant scratched his chin. "I think I know that horse. We were calling her Minnie, on account of her being so small. Spooks easily and afraid of people. How do you know her knee hurts?"

"I just do."

"Fair enough. Did she let you get near her?"

"Kind of."

"Then you must be pretty special."

Coco shrugged. Lana was about to usher the girls away when Coco said, "Can you come teach us how to be cowboys?"

Marie shot Lana a worried look. Explaining why they had a Japanese man and his son living with them would be tricky, at best.

"Major Bailey is busy bolstering up our defenses in case of an invasion, so let's let him do his job. Now is not the time to play cowboy," Lana said.

Grant said, "Actually, I would love to."

"I appreciate your kindness, sir, but we have other things to focus on."

"Like what?" Coco whined.

Just this morning her mind had been stuffed full of worries, like how to keep Mochi alive and how to reach the Wagners and how soon another attack might come. But standing here now, she couldn't come up with one darned thing to say.

Thankfully the two younger soldiers walked out of the dining hall and stopped for introductions. They had freshly clipped hair, pressed uniforms and a bit of swagger in their steps. Maybe Grant would drop the cowboy idea and leave with them. Both guys were tripping over each other to shake hands with Marie, who was probably the only blonde this side of Hilo. After a few minutes of chitchat, the soldiers moved on.

Grant stayed put. "What you said earlier, about

me being busy, that's true. But when I start something, I like to see it through. Truth be told, we could actually use the horses for patrol along the pali. I could get them rounded up and check on 'Ohelo if she'll let me. The last stretch of fencing needs to be put up, too."

Coco jumped up and down. "I could be your helper."

"No," Lana said, more forcefully than she meant to.

Grant persisted. "I swear I won't get in your way at all."

"Major—"

He held up his hand. "Look, I know you don't want to impose on me, but think of it as helping in the war effort and doing *me* a favor, honest to goodness." He put his hand on his chest. "I miss the ranch something fierce. This way I can sneak away and get my cowboy fix. Not to mention making a pretty little girl's day."

Coco beamed up at him. How could Lana say no to that? There were no rules that said she had to invite Major Bailey into the house, were there? Maybe Mochi could stay indoors and they could concoct a story about Benji, say he lived nearby and was helping out. It was foolish and she knew she ought to put her foot down and keep him at a safe distance. *But.*

"I can see you're used to getting your way," she said, feeling more than a little flustered.

"No comment," he said with a wink.

"Can you come tomorrow?" Coco asked.

"Not tomorrow, but Saturday. Will that work?"

This was a losing proposition. "Fine. We'll see you at 9:00 a.m. sharp," Lana said.

That gave her two days to figure out how to steel herself against his charms. Surely he had someone waiting at home. Though he wore no ring. Not that she meant to be nosy, but it would have been impossible not to notice, especially when their hands had been mashed together. Truth be told, he had been entering her thoughts more than she liked.

"Saturday it is," he said with a huge grin.

Lunch went on without a hitch. Coco stuffed herself nearly sick with baked macaroni and cheese, Sailor was escorted outside to gnaw on a cow knuckle bone, and Uncle Theo came back to sit with them for the remainder of the meal. When it was time for goodbyes, he whispered in Lana's ear, "Major Bailey is good stock. Your father admired him."

THE ROUNDUP

Listening to the staticky voices on the radio, it was hard to tell what was rumor and what was real. Jeb Hartman in all seriousness reported that, on the morning of the attack, Japanese agents in Hawaii had infiltrated the bases on Oʻahu and slit the throats of American servicemen. People were calling in at all hours reporting submarines spotted off the coast and mysterious lights offshore. The consensus seemed to be *when,* not *if,* the enemy bombers or ships full of troops would strike again. Jeb reminded listeners that Germany and Japan were in cahoots, and an East Coast, West Coast, Hawaii siege was imminent.

Lana shut down the radio after that, certain the whole house would be having a round of nightmares tonight. The need to know was at great odds with not wanting to hear anything about the war. Would it be possible to exist up here in their own bubble for much longer?

Once the kids were asleep, Lana told Mochi, "None of this feels real to me yet. I find it hard to fathom Japanese troops actually coming ashore and murdering or torturing us, and yet all the news about China and how brutal they were in Manchuria gives me chills."

Mochi poked at the fire with a stick, bursting cinders. "The only thing real is the two of us sitting here at this table. The flames, the crickets singing outside. Can you hear them?"

Lana listened. The fire hissed and spat, and beyond that, the steady chirping of crickets singing into the night. "That doesn't change the fact that there is a war going on."

"That is true. But worrying about what *might* happen is futile. It won't prevent the inevitable," he answered.

Men always said that kind of thing, and it annoyed her no end. Worries were not faucets and could not be turned off and on as you pleased.

"Is this part of your Shinto religion?" she asked.

"Shinto is more a way to exist than a religion. One in which we are part of the natural world, not separate from it."

In the firelight, big shadows formed under his cheekbones. Since they arrived, he looked thinner, and yet that quiet strength he always had still emanated from him. Maybe he was on to something.

"I get a sense of that every now and then," Lana said.

"Pay more attention."

"To what?"

"The moment."

Weariness hit, along with the impossibility of what he was saying. Right now the only things she could pay attention to were the girls and Mochi and Benji, and keeping them all safe and fed. Sailor and the geese, too, to be fair. A knot formed in her stomach. Her mind was also annoyingly distracted by thoughts of Grant and the smooth lines of his muscular forearm.

"I should warn you that Major Bailey from the military camp is coming here on Saturday morning. He's a cowboy, and Coco persuaded him to come help with the horses."

"He's the one who fixed up the bike?" Mochi asked.

"Yep."

"I will keep out of sight."

Was she imagining it, or was there a touch of a smile in his eyes?

They spent Friday searching for berries and exploring the outlying terrain near the house. And after that Lana took them out back to the hives and explained the basics of beekeeping and how to harvest honey. The air around them vibrated as she spoke. It had been some time since her father had checked on the bees, and honey dripped from the boxes.

"Look at the honey from this one. It's reddish," Coco pointed out.

Jack used to say that red honey was as rare as wild snipe, and it took Lana years to figure out that snipes were not real. "There's an old wives' tale that during volcano season the honey glows red as the lava. My father believed it was from the bees drinking too much 'ōhelo berry nectar, and that red honey carries quadruple the healing properties," she said.

"When is volcano season?" Coco asked.

"It's when the volcano is erupting," Lana said.

"But it's not erupting right now."

Marie rolled her eyes. "She said it was an old wives' tale—that means it's not true."

Lana gently corrected her. "There's usually some degree of truth to an old wives' tale."

Coco asked a hundred and one questions about dealing with the bees, though Marie looked ready to bolt.

"The main thing to remember is that bees pick up your energy. So you need to be relaxed and think loving thoughts when around them," Lana said.

With these two it would either be a disaster or a miracle. She could imagine Coco talking to the bees the way she talked to all the animals, and lulling them into complacency.

"We'll need to find more jars and containers to collect it in, so don't throw anything away," Lana instructed them.

Later Coco insisted that Lana try her parents again. They all drove down to Kano Store, but this time there was no answer. They went to a yard near the village where Lana had remembered an apple tree, but there were a couple of loose, scroungy dogs guarding their territory.

No one said it outright, but they were all looking forward to Saturday morning. When it dawned, Lana was sure that if the temperature dipped any lower, it would snow. She bundled up in half of the clothing she owned here and went outside to sit with the sleeping geese. Their heads were tucked away in their feathers in a way that made Lana wish she could do the same. Gin moved enough so that he could open his eye and see her, but Tonic didn't budge.

Early morning had always been her favorite time. Jack's, too. He used to tell her that dawn was enchanted. As always, he tried to explain it in scientific terms: *The sun's energy is just beginning to spread through the atmosphere, and it fills us with vital particles. Everything is more conductive.* As a child, all Lana knew was that in the mornings the world felt ripe with possibility.

If morning was enchanted, night was surely haunted. Those were the hours of magnified darkness and bad thoughts. Last night there had been more sobbing from Coco. Poor thing. Lana felt it, too. She had woken in a sweat, heart racing. Nothing she told herself could calm her down, and she lay awake for hours ruminating about every fear possible.

As the sun came up, the sky turned a violet hue and birds wove invisible pathways through the trees. She remembered being so frustrated as a girl, trying to glimpse one for more than a second. Jack used to joke that they were faster than the speed of light.

A few minutes later Coco came marching up the drive, a blanket wrapped around her whole body. Sailor was by her side.

"What on earth are you doing out here so early?" Lana asked her when she reached the top step.

"Seeing if I could find my parents."

Lana sat stunned for a few seconds, unsure of how to respond. "Um, well, how did it go?"

"They are still alive," Coco said with a definitive nod.

"Of course they are. You didn't have to go out in the cold and the dark to know that."

Rosy spots had formed on Coco's cheeks, and the way her hair was matted to her head with leaves in it, she looked like a feral child come out from the bush. "The sky crack was there again, and sometimes I find things out when I see it. The closer I am the better."

"What else did you find out?"

Coco frowned and sat on the step. "Nothing."

Lana surveyed the sky for any signs of a crack. "Is it still there?"

"Yes, but you won't be able to see it."

"Why not?"

"Because you don't believe, not really."

"Believe in what?" Lana asked.

"Magic."

It had been so long since Lana had thought much about magic. Not since the days of Jack, though he rarely used the word *magic*. His scientific mind preferred *unexplained phenomena*. Since then, time and pain and distance had eroded her belief. All she was left with was the sense of knowing when a disaster was on the way. Some kind of magic that was.

"Perhaps you can help me?" Lana said.

Coco shook her head vigorously. "No."

"Why not?"

"It doesn't work that way."

"Tell me, then . . . how does it work?"

"I'm not sure, but I do know you have to believe."

How could such a wee thing know so much?

After picking at his porridge topped with 'ōhelo berries, Mochi returned to his bedroom with a dog-eared copy of *The Good Earth* and a mug of tea. He had slept late and his breathing sounded ragged at breakfast, and Lana could tell he was eager to lie down again. This arrangement with Major Bailey gave him the perfect excuse to spend the morning in bed. Though she was worrying more and more that she needed to find a doctor. Was it an infection? Something treatable? It would sure help to know.

She and the girls were out back working at the beehives when Sailor's ears perked up. Lana listened for the sound of a motor but heard only the hum of thousands of tiny wings. Honey dripped from the comb, and the girls were eager to collect a jarful. As far as she was concerned, one could never have enough honey in the same way that one could never have enough love.

"It's Major Bailey," Coco said, grabbing ahold of Lana's hand and pulling her toward the house.

"We would have heard the car."

"He's not in a car."

She rushed over, just in case Coco was right, in order to avoid any nosing around on his part. Benji was with Mochi, and they had decided he would show up later, under the pretense of coming to help. Instead of the rattle and rumble of an engine, she heard the thud of hoofbeats. Sure enough, Grant was in the grassy turnaround sitting atop one of the largest horses Lana had ever seen. He had a rangy palomino roped behind him, all saddled up.

He tipped his hat and rode over to them. "Aloha!"

Coming from him, it sounded goofy. Visitors never seemed to get the word quite right. "Howdy," she said back.

In a quick swoop, he was off the horse and standing a foot away. He smelled like cinnamon

216

and leather with a dab of sweat. Lana took a step back, while Coco moved toward the palomino. "Is this one mine?" she asked.

"This here is Lady, and you can ride her once we make sure you are checked out. I take it you've been on a horse before?"

"Twice."

"An expert," he said, winking at Lana. "How about you, Mrs. Hitchcock—when was your last ride?"

Hearing the name made her neck itch. "Again, it's Lana. And for the record, I'll be changing my name back to Spalding once things settle here. Last time I rode a horse was up here when I was about sixteen. We rode from Hilo."

The faintest of smiles passed over his face. "Another expert. Glad to know I'm in good company."

Lana rolled her eyes. "Hardly, Major."

"Where did you get these horses?" Coco asked.

"The ranch behind the camp. Starts with a *K*, and I'm not even going to try to pronounce the name. I've gotten friendly with the foreman."

"Keauhou," Lana said.

"I need lessons on how to say these Hawaiian words. It would give me some credibility with the locals," he said.

The thought of sitting alone with Grant was appealing, if not impossible. "They're easy, once you know the vowels."

"As easy as it might be for you to round up a wild horse," he said, nodding at Sailor. "Is the dog well trained? We may be able to use it."

"Sailor is a girl, not an *it,* and she listens well. She's kind of a scaredy-cat, though," Coco said.

"Fair enough. By the way, you okay to wear that riding?" he said.

While Grant was in Levi's, a worn plaid shirt and a cowboy hat, Lana and the girls were a hodgepodge of skirts, overalls and blouses, layered with coats and sweaters. Lana had not packed for horseback riding, and all her skirts were white.

"It's all we have."

Grant gave the girls a refresher on riding and said they could take turns riding Lady down to the pasture. "But maybe for today, you two can work with Sailor and guarding the pasture, while your mom and I see if we can find some horses."

Coco's eyes went wide at the reference and looked about to say something, but she caught herself.

Lana suddenly felt that she ought to tell Grant the truth. But could she trust him?

"I'm the last person you want out there. I won't be much use," she said.

He jumped onto his horse, who he called Boss. "I doubt that."

Lana felt a rush of heat on her cheeks. "By the way, one of the boys in town has been helping out down here. His name is Benji, and I asked him to come over, in case we work on the fence," Lana said.

"We can use all the help we can get," he said.

Coco rode first as they walked the path to the pasture, and when it came time to switch with Marie, she refused to get off. Lana flashed back to her riding times as a girl, when riding a horse was as much of a thrill as riding a unicorn.

Marie, who usually gave in to Coco, stood her ground. "It's my turn."

"You can ride later."

"We're almost to the pasture . . . get off," Marie said.

The look on Coco's face said she was weighing the possibility of making a run for it. Grant must have seen it, too, because he rode up next to her and grabbed the reins. "You'll get your chance again, promise. Now, switch with your sister."

His tone was hard and soft at the same time. Coco slid off without a word, falling in line behind Lana. A few minutes later she began humming. Nature had a way of doing that to you. You could walk into a forest blue or irritable, and minute by minute, the trees would strip you clean. On O'ahu, she'd been too caught up in the city life to remember the feeling.

When they reached the pasture, two horses were grazing. One white, one black. Both raised their heads and eyed the group warily.

"That's her!" Coco cried.

The white horse flared his nostrils and circled around. 'Ohelo bolted. Grant made a bunch of clicking noises and utterances, and his horse came to a halt. By then 'Ohelo was long gone.

He jumped down and ordered Marie off. "We want the horses to get used to us first, so give him space."

"What about 'Ohelo?" Coco asked.

"She won't go far. Horses like to stick together."

They surveyed the pile of fencing and fence posts, which was right where he said Jack had left it. "Once we get this up, we can keep 'em here. The pasture is big enough for the herd."

Lana was beginning to wonder what the point in all this was. "I appreciate your enthusiasm, but to be honest, I have no idea how long we'll be staying. This all seems like a lot of work with so much uncertainty."

"Last I checked, life was uncertain. Are there any guarantees about anything?" he said.

In the past week, her life had moved in a whole new trajectory. But even before that, her safe and neatly planned life with Buck that was supposed to be full of abundance and love and children had evaporated. There was no accounting for potholes in the road and unexpected detours.

"You may be right about that, but still, why bother? Maybe we can satisfy our cowboy urges by riding these two horses and seeing if we can help 'Ohelo," she said, reaching out and squeezing Coco's bony shoulder.

Grant cocked his head and smiled. "Cowboy urges? Now there's a term I haven't heard before."

"I definitely have them," Coco said, bouncing up and down.

Lana had to laugh. "I mean this little one's desire to ride the horses and do whatever else it is that cowboys do."

"What about your desire?" He skipped a beat before continuing. "To ride, I mean?"

She stammered back. "I . . . well . . . I enjoy riding, but right now the horses are not my top priority. There's so much to worry about—"

"You said that the other day. Tell me what you're worried about and maybe I can help."

She wasn't about to tell him her more troubling concerns. "Making sure there's enough to eat, for one."

"Let them be a distraction, then. There might be a war going on, but that doesn't mean you have to stop living," he said with his hands shoved in his pockets.

Jack would have said the same thing.

"Fine."

"How about this. You two girls and Sailor form a living fence along this boundary, and Lana and I will go see if we can find 'Ohelo and any others. We'll circle around behind them and send them this way. Your job is just to hang out and very casually keep them from going past you."

"How do we do that?" Marie asked.

"Don't make any fast or big motions or you'll spook them. Just being there should be enough. Let's hope Sailor's instincts will kick in."

Sailor tipped her head at the sound of her name, ears up. Lana had her doubts about Sailor's ability to maintain her cool in a herd of horses. If anything, she was likely to hightail it out of there. As Lana and Grant rode away, she heard Coco mumble something to the horse.

Lady might have been pretty, but she had a choppy trot that made Lana feel as graceful as a rag doll. She fell in behind Grant and watched how he moved. His wide shoulders tapered to narrow hips. His lower body looked to be part of the horse, while his upper body cruised along smoothly.

They drifted through a damp koa forest with akala berries—the Hawaiian raspberry—and came out the other side to a smaller pasture sprinkled with trees. Blue sky stretched out above. There was no sign of horses. Grant broke into a canter across the pasture and Lady followed, providing a much smoother ride. Every now and then they passed a patch of lava, but Lady avoided them. A fullness rose up in Lana's chest that made her want to laugh and cry at the same time.

When they came to a stop in front of a grove

of pines, Grant was watching her intently. "You okay?"

Her hand automatically went to her cheeks to feel for tears. Had she been crying and not realized it? "I think so, why?"

"No reason. Just that huge smile on your face."

It must have been catching, because he was grinning right along with her, his whole face transformed. It felt as though she had her own personal riding teacher and tour guide.

Distractions.

"It's been a while since I've had any reason to smile. I guess I couldn't help it," she said.

"Lana?"

"Yes?"

He moved his horse close enough that their legs were almost touching. She noticed a half-moon scar above his eyebrow. "Don't ever apologize for smiling. It lights you up from the inside out."

She blinked. Wanted to ask him to please repeat himself. Instead she felt a swell of tears coming on. *Lord, what is wrong with me?* Unable to stop them, she covered her face with her hands, which she now realized were trembling.

"Ah, hell, I didn't mean to make you cry," Grant said.

Lana shook her head. "It's not you."

They were silent a moment, then he said, "What is it then? Sometimes it helps to just get it off your chest."

She moved one of her fingers to the side and peeked out at him. His hand ran up and down his horse's neck in a way that made her wish it was her neck he was stroking.

"It's a whole string of things that started long before I arrived on this island. I don't want to bore you with details when we have a job to do, and the girls are waiting for us."

He swung his leg over so he was sitting sidesaddle and facing her. "Don't look now, but 'Ohelo is under that far koa tree, watching us. So we'll just rest here for a bit and act uninterested. Which means we have time."

He was right about 'Ohelo, and she hadn't even noticed. "How did you know she was there?"

"Years of practice. And don't try to change the subject."

Lady blew out a breath and repositioned herself, smashing Lana's leg against Grant. "Ouch!" she cried, but it was more out of nervousness at touching him again than any pain.

Grant slid off Boss and held out his hand. She stared at it as though it were lathered in poison and made no move to dismount. The thought of her hand in his made her tingle.

"What are you so afraid of?" he asked.

You.

"I appreciate your kindness, but can we stick to the task at hand? Please?" she said, attempting a smile.

A gust of wind rustled the trees around them, causing the red 'ohi'a blossoms to dip and sway as though they were doing their best to fall. Good thing they didn't or else the rain was bound to come.

He squinted up at her. "No more personal questions. I swear. My mother used to get on my case for not knowing when to stop. She used to say I was worse than a badger when I wanted something."

"I suppose it could be both a blessing and a curse. My father used to tell me I was more stubborn than an opihi, so I guess that makes us even," Lana said as a peace offering.

"Opihi?"

"A type of shell that's nearly impossible to pry from the rocks. With a little salt on them, they're about the best thing you've ever tasted."

"I suppose we wouldn't find any up here, would we?" he said.

"Not a chance."

And just like that, the air between them had lightened again. He might be tenacious, but he did have a knack for making her want to talk. A part of her wished she could plop down on the soft green grass with her head in his lap and spill all her troubles and secrets.

Grant tipped his head back toward 'Ohelo. "Looks like curiosity is winning. Why don't you get off and just start rubbing Lady's back and neck. Just act real natural."

He did the same with Boss, leaning into him and almost massaging the giant horse. Boss pushed back and nickered. Lana didn't want her feet crunched, so stood out a bit and tentatively touched Lady on the shoulder. Sunlight glinted off her lashes, which were long and curved, and Lana could see why they'd named her Lady.

"You sure are a pretty thing," she said.

The horse swished her tail and let out a big exhale. In turn, Lana felt her shoulders soften and her chest unwind. Something about the warm and big presence of the animal pried open her heart. Within minutes she felt herself lulled into a trancelike state. Palm running across muscles, fingers through a wiry mane. When she looked up, 'Ohelo was standing ten feet away from Grant and Boss.

"First thing is we want her to feel safe. Something spooked her early on and she doesn't trust humans," he said to Lana, low and slow.

"She sure seemed to feel comfortable with Coco the other day."

"Kids are less intimidating. They're an open book compared to us adults. Horses are masters at reading body language and intentions," he said.

Boss, who clearly was curious about this new horse in the mix, sidled over and the two shared a few breaths. Then Boss leaned down and started munching on grass as though she weren't even there.

"You'd think they know each other," Lana said.

"They might. A lot of these horses originally came from Keauhou Ranch. And 'Ohelo is small, but she's older than she looks."

Now it was Lady's turn to trot over and sniff around. Lana watched Grant watch the horses. He looked completely at home with a rip in his jeans and scuffed boots. His jaw muscles flexed as he chewed on a piece of grass, glancing at 'Ohelo every so often, as though he knew she was there but wasn't too interested.

"Hello, gorgeous," he finally said.

'Ohelo, who was now grazing with the other two horses, eyed him cautiously but remained in place. He took a step closer, and another, until he was standing about an arm's length away from her shoulder. She sniffed at him and then backed off.

"A little bird told me you have a sore knee. Any chance you'd let me have a look?" he said. He turned to Lana. "I won't try to touch her today, but it's good to let her get used to the sound of our voices. I'm sure she remembers me, but it's been a little while. Go ahead, say something."

"Um, good morning." Her mind went blank. Alone, she felt she could talk all day to a horse, but something about the way Grant kept his eyes on her made Lana unable to think straight. "I met you the other day, and I think it would be lovely if we could be friends. We live up the way."

227

Could she have sounded any duller?

Grant chuckled. "A real proper introduction. I like it."

"Do you know what might be wrong with her knee?" Lana asked.

"Hopefully just a hygroma—it's when a pocket filled with fluid forms. They can be mighty painful but aren't serious."

"How would you treat it?"

"Drainage and bandaging would be best. But we'll see how she takes to me."

Lana was impressed. No wonder Jack had liked him. "You could do that?"

He shrugged. "When you're out in the wild for weeks on end, you get real good at taking care of your horses. They break down, you're stranded. I could do it with the right equipment."

A step closer. 'Ohelo raised her head and sniffed the air. Her nose went to Grant's jeans pocket and she began to nibble with her big square teeth.

"She likes you!" Lana said, laughing.

He pulled out a purple carrot and handed it to the horse, grinning. "She wants me for my carrot."

Lana was again at a loss for words. She watched as flecks of carrot fell out of the horse's mouth. She didn't dare look at Grant. At least they had made some progress. "If you could help this horse, you'd have a fan for life in Coco.

She loves animals more than the average person does."

"Something we have in common."

They decided to continue on to look for any other horses but after about fifteen minutes turned around. Lana didn't want to leave the girls alone too much longer and figured Benji might be there by now. Grant didn't want to push it with 'Ohelo, so they let her be, though he reckoned she might show up in the fenced pasture again on her own, looking for friends.

When they got back, Coco was sitting in a tree and Marie and Benji were bent over digging. Benji stood up and waved. Lana waved back but Grant didn't.

"What about your human fence?" Lana said as she came to a halt and jumped off.

"We got bored. And then Benji came and we figured we'd start on holes for the fence post," Marie said.

Five seconds later Coco was by her side. "Did you find 'Ohelo?"

Grant stayed on Boss, his face unreadable. He seemed to be off in his own world. Lana told her about their encounter with the horse. "Thanks to you, she's going to get treated."

"If she'll let us," Grant said.

Coco kissed Lady delicately on the nose.

"Grant, this is Benji," Lana said.

Benji walked over, shovel in hand. His face

was red and lined with sweat and dirt. "Pleased to meet you, sir. We've been spacing them as even as possible, but in some places the lava's made it hard," he said.

It was as many words as Lana had heard him utter at one time.

Grant did not greet him but said flatly, "It happens."

She saw the hurt in Benji's face. "Thank you for getting started. Hole digging is one of my least favorite things, and I'm sure Major Bailey would rather use his talents elsewhere," she gushed.

In her mind, there were two kinds of people: decent, or downright rude and unjust. And in this moment, she felt like Grant was about to reveal his true character.

"I don't mind getting my hands dirty, for a good cause," Grant said.

He was sidestepping the issue, and Lana felt herself growing angry. "Down here, we all help out—family, friends, neighbors—so if you have a problem with that, you can head on back to camp. In fact I think I need some water. You can see yourself out."

He looked as though he'd been slapped in the face. The kids were all staring at her, eyes wide. All she could think of was getting Grant away from there. She hopped back onto Lady, kicked hard, and took off in a cloud of grass and cinder. The sound of hoofbeats and the wind on her face tasted of freedom, and she had half a mind to keep on going, past the house, past 29 Mile and back to Hilo, where this whole nightmare began.

A ways before she reached the driveway, Grant and Boss caught up to her.

"Lana, stop," he yelled.

She kicked on Lady again, but Grant was next to her and he grabbed her reins, easing Lady back. "What has gotten into you?" he said when the two horses had slowed to a trot.

She spun to face him. "You, that's what. Your rudeness back there was a disgrace. You don't even know that boy and yet you've already judged him as an enemy. I could hear it in your tone."

"That's not—"

"What you are doing is cruel and unfair. Can't you see that? You probably don't have any Japanese people in Wyoming, and since you're fresh off the boat, I wouldn't expect you to understand. But the majority of the people you are suspicious of and locking up are just plain folks doing their best at living. They are part of us."

He pulled up the reins so they were at a stop. "Look, I'm sorry if it came across that way. I was just a little shocked to see he was Japanese. You have to see that everything being done right now is to protect our country, our people."

She was fuming. "We don't need protection

from people like Benji, he is *our people*. We need protection from the likes of you. He's a kid, for crying out loud. And he was born on this island, which is more than you can say."

"I have nothing against him, I swear it. That there was a knee-jerk reaction. You know, I lost a few close buddies at Pearl Harbor, and I would gladly kill any of those bastards responsible. I'm not gonna lie. But with the locals, I'm learning to recognize the difference," he said.

"You'd better learn fast," she said.

The wind had kicked up several notches from earlier gusts, and branches waved around wildly. An old woman in Chinatown had once told her that the wind brings in ten thousand evils, and it sure felt that way. Their lovely morning had taken a horrible nosedive. It was hard to think straight with her hair in her mouth and her skirt billowing around her.

He continued. "All I ask is you put yourself in my shoes. Lana, they ambushed us while we were sleeping. We can't be careful enough."

"There's a fine line between careful and paranoid. And in my opinion, it's been crossed. *They* does not mean all of them," she said, sliding down Lady and starting off on the trail.

"I know that," he said.

"Well, then, act like it, and if you wouldn't mind, please see yourself out," she said, hurrying toward the house and not looking back.

The tall grass pulled at her skirt, nearly tripping her on several occasions. The air was stirred up the same way she was, with fits and outbursts and a cool bite. She took the steps two at a time. Once inside, she slammed the door behind her, leaning back against it, chest heaving. Mochi was sitting by the fireplace, eyeing her with concern.

"Well, that went well," she said, wiping her hands on her skirt and smoothing her hair back.

His brows were pinched. "What happened?"

"Don't worry, the kids are okay. It's Major Bailey. He and I got into a terrible disagreement and I don't want to be around him anymore."

Windows rattled, which was rare here at Volcano.

"But you hardly know the man."

Lana didn't want to offend Mochi but figured he would want to hear the story. "When he saw Benji, his whole demeanor changed. Like he could barely stand the idea of all of us working together."

"Did he say something?"

"It was more of what he *didn't* say. He's been so warm and charming with me and the girls, but he could hardly look at Benji," she said, sitting across from Mochi. "Benji is quiet, and I thought maybe Grant could draw him out, get him talking. Boy, was I wrong." The heat from the fire felt welcoming against her chilled limbs.

"So why are you here and they there?" he asked.

"I gave him a piece of my mind, and then I took off," she said sheepishly. "I may have been a little harsh, but he deserved it."

Mochi reached out and placed his palms in hers. They were cold as snow. "People not raised here won't understand. Maybe you need to teach him. Matching anger with hatred never helped anyone. And why do you care so much what he thinks?"

His words stung. But Mochi was usually right. Her mind went to that first day in Kano Store. While his sidekick had been a jerk, Grant had remained professional. He'd been cool, but not outright disrespectful. Maybe he was just doing his job. *Don't make this harder than it already is,* he'd said.

"Too late now. I'm sure he won't have anything to do with me after this, which is perfectly fine," she said.

Letting another man into her life was about the stupidest thing she could do, so it was better this way.

"Everyone's walking on eggshells. If he's a decent man, he'll understand."

"He seems decent in every other way. That's why I agreed for him to come down here."

Mochi slurped his tea. "You didn't answer my question."

"Which question?"

"Why you care what he thinks."

234

Grant was a conundrum. Call it some peculiar form of chemistry, but it felt as though a spell had been cast. The horses running on his arm, the bow in his legs, and how he smelled of cinnamon and longing.

"I honestly have no idea."

"But you do."

She nodded slowly, meeting his eyes. "More than I should."

THE ROOM

That night while Lana and the girls were preparing dinner, Coco discovered a curious thing. Lana had pulled out the envelope with her childhood drawing of the horse to show Coco, and the plans for the house were lying on the counter. Lana was washing the rice, and Marie was chopping ginger and sweet potato for the stew.

"The horse looks like Sailor with all its spots. Do you think it's still up here?" Coco said.

"That was a long time ago. I doubt it."

Coco then turned her attention to the plans. "How do you get to this room?"

"Which room?"

"The one under the kitchen."

Marie stopped. "There's a room under the kitchen?"

They all crowded around the plans. On the elevation drawing, it showed a small room. There were even stairs leading down from the kitchen. When Lana had first seen the plans, she had only glanced at them, more concerned about the directions and the fact that a house existed at all.

"But there's no stairs here," Marie said.

This was typical Jack. Hidden compartments and mysterious rooms were the kind of things he lived for. "If he was building this as a hideout, this would make perfect sense. There's got to be a door somewhere."

Coco immediately began nosing around the kitchen, opening cabinets and examining the floor for any sign of a door.

"That's strange. He must have changed his mind," Marie said.

"I bet it's here somewhere. We just need to look harder. Maybe Benji can help us. But let's eat first," Lana suggested.

Lana was famished. All that riding and then an afternoon spent clearing several large patches of earth for planting had stirred up an appetite. Or maybe it was the ruminating over how she'd handled herself with Grant. A breakdown and analysis of each word spoken.

With nightfall the winds had turned from the south and the air was visibly warmer. Balmy, after the biting cold of the past few days. The stew was simple and hearty, but Coco picked at it as though it were full of bugs. She held up a chunk of sweet potato with her fork, which had turned gray in the cooking.

"What's this?"

"Sweet potato."

She dropped it. "Yuck."

Marie kicked her under the table.

"You can't live on peanut butter. And with our food supply cut off, we need to get used to eating things we can grow here," Lana said.

Coco looked to be considering what that meant. "Are there peanuts in Hawaii?"

"No peanuts. No wheat for flour, which means our bread is limited to what we can bring in. No a lot of things. So you're going to have to expand your eating horizons, young lady."

"What about Christmas? Will it be dangerous for Santa to come?" Coco asked.

Christmas. Just hearing the word made her heart hurt. It was less than two weeks away, and it had not crossed her mind even once. War did not care about Christmas.

"I hadn't thought of that. I'm sure he travels far higher than any airplanes, and he's got the reindeer to lead him safely," Lana said, looking to Mochi for help.

"But we wouldn't want him to lead the Japanese to us," Coco said.

Mochi spoke softly. "Santa can become invisible when he needs to. He's been in and out of wars before and in far more dangerous situations, but he always shows up. You can count on that."

Lana saw Benji and Marie smirking at each other, obviously old enough to know the truth about Santa Claus. But Coco seemed genuinely concerned.

"We finally have a chimney for him to come down," Coco said.

Lana smiled. "We'll just have to make sure to put out the fire on Christmas Eve so he doesn't burn his *okole*."

"And keep Sailor in bed with you so she doesn't scare off the reindeer," Benji added with a hint of sarcasm that flew right over Coco's head.

"Our parents will be here by then, won't they?" she asked.

"I hope so, sweetie."

Coco blinked rapidly, bravely fighting back tears. "I'm going to make a list for Santa, and that's going to be at the top of it."

"Let's do that. Tomorrow we'll start getting ready for Christmas. We can find a tree and make our own ornaments and maybe even make some cookies for Santa," Lana said, grateful for another distraction and wondering how on earth they would manage Christmas this year. No husband, no parents, no Christmas cheer.

It would take a miracle.

After dinner they all gathered in the kitchen. Coco was still hungry so Lana let her open a can of mandarin oranges. She had been extra quiet since the topic of Christmas had come up. The house plans were laid out and Mochi and Benji took a look.

"Jack always was a smart buggah," Mochi said.

"But there's no way in," Marie said.

Mochi waved his finger. "Guaranteed, there is."

"It looks like the stairs come up somewhere behind the pantry. What's on the other side of this wall?" Benji asked.

"I think it's the bathroom," Lana said.

They examined the pantry walls and floor, which were well crafted, without any visible cracks or crevices that didn't belong. No extra notches or handles or buttons. Lana and Marie went into the bathroom to see if they could find evidence of any hidden doors. But no one found anything.

"In theory, it was a good idea. But it looks like he never built it. Maybe he ran out of time," Lana said.

Mochi disagreed. "Doubt it. We just haven't looked hard enough."

"Well, I'm tired. We can look more tomorrow," Lana said.

Coco spoke for the first time since dinner. "Tomorrow something's going to happen."

A chill ran up the back of Lana's legs. "What kind of something?"

"With Mama and Daddy."

"Can you tell us what you mean?" Lana asked.

Coco shook her head.

Lana felt for her. Knowing things like Coco did seemed a burden, and yet less so up here. Up here, it felt almost natural.

. . .

In the morning Lana woke to light snoring impossibly close to her head. She opened her eyes and not two feet away was Sailor, black nose twitching. Sleeping on a mattress on the floor made her an easy target. But the snoring had a lulling effect, and Sailor added warmth to the bed. Lana reached out and stroked her. Sailor opened one sleepy eye.

"You're a real sneak, you know that?"

Sailor blew out like a horse, shut her eye and kept right on snoring. The dog was an accomplished sleeper, and Lana wished her own slumbers could be so serene. Instead there were nightmares of Japanese soldiers in the rain forest and Zeros strafing the pasture, or she'd wake up and her mind immediately took off running to every worst possible scenario imaginable. Lana slipped out from under the covers and went to the kitchen to start the hot water. Then she wrote up a list for a Volcano Christmas. Less than two weeks to go. Before everyone was up, she switched on the radio.

"*US freighter* Lahaina *shelled by a Japanese submarine eight hundred miles northeast of Honolulu. With a crew of thirty-four, there are thought to be no survivors. Nazi Germany and Italy have declared war against the United States, and the entire West Coast is now a theater of war.*"

Nothing but bad news. What had she expected? Yet with the ocean still crawling with Japanese submarines, each day that went by without another attack was a good day in her mind.

With hot coffee in hand, she went outside and made her way around back to check the hives. The morning buzzed with a smattering of bees. With the sun just coming over the treetops, the whole yard was draped in a honey-colored light. Gin and Tonic spotted her and waddled over.

"Did my father mention any secret room to you two? Oh, I wish you could talk," she said.

The rock foundation was solid all around the base of the house, with no signs of any room. The only difference was in terrain. A narrow patch of lava went off from the corner of the house where a room might be, making her wonder if he'd been able to dig down through all that rock. Usually, once Jack had his mind set on something, he never gave up.

She remembered the summer her father decided they were going to walk into Waimanu Valley. Lana was fourteen. By all accounts it was a rigorous all-day affair that smart people did on mules. You had to park at the top of Waipi'o Valley, walk down the nearly vertical road carved out of sheer cliff, cross a wide and swift-flowing river and long beach, then switchback up the other side. When they reached the top, Lana was ready to curl up under an ironwood tree.

She could hardly breathe and her thighs felt like wooden logs.

Jack hadn't even seemed winded. He stood at the edge, looking out to sea lost in thought. His wiry frame leaned up against the tree as though he were part of it. At that moment Lana realized Jack was driven by some unknown force to unlock every minute detail of the world, to understand nature in all its complexities.

The walk of misery continued as they made their way through thirteen more valleys. Every time they went down, Lana knew they'd have to go back up. It wasn't until they were halfway there, when they stopped for lunch, that they realized Lana had forgotten to pack half their food. Jack didn't reprimand her; in fact, he acted as though it was no big deal. At about the same time, skies turned gray and the air smelled thick with rain.

"We should turn back," Lana said.

Jack looked genuinely confused. "Why would we do that?"

"Why wouldn't we? We have no food and there's a storm coming," she said, trying not to cry.

He tapped his head. "This way, we get to see what we're made of. Have a little faith."

By the time they reached the cliffs of Waimanu Valley, waterfalls poured over the trail and their shoes were soaked through. They descended in near darkness. Huge surf crashed into the boulder-filled beach, and they set up their tent in a small patch of mud. Lana was sure they would be taken out by either a giant wave or a flash flood. Jack seemed unfazed. Even when a long centipede crawled over his foot, he just laughed.

"We're in his territory."

After eating brownies for dinner, Lana collapsed into her wet sleeping blanket. It was the worst sleep of her life. When dawn finally came, the skies had dried, the surf settled, and the day broke blue and cloudless. Lana ignored Jack when she got up. She was furious at him. As a peace offering, he made hot chocolate spiked with coffee.

"Here's a secret, Lana. When you think all is lost and you're about to give up, when you want more than anything to turn around and quit, don't. Keep going." He paused for effect in the way he always did before he was about to reveal some great discovery. "That's when the magic happens."

The rest of the trip was beautiful and memorable and perfect. So many of their experiences had been like that. That was Jack to a T.

Lana walked up the trail behind the house to investigate the outdoor shower. After days of ice-cold showers and sponge baths, Lana decided it was time to figure it out. Water was piped over from the big tank to a smaller holding tank which had a cast-iron box underneath it. From the looks of it and the way it was crudely welded together, Jack had made it. Lana opened the door and saw ashes and chunks of burned wood. At least it had been used before; that was hopeful.

She went back to the house and grabbed a towel, a basket of firewood and an ax. Then she came back out and split the wood into smaller pieces and lit a fire in the box. It took her several tries to get it going, and once she did, she turned the shower on. It took some time to warm, and as water was valuable, she stepped in while it was still lukewarm. After the past few days, lukewarm was fine with her. The act of taking a proper shower made her feel human again. Layers of sweat and grime and heartache rinsed into the rock beneath her bare feet.

While she stood there, with the water running on her face, she heard a small voice. "Can I go next?"

Lana peered over the shower door to see Coco standing there with a towel. "Why, of course you can. I was just warming it up for all of you."

Coco had developed several big tangles in her hair, which now had a greasy sheen to it. And despite the sponge baths, she had developed a musty smell. This hot shower was about the best thing to happen to them in days. By now the water was properly hot and she had to add some cold. Lana wrapped herself in the towel and stepped out.

"Do you need help?" she asked Coco, not really sure how much to mother her and how much to let her be.

"I can do it myself."

"Make sure to wash your hair twice."

Lana went in to tell the others and get another load of firewood. When everyone had had their turn, they sat down to eat. The mood around the table was several notches lighter, and the room smelled like spring.

After breakfast, Benji and Marie insisted on walking down to the pasture and working on the fence posts. Some invisible line had been removed between the two, and now they acted as though they had known each other for years. Getting your hands dirty side by side had that effect on people. Coco and Sailor trailed along.

Lana took off in the truck for Volcano House. As much as she was getting used to having a house full of people, stolen moments alone gave her space to breathe. She was lost in thought, passing through the Sugi pine grove, when she spotted something peculiar up ahead. A white object was suspended in midair. She stopped the truck and climbed out. A handkerchief tied to a piece of twine hung from a branch. Cinnamon filled the air. She pulled it down and noticed words scrawled in permanent marker.

Volcano House. 1700. GB.

Lana felt as though she might hyperventilate.

He certainly was bold, demanding her presence without any explanation. But on a white flag. She couldn't help but smile at his truce attempt. Yesterday he had been rude as all get out, but Mochi's words played in her head. *Maybe you need to teach him.* She stuffed the handkerchief in the glove box and continued on to Kano Store. She could decide later.

Mrs. Kano was outside, arranging anthuriums. Either she had forgotten to take her hair net off, or she just didn't care. The scarlet flowers reminded Lana of Christmas, and though there was no extra money, she grabbed a bunch. Pretending something was true often went a long way in making it actually feel so, she had learned over the years.

"You here to call those Germans again?" Mrs. Kano said.

"I have to keep trying. Say, would you mind doing the talking this time? You could ask for Mr. Wagner and save me the trouble of having to speak to that awful Mr. London."

Iris walked out from the back. "I will, but first you should see this," she said, leading her inside. She slid a piece of paper across the counter. It was facedown. Lana got a sense of foreboding. She flipped it.

Wanted for Questioning:
Mrs. Lana Hitchcock, of Oʻahu, in con-
nection with the kidnapping of Coco (8)

and Marie (13) Wagner of Hilo. Both girls were last seen in their home on Kīlauea Avenue on December 7, in the company of Mrs. Hitchcock, wife of Buck Hitchcock. Anyone with information on their whereabouts should immediately contact the sheriff's office or the FBI.

Lana's whole body went numb. She said, "You must know I didn't kidnap these girls. Who put this up, and when?"

She had known this was a possibility but had doubted Mr. London would actually go through with reporting her to the authorities. He must be more of a creep than she realized, and far bolder.

"Yesterday afternoon, two men in suits."

"Did they talk to you?"

Mrs. Kano shuffled in and said, "Iris wasn't here. They asked if I knew you and I said no. I don't know you. But I knew your dad and I liked him."

Lana needed to straighten this out right away. "Thank you for taking it down, and for telling me. You did the right thing."

Mrs. Kano's expression was unreadable. "No one saw it. But better you lay low for now."

When Iris dialed the Wagners' number, the phone rang and rang and rang, just as Lana had feared. But right before Iris was going to hang up, someone finally answered. A man's voice.

"May I speak with Mrs. Wagner please?" Iris paused to listen. "Okay, thank you very much." She hung up with a dull look on her face. "They're still being held by the authorities."

The shelves in the store had not been replenished since Lana's first visit, and they were almost empty now. Several twenty-pound bags of rice, corned beef hash, tuna, flour, a few other nonperishables and five jars of peanut butter. Iris said they didn't allow any hoarding, so Lana took one of each. Out back, there were crates and barrels of sweet potato, greens, eggs and plums, which they were more generous with, since they had a continuous supply up the road.

"Do you sell seeds?"

"No," Mrs. Kano said.

"Normally we don't, but I have some I could give you," Iris added. She disappeared into the back of the store for a minute and came back with a couple of small brown envelopes that she handed to Lana. "For sweet potato, all you need are cuttings. I have a bunch up at the farm. Can you swing back this afternoon?"

"Sure."

For the first time in her life, Lana was afraid of not having enough to eat. And worse, that the girls would go hungry. Except for the occasional storm, the barges with food usually arrived promptly, providing the islands with a never-ending stream of sustenance.

"Any idea when you'll get more food?"

"All the ships have been taken over by the military and food is going to the troops. With the Japanese subs out there, it's a big risk to come anywhere near these islands."

Lana and the kids spent the rest of the day organizing and labeling rows in the garden and planting the seeds. The geese seemed overly interested in the seeds, and Lana asked Coco to ask Sailor to keep them away. Lana kept the flyer to herself. She wanted to tell Mochi, but he didn't need anything else to worry about. Thank God Mrs. Kano had lied for her. She wanted to straighten things out, but the thought of the girls going back with Mr. London made her sick to her stomach.

Mochi sat in the shade of a nearby 'ohi'a tree and offered up advice now and then. "You need to make mounds for the sweet potato, and not too close together. They like to crawl."

Coco rolled her eyes. "Plants don't crawl, silly."

He smiled so tightly his eyes were closed. "Oh, but they do—they just do it a little more slowly than we do and when we aren't watching."

Several times Lana noticed Coco mumbling to the seeds. "What are you saying?" she finally asked.

"Just singing to them."

So what if Coco was quirky? It made life more

interesting. And Lord knew they could use any kind of entertainment to keep their minds off of the situation at hand.

Speaking of situations, Lana had been changing her mind every five minutes about whether or not to meet Grant. *The man was presumptuous. He deserved another chance. She shouldn't leave the house for too long. Everyone would be fine without her for a couple of hours. She was too busy now, with Christmas and all.* But the way she felt on the inside when he looked at her was almost too much to bear. The fact of the matter was she really didn't have any choice.

At Kano Store, there were two bucketfuls of vines waiting for her on the front porch. When Lana poked her head inside to say hello and thank them, Mrs. Kano was propped up against the wall with her eyes closed. Lana was about to tiptoe back to the buckets, when Mrs. Kano said, "We saw them."

"Excuse me?" Lana said.

"The Germans. They came by in a squad car."

Lana felt herself go numb. "You sure?"

"Until now, only Japanese in the back of those cars. Not today."

Lana walked closer to the counter. "The Wagners are my dad's neighbors, the ones I've been trying to reach on the telephone. The girls' parents. Some of the nicest folks you'd ever meet. But you saw firsthand how the government isn't taking chances."

"Germans in Hilo. How much of a threat can they be?"

"Good question."

Mrs. Kano squinted and looked her up and down. "Why you all fancied up, girl?"

"Me? I only brought a few things with me from O'ahu, so my options are limited."

"No, I mean the lipstick."

"Oh, that. Habit, I guess. I'm going to Volcano House to see Uncle Theo." Lana thanked Mrs. Kano before she could ask any more questions, threw the buckets in the truck and took off in a cloud of dust. She arrived in the parking lot at five minutes to five. She checked the rearview mirror, dabbed her coral lipstick with the white handkerchief and checked again.

A loud tapping on the window. Her hands flew down and she jumped, head nearly hitting the roof of the truck.

Grant's face was six inches from the glass, and he was smiling. "Hey there."

"You scared me half to death. I didn't hear you drive up," she said, feeling flustered and caught in the act.

"Sorry about that. I rode over." He motioned toward Boss, then opened her door.

When she climbed out, he was still standing there, awkwardly close. Was he expecting a hug or, God forbid, a kiss? Lana stood with her arms at her sides, straight as a plank and angling back toward the truck. "Hello, Major."

"You're still upset," he said.

A troop of honeycreepers landed in the tree behind them and started chirping away. He glanced up, then back at her. A shadow of stubble ran across his chin. Lana found it impossible to turn away.

"That remains to be seen," she said.

"Then I'm glad you came. Shall we go inside?"

They walked in side by side, him dressed casually in jeans and a tan corduroy jacket and Lana feeling overdressed in a white skirt and pink checkered blouse. But it was her only long-sleeved shirt. Thankfully the lobby was empty. The two of them being seen together was likely to cause talk. On one hand, she didn't want to be a spectacle, on the other, she was beyond caring.

They sat in the rocking chairs overlooking the caldera. Grant pulled his close. "Thank you for coming," he said. "To be honest, when I saw your truck in the lot, I was a little surprised."

"I figured it wouldn't kill me to show up."

He laughed. "I'm that bad, huh?"

"No comment."

Her eyes went to Mauna Loa, and the bands of sunlight darting into the sky behind it. Grant's foot started tapping a mile a minute. Sitting here this close to him, it was tough to stay mad, though she was trying her darndest. *Remember what he's done. Who he is.*

He chewed his lip and then said, "I owe you a proper apology for how I came across yesterday. I know you don't get another chance at first impressions and all that, but I honest to God, cross my heart simply came up short for words. I have nothing against that kid. Nothing at all."

"It sure seemed like you did."

"Look, I didn't expect him to be Japanese, though in hindsight it's not surprising. Most people up here are. With what we have going on over at the military camp, it complicates things," he said.

Lana cleared her throat. "What exactly is going on over there?"

"We're holding the detainees in the barracks until we get word from the Feds how to proceed. Right now everyone on the island is being brought here."

Here was her chance. "All Japanese?"

"Almost. We got a German couple today brought in from Hilo. Turned in by a friend for being sympathetic to the Nazis."

Her heart skipped along double time. "Are they really?"

"They seem like decent people, but we're at war now. This friend had some information that didn't bode well for the couple."

"How do you find out for sure if someone is a Nazi or a Japanese spy?" she asked.

He fingered his collar nervously. "It takes some digging, I guess, but that's up to the police and the Feds. I just make sure the camp is running smoothly and keep the guards in order. I'm also helping secure the park from any future invasions or funny business."

"So the camp has turned into a prison?" she asked.

"More of a holding cell. While people are being investigated."

Lana grew quiet. He sure was right about one thing: what was going on at Kīlauea Military Camp certainly did complicate things. Especially now that she knew the Wagners were there.

Grant leaned back with his head in his hands, rocking the chair gently back and forth. He stared out at the expanse of lava and sky. "Can I ask you a question, Lana?"

It was too late to back out, but she was feeling exposed in a way she never had before. Raw and naked. "You can ask, but whether I'll answer is another matter."

He stopped rocking and put his hand on her arm. "So here's the strange thing. Pearl Harbor has been damn near annihilated, the islands are on high alert and carloads of new suspects keep arriving at our camp. I've hardly slept a wink, and yet there's one question that's been keeping me up at night."

Lana wasn't sure she wanted to know. "Is it something I can answer?"

Their eyes locked.

"I know you said you'd be taking back your old name, but what I'm dying to know for certain is if that husband of yours is still in the picture at all," he said, giving her arm a slight squeeze that sent shivers down to her toes.

The moment felt surreal. A point in time that all else hinged upon. *Yes* would be an easy way out. Keeping her safe and untouchable. *No,* on the other hand, would open her up to all kinds of possibilities, some of which made her blush. There was no way to avoid an answer, but she hedged. "Why is it you want to know?"

"Maybe I can answer that with a story about your father," he said.

"My father?"

He nodded. "One day there was the Tomato Can Tournament over at the golf course. We drew names out of a hat, and Jack and I ended up being partners. Wherever we went, this dang cow was following us, and every time we made a shot, we had to shoo her off the fairway. The cow paid no mind to Jack, but I was able to get her moving. That got him talking about the house he was building and his plans with the horses and a few cows, too. He had never mentioned it before, but he said he felt like he could trust me.

"He told me that when General Short urged people to build bomb shelters and make plans for evacuating civilians out of high-risk areas, he knew he better get cracking. I thought a hideaway house seemed pretty outlandish and that he was all talk. But soon after the golf tournament, he had me come down to see for myself. The framing was up and I realized he was serious. 'Oh, I'm serious, all right,' he said. 'Now I just have to figure out how to get my pigheaded daughter over here when the time comes.'" Grant stopped there but looked as though he wanted to continue. Lana waited for a moment, but he didn't go on.

His imitation of her father carried just the right intonations, and it made her homesick for Jack and his zany ideas and contagious passion for whatever project he had going on at the time. Especially sitting here in a place he used to bring her.

"He actually said that?"

Grant gave her a one-sided smile. "Sorry, but pigheaded was exactly the term he used."

"No, I mean he was concerned about getting me here?"

"Very. He hated the fact that you were on Oʻahu, and so far away. And I don't know what happened between you, but he mentioned that he planned on going over there and setting things straight, sooner rather than later."

Lana thought about the last time Jack had called and spoken to Buck. Lana had been out and she'd meant to call him back, but as usual never did.

The problem was every time she thought about Jack, she felt an agonizing and searing pain in her lower abdomen. It was far easier to avoid him than to face the misery that he stirred up, and yet now she would give anything to have him back.

"I admit I've been pigheaded and not the best daughter, but there's a long story behind it all. One I don't feel like talking about," she said.

He seemed to be wrestling with a thought. "We all have our stories. But, Lana, you may want to know that the last time I spoke to Jack, we were out riding. The sun was going down just like it is now, with that orange ribbon of light along the summit. He stopped and out of nowhere said, 'If something should happen to me in the war, can you find my daughter and bring her here? Help look after her?' "

All the air went out of Lana's lungs. Grant was watching her closely, his eyes catching the day's final light. Mauna Loa was fading into shadow.

"No offense, but what made him think I would leave my house and run off with a stranger?" she said.

He shrugged. "I can't answer that, but I do know he thought you belonged here, not on O'ahu."

A nagging voice told her that Jack had been right. O'ahu was not home, never had been, and despite the circumstances, there was a strange feeling of rightness here. "I guess I saved you the trouble," she said.

"I promised him, and my promises stand. I would have found a way."

"How was he so sure that there was going to be a war? People don't just go around building houses based on rumors and hearsay," she said.

"He said he was tuned in somehow. He tried to warn people, but no one listened. People dismissed him as an eccentric."

"He was an eccentric."

"Eccentric and wise."

Grant seemed to have a real fondness and understanding of her father. "You really cared about him, didn't you?" she said.

"Sure did. And that leads me back to my original question." He paused for a few breaths. "Is Mr. Hitchcock still around?"

Lana had begun to think he had forgotten. But now, in light of the new information, his question made more sense. He felt an obligation to look out for her, based on a promise to a friend. She owed him an honest answer. "Mr. Hitchcock is on O'ahu and we are separated."

"A permanent separation?"

Now that she was removed, looking at her situation from the other end of the island chain, it seemed so clear. It had simply been a matter of her head catching up with her heart. Even if this war hadn't happened, she would have found a reason to stay here. Returning to Buck was an impossibility, like breathing underwater. It was no longer an option.

"Not formally yet, but I won't be going back."

As the words lifted off her tongue, she felt lighter and more spacious. There was even a faint hum in the room that seemed to be emanating from somewhere inside her chest. Could he hear it? She could have sworn Grant smiled, but it was so fast, it quickly disappeared.

"So then it wouldn't hurt to have someone up here keeping an eye on you," he said.

"I appreciate your concern, but as I mentioned before, I have things under control."

Losing Jack was like losing the whole backdrop of her life. There was no going back and no longer a heart to which you were tethered unconditionally.

Before Grant could respond, Uncle Theo appeared in the doorway. Lana was both relieved and disappointed.

"Greetings, my friends!" he bellowed. "Sorry to intrude, but I'm going to have to draw the curtains lest we attract any enemy planes with our fire."

"I should be going anyway. I need to feed the girls," Lana said, pushing her chair out and standing to kiss him.

"You ladies are always welcome here for dinner. Just give me notice so I can prepare a feast. I can make my famous moussaka, a Greek version of lasagna. Maybe Major Bailey would like to join us?" Theo said, hitting Grant on the back so hard he nearly toppled forward.

"That'd be nice, sir," Grant said.

They said goodbye and walked out into a cool and star-kissed sky. She could feel him next to her, a presence as big as the volcanoes all around them. Neither spoke. Nearby, a cricket turned up the volume and a motor rumbled in the distance.

When they reached her truck, he opened the door but stood blocking her way. "What do you say we try again? Not only with the horses and getting 'Ohelo's knee fixed up, but you and me. It feels like we got off to a rocky start and it only went downhill from there. I'm not asking for anything in return," Grant said.

She knew she should say no, but the word would not come. "That would be fine."

There was still enough light to see him smile, then quick as a hawk, he swooped in and kissed her on the cheek, one hand on her lower back. Before she could even react, he had pulled away.

"I'll be there tomorrow at sixteen hundred hours. Sweet dreams," he said, disappearing into the night.

THE COOKIES

The next morning, marshmallow fog crawled in and settled over everything, distorting all sound. Birdsong was captured in its white confines, horses galloping out in the pasture sounded six feet away and the hum of the beehive vibrated the whole house. Lana refused to let the girls out, lest they get lost. Instead they decided to bake cookies with the ingredients they had. Coco wanted peanut butter, Marie swore that chocolate chip cookies were the new best thing and Lana was partial to Russian tea cakes. They were low on sugar, so honey would have to suffice.

"Since we don't have chocolate chips and we want to ration our peanut butter, let's get creative," Lana suggested. They did have a chocolate bar squirreled away, and Lana found cinnamon and nutmeg in the spice jars she'd brought from the Wagners' house. "How about chocolate and spice swirls?"

"Yes!" Marie said.

Coco didn't look as thrilled. "My mama says that you can bake hopes and dreams into your cookies, and then when you eat them, they come true. Do you believe that?"

"What a nice idea," Lana said. "I haven't heard that before, but I think it's worth a shot. Have you tried it before?"

Coco nodded. "A couple times, but nothing happened."

"Hmm. One thing I know about hopes and dreams is that they come on their own time. So you may wish for something now that shows up later on."

"Why do we have to wait?"

Lana laughed. "They say the reason for time is so everything doesn't happen at once. Meaning, if all our dreams came true at the same time, we wouldn't be able to appreciate them."

Coco's little face scrunched up in thought. "I would."

"Are we allowed to tell each other what we wish into the cookies?" Lana asked.

"No, because then it won't come true."

Marie said to Coco, "You just said yours didn't come true anyway."

"Give it time," Lana said. "And anyway, hopes and dreams and prayers are all about imagining good things to happen. The more we do that, the better our lives."

Lana realized she sounded an awful lot like Jack, the king of imagination. Maybe being inside these walls had that effect on her. Looking back on recent years, the act of imagining good things had been mostly absent from her life. She'd been too busy rehashing the past and blaming Buck and her father for a childless present. One's own advice was easy to spoon out but so hard to swallow.

In such a big kitchen, all three of them had plenty of space to do their jobs, though with Sailor stretched out on the floor, they had to step over her to reach the table. Marie measured dry ingredients, Coco chopped the chocolate, and Lana beat the eggs and supervised. On several occasions she almost told the girls about their parents but decided to wait until she knew more.

"How about we add some coconut flakes? We have that bunch out back," she said.

They sent Benji out to husk and crack a coconut. He came back a few minutes later with several hunks of perfect waxy, white flesh. Lana sat him at the table with a cheese grater and put him to work. With each passing day, she was more grateful for his quiet competence. With music on the radio, instead of news, Lana found herself swaying along and tapping her foot to the beat. Marie was humming, and Coco asked Benji if she could steal a piece.

Was this how it felt to have a family?

Lana caught Mochi watching from the doorway. She walked over to him. "Can I get you something?"

He nodded toward the kids. "This. Warms the heart."

"They're a good bunch, aren't they?"

After the first batch of cookies went into the oven, the smell of chocolate and cinnamon wafted through the whole house. Lana, Coco and Marie sat at the table and talked about Christmases past. It turned out the Wagners celebrated with a German flair, building gingerbread houses and nativity scenes, and baking stollen and Christmas cookies. Ingrid also brewed a hot cider from apples picked on Mauna Kea. The woman sounded like the mother Lana had always wished for, and wanted to be. To be fair, Jack had done as fine a job with Christmas as could be expected of any single father.

When the timer rang, they pulled out the first batch of cookies. Coco insisted they eat them hot and gooey. Lana took a bite. With the oven on, the kitchen had felt warm and cozy, but she soon began fanning herself. A feverish heat came over her.

"Is it getting too hot in here?" she asked the girls.

Coco had chocolate all over her lips. "No, but you look hot. And what's that on your face?"

Lana's hand went to her cheek, which stung. "I don't know, but it hurts. What does it look like?"

Marie moved closer to inspect. "A red spot. Did something bite you?"

"Not that I remember."

Lana pushed her chair back and ran to the

bathroom mirror. There was a red mark on her skin, more like a burn than a bite, in the exact place that Grant had kissed her. She wiped at it. Nothing happened. She dabbed a wet cloth on it, but that didn't help, either.

When she went back to the kitchen, the plate was empty.

"Did you two just eat all the cookies?" Lana said.

Both girls exchanged guilty looks. The cookies were messy, and not pretty, but the combination of chocolate and coconut was a winner. Lana wanted another one, badly. Benji and Mochi came in as the next batch was coming out of the oven. Before Lana slipped the hot cookies onto the plate, she shoved one into her mouth. The melted chocolate burned going down.

Mochi gave her an odd look. "That good, huh."

"That was rude of me, wasn't it?" Lana said, wiping chocolate from the side of her mouth.

The next batch was gone in a flash. Everyone but Mochi had chocolate smeared on fingers and faces. Even Benji, who was usually so well mannered, practically swallowed them whole. They all looked at one another. Lana felt herself go a shade darker. There had been many thoughts going through her mind as she sought out hopes and dreams. So much wanting. *For the war to end quickly. The Wagners' release. Wellness for Mochi. Her father to still be here.*

And more time in close proximity with Grant Bailey, despite everything.

At four o'clock sharp, they heard the clipped echo of hooves on lava. The fog had been thinning and thickening all afternoon, but now it was as dense as ever. Lana and the girls sat on the porch with Sailor, who made a low rumble in her throat.

"I want to ride with him today. Can I?" Coco asked.

"We'll see, sweetie. In this weather I don't know if any of us are going out," Lana said. All the trees surrounding the house had been swallowed in white, and visibility was down to twenty feet or so.

Through the fog, Grant and the horses emerged like apparitions, and she wondered how they hadn't gotten lost along the way. Coco was down the steps before Lana knew it.

"Aloha!" Grant called.

Lana stood at the bottom of the steps. "Howdy," she said.

He pulled up and dismounted right in front of her. "This whiteout is tough for riding. Lucky we came out here yesterday and the horses know the way."

"We were wondering if you'd even show up."

"I thought about not coming for about five seconds, and then realized I had no way to reach you to let you know."

Coco held up a brown paper bag. "We made you cookies."

"Good thing I came, then," he said, taking the bag. "I brought you something, too. Hold out your hand."

Coco beamed up at him.

"Close your eyes," he said.

Grant reached into a saddlebag and placed something in her palm. Lana strained to see, and when Coco opened her eyes, she held up a small wooden horse. The look on her face was one of wonder and disbelief. It was a perfect replica of 'Ohelo, mane and tail painted on.

"Did you make this?" Lana asked.

"Carved it myself out of sandalwood," Grant said, proudly.

"It's lovely," Lana told him.

Coco stared at it for a while longer, lost in her own world, until Lana finally asked, "What is it, Coco?"

"Nothing." Then to Grant she said, "Thank you."

"Sure thing, little lady," he said, patting her on the head. "Now, I know you were hoping to ride today, but we're running out of daylight, and I want to see if I can find 'Ohelo and see if she'll let me wrap this bandage around her leg. Lana, would you come with me?"

Coco's face fell but she didn't put up a fuss this time, and Marie seemed happy to stay back. They rode off down the pathway, Grant in the lead.

"Stay close," he said back to her.

"Don't worry."

They floated in the fog, down through the pasture, along the tree line and onto the lava. Off in the white, an iiwi squeaked like a rusty door hinge. Another answered. Lady picked her steps carefully and plodded along, hooves crunching the loose rock below.

"I hope you know where you're going," she said to Grant's back.

"Same place as yesterday."

"How can you even tell where we are?"

He held out a compass. "This helps. But most horses have a good sense of direction. I trust 'em."

"I just don't want to end up in a steam vent or crevice," she said.

"Nor does Lady."

When they came upon the next clearing, the fog had thinned noticeably. Patches of pale blue peeked down from the sky. Grant stopped and Lana pulled up beside him. Something about his nearness was reassuring.

"You said you hardly rode, but you seem pretty comfortable on a horse. I'd even venture to say you're a natural," he said.

She felt a rush of pride at the compliment. "I thought I would have forgotten, but it comes back, doesn't it?"

"Sure does. Did you ride up here when you were young?" he asked.

She nodded. "One summer we actually rode from Hilo all the way to the ranch down the way. It took us a couple of days, and I never wanted to stop. I could have kept going around the whole island."

"That must have been something. So why did you stop? Riding, I mean."

"I fell into a different world. O'ahu is more big city and there are more cars there than horses. At least in Honolulu."

"Do you miss Honolulu?"

"I haven't been gone long enough to miss it. But I already know I won't. What about you? When did you learn to ride?" she asked.

He seemed to think that was funny. "I was born with cowboy boots on," he said.

She laughed. "Your poor mother, then."

"My poor mom is right. But seriously, my dad took me riding with him as soon as I could sit up on my own. I can't remember a time when I didn't ride. I was that young."

"It must have been nice."

He shrugged. "Riding and horses and ranches are like breathing to me. That part was nice. My father's temper wasn't."

Lana could tell she'd touched a nerve. "I'm sorry."

"No need to be. That was then, this is now. And look where I am and who I'm with."

Lana thought about her motherlessness, and wondered which was worse: to have no parent or to have one who is alive but incapable of caring for you.

"You could have picked a worse place to be stationed," she said.

He looked at her knowingly. "I believe there are no such things as accidents. Me being here, you being here."

"You sound like Jack," she said.

"That's a high compliment, coming from his beautiful daughter." He rustled around in his saddlebag and pulled out the cookies. "Mind if I have one?"

"Go ahead."

He offered her the bag. "Would you like one?"

She laughed. "No, thank you. I ate half the batch when they were hot out of the oven. I have to warn you they're addictive."

Grant slipped one into his mouth and immediately Lana got a strange sense that maybe he shouldn't be allowed to eat them. Surely they weren't enchanted, but she *had* felt odd after eating them. Not only feverish and ravenous, but the red blotch on her face had flared up, and despite the cold, she had spent the rest of the afternoon in a sleeveless top.

"Dang, that's good," he said, chewing with his eyes closed.

Why was watching him eat the cookie such a

sensual experience? When he was done, he ate another one, chewing slowly and deliberately. This time his eyes were open and he watched her watching him.

"I can see why you ate half the batch," he finally said.

"With Christmas coming up, I thought we better start baking. We have to watch our butter and flour, but the—" *Wagners* almost came out "—my father had several large sacks in his pantry in Hilo. The shelves are almost empty in Kano Store."

"I give him credit for such foresight. Stocking up on things like that," he said, coming closer and looking directly at her cheek. "What happened to your face?"

Lana felt her cheek. Now it was raised slightly. "I must have burned it in the kitchen earlier. My skin is sensitive."

All untrue.

"I hope you don't mind me saying this, but it looks like you got branded," he said.

"Why, thank you, just what a girl wants to hear."

He tipped his hat. "What I want to know is by what?"

She could only imagine what the spot looked like now and wondered if he was just toying with her or being serious. Someone could have taken tracing paper to his lips and then transferred it to her cheek. "What do you think?"

He jumped off. "Come down here. Let me have a better look."

Lana did as she was told. They stood there between the two horses. Her heart thumped uncontrollably. Grant took off his hat. His hand went to her chin, turning her cheek toward the muted light.

"Hmm" was all he said.

Lana could feel his warmth travel across her skin, down her throat, through her dress and all the way to the ground. He moved so his face was two inches away from hers. She could see the bleached tips of his lashes and the moss flecks in his iris. She stopped breathing. No one had ever looked at her this way.

Bottled-up longing made her weak in the knees, but she managed to step back. "Are you okay?"

He squeezed his eyes shut and blinked several times. Lines of perspiration beaded on his upper lip, and he turned to the side. Then he unbuttoned his shirt. All the way to the last button. "I'm not sure," he said.

Her eyes automatically ran down to where his stomach met his jeans. "What are you doing?" she said.

The look on his face said he was just as surprised as she was. "I'm not sure what's happening, but I don't feel like myself. I don't think I should be here right now. Do you think you and Lady can find your way back?"

Something was very off. "You can't be serious. What about 'Ohelo? And this fog?" she said.

He jumped on Boss, who pranced around in a circle, nostrils flaring.

"What do I do with Lady?" she pressed.

"I'll get her tomorrow."

And just like that, he was gone.

THE CRATER

What a failure the venture had been. No helping 'Ohelo, no more information gathered about the Wagners, and Lana and the girls had poisoned Grant with cinnamon and chocolate cookies. Maybe the coconut was somehow tainted, or there was a bug that was catching, but Lana had her doubts.

At least he had been right about one thing. Lady had a great sense of direction. At one point Lana was sure to veer left, but Lady stopped in the middle of the trail and refused to budge. Lana kicked her heels in but Lady stood firm. When she finally let the reins up, the horse took her own route through the unfiltered fog. Fifteen minutes later, they were back at the house.

She found Marie and Benji layered in sweaters and wearing their boots, about to head out and search for her. Apparently Grant had flown past the house in a blur. Everyone wanted to know what happened.

"Major Bailey fell suddenly ill," Lana said, unsure of how else to explain his odd behavior and rapid undressing.

"And he just left you out there?" Benji said.

"I told him I could find my way back."

Coco lit up. "Does that mean we get to keep Lady?"

"For the night, we do."

Mochi remained quiet, but she could tell he had questions. So did she.

With a steaming mug of coffee in hand, Lana stepped outside to check on Lady. Sunlight shone through the treetops, spreading the scent of honey and pine needles through the morning. The sky was wide-open. Bleary-eyed from a night of vivid dreams involving Grant, it took her a moment to register that Lady was no longer tied to the tree. The rope was still there and Lana ran over to check it. *Untied.* Her saddle was hanging from a low branch. She tiptoed through the house to see if Coco was still asleep, and sure enough, her bed was empty.

Lana laced up her boots and set out toward the pasture. The dew-covered grass wet everything below her knees, and pretty soon her boots were soaked. They weren't at the pasture, and Lana was in no mood to go trudging through the forest and across the lava fields. Nor was she dressed for it. But worry strained her heart. The thought of Coco thrown from Lady, or fallen through a crack, was enough to keep her going. She'd ridden bareback only once, but once was enough to know how hard it was.

She passed the barn and crossed the field, looking for evidence of hoofprints. None of the grass had been trampled and the fine layer of water droplets remained undisturbed. Lana stopped. She was out of breath and on the verge of panic. On horseback, Coco could be miles away by now. She thought about what lay beyond the immediate area. Pit craters and desert, and below that the rift zone, a sudden drop of land that spanned the whole coastline. It was futile to keep going.

On the way back to the house, she ran through a dozen horrific scenarios before some of Mochi's words came to mind. *Live in the here and now— that means choosing faith over worry.* When she thought about it rationally, Coco was on Lady, Sailor was with them and both animals had strong instincts for self-preservation. Coco had a tendency to wander, and she always came back. Right away, her mood flipped. Numb toes and a cold and dripping nose. These were real. As were the faraway call of a hawk and the spiderweb between two 'ohi'a trees.

Back at the house, the others were awake. Coco had not returned, so they made breakfast of fried rice and egg with chopped wild spinach, which grew in abundance around the house. Coco hated spinach. Lana kept reminding herself not to worry, and Marie seemed unconcerned, which helped.

After eating, Benji and Marie went outside to check the garden beds, which had begun to sprout. The sweet potato was especially fast-growing, sending shoots in all directions.

Mochi seemed settled in at the table. He had more color today. "What's going on with that Major Grant? First you run off in a huff, and then he leaves you in the fog with his horse," he said.

To admit having feelings for Grant would complicate their neatly constructed sanctuary. But how could she hide it? Mochi saw through falsehoods and pretenses as clearly as he saw through glassy seas to the fish below.

"You'll think I'm crazy, but since our paths first crossed, there's been this invisible pull. The worst part is I just found out the girls' parents are now being held in the camp up here. And Grant is in charge," she said.

He looked at her without judgment. "You still haven't answered my question."

She sighed. "This will sound even odder, but I think the cookies had some kind of effect on us— Grant in particular."

He nodded. "The more we expect the unexplainable, the more we draw it in. Especially up here."

The words reminded her of what Coco had said the other day. *You have to believe.* The two had more in common than one might assume. Both seemed to have an extra helping of faith in the unseen world. One was young and one was old, but kids and old people cared little about what others thought. This was their blessing.

"I used to feel the difference in the air every time I came up here, as though everything was dusted in a strange kind of electricity. But being away for so long, I started thinking it was just a figment of my young imagination."

"It wasn't your imagination."

Hooves thundering down the road caused a jump in her heart. Lana stood to look out the window. Coco and Lady were trotting down the driveway side by side with Grant and Boss. Coco was barefoot and she had a blanket wrapped around her. Grant showing up unannounced was risky for them. As a precaution, Mochi disappeared into the bedroom. It was late enough in the day that having Benji here made sense.

Lana rushed out to meet them. All her plans to scold Coco evaporated when she saw the look on her face—bliss and freedom and a contented heart. Lana knew it well because, as a girl, riding horses or running wild picking berries or combing the beach for shells had had the same effect on her. The secret back door to happiness opened in small moments like these.

"Where have you been, young lady?" she had to ask.

"Not too far. We stayed on the driveway and walked to warm up. It was Lady's idea."

"I'm sure it was."

Grant waved. He would hardly make eye contact with Lana. "Coco's a natural, I'll give her that. It's like she's been riding her whole life, bareback."

"How did you get on?" Lana asked.

"The stump," Coco said, pointing to the remains of a Norfolk pine to the right of the lanai.

Grant slid off and held his hand up to help Coco down. "I'd love to stay and chat but I need to get going. We're dropping boulders today to block Boles Field and that old airstrip right next to the crater."

"Has something happened?" Lana asked.

"Just precautionary."

Lana remembered the old landing strip he was referring to, which had been built by the military on volcanic sand just south of Halemaʻumaʻu crater. Whose bright idea that had been, she wasn't sure, but not long after it was completed, the volcano spewed out thousands of fiery boulders and a towering cloud of ash. Needless to say, they moved the airstrip.

Coco came over and for a moment Lana thought she was going to hug her, which would have been a first, but Coco said quietly, "Want to know a secret?"

"I'd love to."

"I wished for a horse yesterday, on top of—"

Lana knew what was coming next and loudly

interrupted. "—well isn't that something! First you got a wooden horse and then a real one, at least for a bit."

"Can't she stay with us?" Coco asked Grant.

"Lady is borrowed, so she's not mine to give. But I'm hoping soon we'll have 'Ohelo and the others rounded up. Then you can have your pick. Hey, would you mind running along, Coco? I need a moment with your mom."

Your mom. The words dropped like lead between them. Coco froze in shock for a moment, then tore off like a frightened rabbit.

Grant looked confused. "I hope that didn't upset her too much. If it were up to me, I would leave Lady here no problem."

"It's fine. She's a sensitive child."

"I want to talk to you about yesterday." He cleared his throat, looked beyond her and kicked at a tuft of grass before continuing. "Taking off like that was a rotten thing to do. I can't explain what happened other than I ate the cookies and my whole body started burning from the inside out. I remember feeling out of control, like I might do something I'd regret. Leaving seemed the only option."

Seeing the concern in his eyes made her want to reach out and take him into her arms. "Don't worry about it. I made it home and no one's the worse for it."

"Did I do anything offensive? My memory

is pretty hazy, as if I drank a whole gallon of whiskey or something."

An image of Grant without his shirt came to mind. "Not at all."

Lana felt a blush coming on. She looked away and caught sight of his long shadow on the grass, crossing into hers.

"There's something I need to ask you," he said, biting his lower lip.

"Okay."

"I know it's a crazy time, but would you consider meeting me away from here, just the two of us?"

If only he hadn't been so good-looking, maybe she wouldn't have this churning in her stomach. And knowing she should say no made her want to say yes. The strange conundrum of wanting what you should not have.

"It's probably not a good idea," she said, forcing the words out.

He just stood there. *Leave!* she wanted to say. It would be far easier to never get involved than to fall for him and deal with the consequences. She was damaged goods *and* a liar—who wanted that?

"Come on, Lana, give me another shot. Just for a couple of hours," he said.

It wasn't as though he was asking for something huge. Just a bit of her time. And she knew she had a tendency to think too far into the future.

"What did you have in mind?" she asked.

"How about you just trust me? As long as nothing new develops, I can sneak off Thursday afternoon and pick you up at seventeen hundred," he said.

Say no.

"I'll meet you at the end of the driveway. Will that work?"

He broke into a smile. "Absolutely."

The ferns along the trail down to the floor of Kīlauea dripped moisture even though the skies were clear. Lana and the girls passed through groves of ginger, towering ferns and stunted 'ohi'a trees. The newer the flow, the smaller the foliage. Ever since lunch at Volcano House, Coco had been pestering Lana to take them in, and Lana figured it would be a nice outing for the day, a welcome diversion.

In many places, the switchback was only a narrow pathway carved into the cliff, providing for a spectacular view of the caldera; in other spots, trees and bushes engulfed you. Coco ran ahead but stopped to wait for them at a lookout along the way. "The ground is smoking. Does that mean it's going to erupt?" she said.

"It's always like that. Groundwater meets hot rock and causes steam to rise from the cracks," Lana said.

"Like our breath when it's freezing?"

"Something like that."

They continued on and Coco took off running.

"I still can't believe your parents never brought you here," Lana said to Marie.

"Dad was always working and Mom was not the adventurous type. Just going to the beach was a big deal for her. She was happiest at home baking or sewing or doing household stuff."

"Nothing wrong with that. Look how wonderful you two turned out," Lana said, feeling bad for implying anything negative about the Wagners.

"She always worried about Coco and wanted to give her the most normal upbringing. And now this happened. It's so unfair," Marie said, folding her arms.

"Life has an interesting way of choosing our paths for us. We can plan all we want and then, just like that, the world turns sideways." Lana threw up her hands. "But you know what?"

She wanted to tell Marie her parents were right down the road but forced herself to wait.

"What?"

"I'm beginning to see that the more we dig our heels in and fight, the harder it becomes. We can't always change what's happening in the world, but we can change how we react to it. Does that make any sense?"

Marie stared at the ground as they covered the final downhill stretch. She gave a weak shrug. Lana reached out and squeezed her shoulder. "I guess what I'm trying to say is have faith that everything will turn out. It may not seem that way now, but one day you'll look back and see the lessons you learned."

Lana was only digging herself deeper. Marie was too young to understand. Her parents were locked up in Kīlauea Military Camp, and she was hiding away with a near stranger. Better to shut up.

On the crater floor, shimmering black fields of lava stretched out for several miles. Lana thought back to her final trip to the volcano with Jack in 1924. News had spread quickly that Halemaʻumaʻu was erupting again after years of quiet. Along with half of Hilo town, they rushed up to see the action. She had witnessed previous eruptions, but nothing compared to the brilliant fountains of lava and the molten web on the crater floor. Hot wind and gas made the air almost unbearable, but people still flocked as close as they could get. Jack and Lana were no exception. Lava hissed and gurgled and screeched. Lana was smitten.

When they'd checked in at the Volcano House later that night, word was going around that Uncle Theo and a local guide had gone out the previous evening to see if they could stir up Pele with prayers and rituals. Business had been slow, and Theo was on the verge of bankruptcy. They tossed an ʻōhelo berry lei and a bottle of gin—

Pele was thought to love gin—into the crater for good measure. A few hours later the volcano roared to life. Since then over ten years had passed and no one knew when the next eruption would come.

Coco crouched down at the edge of a crack, peering in. "Does the crater go to the center of the earth?"

"I doubt it," Marie said.

"What's under here, then?" Coco said.

"A whole lot of hardened lava and most likely some lava tubes that branch out from the crater. That's how the lava comes and goes," Lana said. An 'ōhelo berry bush grew out of another crack nearby. "Let's pick a few to toss to Pele."

The air was still and hot and waves of heat distorted the pathway, which was already hard to see. They walked in silence mostly, Coco darting ahead and peering into cracks and Marie falling behind and seeming hot and bored. When they finally reached the edge of Halema'uma'u, Lana's blouse was matted onto her back.

"Careful," she called to Coco.

Coco stopped abruptly. "Does this one go all the way to the center of the earth?"

"It may."

They all approached cautiously. Rockfalls were visible along the far crater wall and yellow banks of sulfur smoked in the distance. Lana loved the otherworldliness of it all.

Coco tossed in her berries and then proclaimed, "I want it to erupt."

Marie nudged her in the side. "Don't say that, stupid."

Coco wanted to hear all about the eruption Lana had seen, asking her to describe where the fountains had been and how high, and whether they were accompanied by earthquakes. "You sound like a regular little volcanologist," Lana told her.

"We learned about it in school."

"The real thing is better—wouldn't you agree?"

"Yes!"

Lana felt lucky to be the one showing them something so rare and special, in the same way Jack had showed her. Being out here under a blistering sun, staring into the mouth of a volcano, and tossing berries to the wind—none of this could be experienced in a classroom.

The way back was uneventful until they were partway up the trail. Both girls' cheeks were flushed red and Coco had stopped running ahead. They were wilting under the Hawaiian sun, even in the middle of winter. They stopped in a shady area, each sitting on a cool, mossy boulder. Lana fanned herself with a fern. She had just closed her eyes when she heard a voice.

"You wahine lost?" the woman said.

Lana opened her eyes. "Auntie?" she said, though of course it was. The old woman had not changed one speck, with gray hair thick as a horse's tail and those haunted eyes that swallowed you up.

Auntie came closer and squinted. "Look at you, all grown up and back in town."

"You remember me?"

"How could I not? The little hapa haole from Hilo with all that strong mana around you."

Lana was blindsided. "You have a good memory."

"We remember what we need to."

There was an awkward moment of silence as Auntie looked her up and down, and what felt like under her skin, then turned her gaze on the girls.

"I'm happy to be back," Lana blurted out.

Auntie glared. "You were in the wrong place. That never works out."

How could Auntie know what she had been doing all these years? Lana must have looked confused, because Auntie went on. "People get knocked off their path all the time. Important thing is you know your *hōkūpaʻa*, your North Star, and you bring yourself back on course. The sooner the better."

Lana thought about the last decade of her life. How completely off course she had been without even realizing it. "I'm working on it," she said.

"If we don't do it ourselves, life will start hurling lava bombs at us to wake us up."

That had certainly been the case lately. Lava

bomb after lava bomb, and yet she still felt lost. The old woman was carrying a cloth sack overflowing with leaves and lichen, and she set it down on a nearby boulder.

Auntie faced Coco and said gruffly, "You, did you offer Pele 'ōhelo?"

Coco looked ready to bolt. "We did."

"All these powerful wahine up here. Pele will be pleased," Auntie said.

Lana asked, "What happens when Pele is pleased?"

The old woman grinned, showing off a couple of missing teeth. "We will see soon enough."

THE DATE

Lana said she had to strategize with Major Bailey on how they were going to handle the horses once they brought them in. A water trough was already set up at the barn, but they'd need to supplement their food. But when she came out of the bathroom in a red sweater and lipstick to match, Marie mumbled something to Benji.

"Excuse me?" Lana said, flooded with self-consciousness.

Marie smirked. "Nothing."

Coco came out of the kitchen, took one look at Lana and said, "You like Major Bailey, don't you? Are you going to kiss him?"

Lana laughed. "I think he's nice, but no, I'm not going to kiss him. We have business to talk about. You all behave while I'm out, and Coco, stay inside."

She felt like a teenager again, and was out the door before anyone could ask more questions. The truck sputtered to life. Cold leather on the back of her thighs reminded her how quickly the temperature could drop once the sun went down. On the drive to their meeting point, butterflies and bats and crows started up in her stomach, to the point that several times she considered turning around. But the look on Grant's face when she had said yes kept her going.

At two minutes past five, Lana pulled the truck off to the side under the big Sugi pine. Grant was not there yet, and she stepped out and began pacing. *Was she overdressed? What if he asked too many questions? Did he plan on kissing her? Maybe her lipstick was too red; this was not Honolulu.* At least the weather was cooperating. Birds were busy and skies clear.

The minute he pulled up, none of that mattered. Before she reached the door, Grant hopped out and sped around, holding it open. When they were both in and doors shut, he stared at her for a moment and said, "Your lips and your sweater match those pretty red flowers everywhere."

Too much lipstick.

The words wanted to stick in her mouth, but she managed. " 'Ohi'a lehua, they're called."

"That's right. These Hawaiian words fall out of my head two minutes after I learn them," he said.

"That's normal. Give it time," she said, wondering how long he would be stationed in Hawaii.

As they rode along, past the roadblock and into the park boundaries, every time she tried to speak, Grant did, too.

"How was—"

"We went on—"

"You know—"

"Have you heard—"

"Today they—"

Lana finally gave up and looked out the window. They had passed the Volcano House and now headed down Crater Rim Drive through the canopied rain forest. She was tempted to ask where they were going but figured she would see soon enough. A few minutes later Grant pulled over at Waldron Ledge. "Here we are," he said.

Outside, they walked to the rim. From this vantage point, though about a mile away from Volcano House, you could see the whole of the caldera, Puʻu Puaʻi to the left and Mauna Loa to the right. A stone parapet guardrail protected them from stepping into the abyss. A considerable landslide at the base of where they stood had occurred in 1913, reminding everyone how precarious life was at the edge of a volcano.

"Takes your breath away, doesn't it?" he said.

Lana looked out at the view. "Would you believe this is one of my favorite spots in all of Volcano?"

He pretended to look hurt. "And here I was thinking I was going to impress you by bringing you to a new place."

"Here at Volcano, that's unlikely."

"Is that a challenge?" he asked.

She smiled. "Just a fact. But I will admit that with all the visitors gone, it has a different feel to it. Like we're the only people on the whole mountain."

"Boy, do I wish that were the case," he said.

They stood there for several minutes, a light breeze coming up the cliff side. Out here in the wild, it was easy to forget what brought them here.

Grant touched her shoulder lightly, sending heat through her body. "Stay here. I'll be right back."

He returned with a used ration box, an army blanket and a grin. "Are you up for a short walk?"

Between the horseback riding yesterday and the hike this morning, she would have been blissfully happy just to sit and sketch all afternoon. "Why not?"

Grant stepped into the bushes, where a narrow pig trail took them along the cliff's edge. "Stay on the path," he warned.

"You needn't worry. I had that drilled into my head as a girl. If there is one place in the world where you follow this rule, it's Volcano."

Pūkiawe branches grabbed at her skirt as they moved along. Grant was as sure-footed as the horses, and she had to work to keep up with him. For such a newcomer, he seemed to know his way around. A few minutes later they came to a small grassy bluff.

He kneeled down and cleared away some sticks. "Before all this happened, I used to ride the crater rim trail a lot. There were always people at the best lookouts, so one day, I decided to find my own."

"Did you ever hike around with my father?"

"No. He was too focused, but he did tell me some of his favorites."

"We were lucky to get to know the Jaggars. Thomas was the head volcanologist when I was little. His wife, Isabel, knew every square inch of the park, and when Thomas and Jack were off tinkering with seismographs or thermometers to measure lava temperatures, she would take us kids out exploring, hunting for olivine or Pele's hair, and sketching."

"Sounds idyllic."

"I didn't realize it then so much, but now I do."

"And to be up here with the Jaggars . . . No wonder you know so much about the place."

"Thomas knows more about volcanoes than anyone alive."

Once he had the blanket down, they sat. Lana made a point to remain a safe distance from him. From the box he pulled out two cans of Primo beer, a sardine tin and a packet of Saloon Pilot crackers.

"Contraband," he said with a guilty smile. "And I hope you eat sardines. My options were almost nil."

Lana would rather eat dirt, but she was touched that he had gone through the trouble of packing food for an outing with her. "I love them."

He began smearing the oily and flaky fish onto the crackers. "Want to know the real reason I brought you here?" he asked.

"I guess you're going to tell me?"

He spoke quietly, as though someone might be listening in. "The other day, you said you love birds, and it got me thinking about this place. You're not going to believe this, but right below us in the cliff is a tropic-bird nest. Or at least there was one a few weeks ago, and they come in for a landing right at eye level. You really need to see it to believe it."

Not only had he remembered she said she loved birds, he had planned this whole date around it. She wanted to kiss him. "Really?"

"Just you wait."

She snuck a glance at his profile as he scanned the horizon for birds. Square jaw, faint dimple in the chin and burnt-olive skin. He was haole but tanned well, not like some of the folks from the mainland who turned cherry pink after five minutes out in the sun.

He turned and caught her watching him. "This place is a far cry from Wyoming, but parts of it remind me of home. The wide-open spaces and all the ruggedness. It's not for the faint of heart."

So true. "Not your typical Hawaii, that's for certain. People with a tough independent streak seem to end up here. Jaggar, Uncle Theo, my father. Not to mention all the Japanese farmers."

Grant took a swig. "These Japanese are a real quandary."

Lana felt herself tense. "Why do you say that?"

"Because they outnumber us ten to one, and I don't know who I can trust and who I can't."

"Have you been able to prove anyone at camp is a spy yet?" she asked.

"No comment."

The back of her neck started heating up, and as much as she wanted to finish the conversation, she also wanted to see the tropic birds and have a nice time with Grant. "I'll just say one thing—try to see them as individuals, not one big collective of enemies. The people I know are some of the kindest, most hardworking and honest ones around."

Grant bit into a cracker, and oil dripped down his chin. He chewed. Contemplated. Swallowed. "That's two things," he finally said with a touch of a smile.

"And that goes for the German immigrants, too," she said.

"That's three."

She couldn't stop. "Tell me you will at least try. Talk to them. Hear what they have to say. For me."

He turned. "For you, I would do just about anything."

The words set her heart into a blustery storm. What kind of man said these things? None she had ever been with. Though to be fair, there had been only two. Alika and Buck. Alika was before, Buck was after. That was how she measured life.

"That's an awfully nice thing to say," she said, suddenly becoming very interested in the hem of her skirt.

"Don't move," he said.

"What?"

"A bird, flying our way."

Lana slowly raised her head. A koaʻeʻkea bobbed on an air current not twenty feet in front of them, white with black streaks painted on its wings and long white tail streamers. If only she could reach out and feel the softness of those feathers. A tangerine sky backlit the picture.

The whole world narrowed to this one and only speck in time. When it was over, and the bird dove down beyond their line of sight, Lana thought of Mochi and how he had said life was nothing but a spool of strung-together minutes, none more important than the next. She still had a ways to go to master that concept, because right now felt pretty important.

Out of politeness, Lana took a bite of a cracker with sardines, washing it down with beer. She had to work not to choke. "Did you know they're considered seabirds?" she said.

"These guys?"

She nodded. "They can fly forever, and they're expert fishers with webbed feet and waterproof plumage."

"You know so much, when this war blows over, you ought to consider giving nature tours. You can carry on what your father was trying to start," he said.

"Who knows when that will be. Maybe years, maybe never. And if the Axis wins, then what?"

"I take it as a good sign we haven't been attacked again. With the whole US military on alert, they'd be hard-pressed to pull off another stunt like Pearl Harbor. They won't win."

His confidence was reassuring.

"I've been praying like crazy," she said.

"You and me both," Grant said, leaning close enough so that his shoulder was an inch away.

They sat like that for a while, listening to tropic-bird screeches and the fullness of warm wind from the crater floor moving through the trees. Grant asked Lana more about her childhood, and she was happy to oblige him. Hilo with its bayfront and all those waterfalls, fishing tales and hula, her father, bursting with outlandish ideas.

She finally worked up the nerve to ask. "Did my father tell you about what happened with us?"

He picked up a rock and tossed it over the edge. "He did."

"Everything?"

"Enough. He said he knew he had made the biggest mistake of his life in sending you away, but he was so scared of losing you the same way he lost your mother that he couldn't see straight. And then he lost you anyway."

Jack had as much as told her the same thing, but Lana had been in no mind to listen. She had been too flattened by betrayal and an all-consuming grief. *Forgiveness* was a word that had come up over the years, but she felt sick any time someone mentioned it. *Lose an unborn child and then talk to me about forgiveness,* she would say.

"Do you think I'm a horrible person?" she asked.

"Would I be here if I thought you were a horrible person?"

"I guess not. I just wish I could have made it back before he died, to tell him that I loved him. As much as he hurt me and I was too stubborn to forgive him, I would have come around. I wanted to, I just didn't know how."

He reached out and held her wrist. "He knows."

Lana turned to look up at him. "What makes you say that?"

"Jack was nothing if not perceptive. He was giving you space because he knew it was just a matter of time. The kind of bond you two had? It was unseverable."

"The thing that haunts me now is that, all this time, I blamed him, but I was the one who went and got myself knocked up. When you look at it like that, he was just reacting, and the whole thing was my fault," she said.

Grant rubbed his thumb along her forearm. "You could spend all day debating who was to blame, but in the end, it was just life. No one has an instruction manual for how to handle the rough patches, we're all just doing our best."

"You sound like you know from experience," she said.

"I've had my share of troubles. My old man left when I was six, and I spent my whole childhood pissed as hell about it. My mama raised me and my brother, Lou, out in the sticks on popcorn and fried squirrel. She existed on air and vodka, so we learned early to fend for ourselves," he said with a shrug.

She felt awful. "I am so rude! So absorbed with my own problems that I haven't even taken the time to find out more about your past. I'm sorry."

"I didn't tell you so that you could feel sorry for me. Just pointing out that no one is immune," he said.

They chewed on that for a while.

"What about women in your life? Have you ever been married?" she dared to ask. She *had* to know.

"Close but no. I was engaged several years back, until I found out she'd been lying to me all along, seeing another cowboy on the side. I wiped my hands and never looked back. So I'm a little gun-shy in that area." He shrugged.

Lana wanted to die. As if her own lies weren't

bad enough, he had already been primed by some woman who obviously did not know how to identify a good man when she had one. "I'm sorry," she said weakly.

He shrugged. "It was for the best."

From the east, a low bank of clouds crept in. Grant raised himself from the blanket. "Fog up here is sneaky. We ought to get going before it rolls in again."

He reached his hand out. Lana grabbed, and he pulled her up as though she weighed no more than a bird. The momentum threw her into him, her forehead knocking into his collarbone. Before she could detach herself, he held both her shoulders. They froze, staring into each other's eyes. Grant bent down and kissed her. Her initial reaction was to tighten up. They broke away and his eyes searched hers. Apparently satisfied with what he saw, he moved in again.

Grant exuded his own gravity, pulling her toward him like a full moon. She had to stand on her tippy toes, and he stooped over with his eyes closed. She felt his belt buckle and the warmth of his skin beneath his shirt. At once Lana decided that whoever had been kissing her before had been doing it all wrong. A peculiar and minty taste on his tongue made her want more.

Wherever he touched her, her skin heated up. Hip, small of the back, neck. This strange chemistry between them caused her to want to curl up in his arms under a downy blanket *and* feel every inch of his skin against hers, naked and taut.

When they finally separated, and she opened her eyes, fog swirled around their ankles. It overflowed from the crater, which had been erased by a dense white cloud. Grant saw it, too. He grabbed ahold of her hand. "We'd better go."

But we just got started, Lana wanted to say.

Along the way, she wondered if he had planned on kissing her, or if it had been an accident. She felt guilty for not being honest with him and debated blurting everything out right then. *I am housing a Japanese man and his son, and you are housing the parents of my two girls.* But the words remained lodged in her windpipe.

They made it back to the jeep without incident. Lana walked to her side of the car, still feeling the weight of his kiss and his minty breath. She felt cheated by the fog. Now they both seemed to have regained their senses.

"I should get back," she said, worried if they started up again, they might never stop.

He pulled out his keys. "Sure."

Day had entirely drained away. They bounced down the road, blue cellophane covering the headlights and casting an eerie glow on the forest. All Lana could think about was why he hadn't tried to kiss her again. Should she have kissed him?

"Have you heard about the ID cards?" he asked.

Mochi had mentioned something about it yesterday. "I did."

"Tomorrow they will be setting up at Volcano House for local residents to come in. You should bring the girls."

"We have ID cards."

"Everyone needs a new one, with fingerprints. And they'll be handing out gas masks, too," he said.

Lana winced. "Sounds like a fun time. The kids are getting fingerprinted, too?"

He paused for a beat. "For identification purposes."

She pictured Coco's small, nail-bitten fingers and Marie's soft hands. The thought of either of them in bad enough shape to require this kind of identifying gave her the chills.

"We'll come."

Neither spoke the rest of the drive. When she reached for the handle, he stopped her. "Look, Lana, I need to get something off my chest. These past days, I've come down to your place under the guise of cowboy business and rounding up horses. But the truth of the matter is I wanted to see *you*."

At least one of them had guts.

He continued. "And what happened back there on the bluff—that was not planned. In case you haven't noticed, you've been hard to read, even though I've been trying my hardest. I hope you would tell me if I'm out of line."

"You're not out of line."

She swore he was smiling, though it was too dark to tell, and the air in the cab was suddenly hard to take in. Without another word, Grant jumped out and came around to her side. She opened the door and turned to him. Cool air rushed in. This time he positioned his body between her thighs. Lana heard nothing but the beating of his heart and a faint buzzing somewhere deep inside. Her hands gripped his back, which was solid as the rock wall holding up their house. His lips covered hers.

So this was desire.

With Alika it had been a case of friendship turned curiosity turned romp in the sheets. And that went downhill fast when she got pregnant. Buck, on the other hand, showed up when Lana was most vulnerable and searching for someone to save her. He'd been careful and safe and wealthy. Most important, though, he helped her forget, at least temporarily. Now she hoped Grant wasn't just a bad case of loneliness.

Something told her otherwise. Never had she experienced such a continuous stream of thoughts about a man. *Scrambling eggs and wondering what he eats for breakfast. Walking and imagining his bow-legged stance. Dreaming about his well-defined stomach while she's half-*

awake in the morning. Grant had woven his way into her mind, and there was not one thing she could do about it.

He kissed her harder, one hand lifting from her waist, tracing a line from her navel, along her sternum and across each collarbone. Lana opened her eyes and counted stars to keep herself sane.

He pulled back. "Damn, woman."

"I should probably get back to the house. I don't want the girls to worry."

Lana was the one that was worried—terrified, in fact, that he would run his hand up her skirt and she would do nothing to stop him.

"Will you promise me something?" he whispered.

"That depends."

"One of these days, I want a big chunk of time with you, when neither of us has to run off. You think we can make that happen?" he said.

The thought of a full day with Grant made her head spin. "Absolutely."

THE CARDS

Word on the radio was that ID cards would be issued and anyone not complying faced arrest. Elderly, adults, small children; Japanese, Chinese, Filipino, haole; no one was exempt. Obviously, Mochi couldn't go, but what about Benji?

"Can't we tell them that you adopted him, too?" Coco asked at the breakfast table.

"Or you run an orphanage," Marie suggested.

It almost felt that way. Maybe it was something to look into—a volcano orphanage. There were likely to be others with imprisoned parents all throughout the islands. Where would those children end up? The thought filled Lana with something close to despair.

"I would still need to show birth certificates," Lana said.

Mochi set down his teacup. "Not if you tell them all their paperwork is on O'ahu."

The thought of going in there made her nervous. People in Hilo had to know about the so-called kidnapped Wagner girls. But without photos, no one had any proof. If she and the girls acted perfectly normal, there should be no cause for alarm. In the end, it would be safer than not having ID cards.

"It would work for the girls, but I already told Grant that Benji lives here and is just a neighbor. And what about you? If this war drags on, how will you explain your lack of ID card?"

Mochi was still frail, but the volcano air seemed to be doing him well, cold as it was. "I can only take each day as it comes," he said.

He might be spiritually advanced, as Jack used to say, but sometimes his lackadaisical attitude annoyed her. "That might be fine for you, but Benji?"

"I can make us cards. See if you can grab some blank ones," Mochi said.

Lana fumed. "That's a stupid idea. If I go to jail, then what? You're not in any shape to take care of these kids."

"I meant only if the opportunity arises."

"Fine."

Coco had already woken up on the wrong side of the bed after a fitful night of bad dreams. She was solemn and puffy eyed, and she picked at her porridge. Going to get fingerprinted was not helping matters. To cheer her up, Lana suggested they go find a Christmas tree afterward.

On the way to Volcano House, they rehearsed their story again. The girls were not to speak unless spoken to, and if asked, they had flown over to see Grandpa Jack Spalding on Saturday, the day before the attack. She imprinted their birthdays front and center in her memory. Lana wanted to get there early, before any crowd.

Gray skies and a light drizzle spread over the mountain. There were a couple of cars in the parking lot, but not hordes of people like she had been worried about. They'd brought Sailor along for the ride, but Lana insisted they leave her in the back of the truck. Inside, next to the fireplace, two tables had been set up, one with rows of cards and ink and pens, the other with gas masks. A small man in a big hat sat at the table.

"Good morning. We're here for identification cards," Lana said, herding the girls over.

The man put on a thick pair of spectacles and examined them as though they were a small herd of cattle. Without even saying hello, he launched into a monologue about keeping the cards on their persons at all times and about curfew and blackout and rations. Clearly, he had worked to memorize this little speech.

"How old is this one?" he asked.

"Eight," Lana said at the same time Coco did.

Lana shot her a look. Coco shrunk back.

"I'll need your birth certificates."

Lana glanced at his name tag. Dick Jones. "Mr. Jones, we came over from Honolulu to see my ailing father on December 6. Needless to say, we are stranded here until further notice, and all our paperwork is over there."

His whole face pinched into a frown, giving him a ratlike appearance. All he needed was a set of whiskers. "This is highly unusual," he said.

"I have my driver's license," she offered.

"You are supposed to report to your voting precinct to register," he said.

"That's not possible."

"Then I'm going to have to call this in," he said.

Wherever had they found this unpleasant man? "Call it in to whom?"

"That is no concern of yours, ma'am. Procedures must be followed." Dick shoved three papers her way. "Fill these out, please."

Lana leafed through her wallet for her license while the two girls stood mute behind her. She could feel their discomfort at being here, which made her angry.

Dick set the pad of ink in front of her and sat down at a typewriter. "Your full name, please," he said.

"Lana Hitchcock," she said, hoping for once that her name would carry some clout. Upon hearing her name, he stared at her for an extra beat. One way or another, he had heard it before.

"Spell it."

He asked her height, weight and age, which she had written on the paper but wasn't about to point out. He then smashed her thumb into the ink and set her card aside to dry. When it came to the girls, he studied them again for a moment. Studied her.

"Are these your biological children?"

There was no way around more lying. She had told everyone else they were adopted, but to say that now would likely send him down a long road of questions. She was banking on Mr. Jones leaving as soon as he finished his business.

"They are," she said, looking him in the eye.

"Where is your husband?"

"On O'ahu."

He must have believed her because he started clacking away on his typewriter again, asking for names and stats. Then, out of the blue, he said to Marie, "You must take after your father. What's his background?"

Lana wanted to keel over and was about to give an answer, when Marie calmly said, "My father was born and raised on O'ahu. His family is English and Dutch."

Jones considered this. "Well, then."

Lana almost cheered, and just like that, Coco and Marie Wagner officially became Coco and Marie Hitchcock. Lana turned to go.

"Not so fast, Mrs. Hitchcock. Two things you need to know. One is how to use your gas masks and the other is that all civilians are required to build a bomb shelter at their residence."

She was so eager to leave that she'd forgotten about the gas masks. He motioned them over to the table with masks of assorted sizes. The contraptions were heavy, with a partial helmet that went over the head and face and a canister hanging down in front of the chest. Jones had them each try several on for fit and showed them how to adjust the straps, but none were small enough to fit Coco's head. Coco was near tears.

"I'm going to be poisoned," she said to Lana.

"No, you're not. I bet Major Bailey can find us one."

Jones added, "We're still waiting on the kid ones, unfortunately."

He then explained how to construct a bomb shelter. It was easy, he told her; they just needed to dig through six feet of solid lava and have a hundred sandbags on hand. That way, they would be immune to flying objects and fire. Lana noticed Coco staring at the masks, clearly working something out in her head. *Please, don't say anything.* Jones was searching through a crate under the table for something when Coco said, "Excuse me, mister, but we need one for our dog, too."

That got a laugh. "Sorry, but the masks are only for humans," he said.

"Why not dogs?"

At that very moment, Lana heard voices behind them. An older Japanese couple and Auntie had walked in. Lana said hello, grabbed their masks and ushered the girls out the door. She let out a huge sigh. It felt as though she had been holding her breath the whole time they'd been in there. When they sat down inside the truck, Coco pulled something out of her pocket and held her hand open.

Blank identification cards.

Lana felt unhinged at the thought of Coco stealing these and the possibility of getting caught. "How did you get those?"

"Easy. Mr. Dick wasn't looking."

"But how did I not see?"

Coco shrugged. "People see what they want."

Back in the truck, Marie and Coco wanted to talk about bomb shelters and the secret room under the house, and they all reasoned that if indeed it was there, that was its purpose.

"When the Japanese planes come back, do you think they will see our house?" Coco asked.

Lana noticed she held the wooden horse from Grant in her lap. The poor horse was in a death grip.

"Our military won't let them come back. And if they did, no planes will be flying out here in the boondocks. They go for the big military bases and boat harbors," Lana said.

"Our parents are in Hilo," Marie said.

Lana had already done enough lying for the day and the residue left her feeling tainted. The girls deserved to know.

She took a deep breath. "About that. I just learned something about your parents and I was waiting to find out more details before I told you, but I haven't had a chance. Your folks have been transferred to the camp up here."

Lana was hit with a blast of questions: "How do you know?" "What kind of camp?" "Can we see them?" "Do they know where we are?" "How come you didn't tell us?" "When are they getting out?"

"The Kīlauea Military Camp. Mrs. Kano saw them driving past, and Major Bailey confirmed that a German couple from Hilo had been brought in. I've been trying to find out more without telling him who you are, but I think I'll just have to come out with the truth," Lana said.

Coco started quivering. "They aren't getting out, are they?"

"Don't say that!" Marie said.

Lana patted Coco's leg. "The good news is they are close, and we know someone at the camp who might be able to help us," Lana said, praying that Coco was wrong.

"Why do they call it a camp if they keep prisoners there?"

They rounded a bend in the road and passed the sulfur banks and steam vents, where clouds rose out of holes and cracks in the ground.

"It used to be for military to come on holiday.

The name stuck. In fact we'll be passing by it on the right soon."

She wanted to slow the truck, but thought the better of it. Now that it was a military installation, guards were likely to be on the watch for anything suspicious. Not that a truck of women and a dog was a threat, but one never knew. Marie rolled down the window, and the smell of burning kiawe wood wafted into the truck. Since Lana's last visit, a barbed-wire fence had been set up around the perimeter. Same stone buildings, new occupants.

As they passed, Coco was on the edge of her seat staring out over Marie's shoulder. "Do you think they lct them play cards? My parents love to play cribbage," she said.

"Maybe we could find out," Lana said.

She could feel the longing in both girls as sure as the vibration of the engine on the back of her thighs. To have their parents just on the other side of a fence and not be able to see their faces or hug them was unthinkable.

"We'll find a way in. I promise," Lana said.

Thank heavens for the Christmas tree search. Mrs. Kano had told Lana there was a small grove of Norfolk pines out near the golf course. Both girls were distracted by not only the trees but the sheer number of blackberry brambles loaded with dark, juicy fruit. It was a bit late in the season, but at Volcano, nothing was ever certain. Bees made honey on their own sweet time, berries came and went depending on the rain and sun, and 'ohi'a lehua bloomed haphazardly.

"Benji told us the Japanese submarines torpedoed the boat that brings the trees," Coco said as they walked through the forest.

Mochi had mentioned hearing that on the radio. Though another account was that the freighter was sunk by angry seas off Oregon. Lana didn't know what to believe. The newspaper that day had declared "Maui Shelled by Japanese Submarine. General Short and Admiral Kimmel Relieved of Duty."

"Most likely rumors. The thing is people start talking about what they *think* happened, and they tell a friend, who then passes it on to a neighbor, and pretty soon that idea has become fact. So we have to be careful what we believe."

"I wish Benji was with us," Marie said. "I feel bad for him having to stay home all the time."

"Once he has an ID, we can bring him with us."

"But then Mochi has to stay alone," Coco said.

Lana was touched by their concern. "We'll sort it out. Mochi doesn't mind being alone some of the time. He needs to rest."

"Is he going to die?"

"I don't know. It all depends on if it's his time or not. Sometimes people stay alive against all odds, and others surprise us by dying suddenly. Only God knows the answers," Lana said.

"Like what happened to your father," Marie said.

"Exactly."

Coco had on her contemplative face. "I want Mochi to live."

"We all do, honey."

When all was said and done, they left with a bucketful of berries, purple smudges covering mouths and hands, and a lopsided but perky tree. Even Sailor was stained red and purple. It took the three of them to haul the tree into the back of the truck.

"Can I make a star for the top?" Coco asked.

"You betcha."

No one was going to take Christmas away from them.

When they reached the road to the house, once again there was something hanging over the middle of the road, same tree branch.

"What is that?" Coco said, instantly alert.

"I think I know," Lana said.

This time it was a sardine tin. Lana let Coco open it. Inside was a note. *Saturday 1600 hours. Your place. GB.*

"We can tell him to let our parents out!"

"First we have to tell him they're your parents, remember? But let me do it. It's a touchy subject.

319

Promise me you won't say anything, okay?"

Marie sounded angry. "Our parents are not Nazis. You think they are, don't you?"

Lana was taken aback by the force of her words. "I never said that. But right now, Major Bailey believes I adopted you long ago, so I need to be able to explain why I lied to him. People don't like being lied to."

It was going to be an uncomfortable conversation, but he seemed so reasonable and level-headed. And teachable. She was banking on that.

"So why *did* you lie?"

Lana grew defensive. "You saw how it's been. No one knows who to trust and everyone's scared of being arrested—or worse. It seemed right at the time. I had no idea that Major Bailey would become friends with us."

That night they made grilled tuna sandwiches with fresh tomatoes from Kano Store, and sautéed wild spinach. Coco complained about having tuna again, but they had run out of peanut butter and no one could say when the next shipment would come in. The girls had told Mochi and Benji all about the day, and after eating, Coco produced her contraband for them, along with the ink they had borrowed from Mrs. Kano. There had been none left on the shelves, but Lana promised to return it the next day. Mrs. Kano didn't ask what it was for.

"What about a typewriter . . . you got one of those on hand?" Mochi said.

Lana leaned in. "No, but Mrs. Kano said I can use the one at the store tomorrow."

After fingerprinting Mochi and Benji and deciding on the new last name *Hamada*, the kids set off examining every inch of the kitchen again for a way into the hidden room. Lana busied herself with a crust for a blackberry pie. Earlier, a program on the radio had played Christmas music, and now she couldn't get the tunes out of her head.

When she went to wash the berries, someone had thrown part of the stem in and she pricked her finger. She rinsed the blood away and kept working. Before she knew it, she was lost in a daydream about Grant and the way he had touched her. Everything about him felt magnified.

Coco brought her back to the kitchen when she said, "I found something!"

She had wedged herself in the pantry. Everyone crowded around to look. On the bottom of the wall with no shelves, behind bags of rice, there was a long crack. With her scrawny arms, Coco moved the rice to the other side, no problem.

"Let me have a look," Lana said.

Coco came out and Lana went in. She ran her fingers along the edges of the wall, and right next to the door frame, something stopped her hand. She pressed on a small lever. Nothing happened.

Then she pressed again, the other way, and the wall sprung open.

"A door!" Coco screamed.

Narrow wooden steps led down into a pool of darkness.

"Who's going to go first?" Marie said.

"Me," Benji offered.

"Grab the flashlight."

Lana followed Benji, with Coco holding on to her shirt. Mochi said he'd stay and keep Sailor company. The wood was unfinished and wall studs were exposed. Benji stopped at the bottom and shone the beam around. About ten feet long and twenty feet wide, a room stretched underground. One wall was lined with rifles and gas masks, the other had a desk with a tangle of radio equipment and wires and stacks of legal pads. The third had shelves of rice, flour, lard, food cans and empty jars.

"Whoa," Benji said.

"I guess we don't need to dig a bomb shelter," Marie said.

"Look at all this food!" Lana said, thrilled at the thought of having extra everything, since no one knew when the next shipments would arrive. And the jars would come in handy for the honey.

She inhaled. Along with the mustiness, the room smelled faintly of her father and his trusty Barbasol shaving cream. She took the flashlight from Benji and walked over to the desk, curious what was on the papers. Illegible scribbles and sketches filled the legal pads. A framed picture of a young Lana and Jack standing at the edge of the crater hung on the wall over the desk. A plume of smoke lifted up behind them.

Marie leaned in. "That's you."

"It is."

"You look so young."

"Getting older happens to the best of us."

Right then, the brunt of missing her father slammed Lana full force. The amount of love he held for her, even with her refusing to return, caused a rush of tears. He had refused to give up on her. Some small part of her believed he would always be there, and that when she was ready, she could go back. It was a risky way to live, she realized.

"Are you okay?" Marie asked.

She felt choked up. "I just miss my father."

A small hand grabbed onto hers. "Don't be sad, Aunt Lana. Jack said he knew you loved him and that you'd be coming back one of these days."

It took a moment to register that Coco was holding her hand. "He told you that?"

Coco nodded. "He also said I reminded him of you, and that made him happy."

That warmed her insides. "Sounds like the two of you were close."

"He was around more than Daddy because

Daddy was always working. And now I miss them both," Coco said.

"I'll tell you what, girls, and this goes for you, too, Benji. If you have a disagreement with someone you love, never, ever put off making things right. It could be a big disagreement or it could be tiny. But the worst thing is to go through life wishing you had done things differently. Love deserves more."

Coco tugged on her hand. "The morning Papa got taken away, I told him he was bossy and mean, and now he's gone. I want him to know I won't bring caterpillars and lizards into my room anymore, and how sorry I am."

"You'll get to tell him," Lana said.

Marie confessed, "Mama was mad at me because I've been walking home with Bobby Kanuha and I never told her."

Benji surprised Lana by adding, "I hardly remember my parents, and I feel bad about it almost every day."

Lana drew them in for a group hug. Marie felt so strong and sturdy, and Coco was a pack of bones. Benji went rigid at first, but none of them pulled away, and she felt a big helping of love surround them. For a moment she swore her father was in the room, too.

When they came apart, Coco was staring at the wall. "Why so many guns?"

All the guns gave Lana an uncomfortable

feeling, too. "For protection. Remember, he was counting on an invasion. He wanted to be prepared. Promise me you won't touch them, okay?"

"He must have started building this a long time ago, though," Benji said.

"My father might have seemed eccentric, but he was always one step ahead of everyone else."

"But how would he have known so long ago?"

Lana thought back on events over the past few years. The Japanese attack on USS *Panay*, the Nanking Massacre and their invasion of French Indochina. Then in 1940, when Roosevelt ordered the Pacific Fleet from San Diego to Hawaii, she could imagine the workings in her father's mind. He picked up on patterns that others missed. He probably started the house before hearing from General Short.

"The signs were there, I suppose. You just had to know where to look," Lana said.

She would be curious to read through his notes and see what he'd been doing with all the radio equipment. Now all civilians had been strictly ordered to suspend operations.

Marie asked, "Should we see what's behind that door?"

There was another door on the far wall. Lana walked over and opened it. On the other side, a long tunnel led off into the dark.

Coco shrunk back. "It looks scary."

"It's a lava tube," Lana said, shining the light down the corridor. "We'll see where it leads in the morning."

"I'm not going," Marie announced.

"Main thing is we know how to get down here now," Lana said. *In case we need it.*

As soon as the sun was up, Lana, Coco and Benji headed back downstairs. She wanted to find the tunnel's end before Grant came. The lava tube was high enough to stand up in, and Lana stepped in. "Who's coming?"

Benji and Coco looked at each other and then followed. The floor was uneven, with fallen rocks scattered about. One was a large boulder. As long as there were no earthquakes, they should be fine. Farther along, a section of roots hung down, dripping moisture onto the ground. Lana could hear her breath and imagined fleeing soldiers along this same path. She prayed with all her might that it never happened.

"It's creepy," Coco said, reaching for Lana once again.

Lana grabbed her hand. "This is an escape route, should we ever need to flee. Don't you want to know where it ends up?"

"Not really."

After what felt like an hour of walking but was more likely five minutes, the tunnel made a turn. Up ahead, light shone from above. A skylight.

A whole section of the roof had caved in, and Jack had bolted a sturdy wooden ladder to the rock wall. Benji went up first. Grass and lantana spilled over the sides.

"We're by the pasture," he called down.

Coco went next, and Lana followed. Sure enough, they were in a small clearing just off the closest horse pasture. Golden morning rays lit up the dew. Once again, Lana was struck by her father's ingenuity and how much thought went into his hideaway. If anyone stood a chance of surviving, it should have been him.

THE LEMONADE

They spent the rest of the morning fashioning a tree stand, using lava rocks in a metal bucket to hold the tree upright, and making decorations to hang on the branches. The girls foraged for pine cones, cut out paper snowflakes, and collected sticks to make ornaments. Mochi was up and about and looking more clear-eyed than he had since he'd been with them.

"What about presents?" Coco asked.

"I told you, Santa will get here."

"I mean for us to give. Can we get presents into the camp?"

"We can make presents, and I'll work on finding that out."

As the time drew near for Grant to arrive, Lana caught herself ruminating over how and when to tell him about the Wagners. And what of Mochi and Benji? She wanted to come clean on everything. Whatever it was that was happening between them, she didn't want it built on untruths. Nor did she want Benji to be hidden away every time Grant came around. But telling him was risky. She decided to bring Benji anyway. This was her property and she could have who she wanted here.

In the stillness of the early afternoon, it sounded like a stampede coming down the driveway. Coco ran outside wearing pants underneath a sleeveless polka-dot dress. Barefoot again. She sprinted up the driveway like a mad fairy. This time, Grant brought three other horses. Lady, a big buckskin and a painted mare.

"I wrangled a couple more horses this time. I figured we could use a few extra cowgirls," he said when he hopped off. He looked at Benji and said without missing a breath, "And cowboys. The two girls can ride together."

Benji smiled with a look of relief.

"I want Lady," Coco said.

"Lady is taken," Lana said firmly.

Coco didn't argue, but she stuck her tongue out at Benji, who stuck his tongue out in reply and walked right up to Lady and held his hand out under her nose. She sniffed.

"You ride?" Grant asked him.

"No, but I'm a fast learner."

Grant showed him how to mount and gave him some basic instructions and treated him like one of the gang. Lana wanted to hug him for it. He looked extremely kissable, too. His skin was several shades darker than when she'd last seen him, and he was wearing a long-sleeved red palaka shirt.

"You look like a real paniolo," she said.

Grant grinned. "Tryin' my best to fit in."

Now that the lines were blurred between them, Lana wasn't sure how to greet him. But Grant gave her an innocent peck on the cheek as he had every other time, and a wink that caused her knees to weaken. Coco eyed them closely.

They set off with Coco and Marie on the buckskin, Lana on the palomino and Benji on Lady. As they rode along, Lana imagined herself leading tours through the park and sharing every ounce of her experience with the guests. It sure would beat attending parties in Honolulu where the men gambled while the women gossiped about who had come on the last ship. In her mind, Grant would be part of the deal, as would Coco and Marie and Benji. The thought of not having them here caused an ache under her ribs. Maybe war did that to a person, quadrupling every potent feeling so that what mattered most was impossible to ignore.

Time slowed down. Love sped up.

As luck would have it, the wild horses were all in the barn pasture. 'Ohelo, the white horse, and four other stunners. They all looked like they wanted to bolt, but there was only a short stretch of fencing needed to close the gap. Grant immediately had the group line up to block it. The wild horses trotted to the far corner, stirred up and anxious.

"We need to finish the fence and then see if we can lure 'Ohelo over here," he said. "Lana and

Benji, I need you with me on the posts. Girls, you keep your horses and Sailor between the others and the gap. Let me know if they give you any trouble."

"Can I talk to the wild ones?" Coco asked.

"By all means, but gently," Grant said.

Grant and Lana went to the barn to collect the rest of the posts and fencing. The minute they stepped behind the wall, he pulled her close and kissed her, long and slow. Lana stepped backward until she was up against the wood. A small groan escaped. He tasted salty. She was pinned to the post, unable to move, unable to think. When he pulled away, he whispered into her ear, "I've been dying to do that since the minute I left you the other night. You've been making it hard to work."

Lana grabbed his hand and laughed. "Behave yourself, Major."

He twirled a lock of her hair around his finger. "You know, I was hoping to run off with you alone in the woods today, but I knew how much Coco wanted to ride, and we have work to do. Can I get a rain check on that?"

"Deal," Lana said.

"Let's get this stuff out there before they get suspicious. Kids know way more than we give them credit for," he said.

"Why are you so good with them?"

He shrugged. "My niece and nephews back home. They keep me honest."

"And Benji is happy to be included."

"Seems like a hardworking kid."

"He is."

"Good to have around in times like these, and if you trust him, then I trust him," he said.

Lana smiled.

It was hard to imagine Grant in another place, in another life. She wanted to know every small detail of his life, who he loved, and who loved him. Whoever they were, they were probably sick about him over here in Hawaii.

They spent the next hour digging holes and setting posts. Coco and Marie looked happier than she'd seen them in days, and Benji had dug three holes by the time Lana finished one. The horses ripped and crunched on the grass, unfazed by the weight on their backs. Coco was chattering away, and every now and then Lana caught fragments of her words. *My name is Coco . . . love horses . . . best friends . . . there's a war . . . safe.*

At one point, Grant leaned on his shovel and observed. "She's a special kid, that one. See how the horses are completely at ease? I reckon they like the conversation."

"Who knows what goes on in that little mind of hers. But I agree, she's one of a kind."

"Has she always been this way?"

A bug flew into Lana's mouth and she coughed. "Since day one."

Tell him! urged an inner voice. She glanced

over at Coco and Marie, and 'Ohelo, with her swollen knee, then back at Grant, who had rolled up his sleeves and was unspooling barbed wire. Sweat ran down his neck, dampening the collar of his shirt. He was completely focused. She'd tell him in private, before he left for the night.

"Any Christmas plans?" he asked.

"Part of me just wants to forget Christmas. But with kids, that doesn't work. We cut a tree and made our own decorations, but Coco was worried about Santa being scared away by the Japanese."

He squinted into the sun. "I hope you told her he'd be here?"

"I did. But where am I going to find presents?"

"Hmm. Let me think on it."

They worked some more, Grant and Benji easily hoisting posts that Lana couldn't even budge. Grant had rolled up his sleeves, and veins snaked up his forearms. He was a different breed altogether than the men in Honolulu, who spent most of their time pushing paper. Grant was the kind of man you wanted by your side during trouble.

After the final post was in, and the barbed wire nailed on, Lana finally looked around. Coco was no longer with her horse, but on the far side of the pasture crouching beside a large rock. A smooth and shiny rock. Lana looked closer, confused as to what she was seeing.

She pointed. "Is that 'Ohelo lying down?"

Grant spun around. They watched. Coco was walking along the horse, stroking the length of her body, and then starting again at her head. "Well, I'll be . . ." he said.

"You hardly ever see horses lying down. Is 'Ohelo all right?" Benji said.

"She looks fine. My old horse was a sucker for a sun bath. Just put her in a grassy field and she was down, lolling about and lazy as a fat baby."

They approached Marie, who was now leaning against a small eucalyptus tree, catching some shade. Sailor was stretched out next to her. "As you can see, Coco's at it again, making friends with the animals," she said.

Coco spotted them and waved.

Grant said, "I made a liniment for 'Ohelo's knee. And if that doesn't work, I'll try to wrap it once she's more used to me. You two hang back here."

He walked slowly toward Coco and 'Ohelo, talking in a soothing voice the whole way. Lana admired his mix of toughness and tenderness. An ache ran through her.

She and Marie and Benji watched while man and girl and horse bonded over sunshine and tall grass and alfalfa cubes. Grant eventually leaned down and rubbed his hands along 'Ohelo's knee, while Coco stood by her head. It looked like she was saying things into the horse's ear.

"My sister would bring that horse into her bed if she could," Marie said.

"I would have done the same as a kid."

Marie turned her lovely blue eyes to Lana. "Thank you for being good to Coco, Aunt Lana. Kids made fun of her at school. Even her teachers thought she was odd and ran out of patience with her."

Lana considered Coco a blessing. "It's all about finding your kind. Being with people who let you be your wonderful, peculiar, unique self."

"Our mom was good at that. Papa not so much."

"Tell you what—when he gets out, I bet he'll have a change of heart," Lana said.

Marie was teary. "I feel the same way. I want to be the best daughter in the world."

Lana hugged her. "Oh, sweetie, you already are."

When all was said and done, 'Ohelo got a good rubdown and a knee full of liniment, both girls were burned pink from the sun, and Grant and Benji looked as though they'd taken a dust bath. Lana figured she probably looked the same.

Marie said she wanted to walk back and set off with Sailor. Once the rest were mounted, Grant said, "Race you back!" He kicked Boss, who took off like a bullet.

All the other horses lurched forward without any prodding. Lana leaned down and hung on. At first she was tense as a fiddle string, but she soon loosened. Her horse, Hoku, carried her along smoothly, wind pressing against her cheeks

336

and the thunder of hooves running up her center. Nothing else mattered, not Grant or the Wagners, not even the war.

Coco's horse was one body length ahead, but Hoku was gaining. Grant and Boss were nowhere to be seen. They tore through the trees and up the driveway when a loud whistle rang out. Out of the side of her eye, she saw Grant standing in the yard. Lana pulled back on the reins. Hoku came to a stop, but Coco kept on going.

Grant wore a huge smile. "See what I mean? These horses keep me sane."

The intoxication was undeniable.

"What about Coco? She's gone again."

He laughed. "That look on her face. Half-mad with delight. I say you've got a true cowgirl on your hands."

"Shouldn't you go after her?"

"Nah, she'll be back."

Benji and Lady soon trotted up, followed by Marie with Sailor trailing not too far behind. Sailor's tongue hung out to the side and she was panting. A few minutes later Coco appeared. They all circled up near an old whiskey barrel that the horses drank from. Even the two geese joined them. Grant appointed Coco as the keeper of the newly fenced-in herd, and she beamed at her new responsibility, asking ninety-nine questions.

A crisscross pattern formed on the grass the

minute the sun dipped behind the trees. The sky began to buzz, faintly at first, and then the sound hummed through her body. Lana shivered. Not as strong as the days preceding the last disaster, but too strong to ignore. She tried to shake it off, but the feeling stuck.

On a regular afternoon, she would have invited Grant in for dinner, warmed up in front of the fireplace with logs crackling, offered him cider and a hot meal. Maybe she would have even kissed him. None of that was about to happen anytime soon. She was about to tell the girls to go inside so she could speak with Grant alone, when Coco said, "Wanna come in and see our tree? We started decorating it this morning."

"Sure, but—"

Lana jumped in. "I'm sure you have to get back to camp, right?"

He shrugged. "I can spare a few minutes. I'd love to."

If Mochi had any sense about him, he would be making himself scarce. Lana took mental inventory of what was out in the house.

Benji turned toward the house and hurried away, calling over his shoulder, "I have to use the bathroom. Excuse me."

"Shall we tie up the horses, then?" she asked Grant, dragging her heels over to Lady and rubbing her rump.

"They won't go anywhere," he said.

Attempting to slow time, Lana sat on the bottom step and began to unlace her shoes. Some people on the mainland never understood why people in Hawaii took off their shoes before entering a home, but Grant followed suit without a word. He sat next to her, hip touching hers. The air felt thick and syrupy as she walked up the stairs. Coco was waiting at the top with a guilty look on her face, as though she had just realized her error. Marie stood in front of the door as though blocking it but slowly opened it when they approached.

Inside, the fire was roaring. Benji hunched in front of it with the bellows, pumping away. There was an indentation in the air where Mochi had just been. Lana could feel it.

If Grant noticed the mature fire, he didn't let on. Instead he went to the tree with Coco and admired the handmade ornaments. Lana stole away into the kitchen. The pantry door was shut, thank heavens. She pulled out the pitcher of lemonade they'd made earlier and brought it out to the table by the fire. Sweetened with honey instead of sugar, it was tart enough to make you pucker, but still drinkable. Refreshing after a hot and sweaty afternoon.

Coco was telling Grant, "Did you know that Sailor really likes you?"

He raised an eyebrow. "Did she tell you that?"

"I just know."

He reached down and scratched Sailor's ears. "I like her a lot, too. She's an exceptional dog with a lot of spunk. Will you tell her I said so?"

Coco smiled up at him and then said in the most nonchalant way, "Do you think we could bring her to camp one day soon?"

Lana gave her a harsh look. "Coco, it's not that kind of camp, remember?"

Grant guzzled down his lemonade. No one else had had a sip yet. A few seconds later, he was yawning and blinking and rubbing his eyes. He sunk down on the bench, leaning on his elbows. "Gosh, I'm wiped out all of a sudden."

"Must be the fire," Lana said.

His eyes were closed. "And a long day."

"Do you want me to drive you back?" Lana said.

"No, I have to return the horses. The foreman was irked I left Lady overnight last time."

Grant leaned all the way down and rested his head on the table. He looked so peaceful, as though he could have stayed there the whole night. Lana's palms started sweating. Her mind went to the lemonade. She and Marie had squeezed the lemons and Coco had stirred in the honey, a batch of dark red that turned the lemonade almost brown.

A twitch of his leg and he bolted to standing. "Look at me, falling asleep at your table. Ladies, I'm sorry, but I should go while I can still see," he said.

Lana ushered him outside and was surprised to see sheet lightning flashing above Mauna Loa. It was hard to tell approaching night from the storm clouds stacking up—ash, charcoal and inky black. Grant moved like an eighty-year-old man. She thought she may have to help him onto Boss, but he managed.

Even in his condition, he had all the horses rounded up in less than thirty seconds. He then swung past her again, swooping down and kissing her on the top of her head. "Good night, my beautiful dream," he slurred.

She sprinted back inside, oblivious to the cold on her bare feet. Coco and Marie were sitting at the table across from each other. Neither had touched the pitcher.

"Did you do something to the lemonade?" Lana demanded.

Coco shrunk back. "No."

Marie came to her sister's defense. "Coco hasn't been sleeping well. Neither of us have, really. Half the time she wakes up crying from her dreams and then I wake up and neither of us can sleep. Could you have been thinking about that when we mixed it? Wishing for a good sleep?" she asked Coco.

"I might have been," Coco said.

Lana called into the secret room that the coast was clear, then returned to the table. Frustration boiled up. "That's the second time poor Grant has been oddly affected by what we've given him. Pretty soon, he's going to start thinking we're doing it intentionally. And inviting him in here with Mochi? What were you thinking?"

Coco sat there with her shoulders slumped, staring at the flames. The sudden rise in humidity caused her ringlets to coil. "I want him to be our friend. That way he'll be nicer to our parents."

Lana's stomach did a slow flip.

"When are you going to tell him?" Marie asked.

"I was about to tell him when Coco invited him in. I'll go tomorrow and clear things up once and for all."

From out of nowhere, a clap of thunder ripped through the house. They all jumped a foot off their seats and Sailor slid under the table. The air tasted metallic and highly uncertain. Lana thought of Grant riding back with the horses. In her experience, thunderstorms brought on change. Changes in mood, changes in circumstance, changes in heart.

THE HOUSEGUESTS

"Whatever you do, don't drink the lemonade,"
Lana had advised everyone. But after tossing and
turning for an hour straight, she snuck into the
kitchen and poured herself a tall glass. It seemed
tarter than she remembered, with hints of honey
and heartache. When she tucked herself back in,
she saw one flash of lightning and was out cold.
The sleep was absolute.

In the morning she peeked out the window.
The sky was plump with water, streams rushed
from the downspouts, and trees were heavy and
drooping. So much moisture you could wring out
your bones. The whole world was underwater.
Lana dove back under the covers, snuggled with
a still-snoring Sailor for a few minutes, then
dressed and tiptoed out to the truck.

Yesterday Mrs. Kano told her they'd have
homemade sweet bread in the morning, and
Lana planned on surprising the gang with French
toast and 'ōhelo berry syrup. But the bread had a
reputation, and you had to get there early to nab
a loaf. When Lana arrived, there was only one
left. She returned the ink pad, carefully typed out
Mochi's and Benji's ID cards in the store's back

room, and bought the loaf, fresh eggs and butter.

"A Japanese submarine opened fire on Hilo last night, did you hear?" Mrs. Kano said in her squeaky-door-hinge voice. She was sitting at the counter cracking mac nuts.

"Was anyone hurt?"

"Just a chicken. Ten rounds they say. Damaged a seaplane tender and burned up some land near the airport. Good thing you folks came up here."

"You're right about that. Any other news?"

"Maui and Kaua'i got hit, too. The pineapple cannery, a gas storage tank and Nawiliwili Harbor."

None of this sat well with Lana. Knowing those subs were still in Hawaiian waters raised all kinds of questions. Her stomach churned. Were they planning another all-out attack? Where next? Even though the islands were crawling with military and civilians on high alert, the Japanese navy could not be underestimated. Lana felt sure of that.

When she ran back to the truck, avoiding puddles, she noticed a black Ford Super Deluxe parked in front. Two figures sat inside blurred by rain sheets on the windshield. The car smelled of government. Soaked and suddenly ravenous, she shivered the whole way home.

Everyone was up, and in Lana's absence, Coco had felt the need to construct a shelter for the geese on the porch. She had rounded up two crates and a scratchy, moth-eaten blanket no one wanted to use.

"They're geese. They're designed for water," Lana told her.

As if that made any difference. Coco's mind was set, and no amount of reasoning could sway her.

"Not this kind of ice-water rain. They'd rather be inside with us," Coco said.

"Your nest will be perfect for them."

Lana rather enjoyed the geese; they reminded her of Jack, but didn't need them in the house pooping everywhere. She found Mochi and Benji at the kitchen table, sipping honey with tea in it. She liked to tease them about that when she saw them filling their glasses with more honey than tea. A small voice also told her that the honey had something to do with Mochi's improving health, and she made sure to always give him the red honey—she thought of the old wives' tale again—the volcano-season honey. Having them around somehow made her feel more at home and that everything would turn out fine, even though the odds seemed slim.

"Am I going crazy, or have you put on weight?" she asked, noticing a new layer on his face.

"I was just telling him that," said Benji.

"Could be your cooking. I haven't had a woman cook for me since Mari died."

Mochi had lost his wife when Lana was young. And that was that. He never sought another woman again. The only memory she had of Mari was a mirage—a waif of a woman with jet-black hair and a laugh like sunshine. And always the powdery scent of fresh mochi brought her to mind.

She told them about the Japanese submarine as she whisked the eggs. News that no one wanted to hear, but they deserved to know. Marie came in and volunteered to slice sweet bread. Benji turned on the radio and was scanning the stations when Sailor erupted in barking. A car door slammed.

"Are you expecting someone?" Mochi said.

Lana shook her head.

Benji stood and took Mochi's hand. "We'll go downstairs."

Jack had built the place as a refuge from Japanese soldiers, not a place to hide his friend from his own countrymen. He'd be somersaulting in his grave about now. Lana hurried to the front door, hoping it was Grant. Coco and Marie stood by the window, peering out, and the look on their faces said it wasn't. A stone formed in her throat when she opened the door and saw the large black truck right in front of the house, and two men in suits coming up the steps. Another car had pulled up, too.

Sailor stood beside Lana, growling. Lana stepped forward and shut the door behind her, holding her hand on Sailor's neck.

"Ma'am, is the dog friendly?" one man said.

Her hair was on end. "That depends on who's asking."

They stopped just under the eaves. The tall one flipped open his badge. "FBI, ma'am. I'm agent Williams and this is agent Franklin. We're looking for a Mrs. Lana Hitchcock. Are you her?"

"I am." For the first time since Lana had known her, Sailor bared her teeth. "It's okay, Sailor."

Sideways rain pelted them all.

"Would you mind if we step inside? We have some questions for you, Mrs. Hitchcock," Williams said.

"Can we do this out here?" Lana said flatly.

Franklin, whose mother might have been a pit bull, said, "Let me rephrase that. We need to come inside and have a word with you."

Her mind ran through alternate reasons of why they might be here, but the obvious answer caused her knees to wobble. *The girls. Mr. Dick reported them.* She steadied herself as she turned to let them in. Coco and Marie were sitting at the table playing cards.

"Girls, we have visitors."

Coco had gone white, while Marie gave a lackluster smile. "Good morning, gentlemen," she said.

"These your girls?" Franklin said.

Lana hesitated. She had a hunch they knew the truth. Why else would they be here? And then the sudden thought arose that maybe something had happened to Grant on his way home the other day. "Does this have anything to do with Major Bailey?" she asked, hands trembling.

Franklin and Williams exchanged glances. "No, ma'am."

Lana looked over at Coco and Marie and felt protective. They might not be her own flesh and blood, but in the past weeks, their hearts had been stitched together like an old quilt. And in that moment, Lana understood a fraction of what the Wagners had endured when they were hauled off. An explosion of helplessness went off inside her.

"Girls, how about you go in the kitchen?" she said.

They did as told, eyes on the floor. Whoever had been in the other car tapped on the door and then walked in.

"Would ya look who it is," Dutch London said with a smug look on his ruddy face.

Williams set his hat on the table and started in. "Mrs. Hitchcock, word on the street is those are not your girls and you have kidnapped them. Would you say that's accurate?"

Her skin bristled. She refused to look at Dutch. "I would say that is one-hundred-percent false. The part about me kidnapping them, at least."

"So you admit they aren't yours?"

"They aren't mine, no."

"Why did you try to pass them off as yours

during the fingerprinting? You lied to a government official and tried to falsify documents. That could land you in jail."

Dutch waved a stack of papers. "I'm the keeper of everything that belongs to the Wagners, including the girls."

Lana sank down to the bench, unable to stand on her own two legs. "I was with the Wagners when they were taken in. I told them I'd watch the girls. And then we left in a hurry, running from the Japanese. I had no idea that their parents would be held for so long."

"Being a Nazi is a serious crime," Williams said.

"It is," Lana said.

Franklin glared. "Didn't you speak to Mr. London here that afternoon, and he told you Mr. Wagner had asked him to take over?"

"Kidnapping is a felony. Are you aware of that?" said Williams.

Their rapid-fire questioning was getting to her. "I didn't kidnap them! You can ask their parents. They're being held at Kīlauea Military Camp, but you probably already know that."

"How do *you* know that?" Williams said.

"The camp is no secret."

Dutch came closer, the faint smell of cheese wafting off him. "The Wagners are up here? I thought they were taken to Oʻahu," he said with a frown.

"Nope, they're right up the road," Lana said, proud of her small victory.

He continued. "The way I see it is that the Wagners are neck high in trouble and they've entrusted me to handle their affairs. As if they need more to worry about. I'll just take the girls and bring them home to Hilo."

"Why don't we go talk to the Wagners? They should have a say in this," Lana said, remembering how Ingrid had looked conflicted when Fred mentioned Dutch. If only she had spoken up back then.

Lana could picture the look on Grant's face when she showed up with two FBI agents. Not much she could do about it now.

Franklin ignored her suggestion and sniffed the air. "This is a big house. Do you have anyone else here with you?"

"Just us."

"Mind if we take a look around?"

A twitch developed on the side of her eye. Yes, she minded. If Mochi or Benji had left one thing out of place, it would be obvious. "There's not much to see."

"Are you aware that one of your father's Jap friends went missing after the attack? He wouldn't happen to be up here with you, would he?"

Both men watched her intently.

"No and no."

The fire spit an ash onto the floor. Williams

stomped it. Lana met their gaze with as much false confidence as she could muster. Their questioning reminded her of being interrogated by the principal for skipping class and meeting up with Alika behind the banyan tree.

"Show us around, please," Franklin said.

Dutch made himself at home by the fire, crossing his arms over his gut. His shirt was one size too small, and his waist several sizes too large. She wished she could blot him out with pen and ink or add whiskers to his already beady eyes. Lana stood on wobbly legs.

As they passed the kitchen, she poked her head in. "Would you be good hostesses and pour these gentlemen some lemonade, please?"

"Why is Mr. London here?" Coco hissed.

No point in lying. "He says I kidnapped you—"

"We don't like him," she said.

Lana gave them a firm look. "Don't do anything silly. I'll handle this. Trust me."

Outside, the rain started up in earnest. Raindrops peppered the tin roof like pebbles, and the rush was deafening. She led them into her room first. Williams took a side trip into the bathroom, slamming cabinet doors around. He came out holding up a bottle of Barbasol shaving cream, which ironically had been Jack's.

"This yours?"

"That belonged to my father. I haven't had the heart to throw out his stuff yet."

They looked under mattresses, through drawers, out windows, all without saying anything. Franklin slow and methodical, Williams hasty and erratic. She was equally impressed and terrified at their thoroughness.

In the girls' room, Coco showed up holding two glasses. "We made this from scratch."

If they had any qualms about drinking cold lemonade on an arctic morning, the hopeful look on Coco's face squelched it. Both men willingly accepted. Williams sipped; Franklin swigged.

"Who sleeps in here?"

Coco started up. "Me and—"

"Coco and Sailor. Marie sleeps in the next room," Lana said.

Coco stood there with that look on her face that said she was fixing to say something dangerous. Lana nodded sternly toward the kitchen, but it was too late.

Her small voice carried a tremor. "My dog, Sailor, really wants you to leave. This is not your house, and it's mean of you to force your way in and look at all our private things. And for your information, Aunt Lana is nothing but good."

Wearing knee-high pink socks and a polka-dotted sweater, Coco looked as threatening as a bunny rabbit in an Easter basket. But her arms were crossed and she meant business.

Franklin set down his nearly empty glass and rubbed his eyes. "Sorry, little miss. We have a job to do. Mrs. Hitchcock has some serious allegations against her, and we need to sort it out."

Lana had the sudden horrific thought they might lock her up with the Wagners and other offenders who were mostly guilty of being born in the wrong country.

Apparently Coco did, too. "You can't take her!"

"Like I said, Coco, trust me. Everything will be fine once we talk to your parents," Lana said.

"Then I want to come."

"No visitors," Franklin said.

Williams began to yawn, one after another. "Show us the next room so we can vamoose. This weather's getting to me."

Coco clung to Lana's blouse and followed them in. Lana pulled her close. She was trying to look calm when inside she was close to full-blown hysteria. The room was astonishingly void of signs. No clothing, no shoes, no empty tea mugs. By now the agents had lost the thrill of the hunt. They barely checked the kitchen and fortunately didn't even open the pantry door. Marie was at the table, hands neatly folded.

Out in the living room, Dutch downed the last of his lemonade. Franklin leaned on the door frame. The skin over his eyelids was sagging. "I'm not feeling so hot. What do you say we just take them all in to the camp and let them fight it out with the parents."

Dutch stood. "I have custody. So just give me the girls and you can deal with Mrs. Hitchcock as you see fit."

Coco's eyes blazed. "I'm not going with him."

Sailor sat upright in the middle of the room. Her gaze went from man to man, never taking her eyes away from them. Coco went and stood by her. What a great team they made.

Williams thought for a moment, then said, "We're taking you all in. Grab your purse, ma'am."

Coco looked ready to bolt. Part of Lana wanted her to stay put, and part hoped that she ran. If they arrested Lana, the girls would be with Mr. London, and that would be unbearable. Surely the Wagners would be able to clear up this horrible mess given the chance, but she remembered that Fred had been adamant about the girls needing a man around. Not all men were created equal— did he not see that?

"What about Sailor?" Marie asked.

"I'll take Sailor with me," Dutch said.

Coco made a sour face. "Sailor doesn't want to go with you."

There was no room for Sailor in the car, with Lana and the two girls.

Franklin suggested, "We can pick up the dog later."

Lana didn't like the sound of that. She stepped into the kitchen for her purse and called out louder than necessary, "Coco, why don't you bring your owl Hoot, since we don't know when we'll be coming back from camp."

Coco disappeared. When several minutes had gone by, and she still hadn't come out, Williams called, "Hey, kid, hurry it up."

Nothing. He looked at Lana. She shrugged. They went back to the bedroom and found the window open. Cool air filtered in and there was no sign of Coco.

"Coco?" Lana called.

"Great. We got a runaway kid on our hands," Williams said.

Just to be sure, they searched the other rooms. Lana knew they wouldn't find her. "The girls don't like Mr. London, in case you missed that small detail. You ask me, some men shouldn't be left in charge of young women."

He raised an eyebrow. "Nor should they be alone out in the boondocks. Any idea where she might be hiding?"

Lana had several ideas. "Nope. The girls stayed indoors much of the time, afraid of falling in cracks or steam vents, that kind of thing."

Back in the living room, Franklin was now leaning sideways on the table, ready to fall asleep. Dutch rubbed his eyes.

"Fellas, the kid took off out the window. How about you stay here, Franklin, and search the area, and I'll take Mrs. Hitchcock and the older girl in. Mr. London, you can follow us," Williams said.

Lana felt extremely uneasy leaving Coco behind, and Franklin there alone with Mochi and Benji in the secret room, but she wanted to get to the Wagners and explain her case. As loud as she could, she yelled out the window, "Coco, Mr. Franklin is staying here, so you won't be alone!"

She grabbed Marie's hand as they walked out the door. Marie had gone pale and mute and shaky.

"We will work this out," Lana said.

If only she could be sure.

THE CAMP

The skies continued to weep. Gullies had formed in the center of the road, creating rivers out of ruts and pools out of potholes. Lana and Marie rode in back trying to remain calm. Every so often Lana checked her wrists to make sure she wasn't in handcuffs. But the truth was that Williams and Franklin were investigating a kidnapping. Their main concern was the girls' safety, not some lying housewife.

Marie looked miserable, and Lana couldn't blame her. Going off alone with Mr. London would be an awful fate. Though Lana was sure that Coco would come to her senses and return. There was only so long she could hide out. Running away usually seemed like a brilliant idea at the time, but when darkness came, the thrill quickly faded. Lana knew from experience.

When they arrived at the camp, a guard waved them through the gate, which was wound with enough barbed wire to fence five pastures. Hair rose on the back of her neck. They parked in front of a large stone house with smoke streaming from the chimney. The surrounding lawns and fields were submerged in rainwater.

Williams held out his hand. "I need your ID. Wait here." He waded up to the red door and disappeared inside.

Beyond the building, another fence surrounded the barracks. Two guards in rain gear walked back and forth, bayonets leaning on their shoulders. A roughly constructed bell tower with a machine gun loomed over the place. Lana craned her head but saw no sign of life other than a group of wet mynah birds.

Williams came back drenched and yawning. He drove them to a large wooden building with a wraparound lanai. The theater was just down the way, and Lana recalled her last time there. There had been hot buttered popcorn and a rowdy audience of soldiers on R and R. She shuddered.

He led them inside and sat Lana down on a wooden bench facing a window. Marie sat with her.

"You, come with me," he said to Marie.

"Why can't we stay together?" Lana asked.

"It doesn't work that way."

Lana squeezed her hand. "Just do as they say."

Williams led her off, and they disappeared around the corner while Lana waited. A secretary click-clacked away on a typewriter, and uniformed men popped in and out of doorways. She pulled her hood as far forward as possible, staring down at the dust in the floor cracks. Breaths were hard to take. If only she could tell

Grant on her own terms, not have him find out this way. Please let him be off submarine spotting or setting up booby traps for Japanese invaders.

Get ahold of yourself. There were far bigger issues here than Grant. Other people's lives were at stake. Everyone's life was at stake, for that matter. This was a different world and she'd better get used to it.

After a time, when it seemed that no one else was around, Lana stood to look out the window. She could see an area between the buildings where several Japanese men were walking back and forth under a deep eave. They could walk only the length of the building without getting rained on. She was too far away to see their faces, but their hunched shoulders and sluggish pace told her all she needed to know. She was tempted to sneak out and offer up her raincoat and an encouraging word, as if that would do any good.

Ten minutes later a young guard came in and ushered Lana into another building, where she was placed in a small room. He said nothing to her, and when he went to shut the door, she could hardly stand his silence.

"What's going on?" she asked.

"Sorry, ma'am. I don't talk to prisoners."

"But I'm just here to clear up a misunderstanding."

He shut the door in her face. The room was eight

paces across and ten long. There was a cot with a folded army blanket, a small table and two chairs, and a barred window on one side. Another door opened into a closet-sized bathroom. Her view was of a grassy field and a barbed-wire fence. What the hell was going on? Had Williams lied to her in order to get her in here without a big fuss?

Lana sat on the chair, paced the room, counted the floor boards and finally, what must have been hours later, lay back on the cot. She thought about Coco and wondered where she was at this moment. In the secret room with Mochi and Benji? With the horses? And poor Sailor, she was probably anxious and confused without all her people.

Lana got up and pounded on the door. "Someone, please tell me what's going on!" she cried, pressing her cheek to the cool wood.

But no one came. With the cloudy skies, it was impossible to tell what time it was. Minutes passed like hours, and Lana created an assortment of scenarios in her head. *The Wagners had indeed been taken to O'ahu. They were arresting her for kidnapping and there would be no trial. Mr. London knew someone at the camp and pulled strings to keep Lana locked up, while he made off with the girls.* It was frightening to think that he was in charge of all of the Wagners' affairs—house, actually *houses,* now that the Wagners owned Jack's house; business; girls; and by default Sailor and the geese. Greed seeped out of him in the house earlier, and Lana finally understood that it was far more than just the girls that he wanted.

When the skies darkened, a different guard brought her a plate of spam and rice with watery greens and warm juice.

"Sir, please, can you tell me why I'm still being held? Williams and I were supposed to talk to the Wagners. Are they here? And what about Marie, the girl who came with me? Do you know where she is?" she blurted.

The soldier was hardly older than Marie. "No, ma'am."

This one seemed more pliable, and she was about to interrogate him further, when she heard footsteps in the hallway. The air began to hum at a higher frequency, as if someone had unleashed a swarm of mosquitos into the building. She knew who was coming. Sure enough, Grant stepped into the room beside the guard.

"What's this all about?" he said in a very buttoned-up way. "Why are you here, Mrs. Hitchcock?"

His formality stung. *Give him the benefit of the doubt,* she ordered herself. But this was not the Grant she knew.

"I was accused of kidnapping—"

"I know what you were accused of. Do those girls belong to the Wagners and not you?"

Lana wanted to tell the guard to scram, but he remained planted.

"Yes, but I didn't kidnap anyone! I brought the girls up here to save them. The Wagners are my father's neighbors and they were taken away—"

"I know the story. But all this time, you led me to believe they were yours. Why not just tell me?"

Lana felt the need to stand up for herself. "I never expected things to happen between us like they did, and I was scared. Our islands were under attack, and the man supposedly responsible for the girls was a louse. The girls hate him. I acted on instinct. I was just trying to protect them."

Lana thought about the trail of Grant's touch, his smile and the way he looked unflinchingly into her eyes. He had been nothing but kind and helpful and *interested*. He didn't look that way now.

"I was over there helping y'all out, and you didn't have the decency to come clean with me."

"I was planning to tell you today. I swear it!"

Grant shook his head and stepped away. At the door, he turned and locked eyes with her. "I will say this—nothing loses my interest quicker than someone lying to me. You of all people should know that."

And just like that, he had shut her out.

"Wait," she begged. "What are they going to do with me?"

"That's not up to me now," he said flatly, and left the room.

Alone again, Lana flung herself facedown onto the cot. She had meant to tell him, and would have, if Coco hadn't interrupted her plans. Though she knew that she should have had the difficult conversation sooner rather than later, since sometimes later never came. Every person makes mistakes . . . that's why there is also forgiveness. And as far as lying went, if her reasons were to keep the children safe, then how could she be faulted? If Grant didn't come to his senses on that, she didn't want him anyway.

A sob arose, and soon she was curled up in a ball, weeping. The cot was soaked, her hands were soaked and her hair dripped with tears.

When the sun had gone down completely, Lana sat in the dark, shivering. Even prisons were on blackout. The worst part was she had no idea where the girls were. Had Coco turned herself in or was she still hiding? Had Mr. Wagner been furious that she brought the girls to Volcano without his permission, mere *woman* that she was, and then sent them home with Dutch London after all? A shudder ran down to her toes.

She kept listening for footsteps, hoping and praying that Grant would have a change of heart. She wanted to tell him that Coco had run away, appeal to his human side. Even if he wanted nothing to do with her, one would think he would want to help the girls. The sound of rain on the tin roof started up again, and Lana thought she heard voices. She ran to the door and pounded. No one came.

Her thoughts turned to every bad scenario imaginable. If they kept her imprisoned, who would watch the horses? Would Mochi and Benji be able to stay hidden in the house? Could they take care of each other well enough without her help? And what about the geese? Her mind simply would not shut off, and she felt her body twisting into one big knot of misery.

Rain dripped outside her window on the grass, and she tried to focus on that. At some point, she fell into a cold and restless sleep, waking up dazed and panicked and remembering. In the quiet hollow of night, she thought back to that first night at the house. How alone she had felt, even with a houseful of people. Back then the girls and Benji had been mere strangers. Now they were family.

In the morning her eyes shot open. Someone was at the door, jiggling the lock. *Please, let it be Grant.* A man walked in. In the dim morning light, it looked like Williams. He flipped on the light and her eyes burned. He was rumpled and creased and smelled like stale bread, or maybe that was her own breath. No one had been kind enough to leave her a toothbrush.

"Mrs. Hitchcock, sorry to keep you waiting.

The Wagners were at a hearing in Hilo yesterday, and, wouldn't you know it, a kind of illness overtook me last night and I couldn't stay awake. You know anything about that?" he said in a slow drawl.

"How would I?" Lana said.

He scratched his chin. "Just thinking out loud."

She ignored him. "Where are the girls?"

"The kid showed up at dusk last night, worried about her dog and her sister. Franklin brought her in."

Lana gulped down air. "So the girls are together? Here at the camp?"

He nodded, and she realized he was wearing the same suit from yesterday. "With the dog. Kid threw a fit when it came to leaving the dog overnight."

That sounded about right. "The kid's name is Coco," Lana said.

"Anyhow, I'll need you to come with me."

"What about Mr. London?"

"He stayed at your place. Hope you don't mind. In case he needs to bring the girls home with him today. Come on."

"Give me a minute," she said.

Lana hung on the words *in case*. They hadn't decided yet, thank heavens. Williams stepped out and she used the bathroom, splashing water on her face and rinsing out her mouth. She looked as though she had aged five years overnight. He

365

took her outside and back to the first building from yesterday. Franklin was already in the room, reading a newspaper. A cigarette burned next to him. He looked worse than Williams.

"Have the girls seen their parents?" she asked.

"The girls are fine. And no. No visitors allowed. We told you that," he said.

He obviously didn't have kids of his own. She felt carved out and empty and ready to burst into tears at any moment. A few minutes later, armed guards came through the door with two prisoners in tow. Lana looked at them and froze. This was not the Ingrid Wagner of two weeks ago. Blond hair turned to ash. Eyes smudged. Red blotches on her skin. Their eyes met. Lana fought back a sob.

"Lana, is that you?" Ingrid whispered.

Lana jumped up and rushed toward her, but the guard blocked her with his rifle. "No touching."

Fred trailed behind. If Lana had run into him on the street, she would not have recognized him. A two-week beard, hair sticking out in all directions and all hope washed from his expression. Williams motioned for them to sit. The room had a card table set up in the middle. The guards stood by the door while the rest of them sat.

Franklin opened a manila folder. "I'll cut to the chase. You signed temporary custody of your daughters over to a Mr. Dutch London. Mr. London reported them kidnapped, and they just turned up with Mrs. Hitchcock in a house near 29 Mile. What do the Wagners have to say?" he said.

"Are they all right?" Ingrid said to Lana.

"They miss you, but they're fine. They're wonderful girls. We have Sailor, too, of course."

Fred Wagner ran his hands through his oily hair. "When they took us away and had us sign papers that they wouldn't let us read, I had no idea what was in store. I figured Mr. London could take care of the house, the girls, my business for a few days."

"Based on your hearing yesterday, it looks like you won't be getting released anytime soon. But we need to know if Mrs. Hitchcock had any kind of approval for taking the girls or if it was outright kidnapping."

"I suggested it," Mrs. Wagner said.

Fred avoided looking at Lana. "I wouldn't say it was outright kidnapping, no. But I told her Mr. London was in charge of everything."

"How are you all acquainted?" Williams asked.

"My father was a neighbor."

Franklin flipped through his notes.

Ingrid filled in more. "Lana's father had just passed, and she showed up the day before the bombing. He lived next door to us, and she was at our house when your friends took us away," Ingrid said.

"Your father was Jack Spalding, correct?" Williams said.

"Correct."

Lana expected him to say something else about Jack, but he continued his line of questioning. "Mrs. Hitchcock, how come you never told Mr. London about your plan to bring the girls up here, and then tried to pass them off as your own?"

This whole thing was one big screwup, and Lana was growing annoyed. She could only imagine how the Wagners felt. "Because the man is not an appropriate guardian. No offense, Fred, but both girls are scared to death of him. They told me so, and I wasn't about to leave them in his care. Nor was Hilo a safe place to be."

"Why didn't you tell anyone?" Williams said.

"Who was I going to tell? Those men that took the Wagners away said they were going to question them, not lock them up indefinitely. And the whole world was upside down. The girls are safe and being well cared for and I stand by my decision."

Franklin took a drag of his cigarette, blowing smoke out his nose. "I guess what I really need to know is—do the Wagners want to press charges for kidnapping? And if not, who do they want the girls with?"

Simultaneously, Ingrid said, "Mrs. Hitchcock," and Fred said, "Mr. London."

Lana refused to back down. "I don't know if anyone told you, but Coco ran away yesterday when she found out she might have to go with

Mr. London. She's back with Marie now, and safe, but that should tell you all you need to know. The girls are comfortable with me, and to move them now will be horribly disruptive. We have Sailor and the geese and there are horses at my place, too."

"Coco does love horses," Ingrid said.

Fred looked unconvinced. "And what if there's an invasion, Mrs. Hitchcock? Are you prepared to fight off the Japanese soldiers to keep my girls safe?"

"My father built a hideaway up here, and we have a bomb shelter and guns and everything we need. Not to mention the army unit that is set to be moving in any day now, right up the road," Lana said.

"Never trust a female with a gun," Fred said nervously.

"I could outshoot Mr. London any day, I'm sure of that," Lana said.

She had never fired a gun in her life.

Ingrid surprised Lana by saying, "I'm putting my foot down. I don't want the girls going with Dutch. They need a woman more than a man right now, and if they don't like him, why force it?"

Lana wanted to reach out and hug Ingrid. The pain of being separated from Marie and Coco and not knowing where they were or how they were doing must have been crushing the life out of her.

Williams appeared not to care who had the girls, as long as he could wipe his hands of them. "The Wagners will need to sign papers assigning new custody."

He addressed them in third person, as if they weren't in the room. Lana felt like screaming, *Have some decency, man!*

Ingrid's hands trembled on the table. "I worry how Coco is taking this. Can we see them?"

"No visitors in the camp," Williams said.

The unfairness set Lana ablaze. "Funny that everyone calls it a camp. Why don't you call it what it really is? A prison. *Kīlauea Military Prison,* that way there's no confusion," she said, folding her arms over her chest.

You could have heard an ash drop. No one spoke for a moment, and then Williams and Franklin both started talking at once. "It's a holding cell, not a prison." "They're awaiting trial and treated decently." "We're doing what we must to keep the country safe." "War has its own rules."

"Can they at least write them a note—is that allowed?" Lana asked Williams.

"Generally, Nazis don't get any favors, but since it involves kids, I'll allow it. Make it short and in English."

Williams's eyelids had begun to droop, and Lana got the sense he wanted to be done with this. He tore off the bottom of a form and pushed it to Ingrid. Her hand shook like a ninety-three-year-old's as she wrote.

Williams produced more forms for everyone to sign. He took the scrap of paper that Ingrid had written on, read it and then handed it to Lana. Unable to stop herself, Lana reached out and grabbed Ingrid's hand. It was cold as snow. "Are they treating you well here?"

She squeezed and Ingrid squeezed back. "I'll have them write you letters and get them in here. You do accept letters, don't you?" Lana said to Williams.

"As long as they're in English. And all mail is censored."

"I doubt that'll be a problem, coming from an eight-year-old and a thirteen-year-old."

The guards led the Wagners out, and Williams walked Lana to the original bench she had sat on yesterday. Dutch London was planted on it. When he saw them, he stood.

"So?" he said.

Williams seemed annoyed. "The girls are staying with Mrs. Hitchcock. This has been a big waste of time. I suggest you go back to Hilo, Mr. London."

Dutch looked offended. "A man has a duty, Mr. Williams. I would think you know that."

"We're done here," Williams said with force.

Lana watched Dutch's mouth open and close a few times, and before he turned to go, she gave him her sweetest smile. "Goodbye, Mr. London," she said.

Williams had Lana wait on the bench as he showed Dutch out. She would be thrilled if she never saw his face again, but she worried what he'd do with the houses and business. He seemed to be the type to take advantage of another man's misfortune.

The storm had eased sometime in the night, though the clouds still looked laden with rain. Lana heard a door slam down the way, and voices. Then the sound of dog nails clicking on the floorboards.

"Aunt Lana!" Coco howled when she saw Lana, sprinting down the hallway and hurling her little body into Lana's arms. She hugged her fiercely. Coco's hair smelled like cigarette smoke and wet dog fur. Lana stood and pulled Marie and Sailor in, too.

"Come on. We're going," Lana said.

Lana had never been happier to return home. Hale Manu had gone from escape house to refuge to home in a span of less than two weeks. Her sense of time had been warped by the war. The minute they arrived, they rushed to the secret door.

Lana called down, "It's safe to come up now!"

Benji and Mochi soon emerged, squinting into the daylight. "That was a long twenty-four hours.

But Benji went out in the night and got us water and berries and honey. My boy is resourceful," Mochi said.

Lana recounted her story. "And I can't believe they let Dutch London stay here. We need to wash the sheets."

"From the sound of it, he passed out on the floor in front of the fireplace, and Franklin couldn't wake him," Mochi said.

"How do you know?" Lana asked.

"We listened through the door."

Coco confirmed it. "When I came back for Sailor, he was sound asleep. He sounded like a whole family of wild pigs digging for roots."

Benji made a fire, and everyone crowded around the table with steaming mugs of mamaki leaf and honey tea.

Lana pulled the note from her pocket. "This is from your mom. She wanted me to tell you that they are being treated well and have plenty to eat, and that they love you to the stars and back. And so you know, she didn't have much time or any privacy to write this."

Marie took it and read, "My lovely daughters, your father and I miss you very much. We are doing well and hope to be with you again soon. I hope you are minding your manners with Mrs. Hitchcock, and taking good care of Sailor. Give each other a hug and keep your chins up. All our love, Mama and Papa."

When she finished reading, there wasn't a dry eye at the table. The words *hope to be with you again soon* spoke to the uncertainty of the Wagners' plight. When they would be released was anyone's guess, but the fact that they were still being held after their hearing did not bode well. And how much to tell the girls? Lana was not well versed in raising children, but in her mind, especially after what she'd just been through, the more truth they knew now, the better.

She put her arms around them. "Listen, no one is saying when your parents will get out, and I hope it's soon, but if not, know that you will be with me for as long as it takes. I'm not going anywhere."

Sailor seemed to think she was missing out and came and leaned into them with all her weight, groaning. They were one big pile of tears.

THE DEPARTURE

Heartache coated everything in the house that night, draping itself on the furniture and covering the walls. Lana felt it behind her ears and in every finger and every toe. She wasn't the only one. Coco refused to let go of her mother's note, reducing it to a crumpled mess.

As she washed out the pitcher, Lana thought about the lemonade. There was something to the honey; that she knew. She was still unsure exactly what. And she was fine with that. Not everything was meant to be understood. In fact a world where everything made sense would be dull and boring. *Mystery unlocks the imagination,* her father used to say.

Boy, was that the truth. There was the time Thomas Jaggar called Jack up to discuss his idea of an automobile that drove on land and sailed the seas. Others told him he was crazy, but Jack showed up at Volcano the next day. He and the boys in the machine shop worked furiously to modify a motorcar with a wooden hull and balloon tires. After months of experimentation, they named her Ohiki and announced her launching in Hilo Bay to all of Hawaii. And not only did she float, she chugged along at a whopping four miles per hour. Jack pranced around like a rooster for days after that.

Lana felt a soft spot for him. Being at the volcano had stirred up so many memories and so many emotions that she now realized she had tucked away and kept hidden, even from herself. A talent that didn't serve her well, she was coming to see. But Jack was spilling out everywhere here, impossible to ignore. Maybe the message was to forgive him, and, more important, to forgive herself.

Bouts of thunder shook the house that night. Sailor left Lana's mattress to seek shelter underneath Coco's bed, which was where they found her in the morning. They had to lure her out with a hunk of steak.

Tuesday was even bleaker than Monday, with the addition of fog thicker than lemon rind. After breakfast of blackberry cobbler and scrambled eggs—the only way Coco would eat them—everyone milled about the house with nothing to do. Lana had purchased Bicycle cards and a deck of *hanafuda* from Kano Store, but was saving them as Christmas gifts. Today was December twenty-second; only three days to go. The thought made Lana want to crawl back into bed. But with a whole house depending on her, it was not an option.

Mochi, as always, was glued to the radio. The

Japanese had invaded Luzon in the Philippines and were headed for Manila, and the US had expanded the draft to include all men ages eighteen to sixty-five. Closer by, citizens were debating an incident on Niʻihau and making a hot case for the local Japanese population not to be trusted. Many people were of the belief that if three people could be so easily persuaded to help a downed Japanese pilot, then what was to stop others?

When the kids went out onto the lanai, Mochi sat Lana down next to him. He placed his weathered hand over hers, the coarseness of his fisherman's skin familiar. His watery eyes looked into hers. "I'm going to turn myself in, Lana. Me being here is endangering all of you, and the war has just started. I never should have left Hilo," he said.

She stared at him in disbelief. "Mochi—"

"Never mind talking me out of it. It's something I must do."

His decision made sense, and she could tell he felt it was the honorable thing to do, but she was not happy about it. Especially in his frail condition.

"When? Where?"

"Tomorrow. Kīlauea Military Camp. It's the closest."

Anything that Mochi did, he did with much consideration. And while Lana respected his altruism, she selfishly wanted him with her, with the kids. He was her calm.

"I can take you," she offered.

"Drop me at the main road. I'll walk from there. I don't want you tied up in this mess."

"Grant wants nothing to do with me anymore . . . he pretty much said so. And I don't care if people know," she said, trying to sound convincing.

"*Auwe*, give him time. And don't be stupid. Lying to protect the girls is one thing, but hiding a wanted man is something else. These kids need you here."

Lana leaned into him. "The main thing is that you're feeling better and that you stay that way. I hesitate to use the *M* word, but it does feel like one."

"The *M* word?"

"Miracle."

He nodded. "Nothing wrong with miracles. They are merely highly concentrated belief."

"Now you're sounding a bit like Coco."

Lana thought of the force of her emotions toward Grant. How she believed in her heart that there was only one outcome—to be with him. So where was he now?

"We are all born with this ability, but most of us lose it. Few go through life believing in miracles."

"My father spent his life chasing miracles. Did he not believe enough?"

"He did better than most. But there's a fine line between want and need, and hope and trust. If we trust, we are given what we need, because we know that all things are possible."

"Does that mean the Wagners will get out soon if Coco believes they will?" Lana asked.

"It means that Coco will receive what she needs. But here's the catch—all life is interconnected, so you have to factor in what's good for the whole. What you want may not be what the world needs at any given moment, and if that's the case, your want may not happen. Better to step aside and allow."

"Is that Shinto?" Lana asked.

He tapped his head. "No, it's Mochi."

"But look at us all right now—we're a pretty sad lot," she argued.

He smiled, showing all his teeth. "Depends on how you look at it."

"What do you mean?"

"You can choose to either see everything as a miracle or nothing as a miracle. Maybe her parents will be released tomorrow, or maybe she stays with you for a while longer, here with the horses and the bees. Either way, you two have something to teach each other."

A feeling of knowing rose up through her, like a column of smoke. She resolved to do her best no matter what life threw at them. The rain had let up for the moment, and the kids' voices could no longer be heard. Voices that had grown around her heart like vines.

"You know what I worry about?" Lana said.

"What?"

"How my heart will break yet again when I have to give these girls up. I know it sounds selfish, but it's true."

He tapped her forehead. "Sounds to me like you need to get out of your head. Go outside . . . breathe some fresh air into those lungs."

Remarkably, he smelled faintly of ocean. "Oh, Mochi. I'm going to miss you, too. Can't you go after Christmas?"

"I have to go, Lana-san."

She turned and looked into his ink-black eyes, her own eyes flickering with tears. "Well, I'll put in a good word for you, if anyone will listen," she said.

"Will you keep Benji?"

"You know I will. Have you told him?"

"Tonight."

Lana circled around back, past the garden beds which were now mud bogs and would probably need to be replanted, beyond the honey hives and to the driveway. Her best guess was that the children had gone to visit the horses. Grant had left them some liniment in hopes that Coco would be able to get close enough to apply some.

For the first time since the camp visit, she

was alone, which probably wasn't a good thing. Grant's parting words began to haunt her. Stabbing, sawing, cutting at her heartstrings. *Nothing loses my interest quicker than someone lying to me.* The cold coming off him had been palpable. She sensed a wound there. The sooner she could explain herself, the better. But what if he didn't seek her out?

The toe of her boot caught between two rocks and she nearly toppled forward. *Wake up!* the ground seemed to be saying. It was strange; she looked around and almost wasn't sure where she was. Almost at the barn, for the first time she noticed that no birds were singing. Was it too wet and dismal for birds, even? As she moved along the saturated earth, she worked out ways to approach Grant. How much time should she give him before marching into camp and demanding he listen. One day? One week? One lifetime?

Love finds a way. The words landed neatly in her brain as though dropped from the tree branch above. She went right back to her conversation with Mochi. If Grant was her man, things would fall into place. If not, they were never meant to be. Not that she would forget him anytime in the next decade, but one couldn't force feelings.

The kids were nowhere to be found, and the horses were gathered under one tree. Lana filled their water and sat on the fence post watching them. They were experts at relaxation; she had to give them that. Standing around lazily, coats soaked. Two of them decided to show off and rolled around in the mud.

"You silly animals!" she called.

Without Grant, how would she train them? *Damn him.*

Late that afternoon, as a remedy for the blues, Lana dove headfirst into preparing Mochi's last meal with them and making it special. She enlisted Coco and Marie to help, giving Mochi space to speak to Benji alone. Dinner would be garlic shoyu chicken, rice and chopped spinach— which Coco would bury under her napkin—and banana cream pie with flaky coconut topping.

An idea came to her. "How about this. Let's try to think about all the things we are grateful for."

Marie moaned. "Surely you're kidding."

Coco stared out the window, munching on a cracker. A mound of bananas sat in front of her. The note from her mother was set on the table under her glass, as if it might blow away.

Lana placed her hands on her hips. "I am two-hundred-percent serious. Times might be tough right now, but our only way through this is to remember what's good in the world."

"You go first, then," Marie said.

Sweet as she may be, she was still a teenager, with a touch of sass now and then. Lana let it slide. "I am grateful for this roof over our heads, that we have enough to eat and that we finished the fence for the horses," Lana said. "Do you want me to go on, because I could, or does one of you want to give it a shot?"

Coco came back from wherever she had been. "I am happy we get pie tonight."

"Can't you think of something better than that?" Marie said.

Coco stuck out her tongue.

Lana went to her defense. "Actually that's perfect, Coco. Small things are just as good as big things, and often overlooked. Anything else?"

"That you came back from camp," Coco added.

Lana offered up her own silent prayer of gratitude for that. They went back and forth for a while. Talking about all the simple and beautiful reasons to be thankful. Horses in the pasture, Mochi feeling stronger, Sailor, the secret room, no invasion as of yet, the forest full of birdsong, and, of course, Grant.

"When is Major Bailey coming back?" Coco asked.

Lana did not want to think about Major Bailey, let alone discuss him. "Sounds like they're keeping him busy at work, so I have no idea."

"Did you see him today?" Marie asked.

"Briefly."

Coco started mashing the bananas as if her life depended on it. "If we write a letter to Mama and Papa, would he give it to them?"

"I'll bet he would. You can each write one after dinner."

They worked in silence for a while, until Benji and Mochi came in. From the red around Benji's eyes, it was clear Mochi had told him he was leaving. Lana admired the way he maintained calm under such weighty burdens.

Lana realized an hour or so too late that there was no way around the sadness. They would just have to plow through it. The evening turned into a sorrowful, weepy affair. Every time Lana opened her mouth to say something, a sob escaped instead. Even the men were crying. Sailor watched from her spot in the middle of the floor, an alarmed look on her face. And the strange thing was—all that grieving in one place, it felt good for the soul.

In the morning Lana dragged her heels. No one wanted to admit that Mochi would no longer be sitting in front of the fireplace drinking tea with the radio turned up a notch too loud. Benji, who was usually a good sport, sat on the front porch, whipping pebbles at the Norfolk pine.

"If you hit the geese, I'll punch you," Coco warned him.

Mochi chuckled. "I like your spirit, little one. Can I get a hug before I go?"

For a moment Coco stood immobile. Hugging strangers and old people was akin to kissing boys.

Distasteful and scary. But a second later she dove at him and burrowed in. Mochi shut his eyes. The sheer amount of anguish on his face split Lana's heart down its seams, and if she hadn't already shed every tear her body could produce, she would have been a bawling mess.

He hugged Marie next, then Lana. "Your father would be so proud of you," he whispered into her hair. "Bringing us all up here and turning an escape house into a home. I promise I will be back."

Those words meant everything to her.

"I know you will," Lana said.

The whole gang insisted on riding in the truck to the main road. The skies were still blanketed with clouds, but the rain had ceased. With not enough room in the cab, Coco and Marie rode in the back with Sailor. Coco wanted to bring the geese, too, but Lana nixed that. Sailor, who especially enjoyed sitting under Mochi's chair at mealtime, began howling as soon as they drove off.

"I never thought I would say this, but I sure am going to miss that creature," Mochi said with a smile.

In the rearview mirror, Lana saw Coco leaning on Sailor, howling in unison. They bounced along the driveway, and when they reached the main road, Lana pulled off to the side. They all climbed out. Mochi had a small knapsack, to which she had added three tangerines and a jar of red honey.

"Make sure to eat your honey, and I'll find a way to get more to you," she said.

Benji stood off to the side, arms slack. He stared down at his feet. Mochi gave him a bear hug and ruffled his hair. "You're the man of the place now. These ladies are all counting on you. Think you can handle it?"

Benji raised his eyes, looking at Lana and the girls as they all waited expectantly for an answer. Sailor was off sniffing for pigs.

He suddenly went straight as a fence post. "I'll do my best."

Before anyone could say another word, Mochi turned and began the slow march to camp. He'd worn a suit of Jack's they'd found hanging in the closet. Lana had hemmed the pant legs, but they still dragged on the ground. Despite the suit hanging off him, Mochi gave it all an air of great dignity. Lana knew the stranglehold of this moment would follow her through her entire life.

CHRISTMAS

Cold collected between the blanket and Lana's shivering body. In the night, the winds must have shifted north again, dropping the temperature by at least twenty degrees below comfortable. Once this war was over, she resolved to buy enough warm clothes for an army. Just to have on hand. She thought of poor Mochi in the barracks.

Yesterday had been one of the saddest days on record. No one had felt much like talking, and they moped around the house as though someone had died. Coco decided to climb to the top of the Norfolk pine outside and refused to come down. It took Benji climbing up and bargaining to bring her down.

"What did you tell her?" Lana wanted to know.

"That the minute they allow visitors, we can go see Mochi and her parents together."

Lana touched her eyelids. Swollen and tender. Not only did she miss Mochi, but all day long yesterday, she had been half expecting Grant to come riding down the driveway on Boss. Double the loss, quadruple the pain. Eventually day fell into night, and he never came. Sleep had been elusive and was filled with dreams of soldiers and prisoners and being trapped in the secret room.

Now she layered on sweaters and her father's jacket and tiptoed out the front door, careful not to wake anyone. A deep raspberry sky greeted her, casting just enough light so she could see large shapes and objects. She walked as fast as she dared. The morning quiet was a balm of solace. No birds, no breeze, just the peace of a sleeping volcano.

As Lana walked along, her chest felt like a pressure cooker. Chances were slim to none that Grant had left another note for her, but she had to see for herself. The alternative meant worrying every twenty seconds about whether or not one was there. She needed to get him out of her system and carry on. Today was Christmas Eve. The kids deserved her full attention.

First sunlight hit the summit of Mauna Loa. Lana stopped and watched as golden light melted down the mountain. One thing was for sure— no one could ever deny the sheer magnificence of that mountain. She pulled her jacket tight and continued on.

By the time she reached the Sugi grove, she could scarcely breathe. Nerves had taken ahold of her lungs and pressed in from all sides. One second she was sure there would be a note, the next second sure there wouldn't. A pale light filtered through the towering trees. Enough light to see. The branch was empty.

Maybe this whole thing with Grant had been more one-sided than she'd thought, nothing more than a passing fancy, making her easy to walk away from. *Men are unpredictable.* A universal truth she could vouch for. But she would have sworn he was different.

With every step back to the house, she resolved to flip this day on its side. At least now she wouldn't have the added burden of explaining to Grant why Benji now lived with them. She was armed with a story but didn't want to have to use it. They were all waiting for her on the porch, the whole motley crew, geese included.

Coco stood at the top of the steps with her hands on her hips. "Where have you been?" she said.

"Out for an early Christmas walk. I picked berries, too. Anyone feel like pancakes?" Lana said.

"Me!" was the unanimous answer. That was the beauty of young people, she was coming to see. Their little hearts were so ready to see the goodness in the world all over again. They had resilience bottled up in reserve. If only she could be more like them.

They followed her into the kitchen, and Marie turned on the radio, a notch too loud. They found a station playing Christmas songs, and before long, there were feet tapping and voices singing in and out of tune. Benji didn't say much at breakfast, but he offered to show the girls how to fold origami animals for the tree. Lana had a few pieces of wrapping paper left over from Kano Store and offered it for the taking.

Lana sat on the porch while they worked, thinking back on Christmas Eve last year. All of downtown Honolulu had been lit in a spectacular fashion, and she and Buck were at a gala at Washington Place—the governor's home. Anyone with an important last name was there. Lana had attempted to feel festive, but inside she was hollow as a shoot of bamboo. Christmas had been hard lately, with no children to open gifts under the tree and no one to hang stockings for.

While all the other women her age were busy being mothers, Lana was busy falling into despair. And no one understood. Some felt sorry for her; others were clueless and kept inquiring when she and Buck would have kids or, even worse, told her she would make a great mother— she really should try it someday. She hated those questions.

Lana and Buck were good at pretending, but signs of decay had begun to show. A complete lack of affection, blazing tempers and the inability to feel. *There is a tipping point for all things, beyond which change becomes unstoppable.* One of her father's scientific phrases, which aptly applied to marriage, as well.

Now she had a house full of children. The sound

of their chatter carried out the window, mixing with the hum of the bees. She peered in and saw them hanging misshapen origami creatures on the tree. The ornaments might have been horses or dogs or geese; she couldn't be sure. Either way, they added charm and sparkle to a dreary day. The world, it seemed, had a funny way of giving you what you wanted when you least expected it.

After lunch and present wrapping in the secret room—Lana forbade any of them from going down there—they fed and watered the horses and collected decorations for the dinner table. Marie showed them how to make a wreath out of juniper and Norfolk, and they adorned it with 'ohi'a lehua blossoms and a'ali'i, which offered the perfect splash of red.

They cut up paper and made cards for their parents and Mochi. Coco also wanted to make a card for Grant, on which she drew purple horses galloping over streams of molten lava. A jagged line cut across her sky.

"What's that?" Lana asked.

"The sky crack."

"I haven't noticed it yet. Is it still up there?"

"Yeah, but the rain clouds covered it." Coco looked up at her, face pinched in thought. "Hey, I just thought of something. Maybe it's how Santa Claus gets around!"

"It could very well be. Brilliant idea," Lana said.

In the spirit of giving, she made her own card

for Grant. It took her all of three seconds to know exactly what she wanted to draw. A white-tailed tropic bird hovering over the crater rim. The picture came easily, but when it came to writing a message, her thoughts ran dry. She started and stopped no less than twenty-two times.

Dear Grant,
Wishing you a Merry Christmas, or, as we say in Hawaii, Mele Kalikimaka. You have been such a blessing during these trying times. I am sorry for keeping Coco and Marie's identity from you. Everything happened so fast and I didn't know who to trust. I was simply doing my best to keep them safe. Believe it or not, I had made up my mind to tell you the very same day the Feds came. Please, give me a chance to explain in person.

Missing you on this
chilly Christmas Eve,
Lana

Without any ham or turkey to be found, and not enough bread to make stuffing, they settled on homemade macaroni and cheddar cheese, and baked green beans with cream of mushroom soup. There was something to be said for food as comfort when most of your other comforts had been taken away.

The table was a picture straight out of *Sunset* magazine, with wreaths and candles and polished silver. It was their first formal dinner at Hale Manu, and for the first time in what felt like days, everyone looked clean and fresh and brushed. The house might be bare-bones, but it wrapped them in its comforting walls and held them close. After a quiet dinner, they settled by the fire. The pile of presents had grown since yesterday but was still meager.

"Our parents let us open a present on Christmas Eve," Coco said.

"Let's wait until tomorrow, since we have so few."

"Won't there be a lot more by morning? After Santa comes?"

Marie gave Lana a concerned look. "Coco, let's wait. Just in case Santa gets hung up someplace."

Benji chimed in. "I say we open one. So what if we have one less present tomorrow? It won't kill us."

"Is that what you all want?"

Two yeses and a shrug. Lana selected three featherweight gifts and handed them out. The way they tore into them with gusto reminded her of the magic of Christmas. Benji held up his first. An ink sketch of Mochi. Lana had done it in a hurry earlier that day. Not perfect, but it captured his toothy smile and the spark behind it. Coco kissed hers before holding it up. Ingrid. Marie had Fred.

"Since we don't have any photographs here, I figured these might be nice to have. And we can try to round up frames. Or maybe Benji can help us make some," Lana said.

"Can you do one of Sailor, too?" Coco asked.

"I'd love to."

Never had her sketches felt more important than in this moment.

Christmas morning broke with a cold snap. Lana checked the lichen on the tree branches for signs of frost. When she got to the living room, Coco was already up and had lit a fledgling fire. She was dressed from head to toe in red.

"He came!" she cried.

"I knew he would," Lana said.

While they waited on Marie and Benji, Coco helped Lana tie red ribbons around jars of honey for Uncle Theo and the Kanos and Auntie. It was strange not to have a whole universe of friends to deliver gifts to. She had half a mind to take a boxful to the camp for guards and prisoners alike. Everyone could use a little honey on a day like today.

Marie and Benji filed into the great room, one after another, bleary-eyed and decked out in all their warm clothes. Benji wore a Santa hat they'd found in the sock box. Both plunked down next to Coco, who was snuggling Sailor by the tree. Lana served hot cocoa and brought out fresh biscuits dripping in honey. She counted her blessings to have these three amazing humans in her care. So why did she feel like crying?

They opened the box of Japanese playing cards, a group gift, and Benji promised to teach them all how to play *hanafuda*. Lana admired his patience as he pointed out the cherry blossoms, wisteria, pine, peony and plum cards, and what the moons and ribbons meant.

"Interestingly, there's a lot of those same plants up here," Lana said. "Hilo is too warm, but Volcano is just the right temperature."

For Coco and Marie, she had wrapped up watercolors and paintbrushes, and for Benji, her father's golf clubs. Lord knew she wouldn't be needing them. For stockings, she had filled some wool socks with tangerines, plums, Japanese rice candy, and a few other odds and ends. The last four presents under the tree were from Mochi. He had used old newspaper and twine for wrapping.

"I miss Mochi," Coco told Benji.

"Me too."

Everyone was doing a fine job of pretending, but the room was so full of missing people that it was impossible to ignore. For each of them, Mochi had filled a palm-sized wooden box with five silver-dollar coins. In Lana's there was also a gold chain coiled around a black-pearl necklace.

"It was Mochi's wife's. He got it for their wedding day," Benji told her.

Lana felt her resolve slipping away even as she reminded herself that adults are supposed to be the ones to hold it together during tough times. Within seconds, tears streaked down her face, and she had to gulp for air. Sailor immediately came and lay on her feet.

"I'm sorry, you guys. Here I go ruining Christmas morning," Lana said, nose dripping.

Coco ran to the kitchen and came back with a box of tissues. In all seriousness, she handed her a tissue and said, "No you didn't, Aunt Lana. It was already ruined and you tried to fix it."

Lana pulled her in for a tight hug, resting her cheek on the top of Coco's head.

Lana was in the kitchen stacking up the honey jars when she heard a motor in the distance. She checked her watch. No one would be out on official business at 9:33 on Christmas morning. Stripping off her apron, she hurried out to the window where Coco was already standing, her nose smooshed into the glass. Lana pulled up next to her and they waited and watched.

"Who could it be?" Coco asked.

Please, let it be him.

"I don't know."

Marie and Benji crowded around them and all their breath fogged up the glass. Sailor barked once, then sat tall with her ears perked up, sniffing the air. A few moments later, an olive-colored military vehicle pulled right up to the bottom step. It wasn't the kind that Grant usually drove. Lana's heart missed a few beats, and she rested her hand on Coco's shoulder to steady herself. Later she would remember the whole scene unfolding like a Technicolor dream.

The first one out, on the passenger side, was a man holding a rifle. He looked seven feet tall. Coco gasped. A half second later, Grant stepped out of the driver's side, slipping off his hat and setting it on the dashboard. His gaze went directly to the window. Instinctively, Lana stepped behind the wall.

Here she'd been, pining away for him, and he was coming to haul her off. Guilt by association. Mochi had been wrong. Grant was not teachable. And then she noticed Coco's eyes go bigger than plums. Lana snuck another glance outside. Standing at the bottom of the steps were none other than Fred and Ingrid Wagner.

Coco screamed, "It's Mama and Papa!"

In a jumble of limbs, both girls were out the door and down the steps before their parents were halfway up. Coco wrapped her whole body around her mother, Marie slammed into them, and Fred pulled them all in with his extra-long arms. Ingrid's whole body was shaking. Just watching them, Lana thought her heart might break with happiness.

Once inside, Lana offered them a seat at the

table, and Grant nodded politely. Sailor was beside herself, howling and skidding as she ran circles around the room. Ingrid was crying and laughing at the same time. Lana rushed off to the kitchen, where she found Benji about to open the hidden door.

"Stay up here with us. You haven't done anything wrong, and I'm done with secrets," Lana told him.

Benji looked surprised but didn't argue. She put on a pot of water for coffee and ran back out. Coco had arranged all of the presents on the table, and Marie was handing her parents their Christmas cards. The room sounded louder than a town hall meeting, with everyone speaking over one another. Grant sat alone on the hearth, and the soldier with the gun stood next to the front door. The man was trying to look relaxed, but his gun ruined all chances of that.

She sat down and joined them. The air between her and Grant was thick as butter. Every time she caught him watching her, he quickly looked away. If only she could pull him aside while the Wagners reunited. But now was not the time. Coco rattled off every detail of their recent lives. "We rounded up horses, there are beehives out back, Lana taught us how to make 'ōhelo berry pie, we saw the crater." She made it sound like summer camp.

"You girls are lucky to have Mrs. Hitchcock

to care for you until we're released," Fred said, nodding at Lana.

"What do you mean *until?*" Coco said.

Ingrid hugged her closer. "He means we have to go back."

Coco looked as though she'd been slapped. "Why can't they move in with us, here?" she said to Grant.

"My job is to help run the camp. The FBI chooses who to keep and who to release. I'm working on getting you visits but can't promise anything." The way he spoke to her, it was clear he cared. "Sorry, kiddo. I wish it were different."

Just then, Benji walked out carrying a tray of steaming mugs. He still wore the Santa hat. "Coffee, anyone?" he said.

Lana was quick to respond. "I would love one. Everyone, this is Benji. He's staying with us for a while."

If Grant was surprised, he didn't let on. Fred and Ingrid surely recognized him from the neighborhood but didn't say anything other than an emphatic *yes* and *hello*. After serving them, he disappeared back into the kitchen and turned on the radio. Lana took a chance and went and sat next to Grant, the fire warming her spine.

"So how did you manage coming here today? I'm sure they didn't let you waltz off for no good reason," Lana asked.

Grant sipped his coffee. "I pulled a few strings."

They must have been fat strings.

"Just so you know, Major Bailey, you saved Christmas. Nothing in the world would have made these girls happier," Lana said.

"The way I see it, kids and parents are meant to be together, especially when the parents are being held on hearsay."

Lana could hardly believe what she'd just heard. "So you've checked into their case?"

"I poked around a bit."

"And?"

He paused. "I can't talk about it."

Sitting with their knees almost touching, Lana longed to close that last inch. Grant being here was a double-edged knife. He had saved Christmas for the Wagners, but she wanted more. Selfish and horrible and true.

"If you wouldn't mind, please keep this visit between us, okay?"

"Of course."

Coco moved from her mother's lap to her father's, though Ingrid still held tight to her hand. Fred stroked her hair as though it were made of spun gold. Seeing them together was like coming up for air after a near drowning. There was still good in the world, if you knew where to look.

The guard at the door pointedly held up his arm and tapped his watch. Grant stood. "Sorry, folks, but our time is up."

Coco wrapped her arms more tightly around

Fred's neck. He stood, carrying her, and they all filed out the door. Ingrid and Marie walked arm in arm, hovering on each step. If you could have slowed time to a standstill, no one would have complained. Lana suddenly remembered her own note and ran back in and grabbed it.

"For you," she said, handing it to Grant.

When her fingers touched his skin, a jolt of static electricity raised the hair on her arm and ran all the way up the back of her neck. He looked surprised. She felt foolish. But for the first time that day, he smiled. A genuine, heart-melting smile.

The Wagners huddled together. Murmurs of love and anguish lifted up around them. Grant gave them another minute. Once again, Ingrid had to pry Coco's arms from her waist. The mood was subdued. Less outright panic and more deep ache. For a moment Lana felt sorry for herself. No one alive loved her that potently.

"I miss you so much the inside of my heart hurts," Coco said.

"Me too, *Mausi*. Me too," Ingrid said.

Tears streaked down Fred's face. "At least we're nearby."

"And alive," Coco said, blinking hard and fast.

That got a chuckle. "Yes, I'm quite happy about that, too," Fred said.

When Ingrid finally broke away and bent over to step inside the car, she exclaimed. "Oh, my!"

Lana looked in. Sailor took up the whole back

seat and had her eyes intently focused on Ingrid.

"You have to stay here, my big girl."

It took Fred pushing on one side and Lana and Coco convincing on the other to get the dog out. Grant stood to the side, hands in his pockets, watching. The way his eyebrows pinched together, you could tell he was affected. He turned his sad brown eyes toward Lana and seemed to be debating whether to say something.

She saved him the trouble by putting her arms around both girls. "Thank you for doing this, Major Bailey. We won't soon forget it."

That was when the buzzing started up. The bees moved in, hovering everywhere, over the muddy garden bed, in the Norfolk needles and hydrangea blossoms, all around Lana and the girls. They were glorious and threatening and golden all at once. Everyone froze, even Sailor. Lana swore she could feel a cool wind from their tiny beating wings. A honey smell filled the air.

"What are they doing?" Marie said.

"Swarming. It's perfectly harmless," Lana whispered.

Even so, Grant inched toward the car. "Merry Christmas, y'all."

He drove away slowly, Fred and Ingrid waving out the back window. Lana and Coco and Marie stood planted long after the car disappeared from sight, bolstered by their closeness and the hum of thirty thousand bees.

THE GLOW

The best remedy for any ailment is usually an animal. After the bittersweet visit from their parents, the girls wanted to see the horses again. No one bothered to smile the whole way there, and Lana had her doubts that the rest of the day could be salvaged. But 'Ohelo trotted right over to Coco, bringing with her a tall white male with gentle eyes. Coco produced a handful of carrots, and within minutes, the whole herd had circled around them. You could feel their calm presence in the same way you felt a hug. So many people loved horses for riding, but Lana was coming to see a whole other side to them—big, comforting beings. And Lord knew they could all use some comfort right now.

In the late afternoon, they delivered jars of honey to Iris and Mrs. Kano, Uncle Theo, and Auntie at her tiny cabin on the crater rim. They found her sitting on a lauhala mat on her porch, weaving leaves into a *haku* lei that was ten feet long.

"This honey is special. I can smell it," Auntie said.

"We collected it ourselves and saved some of the special red kind for you," Coco said proudly.

"The red honey is influential."

"Do you think that's true?" Lana asked.

"You haven't figured it out by now?"

"I . . . well . . ." Lana didn't quite know what to say.

"The volcano has a powerful force all its own. More potent than most people can imagine. Those scientists know all about it. Some kind of magnetic mumbo jumbo."

Lana recalled hearing a theory of a vast sea of iron deep beneath Kīlauea, and how molten lava was conductive. But conductive of what?

Auntie continued. "The bees pick up on it and so do the plants. Everything up here is bursting with it," Auntie said. "And it's stronger when the volcano is erupting."

"But there's no eruption right now," Lana said.

Auntie raised an eyebrow, then said to Coco, "I bet you love those bees, don't you?"

"How did you know?" Coco said.

Auntie got a mischievous smile. "I know things. Just like you do."

Coco stepped back.

"Don't worry. Knowing is a natural thing, but most people have forgotten and get scared when they see it."

"I'm not scared," Coco said.

"And that's why you have it. That, and it's in your blood," Auntie said, eyes boring into Lana, whose skin began to itch.

Lana had an idea. "Say, would you mind if we come talk some more about this with you one of these days? It seems like *we* could use some guidance in this matter." She nodded toward Coco.

Auntie closed her eyes and drew in a deep breath. Her hands shook with age, but you could feel a well of strength hidden beneath her skin. "I will, on one condition," she said.

"What's that?"

"You give me a year."

The house suddenly began to rock, rafters creaking and groaning as the earth shifted beneath them. Coco and Marie rushed to her side. It stopped just as quickly as it started.

"Earthquake. A *manini* one," Auntie said.

"What's *manini*?" Coco asked.

"Small. Nothing to worry about."

Earthquakes were nothing new on this side of the island. Even in Hilo they had their fair share of rumbling. But living on Oʻahu, Lana hadn't felt one in a while. They were highly unsettling, especially in a tiny hut on the edge of Kīlauea.

Lana shook it off. "There's so much uncertainty with the war, I have no idea how long the girls will even be with me. Their folks are in the camp."

Auntie looked through her. "I know."

A narrow black cat strolled up the steps, rubbing on Coco's leg and then Marie's, distracting them momentarily. Good thing they'd left Sailor in the truck.

"Can you *see?*" Lana asked in a hushed voice.

Auntie repeated, "I'll need at least a year."

Lana was struck with the sudden thought that the girls would be with her for the coming year and beyond. How far beyond, she couldn't tell. For a moment she doubted, wondering how the government could justify holding on to the Wagners for so long, but then sureness flooded in. She tasted bitterness in her mouth, along with the sweet taste of honey. She swallowed to try to clear it.

The next thing she knew, Auntie was standing up and ordering the girls to run down the trail and pick her more aʻaliʻi. She showed them a small branch of the delicate reddish leaves and sent them away.

Once they were out of earshot, Auntie said, "It's time you know."

She was so close Lana could smell her earthy breath. "Know what?"

A small aftershock rattled the windows.

Auntie reached out and held Lana's hand. "Your grandmother was my sister."

Lana went perfectly still. A cool breeze shot up from the crater. For someone who had a tendency to *know* things, she felt an incredible sense of ignorance. Her mind went back to those early days at Volcano, all the run-ins, all the haunting looks. Auntie always just around the next bend, or behind the next 'ohi'a tree, ready to dispense advice on proper volcano etiquette and life in general. Was it surprise or betrayal or a blend of the two that she felt? Whatever it was, the skin on the back of her neck heated up.

"Have you always known?"

Auntie's hand warmed up. "Always."

Anger stirred. "Why didn't anyone tell me?"

"No one here knew. I left Kaua'i when I was sixteen and traveled to New Zealand for a time. When I came back, I knew I needed to be here at Kīlauea. I wrote to Anuhca—your grandmother—from time to time, and I called her when I found out that your mother died. She told me everything and how they blamed Jack and pushed him away and he refused to let them see you. She asked me to keep an eye on you."

Blame. A useless sentiment if there ever was one. No amount of blame has ever solved anything the world over. Poor Jack had taken the brunt of all that fierce and angry blame, and a second dose from Lana. While they had all been stuck in the past, Jack had tried to move forward. She saw that now.

Part of Lana wanted to run away; the other half needed to know. "How did you find out my mother died?"

Auntie closed her eyes and squeezed Lana's hand tight. Her bent and calloused fingers were surprisingly strong and warm. "I heard her last words."

Those were Lana's private words. They belonged to her and Jack and no one else. "I don't believe you," Lana said.

"I had no children of my own, and your mother used to come visit me and bring me lilikoʻi and dried mango and honey. Every time she came, we talked for hours. Not often, but we had a bond. She was beauty and goodness and aloha all wrapped into one woman."

Auntie held firm to Lana's hand. "What did she say?" Lana demanded.

"You know."

Her voice was barely a whisper. "Tell me."

Auntie opened her eyes and let out a long, deep breath. " 'She is my *ha*' was what she said to Jack before crossing over."

She stared into Lana with those haunted eyes of hers. Blue as the sea and brown as the earth. *How could she know?* Lana blinked back tears. And still Auntie did not let go. Lana knew that even if she tried, she would not be able to pull away. There was too much holding them together.

"Why didn't you tell me when I was younger? Surely Jack would have understood."

"I knew how much he had lost. Sometimes you have to know when a soul has had enough. When to fight and when to sit back and wait. You were all he had left, and I didn't want to interfere," Auntie said.

"No one ever thought to ask me?"

"You were too young. I knew the right time would come."

Lana's knees felt watery. She sank down to a nearby stool, and Auntie let go. The old woman looked spent, too. She crumpled to the floor, legs folded up, and leaned against a faded wicker love seat.

A full minute passed before Lana said, "This is a lot for me to take in right now, on top of everything."

"Just know that you coming back here to Volcano was no accident. You are a part of this place and this place is a part of you."

"It has always felt that way," Lana said.

Auntie patted the spot above her heart. "And now look. You've brought others along with you. People who need an extra dose of care. You are stronger than you know, girl, and even more so when you're here."

Chattering voices announced the girls' return. Coco and Marie came to the porch holding branches full of red leaves, their cheeks flushed. "We felt another earthquake. Did you feel it?" Coco said.

"We did," Auntie said.

Coco frowned. "Aren't you scared your house might fall off the cliff?"

Marie said, "We saw a big rockfall just down the way. This seems like a dangerous place to live."

"Fear is purely in our minds," Auntie told them, already back to work layering leaves into the lei.

"That rockfall looks pretty real," Coco said.

"The rockfall *is* real. It happened. But my house is still here on the edge of the cliff. So I don't waste my time worrying about something that may never happen. Nor should you."

Lana wasn't so sure about that logic, but didn't have the energy to resist. "Auntie has invited us back. We can talk more about it then," she said.

Coco gazed down at Auntie with a puzzled expression, and Lana knew she was going to come out with a big question. "Don't you have a first name? It seems weird to just call you Auntie. Our mother has two sisters and we call them Aunt Heidi and Aunt Emma, even though they live in Munich."

Munich came out very guttural.

Auntie looked at Coco, then at Lana. Her mouth puckered up and the creases around her eyes deepened. For the first time Lana could recall, she seemed unsure of herself.

"My first name is Lana."

Coco frowned, taking in Auntie and then Lana. "You have the same name. Is that on purpose?"

"It is."

Lana's mouth had gone dry.

"Did my father know about any of this?"

Auntie shrugged. "She said she was going to tell him. But you ask me, he already knew."

All Jack's books, and his fascination with unexplained phenomena. They made sense now. Lana had a lifetime worth of questions, but right now, her concern was for the girls, especially Coco. "Can I come back soon and talk more?"

"There will be time. Come when you are ready."

On a Christmas Day long ago, Jack and Lana had taken a drive up Mauna Loa Truck Trail with Isabel and Thomas Jaggar. A small lava lake bubbled in the crater, and after dinner Isabel wanted to watch the glow from the slopes above.

"I'd rather have a red Christmas than a white Christmas any day," Isabel had said to Lana as they bumped along the winding road, beneath the wooded canopy and past the knee-high grasslands. They drove higher and higher, until they reached a newer flow with only the sporadic tree poking through the lava. Thomas pulled over to the side, and when Lana turned around, there before them was an ethereal glow coming from the heart of the earth. They sat under an ocean of stars, the adults sipping from a bottle of gin, and Lana munching on Christmas cookies. They watched the lava until Lana fell asleep under a wool blanket, with her head on Jack's lap.

Now the memory kept tugging at her, causing

melancholy to stick in the back of her throat. When she could no longer ignore it, or the throb of missing her childhood, she thought, *To hell with it*. They might not see any glow, but at least they wouldn't be stuck in the house, moping. They were in the midst of preparing dinner when Lana announced, "Okay, everyone, we're having a change of plans. Put everything aside. I want you to dress in your warmest clothes and gather all the blankets. We're going for a drive."

"I don't feel like going anywhere," Coco said.

"Me neither," said Marie.

It would have been so easy to acquiesce. She hardly had any fight left, but if they stayed, she would suffocate. All patience had eroded. "I don't care. We're going."

Coco threw down the wooden spoon, causing chunks of sweet potato to splatter across the floor. "No! You can't make us!"

Sailor went right over and started licking it up.

Benji jumped up from the table. "I'll go get ready," he said.

Lana started trembling, every ounce of hurt and fear and frustration from recent weeks rattling through her body. And the revelations from Auntie. She felt like a human earthquake, about to split at the seams.

Her voice lowered. "I said, go get your stuff. I know this is not how you want Christmas to be, but it's how it is."

Something in her tone must have spooked the girls, because they both shuffled off without another word. Lana put on two jackets, grabbed her wool cap and went to start the truck. The sun had gone behind Mauna Loa, but a piece of daylight remained.

Benji climbed into the back, and the girls seemed torn between riding in a warm cab with a grumpy driver, or freedom in the back. Sailor had already jumped in, and her tail thumped against the cab. They opted for freedom, which was fine with Lana, who wanted time to clear her head. Riding in the truck had become her only time alone throughout the day, and she welcomed the solitude.

On the way to Mauna Loa Road, they passed the military camp. The truck felt collectively heavier. It struck Lana that behind that barbed wire dwelled the other half of all their hearts. No matter how hard they tried to pretend that life went on, nothing would change that awful truth. Tears ran down her cheeks. She pressed the pedal to the floor and shot ahead.

Once they hit the Mauna Loa Truck Road, the going slowed. Eleven miles of twisty, curvy uphill. With gas rations and blackout, this was probably a dumb thing to do, but she saw no other means of escape. They rose through dense koa forests and thinner 'ohi'a drylands, where the occasional hawk hung on the wind. Soon the kids

413

huddled against the cab for warmth. Lana rolled her window down a crack as icy wind blasted her face. Maybe she ought to pull over.

"You guys okay back there?" she yelled.

Heads nodded.

By the time twilight arrived, Lana guessed they were halfway up the mountain. Most of the drive passed in a blur. Her thoughts were purely on Auntie. *Lana.* Not only was she related to the woman, but she was her namesake. It seemed impossible. In Hawaiian, *Lana* meant "afloat," or "calm as smooth waters." Right now she felt more like waters slammed by a kona storm.

Had Jack known about Auntie? Known Lana was named after her? Beneath the injustice of it all, Lana felt the stirrings of a warm and cozy feeling. Auntie was family.

My great-aunt Lana.

A few minutes later, someone tapped on the glass behind her head. She rolled down the window and Marie yelled in. "Are we almost there? Our noses are freezing off."

"We'll stop at the next clearing," Lana called back, feeling guilty for being toasty in the warm cab while they were in the cold, and also for growing impatient with them. She felt so volatile.

They bumped along for another half mile. She wanted to find a bluff where they could stretch out on a blanket, count falling stars and wish for better days. For the kids' sake, she forced herself to concentrate on the task at hand. Then she noticed a staticky feeling in the air. The skies were perfectly clear and yet the hair on her arms stood on end. Something in the air was different.

Lana leaned forward to try to catch a glimpse of the summit. From her vantage point, the top of Mauna Loa was blocked by a steep cliff. When they finally hit a flat spot, she saw it. She slammed on the brakes. An unmistakable glow lit up the whole eastern flank of the mountain. She jumped out and climbed into the truck bed with the kids, standing to get a better look. Surely her eyes had been playing tricks on her. But the glow was still there. A line of chills shot from her toes to the base of her skull. Coco's words sprung to mind. *I want it to erupt.*

"What are you looking at?" Benji asked.

None of the kids had budged from their cocoon. It would have been hard to with Sailor on their feet. The cold air stung Lana's cheeks. "Get up and see for yourselves!"

Orange stained the night sky.

Coco stood behind Lana and grabbed her arm. "Did the Japanese bomb us again?"

"No, honey—Mauna Loa is erupting!"

"Will the lava come all the way down here and get us?" Coco asked.

Marie reminded her, "You were the one who said you wanted it to erupt."

"I said I wanted Kīlauea to erupt."

"Well, someone misheard you, then." Lana intervened. "The lava has a long way to travel before reaching us, and depending on where the eruption is, it could flow the other way."

Though who really knew. Pahoehoe lava traveled fast downstream, forming swift molten rivers. It might be smart to turn around. But they had just driven for an hour through the cold to get here, and they were all mesmerized.

"Will they evacuate our parents if the lava comes?"

"I'm sure they will."

The glow blotted out the stars in half the sky. Lana was reminded how nature always had the last say. Lava built the ground up, while at the same time swallowing everything in its path—trees, roads, houses. There was nothing anyone could do but surrender. Maybe she should take note.

Surrender.

They stood watching for a good five minutes before the girls started whining about being cold. As much as Lana wanted to stay, the blazing sky was spreading down the mountain.

"We should probably head down. I'm sorry I dragged you all this way only to turn around, but I'd rather be safe than sorry," she said.

In the excitement of the eruption, no one seemed to remember not wanting to come. They were all chattering and oohing and aahing. Lana fixed her gaze on the brightest of stars and made a wish. Nothing had gone her way in the past months, but there was always tomorrow. It was absurd to hope for love and happiness amid all this tragedy, but that's exactly what she did.

"I'm sitting in the truck," Coco announced.

"So am I," said Marie.

Benji added, "Me too."

They made a nest of blankets for Sailor in the back, Coco sat on Marie's lap and Benji squished in against the door. Their four bodies warmed the cab within minutes.

On the way down, they passed two trucks racing up. Both had high beams on. With the whole sky ablaze, what difference did a pair of headlights make? Benji and Lana climbed out and took off their covers, too. With all the blind curves, it made for easier driving.

At the bottom, several army jeeps clustered around the gate. She slowed, cursing under her breath. A uniformed man on each side of the road stood pointing rifles at their vehicle. One of them held out his hand, as though he thought she might try to plow on through.

"Halt!"

Lana rolled to a stop and cut the lights. The man pointed a flashlight at her face, temporarily blinding her. She should have seen this coming. In the back, Sailor growled.

"State your business, ma'am. Civilians are not to be out past six o'clock."

Lana held her hand up to block her eyes. "Sir,

our truck broke down on the mountain and it took a while to get it going again, otherwise we would have been down hours ago."

"You're also breaking the law with no headlight covers."

"We just took them off. The other cars had none, and, well, we figured with the eruption, what was the point. I was going to put them on back here at the gate."

All these guards everywhere and suspicion and rules were hard to take. She hadn't realized how good they'd had it in peacetime. Cinders crunched. Another man emerged out of the darkness, on the passenger side. He bent down and looked inside. "Let them pass, Private. I know Mrs. Hitchcock."

That voice.

"Major Bailey!" Coco cried.

"Hey, kid."

Lana turned toward Grant. He gave her a half smile, then said, "Why am I not surprised to see you here?"

She shrugged. "We had to get out of the house. I'm sure you can understand."

"Ma'am, you'll need to move on," the other guard said.

Another vehicle approached from the park side. Grant stepped back, tapped the door frame and said, "Merry Christmas, y'all. I'll expect you to head straight home."

Lana couldn't get out of there fast enough.

THE GIFT

Back at the house, she tucked the girls in, said good-night to Benji and collapsed onto her mattress. Now that Mochi was gone, she supposed she could move his bed in here, but then there would be no room for Sailor, and Sailor had become a fine sleeping partner.

The room was lighter than usual, with tree branch shadows moving like unknown guests across the walls. Lana thought of Grant. As soon as she'd seen him, the rest of the night had fallen away. The look on his face had been hard to read. Had he been concerned about them, or just annoyed? Either way, nothing had changed. He was there, and she was here with a heavy heart.

Drifting off, she heard Jack tapping nails in the floor somewhere nearby. He was working on the secret room again. It was so nice to have him back, but why did he have to build while she was trying to sleep?

"Quiet," she said, jolting herself awake.

Sailor lay next to her, a growl forming in her chest. "What is it, girl?"

A sharp tap. Something hit the window. *What on earth?* Again. She jumped up and ran over, nearly tripping over her blanket. A tall figure stood in the grass, illuminated by just enough moon to make out the face. Lana opened the glass.

"Is that you?"

"It's me."

"What are you doing?" she said in a loud whisper.

His voice stirred up the night air. "I came to see you."

"Hang on. Meet me out front."

Lana half ran, half slid down the hallway in her socks, wearing her blanket over her nightgown and pulling on the yellow wool hat hanging by the door. *Stay cool,* she commanded herself.

Grant was waiting at the bottom of the steps.

He sounded out of breath. "I need to talk to you."

"Am I in trouble again?"

"Thanks to me, you're not. Will you come down here? I don't want to wake the kids."

Lana took each step slowly, sure that she was heading into danger. Once she reached the ground, she remained at arm's length.

"How about that eruption," Grant said.

"It took us by surprise."

"I'll say, and it's a perfect bull's-eye for the Japanese."

A mountain that tall lit up with fire would stand out like a beacon. "Do they know exactly where the flow is located?" Lana asked.

"The crater at the top. It has a name that I will never be able to pronounce. Not if I lived here a hundred years."

"Moku'āweoweo," Lana said.

"Yeah, that."

Lana felt deflated. She couldn't care less about the eruption right now. "Is this why you came, Major Bailey? To talk about the volcano eruption?"

She was acutely aware of his nearness and his warmth. Of his particular cinnamon scent filling the darkness around them. He stepped in front of her, blocking her view of the light.

"Look—"

"Just—" she said.

They both talked over each other in that way that they did, but in the end, Grant won out. "No. It's not."

"So what can I do for you?" she said, standing her ground.

He shivered. "I was a real jackass the other day, and I pray to God I didn't screw things up beyond repair. Seeing you there caught me off guard, and I just reacted. I was blindsided. And all you were doing was trying to protect the girls. I know that. I wanted to come earlier, but it's been mayhem all afternoon and the last two days they had us out patrolling on the cliff all day."

She wanted to be tough and show him she had been perfectly fine without him. "Maybe now is not a good time for us. You have your hands full with the war, and I have mine full with the girls and Benji. I know you promised my father, but he would understand," she said.

Her feelings were still bruised. The humiliation of staying in the room all night, alone. Days of waiting and wondering and dying inside.

"Not a good time, huh?"

She was glad it was dark. "Yes. You and I starting something now would be inconvenient."

He let out a dull laugh. "I'll take fate over convenience any day. That first day at Kano Store when I saw you standing there, I didn't know what hit me. I tried to keep my cool, but I was already a goner. I swear I could feel you before I even saw you."

She thought back to how he helped her out of the bushes after the bicycle crash. The way their hands stuck together, and how his had turned red afterward. Alchemy and chemistry and desire were making him hard to resist.

Grant continued. "I once swore I would never tolerate even one lie. But I can see that lying is not part of your nature. You did it because you had to."

"I hated lying to you."

He grabbed her hands. "You have every right to tell me to drive away and never come back, but please, Lana, give me another chance."

He spoke the words with such tenderness

that she felt a catch in her throat. Her resolve melted. "Seeing that it's Christmas, do I have any choice?"

His smile shone in the moonlight. "Are you toying with me?"

She tried to suppress a laugh. Not forgiving him would be impossible.

"Is that a yes?" he said.

"I think it is."

"You think? Well, let me persuade you."

He swept her into his arms, pressed his face into her hair. His heartbeat was louder than crickets and more wonderful than the glow on the mountain. Lana closed her eyes and let herself soak in all his beautiful warmth and soapy scent. She held his hand, lacing her fingers in his, and pulled him up the stairs and down the hallway.

In the room she kissed him. There was no hurry this time, and his tongue moved softly and surely. He held her tight, as though afraid to let go. Weeks of near misses had her wanting him more than she thought possible.

"I brought you a Christmas present," he whispered.

"Can I open it tomorrow? I won't be able to see it in the dark," she said, though she could see him just fine. He made his own light.

"I couldn't find any wrapping paper, so I'll just give it to you. I hope you don't mind."

Was he serious? "Of course I don't mind, silly."

He pulled something from his back pocket and hung it over her neck. It was heavy. Lana reached up and fingered the cool glass at the end of two cylinders. "Is this what I think it is?"

"It's not a clunky necklace, I can assure you that."

She laughed. "What a perfect gift. Now I can take you and the girls out and show you the birds close up. Thank you."

Handsome and thoughtful and painfully sexy. She moved the binoculars so they hung against her back and reached for him again. His hands found her waist, stayed there for a moment, then moved down over the curve of her rear, leaving a line of heat in their wake. Lana was conscious of the mattress just behind her feet.

He spoke softly in her ear. "Nothing would have kept me away tonight. Not the Japanese, not Santa Claus and, hell, not even a volcano."

How had she ever doubted this? A tear ran down her cheek and she wondered what it was that drew two people together from far ends of the world. An unexplained phenomena if there ever were one. And in that moment her world locked into place.

THE AFTERWARD

A year and a half later,
June 21, 1943

The loud buzz of the telephone rang through the whole house, waking Lana with a start. It was still dark outside. She bolted upright and sat for a moment rubbing her eyes and making sure she wasn't dreaming.

Grant wrapped an arm around her waist and tried to pull her back into the tangle of warm skin and quilt. "Don't get it."

Tempting.

"I have to get it. Who calls at six o'clock in the morning unless it's important?" she said, taking off down the hallway at a full sprint.

In the past months with Auntie, Lana had been learning to still her thoughts and listen from the inside out. Lana had been practicing daily, learning to trust herself, and by the time she reached the telephone, she already knew who was calling.

Life is a stream of days. When you look back, most of those days blend into one another like water in a rushing river. Every so often, if you're lucky—or unlucky—you have one that stands out against the rest. The difference with war is that all the days stand out.

Living on the edge became an all-too-familiar term, and quite frankly, Lana was tired of it. The intervening year had come and gone with no more bombs and no invasions, but a constant threat looming. The victory at Midway helped matters, and people began to loosen up, but only slightly.

At the volcano, after weeks of nail biting, the eruption of Mauna Loa had ceased, but not before someone got the brilliant idea to bomb the vents that were feeding the flow. With a mile-long fountain of lava, which then formed a swift-moving river headed toward Hilo, the military felt they had to do something. It was as though someone had flipped a switch in the night sky and turned on a light over the island, leading the Japanese right to it. Auntie and others were appalled at the army's actions, and in the end, not all of the bombs exploded, and those that did seemed to have little effect on the eruption. Coco said that the mountain was stronger than any bomb.

Lana and the kids lived in their close-knit world to the best of their ability, not traveling much aside from visiting Kano Store, Volcano House, and the small schoolhouse they attended with several other local students. Lana helped there on Tuesdays and Thursdays and found she had a talent for teaching science and art, which she thought had more in common than people realized. By the end of the third month, all the students knew their Hawaiian birds—iiwi, ʻapapane, amakihi, omao, ʻio, koaʻeʻkea—and could identify and sketch each one, rattle off their habitats, and imitate their calls. Lana considered it a victory.

Before long, the Wagners and Mochi were transferred with all the prisoners from Kīlauea Military Camp to Sand Island Detention Camp on Oʻahu, where Fred and Ingrid were separated without an explanation. Days later, Fred was shipped off to the mainland, still in the same clothes he had been picked up in. He and a handful of other Germans and Italians, and over a hundred Japanese men, rode locked in the steerage section of a transport ship to California and then were packed into a train and taken across the country to Wisconsin. Bleak and cold and miserable, the men resorted to stuffing newspapers into their clothing to keep themselves warm. Ingrid heard only rumors of where the men had been taken, and she worried herself sick. Literally. The doctor diagnosed her with hysteria and ordered bed rest, but bed rest was hard in a detention camp.

Letters came sporadically, and the girls and Benji swung between enjoying life with Lana and fretting about their parents and Mochi. As luck would have it, several months later, again with no explanation, Fred was brought back to Sand

Island and reunited with his wife. The pining was lessened by the fact that Lana soon traveled with the kids to Oʻahu for several overnight visits. Lana had managed to track down Baron, who had thankfully been off on Sunday, December 7, and arranged for him to fly them back and forth. The kids all loved him and always fought to be copilot.

Then, in early 1943, following hearing boards in Hilo where lawyers and character witnesses did nothing to sway the council, the Wagners and Mochi were moved to Honouliuli, a hot and dusty gulch in the center of Oʻahu known as Hell Valley. On the Kona wind days, the heat grew as unbearable as the uncertainty. The camp housed separate compounds for Germans, Japanese and prisoners of war. Only family could visit, and the kids would come back with stories of Coco and Marie going to the Japanese side to say hello to Mochi, and on the way passing pup tents full of prisoners of war dressed only in loin cloths.

"They look spooky," Coco would say.

Even Marie swore the place was haunted and came down with a bad case of nerves every time they went. Thank goodness for Mochi, who bought fudge from the PX when he knew Benji and the girls were coming. He told Benji that he could endure the camp and whatever they threw at him, because the alternative was worse. He felt lucky to still be alive and credited his survival to the honey from the volcano, and all that love. Benji teared up when he told Lana.

No one had any idea how or when or if their imprisonment would end.

Lana had made use of the time on Oʻahu by visiting with an attorney and filing for divorce. Once the war began, Buck had wasted no time moving Alexandra into the house and turning the guest room into a nursery. Lana felt nothing. With a man like Grant waiting for her back at Volcano, why would she? When Lana and the kids were away, Grant took care of the animals. Sailor went to work with him and soon became the most popular member of the camp, which, empty of prisoners, now housed the 27th Division of the National Guard as they bolstered defenses of the island from an amphibious attack. Every time Sailor was around, morale skyrocketed. So much so that Grant began bringing her in several times a week. She took her job very seriously. She also had a tendency to mysteriously gain weight during Lana's absence, about which Grant feigned ignorance.

Now that all the troops were in town, the whole landscape of Volcano immediately livened, with Volcano House and every available building in the area occupied by soldiers. On any given day, they could be seen patrolling and training in the lava fields. Lana and the kids found a whole new market for their honey, which they had been selling for a dollar a jar, though now they had to compete with alcohol since the ban had recently been lifted. The red honey they kept for themselves.

Meanwhile, Japanese forces were evacuating in the Aleutians, leaving behind their last main stronghold in the Western Hemisphere. In the islands, blackout rules were eased, allowing lights on until 10:00 p.m., except for ocean-facing rooms. A horrible outbreak of dengue fever spread through Waikiki, which was now off-limits to all servicemen. All in all, the war had infused Hawaii with tens of thousands of soldiers, miles of barbed wire and a bad case of paranoia.

On Christmas of 1942, 'Ohelo officially became Coco's horse. The two were connected at the withers, with Coco riding more than she walked, so it was bound to happen. 'Ohelo still had a tendency to be shy with others, but with Coco she was a different animal. Lana swore the two could read each other's thoughts.

Auntie became a huge part of their lives, and everyone looked forward to the time with her. Being in her small cottage with all of its herbs and knickknacks and animals was like stepping into an enchanted forest. You never knew what you might find. It turned out that Auntie had several cats, a mongoose, a very old white dog who never got out of his bed and a revolving door of forest birds who perched in her rafters.

They spent much of the time in the kitchen,

boiling decoctions out of roots and twigs and leaves they had gathered, or baking honey-infused scones and savory breads and taro cakes. They learned the peculiarities of the volcano and its surrounding terrain. To Lana, the most astonishing part of all was that no one ever complained. Not once. It was like school, only far more compelling.

As soon as it had been safe to drive to Hilo, Lana went and retrieved her father's ashes and brought them back to Hale Manu. They scattered some of the ashes in the wind blowing over Kīlauea crater, where Grant had taken her on that first date. They buried the rest under the big Norfolk pine out front. The one that Coco liked to climb on moody days.

"Now you won't be alone when you're up there," Lana told her.

Coco bent her neck and looked up the tree, smiling. Lana's gaze followed, and for a few seconds, she swore she saw the sky shimmering in a line over their heads. *The crack.* So unmistakable. All this time she had been scanning the skies and looking so hard for it, even when a big part of her had doubted its very existence. Now it seemed to have been there all along.

Lana took a deep breath before picking up the phone. She answered with a standard hello, even though she knew who was on the other end.

"Lana, is that you?"

The past year and a half condensed into a blur, flashing before her eyes.

"Good morning, Ingrid."

Ingrid sobbed as she spoke. "They're releasing us if you can believe it. We're coming home."

On the Monday morning following the phone call, Lana had no idea how to feel. Suitcases were packed, faces scrubbed. Marie wore a button-up dress that matched the berry red of her lips. On more than one occasion, Grant had had to come to her rescue about town, fending off salivating soldiers. Coco had chosen an interesting combination of a dainty yellow dress with knee-high riding boots they'd bought in Hilo. Her freckles had become more pronounced with all her time outdoors.

All day long, Lana felt herself becoming unglued. Outwardly, she fought to appear upbeat. The Wagners were being released after a year and a half of prison life. The least she could do was be happy. And she was—truly. But the happiness perched on the edge of a gaping hole that had been there for more than ten years.

Grant promised to be at the house before three, the estimated arrival time. Coco was unusually quiet, nestling on the porch with the geese and Sailor. She had said her goodbyes to the horses earlier, riding 'Ohelo up and down the driveway with her arms draped around her neck. Remarkably, she hadn't cried. But in between then and now, she'd disappeared into the tree for over an hour and returned with red and swollen eyes.

Lana began checking her watch every two minutes and, at ten to three, finally went out and sat on the top step. The kids all crowded around her. Coco tickled the back of Benji's neck with a Norfolk pine needle, causing him to leap up and dance around, slapping himself silly. It could have been just another day.

Coco clapped. "That's for the time you put one in my bed."

After that first Christmas they'd all shared together, Grant and Lana had a heart-to-heart about Benji and how he came to be with her. Grant had sworn that nothing she could do would sway his feelings for her, and so she told him about Mochi, and how he'd been hiding there all along. It didn't take long for Grant to warm to Benji, and now the two were often together, working with the horses and doing odd jobs on pretty much everything else around the place.

Grant arrived first, joining them on the steps. He kissed Lana firmly on the lips, something she would never tire of, and handed out balls of mochi to the rest of them.

"Mrs. Iwamoto's special," he said.

The minute Grant sat down, Sailor tried to

finagle her way into his lap, tail slapping Lana in the face. The dog might be loyal to Coco, and Lana to a degree, but Grant was Sailor's favorite. He rubbed her spotted belly and gave her scraps when he thought no one was looking. Lana caught him regularly.

After those shaky first weeks and the incident at camp, Grant had been there for Lana and the kids one-hundred-percent. He was her lava rock. And he was interested in her life. Not like Buck, who'd rarely asked about her day. Grant helped them with the hives, learning all there was about beekeeping and the medicinal properties of honey. He wanted to know everything about the birds at Volcano and developed a knack for imitating their calls. He even tried his hand at drawing, which everyone agreed might be a losing proposition. His wooden carvings, on the other hand, took on a life of their own. The main thing was he jumped in and he cared. He was the kind of man to hold on to, steadfast in his love. Lana loved him with every speck of her being.

As they waited, the sun was nearly unbearable. Coco stood up and began pacing.

"Honey, are you all right?" Lana said.

"I don't see why our parents can't just move in here and we can all live together," Coco said.

Lana had considered offering. Anything to keep the sense of family they had acquired over the past year and a half. They had developed such a strong foundation, and now she felt as if someone was coming to take away both of her legs and half of her heart.

"You and your parents are welcome to come and stay with us anytime. Maybe they'll even let you come for summers. Who knows?"

Coco's whole face wrinkled up and her voice went an octave higher. "But I love it here. So does Sailor."

"This place will always be a home for you. Remember what Auntie said? That we carry people and places we love in our hearts. They stay with us forever, no matter where we are."

Coco brightened. "And animals, too."

"That's right."

All those days at Auntie's house had given Coco permission to trust herself and to accept her unique strain of magic. "I'm glad it was you who took care of us."

All of Lana's resolve drained away in that moment. She held her arms open. "Come here."

Coco came over and sat in her lap. Lana rubbed her back as tears turned on and wouldn't stop. "I love all three of you like my own. You know that, don't you? Somehow, I ended up being the lucky one in this war. While everyone else was losing family members, I was gaining them. This house is going to feel empty and soulless without you here, but Grant and Benji and I will keep on going. We have no choice."

"But the house is full of Jack—at least you have that," Coco said.

Jack was there when the front door opened so smoothly. He was in the extra-wide trim and floor planks, and in the huge windows that let the sunlight in. He was under the floorboards and between each rock that fit so perfectly into the fireplace. Lana understood now that her father had been a perfectly imperfect human. Like the rest of us.

"When is Mochi coming home?"

"That I don't know, but we can keep him in our prayers and keep sending letters every week."

"Yes!"

Marie leaned into them from the other side. "We'll come up every weekend."

"You had better. And we'll look forward to it more than all the homemade cookies in the world," Lana said.

The sound of a motor broke through the warm June afternoon. Lana's heart sped up. Her palms began to bead with sweat. Coco jumped up and sprinted down the steps, then turned and smiled. A smile that outshone the blue in the sky and the green of the forest around them. Marie stood up and smoothed out her dress, following her sister.

Grant moved over and put his arm around Lana. This had to be hard for him, too. She caught herself holding her breath, not ready to say goodbye. There is never a good time for goodbye when you love someone. When the car came around the bend, both girls took off running. Lana thought of Mochi and Auntie and channeled all of their combined strength. A particular phrase came to mind. *Life is in the honeybee at the tip of your nose.* The truth of those words hit her square in the chest.

This was not a moment to be feared but a moment to be lived and experienced from all angles. As soon as those car doors opened, she was struck with enough love to cure heartache the world over. Here she'd been all this time worrying about the hole in her heart, when the hole had already been filled up to brimming over. These were her people, this was her place, and that would never change.

LOVE & MAGIC

When I close my eyes, I still see the fiery glow of lava in Halemaʻumaʻu crater. Sometimes if I'm not careful I find myself walking through the clouds while the honeycreepers build nests in my hair. I can't see where I'm going, but I don't care. To be there with my boots crunching on lava is sweeter than any honey from the hives. Bees swirl around me. I still feel my hand in his and hear the sound of his voice whispering in my tired ear, *She has your eyes*.

In the end, we remember those slices of time where we *feel* the most—love, anguish, joy, sorrow, fright. I don't care what the reason. Maybe it was the day you first realized you were mortal or that first moment you saw love walk in the door. Or that no matter how many years passed, you would still be that girl, the barefoot one with long brown hair and a penny in her pocket. Maybe it was when you suddenly realized you had everything to lose and you were too blind to notice. What matters most is what lives in your heart, and if there is one thing I know, it is this: love is the only way.

And magic.

I guess that's two.

AUTHOR NOTE

This book was born several years ago when I first stumbled upon an old house called 'Āinahou at Hawaii Volcanoes National Park. I later discovered that it was built in 1941 as a hideaway in the event of a Japanese invasion. 'Āinahou is on the National Register of Historic Places. It is old and beautiful and intriguing, and I knew when I saw it and heard its story that I needed to somehow write about it. At the time, I wasn't sure how. Fast forward a year or two when I heard from a friend who was talking about my first book to another friend. This woman mentioned that her mother had been a young girl when Pearl Harbor was attacked, and her parents were hauled off by the FBI and kept at Sand Island and Honouliuli for over a year. As it turned out, this woman and her sister were left to fend for themselves. I was able to find her story online, and when I read it, it broke my heart. People know about the Japanese-American citizens held in camps, but fewer know about the Germans and Italians. It was after reading the Berg family's story that my novel started forming in my mind. I also wanted to tie in the detainment center at

Kīlauea Military Camp (KMC), which was the largest camp outside of Oʻahu, and the main one on the island of Hawaii. To my knowledge, there were no Germans held at KMC, and I created this for the sake of the story. *Red Sky Over Hawaii* is purely a figment of my imagination, but it is inspired by these places and stories. It is also true that Mauna Loa erupted—not in December of 1941 as in the book, but in early 1942—and the military bombed it to try to stop the flow, worried that it might hit Hilo and also lead the Japanese navy right to us.

Another part of my story inspired by real life is Sailor. I fell in love with Sailor, a Great Dane with one blue eye and one brown, on Instagram and I asked her mama @love_my_dane_dolly_ if I could make her a character in my book. She said yes. Sadly, several months later, Sailor suddenly passed away. I was heartbroken for her family, but they gave me their blessing to keep on writing. I feel honored to be able to keep her memory alive. I hope I have done her justice!

ACKNOWLEDGMENTS

I feel like the luckiest girl in the world to be able to write books and share them with the world. I am beyond grateful for my agent, Elaine Spencer, who makes it all possible, always has my back, and also does a wonderful job with early edit notes. Also top of the list is my editor, Margot Mallinson, who is amazingly insightful and talented. My books are so much better because of her. The gift of a good editor can never be underestimated. There are also so many people behind the scenes at Mira that I can't thank enough. To have such a wonderful publisher is a dream come true.

Also, thanks to my Authors18 group, whom I could not live without. They are my tribe, and we have been together through thick and thin.

I would also like to thank Helie Rohner of Hilo, who took the time to meet with me and share her experiences of what it was like growing up in Hilo and spending time at Volcano back in the day. Another valuable resource was this publication on the National Parks History website about Volcano during the war years: http://www.npshistory.com/publications/hawaii /wwii-special-history.pdf. It is an extremely thorough and well-researched document, and I encourage anyone interested in Hawai'i Volcanoes National Park history to read it.

On the home front, I am forever grateful to all my friends who listen to my continual book ramblings. Especially Lilly Barels, who has been by my side since day one, and Mia Kresser, whom I can count on to read early copies and give great feedback. Her response is always: *It needs to be longer because I don't want it to end.* Music to an author's ears! Also, to my mother, Diane, who is always there to bounce stuff off of, and Marilyn Carlsmith, who lived through the war here on Hawaii island. Thanks to Lucy (my sweet dog) and Kitty, who supervise all my writing sessions. And last but not least, Todd (Honey) Clark, the man of my dreams, who is always by my side.

QUESTIONS FOR DISCUSSION

1. Suspected sympathizers were hauled away within hours after the attack on Pearl Harbor, some kept for the duration of the war. They were not only citizens of Japanese origin, but Germans and Italians, too. Do you believe this was justified because the country was at war, or do you feel that it was a violation of human rights?

2. Lana puts herself in danger of arrest by sheltering her German and Japanese neighbors and friends and lying about their identities. What would you have done in her position?

3. Lana experiences guilt and regret over not reconciling with her father while he was still alive. Do you feel that her reasons for staying away were justifiable? Do you think she should have forgiven him sooner?

4. Over time, Lana and her housemates grow to be as close as family. Do you have any "chosen family"? Have you experienced bonding during times of great stress? Do you think that she and the girls, and Mochi and Benji, would continue to see each other after the war?

5. Fred and Ingrid Wagner were separated from their two daughters without warning and with no idea of how long it would be for. How do you think you would cope with such a situation?

6. Animals play a big role in the book as both companions and healers. Have you ever thought about what you would do with your animals if you experienced war or natural disaster firsthand?

7. Both Lana and Coco possess intuitive powers that seem to grow stronger at Kīlauea Volcano, a place long considered sacred. Do you believe in the untapped power of the human mind? What about the heightened energy of certain places?

8. War is known to bring out the worst in people, but hardship can also bring out the best, and stories of courage and hope and survival abound. How did the characters in the book react to the pressures of war on their doorstep?

9. Before Pearl Harbor, there were many signs of a Japanese attack looming. If you'd been in Hawaii then, do you think you would have taken precautions and built an escape house or bomb shelter or anything else, or would you have remained optimistic that there would be no attack?

10. Lana does everything in her power to make

Christmas special for the kids, despite her own struggles and grief. Do you think it is important to keep up traditions even in such dark times?

11. Grant is unknowingly caught between working at the detainment camp and getting to know the two Wagner girls. When he finds out the truth about their parents, how do you feel he handled it? Did you want him to try to help them more? Realistically, could he have?

12. To what degree do you think the hideaway house played a role in Lana's journey of self-discovery?

Center Point Large Print
600 Brooks Road / PO Box 1
Thorndike, ME 04986-0001 USA

(207) 568-3717

US & Canada:
1 800 929-9108
www.centerpointlargeprint.com